"*Don't Go* marks the biggest step forward yet by this great storyteller— a novel about war, and the toll it takes on decent men."

—*CT News*

"A compelling and suspenseful thriller. It will keep you guessing right up to the unexpected end . . . I just couldn't put it down!"

—*Portland Book Review*

"A deeply emotional book that explores complex family dynamics. The story powerfully conveys what it really means to be a hero."

—*Deseret News*

Also by Lisa Scottoline

Fiction

Come Home

Save Me

Think Twice

Look Again

Lady Killer

Daddy's Girl

Dirty Blonde

Devil's Corner

Killer Smile

Dead Ringer

Courting Trouble

The Vendetta Defense

Moment of Truth

Mistaken Identity

Rough Justice

Legal Tender

Running from the Law

Final Appeal

Everywhere That Mary Went

Nonfiction (with Francesca Serritella)

Meet Me at Emotional Baggage Claim

Best Friends, Occasional Enemies

My Nest Isn't Empty, It Just Has More Closet Space

Why My Third Husband Will Be a Dog

Praise for *Don't Go*

"Lisa Scottoline is one of the very best writers at work today. *Don't Go* proves it once again. This is a story that is heavily muscled, emotional, and relevant. They don't come any better."
—Michael Connelly

"This stand-alone from Scottoline effectively tugs at the emotions."
—*Publishers Weekly*

"In her first book featuring a male protagonist, Scottoline spins a compelling drama that reads like the literary lovechild of Jodi Picoult and Nicholas Sparks. Readers will fall in love with this war vet father who fights seemingly insurmountable odds, and his powerfully addictive story will haunt them long after the final page."
—*Library Journal*

"Scottoline offers readers a nuanced, multidimensional portrait of a young man in crisis, couched in a page-turner of a story that will appeal to her many fans."
—*Book Reporter*

"This story grabbed me from the very first chapter . . . This is a story about family, loss, love, dedication, conviction, addiction, betrayal, redemption, and so much more. It's a bit of a: thriller, mystery, legal drama, war story, and romance. It's real and human. The characters are so complete and full. These are people that I know, that you know. People that live in our neighborhood."
—*Crochet Nirvana*

"This is a powerful story about how soldiers are changed forever and the difficulties of returning to civilian life. There is also the mystery surrounding Mike's wife's death, which is well-written, and the courtroom battle for the custody of Emily, which is heart-wrenching. Scottoline really delivers with this book."
—*Parkersburg News & Sentinel*

DON'T GO

Lisa Scottoline

 ST. MARTIN'S GRIFFIN ✿ NEW YORK

DON'T GO. Copyright © 2013 by Smart Blonde, LLC. All rights reserved. Printed in the United States of America. For information, address St. Martin's Press, 175 Fifth Avenue, New York, N.Y. 10010.

www.stmartins.com

The Library of Congress has cataloged the hardcover edition as follows:

Scottoline, Lisa.
    Don't go / Lisa Scottoline.—1st ed.
        p. cm.
    ISBN 978-1-250-01007-0 (hardcover)
    ISBN 978-1-250-02599-9 (e-book)
    1. United States. Army—Surgeons—Fiction.   2. Life change events—Fiction.
3. Family secrets—Fiction.   4. Widowers—Fiction.   5. Fathers and daughters—
Fiction.   I. Title.
    PS3569.C725D66 2013b
    813'.54—dc23

                                                                    2013002622

ISBN 978-1-250-01008-7 (trade paperback)
ISBN 978-1-250-05671-9 (Scholastic edition)

St. Martin's Griffin books may be purchased for educational, business, or promotional use. For information on bulk purchases, please contact Macmillan Corporate and Premium Sales Department at 1-800-221-7945, extension 5442, or write specialmarkets@macmillan.com.

First St. Martin's Griffin Edition: March 2014

10   9

This novel is dedicated to all of our brave
men and women in the armed services,
and to their loving families, with
deepest respect and gratitude.

Every war has it own signature wounds.

—Ronald J. Glasser, M.D., Major,
United States Army Medical Corps

Part One

Chapter One

Chloe woke up on the floor, her thoughts foggy. She must have fallen and knocked herself out when she hit the hardwood. She started to get up, but felt dizzy and eased back down. The kitchen was dark except for pinpoints of light on the coffeemaker, TV, and cable box, like a suburban constellation.

She tried to understand how long she'd been lying here. The last thing she remembered, she was rinsing the dishes after lunch, eyeing the sun through the window, like a big, fresh shiny yolk in the sky. Yellow was her favorite color, and she always tried to get it into her painting. Chloe used to teach art in middle school, but now she was a new mom with no time to shower, much less paint.

She heard a mechanical *ca-thunk,* and the Christmas lights went on outside. Red, green, and blue glimmered on the wetness underneath her, which seemed to be spreading. Her gaze traveled to its edge, where her Maine Coon, Jake, sat in silhouette under the table, his ears translucent triangles, backlit by the multicolored lights.

Chloe reached for a chair to pull herself up, but was oddly weak and slumped to the floor. She felt cold, though the kitchen had a southern exposure and stayed warm, even in winter. She needed help, but was alone. Her sister Danielle and her brother-in-law Bob had come over for lunch, then Danielle had taken the baby Christmas shopping and Bob had gone to work. They didn't have children, and Danielle had been happy to take Emily to the mall by herself.

We can pick out Christmas presents for you and Mike!

Chloe closed her eyes, wishing her husband Mike were here, but he was a reservist in the Army Medical Corps, serving in Afghanistan. He'd be home in a month, and she was counting the days. She'd prayed he wouldn't be called up because he was thirty-six years old, and when the deployment orders came, she'd taken it badly. She'd simply dissolved into tears, whether from sleep deprivation, crazed hormones, or worry.

Mike, please, I'm begging you. Don't go.

Suddenly Chloe realized something. The Christmas lights were controlled by a timer that turned them on at five o'clock, which meant Bob and Danielle would be back at any minute. She had to hide the vodka she'd left out on the counter. Nobody could know about her drinking, especially not Danielle. Chloe should have been more careful, but she was a beginner alcoholic.

She reached for the chair and hoisted herself up partway. The kitchen whirled, a mad blur of Christmas lights. She clung to the chair, feeling dizzy, cold, and spacey, as if she were floating on a frigid river. Her hand slipped, and the chair wobbled. Jake sprang backwards, then resettled into a crouch.

She put her hands on the floor to lift her chest up, like a push-up, but the wetness was everywhere. Under her hands, between her fingers, soaking her shirt. It didn't smell like vodka. The fog in her brain cleared, and Chloe remembered she'd been loading the dishwasher, and the chef's knife had slipped, slicing the underside of her arm. Bright red blood had spurted from the wound, and she'd fainted. She always fainted at the sight of blood, and Mike used to kid her.

The doctor's wife, who's afraid of blood.

Chloe looked at her left arm in horror. It was covered with blood, reflecting the holiday lights. Blood. Her mouth went dry. She'd been bleeding all afternoon. She could bleed to death.

"Help!" she called out, but her voice sounded far away. She had to get to her cell phone and call 911. She dragged herself through the slippery blood to the base cabinet, clawed the door for the handle, and grabbed it on the second try. She tried to pull herself up but had no strength left. She clung to the handle.

Chloe spotted her laptop to her right, on its side. She must have knocked it off the counter when she fell. Her best friend Sara was always online, and Chloe could g-chat her for help. She slid the laptop toward her and hit the keys with a slick palm, but the monitor didn't light up. She didn't know if it was off or broken.

She shoved it aside, getting a better idea. She would crawl to the front door and out to the sidewalk. The neighbors or someone driving by would see her. She started crawling, her breath ragged. The front door lay directly down the hall, behind a solid expanse of hardwood and an area rug. She dragged herself toward it, smearing blood across the kitchen threshold.

Hope surged in her chest. Her arms ached but they kept churning. She pulled herself into the hallway. She kept her eye on the front door. It had a window on the top half, and she could see the Christmas lights on the porch. She had put them up herself, for Emily's first Christmas.

The door lay thirty feet ahead, but Chloe felt her legs begin to weaken. Her arms were failing, but she couldn't give up. She was a mother. She had a precious baby, only seven months old.

Chloe moved forward on her elbows, but more slowly, like a car running out of gas. Still she kept going. The front door was only fifteen feet away. Then thirteen, then ten. She had to make it.

Go, go, go. Nine, eight, seven feet left.

Chloe reached the edge of the area rug, but couldn't go another inch. Her forehead dropped to the soft wool. Her body flattened. Her eyes closed as if they were sealed. She felt her life ebb away, borne off in a sea of her own blood. Suddenly she heard a noise, outside the house. A car was pulling into the driveway, its engine thrumming.

Thank God!

She heard the sound of a car door opening and closing, then footsteps on the driveway. They were slow because the driveway was icy in patches, the rock salt melting it unevenly.

Hurry, hurry, hurry.

Chloe remembered the front door was unlocked, a lucky break.

She was supposed to lock it behind Danielle, who had been carrying Emily, the diaper bag, and her purse, but she had forgotten. It would serve her well, now. Whoever was coming could see her through the window, rush in, and call 911.

The footsteps drew closer to the door, but Chloe didn't recognize them. She didn't know Bob or Danielle by their footstep. It could be anybody.

Please God hurry

The footsteps reached the front door, and Chloe heard the mechanical turning of the doorknob. The door unlatched, and she felt a vacuum as it swung open. Frigid air blasted her from the open doorway. Her hair blew into her face, but she couldn't even open her eyes.

Help me help me call 911

She heard the footsteps walk to her, then stop near her head. But whoever it was didn't call her name, rush to her side, or cry out in alarm.

What is going on why aren't you calling 911

She heard the footsteps walk back to the door.

Wait don't go please help me

She heard the sound of the front door closing.

No come back please help I'm—

The latch engaged with a quiet *click*.

Chapter Two

Mike raised the scalpel, about to make the first incision. He always said a prayer before he cut, though his wife Chloe was the religious one. She'd given him a silver crucifix before his deployment, and he kept it in his ACU pocket with a picture of their baby Emily. He was about to send up his homemade prayer when he noticed Joe Segundo, their administrative medical service officer, looking at him funny from across the OR.

Mike returned his focus to his case, telescoping the task at hand and ignoring the anguished moans of the wounded, the constant talk of the docs and nurses, the *whop whop whop* of the Chinook outside, and the *crack pop* of ordnance in the distance. The 556th FST, or Forward Surgical Team, was only three to five miles behind the offensive, but Mike didn't think about that when he operated, staying in the silence of his own mind, his fingers working on muscle memory, a result of the on-the-job training from hell, in hell.

The 556th was a twenty-person surgical team assigned to an Army combat brigade, traveling with three tents that took only an hour to assemble into a surgical facility complete with triage, OR, and recovery bays, as well as medical supplies and materiel to last seventy-two hours, including generators to power the fluorescent lights that shone overhead. The OR reeked of sickly-sweet blood and medicinal iodine wash, and the air was freezing. One of the nurses had decorated an IV stalk with homemade tinsel, but it wasn't easy to make carnage cheery.

Mike was the only orthopedist/podiatrist of the 556th, and the three other docs were general trauma surgeons, now bent so far over their patients that they looked almost headless from behind. There was Phil DeMaria from Providence, chubby enough to be called Phat Phil, and Adam Goldstein, who was in his mid-forties, so they called him Oldstein. Their FST commander was Stephen Chatham, a hotshot from Darien who never shut up in the OR. Mike called him Chatty Kathy, but he called himself Batman. Everybody loved Chatty, especially the nurses, who made him a Batman cape out of a body bag, which he never took off.

Mike never felt like a superhero, and podiatry was far from a prestigious branch of medicine, which was why his nickname was Dr. Scholl's. Ironically, blast injuries to the extremities were the signature wound of Operation Enduring Freedom, due to the overwhelming number of IEDs, so Mike was the busiest doc in the 556th. Supporting the team were three nurses, two nurse anesthetists, three medics, three surgical technicians, and Joe Segundo, who kept track of them and the paperwork the Army loved so much.

Mike focused his attention on his case, Nestor Salinas. Salinas was twenty-one, and his right calf and ankle were riddled with AK-47 fire that had shredded his gastrocnemius, the large calf muscle, and the smaller soleus, underneath. Salinas must've sprinted in high school track, his calves were so well-developed, but Mike didn't have time to think about that. The FST docs limited their surgeries to an hour or two, then evacuated the case to a Combat Support Hospital, or CSH, out of the battle zone, similar to the old-school MASH units. Salinas would end up in CSH Bagram, but the more severely wounded were flown from Bagram to Landstuhl Regional Medical Center in Germany.

Salinas was already being transfused, and Mike needed to salvage as much tissue as he could from the lower leg. His goal was to control any hemorrhage and clean, debride, irrigate, and pack the wounds, emplace a cast or external fixation if necessary and get

Salinas onto a transport. Each minute counted and the FST was in constant motion, but Mike had learned to slow time down while he operated, all the while assessing the variables that meant life or death in combat theatre.

Mike cut around the first wound, a glistening cavern of blown-away flesh, nine centimeters long. The bullets had shredded, burned, and shattered everything in their path, including the tibia and fibula, embedding bone fragments in the remaining tissue. Still it was only a GSW, a gunshot wound, and Mike had gotten used to the idea that a soldier who merely got shot was lucky.

He felt eyes on him as he worked and looked up to see Joe Segundo talking with Oldstein. It wasn't Mike's concern, and he made the cuts he needed, excising the purplish tissue and salvaging the healthy red and pink. The wound didn't smell bad and wasn't that filthy; in contrast, homemade IEDs were stuffed with trash, so when they blew up, they caused bizarrely dirty wounds, embedded with pens, rocks, pins, nails, and even kid's toys.

Mike tied off the veins, noting that the wound was remarkably clear of blood flow, thanks to a battlefield tourniquet by a combat medic, the medically trained infantrymen, the 68W who acted as first responders. Medics were able to stabilize a wounded soldier in fifteen minutes, and the one who had treated Salinas had written on his bare chest in purple marker, per procedure, so that the soldier was traveling with his medical records:

GSW
R LEG
4 HOLES
3 ENTRANCE
1 EXIT
tourniquet 3:15 am

Mike felt as if he were being watched again and glanced up to see Joe Segundo, now talking to Chatty. He wondered what was going on, momentarily distracted. He'd heard that the 556th might get reassigned up north, which would be a problem because they weren't ready to roll out yet. When they had to go, Chatty would tell them the way he always did—*to the Batmobile!*

Mike accepted a roll of Kerlix bandages from his nurse, Linda, and began to pack the wound, which stopped the bleeding by pinching off leaky vessels and pressing them into soft tissue. The technique was called tamponade, from the French, which also gave rise to the word *tampon*. Mike loved knowing stuff like that and he loved being a podiatrist, though they all kidded him because he worked in silence. His nurse, Linda, liked to joke around with Chatty, who was singing, *I'm too sexy for my cape,* and Linda sang back, *I'm too sexy for my gloves*, then Chatty sang, *Who needs latex, it gets in the way,* and the OR erupted in laughter.

Mike kept his hands in Salinas, who would become The Kid With The Lucky GSW. He remembered his soldiers by names he gave them, like The Kid With The Big Freckles, The Kid With The Lazy Eye, and The Virgin. He would never forget The Girl With Hair Like Chloe's, because he had to amputate her left foot after an IED blast. Her injuries scored nine on the Mangled Extremity Scoring System, the tactlessly-named MESS scale, when anything over seven was predictive of amputation. He still replayed that procedure in his mind when he couldn't sleep, thinking of Chloe.

He tried not to think of his wife now, but he wasn't succeeding. He loved his wife and he hated not to be home on their baby's first Christmas. His only consolation was that his tour ended in a month, and he was counting the days. Emily was only a newborn, a month old, when he deployed, and the photos Chloe emailed him showed how much she was growing. They emailed and Skyped when the 556th returned to base to resupply, but the contact only intensified his longing for her, the baby, his home, his practice, his very country. It was all too much, and afterwards, he would block it out, mentally. If Mike was a superhero of anything, it was that. He was the Batman of Compartmentalizing.

Joe Segundo walked to Mike's table, his dark eyes concerned over his surgical mask, which cut into his fleshy cheeks. He was a short and blocky Texan, whose jarhead haircut fit perfectly under his scrub cap. He frowned when he saw Salinas's wound, up-close. "Bone salad, yo," he said, with a touch of a Tex-Mex accent.

Mike glanced up. "What's going on?"

"When will you be finished?"

"Me? My tour is up in one month." Mike was joking, but he could tell by Joe's eyes that he didn't smile under his mask, which was strange. "Joe, what's up? Something on your mind?"

"Can we talk when you get a break in the action?"

Mike thought it was an odd request. "No, I gotta finish this kid, then I got another GSW. Why, are we rolling out?"

"The other GSW isn't an urgent. Oldstein will take him. Come find me when you're done, okay?"

"Okay." Mike let it go, figuring that it was about the FST or Army politics, as usual. Army MEDCOM was always on their case about one thing or another, and Joe loved to vent to Mike, whose odd-man-out status made him like Switzerland. It was probably nothing.

But later, when they told him that Chloe was dead, Mike remembered one thing:

I forgot to say my prayer.

Chapter Three

Mike climbed the jetway at Philadelphia International Airport in a sort of trance, numb. His backpack hung off his shoulder, and his iPod buds were plugged into his ears, though he played no music. He'd turned off his phone in Afghanistan, to avoid the condolence emails and calls from his former partners and friends. The one call he would have answered wouldn't come, ever again.

Mike lumbered into the gate area, where the fluorescent lights hurt his eyes and the Christmas music bled through his buds. It was inconceivable that Chloe was dead. She was worried about him, not the other way around. They'd even made wills and upped their life insurance, in case he died. So it made absolutely no sense that she had died in a household accident, a stab wound, an SW. His *wife*. It wouldn't have happened if he'd been home. He had failed her. Chloe had died alone.

He fell behind the excited and happy travelers, a swollen scrum of scarves and puffy coats who bustled along, rolling suitcases and carrying shopping bags of wrapped gifts. He kept going, head down and one boot in front of the other, past the Jamba Juice and a Gap decorated in red-and-green lights, blue-and-white menorahs, and signs 30% OFF EVERYDAY PRICES. The most time the Army would give him was ten days' emergency leave, so there was a lot to do in a short time, and Mike told himself he'd get it done, just like in surgery. He'd drape the blasted flesh and perform the steps in the procedure, which was burying his wife and making arrangements for the care of their child.

He tugged out his earbuds, tucked them in his pocket, and felt his senses assaulted by the sights, sounds, and colors. Afghanistan was tan and brown, except for what was gray; the dry earth was a gray-brown powder that the soldiers called moondust, and the flat-roofed Afghani houses of the Kunar Valley were hewn from gray-black indigenous rock, built into the mountains and covered with gray stones and grayer rubble. Camp Leatherneck, where he'd first flown in, was in the gray-brown-red desert, but at least it had a portable toilet, and he'd been in camps that smelled like smoke and feces, which they burned, creating a stench all its own.

Mike shook it off, trying to leave it behind, but caught betwixt and between. The aroma of fresh pizza filled the air as he passed the Sbarro's, and he caught a whiff of a flowery scent from a perfume kiosk. It reminded him of Chloe, so he tried not to breathe. He reached the security exit, where the crowd crammed together into a chute. They'd all be dead if they came under enemy fire, and he felt a bolt of reflexive fear. His heart rate picked up until he reminded himself he was home. A TSA lady smiled at him, showing a gold tooth, but he looked away.

"Mike! Over here!"

Mike spotted Bob, who clearly wasn't himself, showing the strain. Robert Ridgeway was a tall, sandy-haired lawyer, usually a commanding presence, but tonight his shoulders slumped in his camelhair topcoat and his brow furrowed all the way to his hairline, with its expensive layers. Mike threaded his way through the crowd and hugged him.

"Hey, Bob," he said hoarsely. He wanted to hold it together, in public. "Thanks for coming."

"I'm so sorry, Mike." Bob hugged Mike back awkwardly, either because of the backpack or the emotion.

"I still can't believe it."

"I know, Mike."

"It wasn't supposed to happen this way."

"No, it wasn't." Bob gave him a final squeeze, then let him go. His smallish eyes were a weary blue, and he looked older than his forty years. "What can I say?"

"Nothing. There's nothing to say. It's not possible." Mike tried to clear his throat, but it wasn't working. People glanced over, seeing it wasn't a typical holiday homecoming.

"Let's go. Did you check anything?"

"Nah, I got it." Mike didn't remark the naïveté of the question, which touched him. He hoisted his backpack onto his shoulder.

"I parked in short-term, so no muss, no fuss. Traffic's crazy." Bob walked down the corridor, and Mike fell into step beside him, trying to recover. Maybe he wasn't as good at compartmentalizing as he thought.

"How's Danielle taking it?"

"Terrible. She was in bed the whole first day, crying her eyes out, but she's coming around." Bob moved quickly, his topcoat flying open. "The baby's keeping her in the game, and she's worried about you."

Mike knew Danielle would be devastated. The sisters didn't always see eye-to-eye, but their differences seemed to dissolve after Emily was born. Danielle was the older of the two and she had helped Chloe with everything. "How's Emily?"

"She's great. Big. She's really cute, wait'll you see her, and she laughs, like, a belly laugh." Bob didn't look over. "Danielle will show you. She makes her laugh."

"Thanks for stepping in. You guys are a Godsend."

"Not me. Danielle did most of it."

"Nah, come on. Credit where credit is due. I saw you in that photo at the waterpark. Where was that, Dorney?"

"No, Sesame Place."

"They have a wave pool?" Mike reached the escalator, piling on behind Bob.

"No. You can't put that young a baby in a wave pool. It was a kiddie pool."

Mike reddened, oddly ashamed. He knew Emily was too young

for a wave pool. They reached the bottom of the escalator, where limo drivers lined up in front of glowing hotel ads. The crowd flowed to the right toward the baggage carousels, and Mike sped up to stay with Bob, who kept talking.

"Glad I bought the snowblower. Snowed yesterday, for six more inches. You believe this weather?"

Mike couldn't make small talk right now, so he didn't try. He knew that Bob felt as awful as he did, but just dealt with it differently.

"I saw online that Kabul and Philly are about the same latitude, so we have the same weather. Weird, huh?"

Mike thought it was typical Bob, who prepared for everything, which he actually liked.

"I was looking at some photos, of Kabul. What a dump! It looks like the Stone Age."

Mike didn't want to talk about Kabul, either. The coffee shops and Internet cafes did business among the rubble and burned-out cars. The children played under the bridges, next to heroin addicts. The Afghani people were grateful, anguished, and angry, in equal measure. The Afghan National Army, ANA, and the Afghan National Police, ANP, were willing but unable. The Coalition Forces were gone or out of gas.

"I looked online. There's, like, *three* cities in the whole damn country."

Mike didn't correct him, unaccountably defensive. Afghanistan was a godforsaken country that he loved. The nights there could be so beautiful it was terrifying. Oddly, Mike had thought none of these thoughts until this very moment. He survived in the FST because he kept his head down and his focus narrowed to one wound, one bleeder, one suture. If he did his job well, he disappeared.

"Did you know that Afghanistan is twice the size of Iraq?" Bob motored ahead. "I read that Helmand Province is about seventy-eight thousand square miles. That's huge. Chloe told us you can hear monkeys howl at night."

Chloe. Mike felt a thud in his chest. Bob said her name, and it was like breaking a spell, or casting one.

"Chloe said you saw tarantulas and mountain lions, too. And vultures."

Mike didn't want to think about vultures. Every war probably had vultures. The birds of Southern Afghanistan were varied and beautiful, but they all scattered the same way when an RPG was fired.

"What a mess, huh?" Bob led him out toward the exit. "We still got troops there. People die every week, but it hardly makes the news."

Mike found his mood worsening, his grief descending like nightfall. They left the terminal, joining the noisy crowd at the pedestrian crossing. The cold air braced him and he struggled to acclimate to the density, traffic, and honking horns. Cigarette smoke wafted into his face, and it reminded him of the soldiers, who all smoked or chewed. They weren't under his care long enough for him to lecture them.

Bob stepped off the curb. "Follow me. I parked where the limos do."

"Will the baby be up?"

"With any luck, she will."

"Good." Mike wanted to hold his baby daughter, a soft little bundle of Emily. She'd barely been as long as his forearm when he left. He would tell her all about her mom. He would make sure she remembered her mother, always. He would show her photos and make sure Emily knew that her mother had loved her to the very marrow.

"Mike, just so you know, we took the crib and toys and brought them to the house. Danielle wanted to keep as many things the same as possible." Bob barreled along, his breath steamy in the chilly air. "Danielle loves taking care of the baby, and that's what family's for."

"Thanks." Mike would have to hire a nanny to take care of the baby until his deployment ended and he'd already emailed agencies. His parents were dead, and so were Chloe's.

"Wait'll you see the new house. We moved in last month. Finally."

Mike swallowed hard, remembering that Chloe had been so happy to have them closer, after they found out he was being deployed. But even that hadn't helped her, in the end. She had died alone. Mike felt a wave of guilt so powerful it almost felled him.

"I told the contractor, I'm not paying the last installment until you're done." Bob stalked through the parking lot, with Mike following. "The only good thing about a lousy economy is that it gives people like me leverage. Cash is king, baby."

Mike hung his head. The Army didn't know any details of Chloe's accident, except that she cut herself by accident. He couldn't listen to another minute of small talk. "Bob, what happened to her?"

"Huh?" Bob turned, his blondish eyebrows lifting.

"Chloe. What happened to her?" Mike heard his voice break. He stopped walking. He didn't want to take another step until he knew everything. The chattering crowd flowed around them, their roller-bags rumbling on the frozen asphalt.

Bob faced Mike, his forehead creased. "Let's talk about it at home, okay?"

"Can't we talk about it here?"

"Mike." Bob looked crestfallen. "Mike, please. Can't it wait? Danielle knows more than I do. She can explain."

Mike understood. They both felt a little lost without their wives, who knew how to make this easier. They were just two guys in a parking lot, trying not to embarrass themselves in front of strangers. "Okay."

Bob turned away, raised his key fob, and chirped his black Mercedes to life.

Mike knew that Bob heaved a sigh because a cloud of steamy breath wreathed his head, rose into the air, and floated off.

Vanishing like a ghost.

Chapter Four

Mike entered the house behind Bob. It was warm and lovely, like something out of a magazine. Crystal lamps shone from mahogany tables, and a navy blue patterned sofa and matching chairs sat around a gas fireplace, flickering behind smoked glass. Holiday cards lined up on the mantel, and a Christmas tree decorated with tiny white lights blinked like electrified stars. Wrapped presents were spread on a carpet of fake snow, and the air smelled of pine, from a scented candle.

"Danielle, we're home." Bob walked ahead, taking off his top-coat.

Mike hung back and tugged down his ACU shirt, trying to make sense of his situation. One day he was covered in blood and he had a wife, and the next he had no wife and he was *here*. He set the back-pack on the Oriental rug, worried it would leave moondust.

"Mike, oh, Mike." Danielle came toward him from the back of the house, throwing open her arms, reminding Mike so powerfully of Chloe that he almost lost it. He met Danielle and hugged her close, knowing if he started crying, he'd never stop. Danielle looked a lot like Chloe but wasn't exactly Chloe, in the way sisters echo each other but aren't exact replicas, and as Mike held Danielle, he felt the agony of losing Chloe and the joy at having her again, even if an echo was as insubstantial as thin air.

"I'm so sorry." Danielle clung to him, sniffling in his arms, slim and vaguely stiff in a white blouse and pressed jeans. "I know you loved her, so much."

"You, too." Mike breathed in her floral perfume and peach-scented hair conditioner, the scents that were almost-but-not-quite Chloe. "I'm so sorry you lost her, too."

"She was my best friend. She was a great sister, and a great mother." Danielle's tone strengthened, recovering. She patted his back. "We'll get through this together, as a family. We'll pull together, and I'll be there for you and Emily, and so will Bob."

"Thank you." Mike released her, managing to keep it together, and Danielle smiled up at him with glistening eyes, her lower lip trembling.

"Everybody sends their love and sympathy. All the old teachers at the middle school, and even some of her old students. Your partners have been calling and they sent a card." Danielle sniffled and managed a shaky smile. "I was so touched by that, because Chloe liked them all, so much. People are posting on Facebook, too, on Chloe's wall, sending you and the baby love and sympathy, which is nice."

"Is she awake?" Mike felt an overwhelming urge to see Emily.

"No, she's not, I'm sorry." Danielle wiped her tears with her index finger turned on its side. "I tried, but she fell asleep."

"I want to see her anyway. Is she upstairs?" Mike went to the staircase and looked up to the second floor, his hand on the banister.

"Yes, she is."

Bob came up, his topcoat off. "Mike, why don't you eat, then go see her. She's not going anywhere." He loosened his tie, making deep wrinkles in his neck skin. "How about it, huh? Come in the kitchen. Danielle made turkey chili."

"I made it the way you like it," Danielle added gently. "I have shredded cheddar. Eat first, then go see her. You don't want to upset her."

"Okay." Mike didn't want Emily to see him such a mess. He was supposed to be a father, not a bowl of Jell-O.

"Here, come with me." Danielle took his elbow. "People have been dropping off casseroles and pies, too. When was the last time you had a good meal?"

"I don't know." Mike let her steer him into the kitchen, which smelled of spicy chili, but he had no appetite.

"Go, sit down, please." Danielle gestured at a pine table with long benches instead of chairs, which reminded him of the mess hall at Bagram. It was set for dinner and stood against a wall of windows. He checked outside reflexively, but they were safe. Snow shimmered in an encrusted carpet, and frosted evergreens were illuminated by spotlights. In Afghanistan, they would say the house needed light security, making itself a target from the air.

"The house is really nice," Mike said, trying to get normal.

"Thanks." Danielle crossed to the stove, which was huge and shiny, of black enamel. Walnut cabinets and glossy black granite counter-tops ringed the huge kitchen. "It was a labor of love."

"Ha." Bob pulled out the bench and sat down opposite Mike. "By love she means money."

"Bob, ahem, I earn money, too, remember?" Danielle shook her head, without rancor. She was a graduate of Penn Law School, but had never practiced and worked as the office administrator at Bob's law firm, The Ridgeway Group.

"Are those Emily's toys?" Mike gestured at the family room, which had a custom entertainment center, tan sectional furniture, and a beige carpet covered with toys, a playpen, and a baby swing.

"Yes." Bob grunted. "The girls have taken over my man cave."

"Bob, really?" Danielle came over with a cup of coffee and set it down in front of Mike. "Here we go, with Half & Half."

"Thanks." Mike didn't take his coffee that way anymore, but didn't say so. He kept looking at the toys, which he didn't recognize, though he'd gone with Chloe to Toys R Us before he was deployed. It was their big shopping trip with a newborn Emily, who slept through the whole store. Still they'd had a blast, going through the aisles.

We need diapers, Chloe had said, pulling him away from the Barbie cars.

But this is automotive excellence. When can we get her one of these?

"You okay, Mike?" Danielle asked, from the stove.

"Fine." Mike turned from the toys, his heart aching. "Danielle, what happened to Chloe? Do you have the details?"

"Oh, honey." Danielle waved him off with a wooden spoon. "Let's talk after. Dinner's ready now."

"No, tell me. Please." Mike braced himself. "I want to know everything. Who found her? Did you?"

"Now, you want to talk?"

"Yes. Please?"

"Okay." Danielle set the spoon on a ceramic rest, lowered the heat, and came over, sitting next to Bob. Her lower lip puckered, and she laced her fingers together in front of her, a smallish bony fist on the table. "I found her. I was out with the baby for the day, to give Chloe a break. I thought it would be nice if you and Chloe got a present from Emily. We got Chloe an ornament, and you a book."

Mike tried to listen without emotion. He didn't want to think about the ornament Chloe would never get, picked out by their baby. He felt broken and woozy. He sipped his coffee, which didn't taste like anything but heat. His hand was shaking.

"The police think that Chloe cut herself on a knife, then hit her head on the counter when she fell." Danielle bit her lip. "You know she fainted when she saw blood."

"So it was an accident, with a knife." Mike knew that much. He wanted to know more, everything.

"Yes. It was on her forearm. I didn't look. She was in the entrance hall, face down. They think she was trying to get to the door." Danielle's eyes glistened, and Bob put his arm around her. "They think she knocked herself unconscious, and when I came home that night with the baby, I found her."

Mike squeezed the mug. He wanted to crush it. He wanted to drive shards into his palms.

"I called 911, and while I was waiting for them I called Bob."

Danielle looked down at her knotted fingers. "They came quickly, in fifteen minutes, but she . . . wasn't alive when I found her."

Mike didn't understand. He had so many questions, all of them coming at once. "Why didn't she call 911 when she woke up?"

"She was unconscious for a long time."

"How long?"

"No, it's not that."

"Then what is it?" Mike shook his head. "Why didn't she call 911? She wouldn't have let herself bleed out." A thought occurred to him, for the first time. "It wasn't *intentional,* was it?"

"No, no, not at all, nothing like that." Danielle's pained blue eyes shifted to Bob. "Honey, you tell him."

Bob turned to Mike, his face falling into somber lines. "She'd been drinking. I saw a vodka bottle on the counter. She was probably passed out for hours. We figure that by the time she woke up, it was too late to call for help."

"*What?*" Mike felt as if he'd been slapped in the face. He recoiled, astounded. "That's not possible. Chloe had wine at dinner, one or two glasses, that was it."

"Mike, she was drunk."

"No," Mike shot back, shocked. "That's not true. She never gets drunk. I've *never* seen her drunk! She hardly even drinks hard liquor."

"I know, not usually, but this time, she—"

"Stop it! *Stop!*" Mike found himself on his feet, jumping up, bumping the table with his thighs, jolting the dishes and glasses.

Danielle gasped, cowering. "Mike!"

Bob raised his hands, palms up. "Relax, Mike. I know, I didn't believe it either."

"I *don't* believe it! I *don't*! You're wrong! She wasn't *drunk*!"

Bob shook his head. "We'd suspected it for a while. Danielle smelled it on her breath once—"

"Stop it!" Mike kicked the bench savagely, a display of violence he'd never shown. "Shut up!"

Bob rose, his hands up, as if he were fending off a wild animal. "Mike, you need to calm down."

"Don't tell me what I need!" Mike exploded. He didn't recognize himself. It was his soul, screaming. "I know what I need! I need my *wife*!"

Bob looked terrified and Danielle recoiled, as if Mike had detonated a grenade in their kitchen, but he still couldn't stop himself, anguished.

"What happened to Chloe? I love her! I *love her*!"

"I loved her, too." Danielle's lower lip quivered. "She was my little sister, my only sister. I looked out for her since day one."

"Aw, sweetheart." Bob sat down and put his arm around her again, and Danielle burst into tears.

"I'm sorry," Mike said, agonized. They didn't deserve this, they were mourning, too. Suddenly he knew what he wanted to do.

He turned away, left the kitchen, and lumbered down the hallway.

Chapter Five

Mike opened the door and knew he'd picked the right bedroom by the slight humidity of the air and the faint scent of baby lotion. He closed the door and walked to the crib, adjusting to the darkness. He wasn't going to wake Emily up. He just wanted to see her with his own eyes, to know she was alive. To prove to himself that not everything he loved could be taken from him, while his back was turned.

He hung over the rail and looked inside the crib, feeling a sort of awe at the sight. Emily lay on her back, wearing a fuzzy blue sleeper, and her head was to the side. Her arms were flung backwards, bent at the elbows, with her hands up, her fingers curled. She was so still he wasn't even sure she was breathing, so he held his hand near her mouth and felt the soft warmth of her respiration, gentle beyond belief.

He flashed on the day they'd brought her home from the hospital. He'd been so nervous, fumbling to buckle her into the brand-new car seat, essentially a plastic bucket. She'd sagged forward, her head flopped so far onto her chest it alarmed even him, who should have known better. He'd driven home as carefully as he could, with one eye on the rearview.

Honey, this is amazing, he'd said. *We have a baby!*

There's four of us now. Chloe had grinned at him from the backseat. *The cat still counts. Jakey was our first child.*

Mike let his gaze travel to Emily's face, which was beautiful. She looked so much like Chloe, with her slim nose and slightly down-turned lips, and her eyes were wide-set, too, like her mother's. Faint blondish curls covered her head, the same color as Chloe's hair, at least in the darkness, and there was a sweet curve to her forehead. Chloe's forehead had been prominent, too.

I hate my forehead, she always said. *It's too big.*

Mike had said, *It's all those brains.*

What are you angling for? Because you're still going to the dry cleaners.

Mike smiled at the memory, so real it felt as if it were happening, right here. It was Emily, bringing Chloe back to him. The baby's eye-lids fluttered, and he could tell by the shape that her eyes were big, like Chloe's. Chloe's eyes were a light blue, but he couldn't recall the blue of Emily's. He tried to remember from the emailed photos, but the color on them was never exact. He knew the stark blue of the Afghan sky, the dark blue of venous blood, and the green-blue of a soldier's tattoo, but he didn't know the blue of his own child's eyes. Chloe would know, but Chloe wasn't here.

I am so sorry, Chloe. I should have been with you. I vowed to be with you.

Mike felt tears come to his eyes and moved his hand to Emily's chest. The sleeper was soft, and her body warm under his palm. He opened his fingers, and his hand covered her entire torso. He bit his lip not to cry when he felt her tiny heartbeat. He wondered if Chloe had ever stood over Emily's crib at night, putting her hand on the ba-by's heart, thinking of him. The husband who had let her die alone.

"Are you okay?" whispered a voice, and Mike looked up to see Danielle standing in the threshold, silhouetted by the hallway light, her hand on the doorknob.

"I'm fine," Mike answered, but he forgot to whisper. Emily started to wake up, moving her head back and forth, then opened her eyes and looked directly at him, something she hadn't done as a new-born. He felt a bolt of sheer joy and on impulse, reached into the crib and scooped her up. "Hi, Emily, it's Daddy!"

Emily started to cry, and Danielle rushed into the bedroom, clos-ing the door behind her. "Don't hold her like that. Support her head."

26 | Lisa Scottoline

"Okay." Mike tried to support Emily's head, but she twisted in his arms. She seemed strong for a baby, and it felt great to hold her, despite the decibel-level. She was tangible proof of life, of Chloe, of family.

"Don't do that."

"What am I doing wrong?" Mike supported the baby's head, but she kept turning away from him.

"Here, give her to me." Danielle reached for the wailing baby, who stretched her tiny arms to her.

"Can't I do something?" Mike asked, but before he could stop her, Danielle had taken Emily.

"Em, it's all right, it's okay, that's your Daddy." Danielle cuddled Emily, and the baby quieted quickly.

Mike felt oddly rejected, though he knew he was being silly. He would've given it more of a try. "What can I do?"

Danielle shushed him, and Emily twisted around, saw him, and started to cry again. "Do you see her pacifier in the crib? It's pink."

Mike crossed to the crib and moved some plush toys around, but didn't see the pacifier. He wanted to hold Emily and comfort her, on his own. "Can I give it another chance? When she was little, I could get her to stop crying."

"Not now, Mike. She's tired."

"What if you turn her around and let her see me, and we turn on the light?"

"I don't think so. Another time, okay?" Danielle kept rocking the crying baby. "You go, and I'll get the binky. She'll be fine in the morning, you'll see."

"You sure I can't try again?"

Emily wailed loudly.

"Okay, right, I'll go." Mike fled past them for the door, opened it, then closed it behind him. Flop sweat had broken out under the heavy cotton of his ACUs, and Bob was coming down the hall, frowning.

"Uh-oh, you woke the baby. Danielle will kill you."

"I know, sorry. I have to be calmer, next time. I got too excited. I guess I held her wrong."

"Don't feel bad, Danielle's got the touch." Bob gestured to the bedroom, where the crying was subsiding. "See? Emily loves her. You have to look it at from Emily's view. You're a stranger to her."

I'm her father, Mike thought, but Bob was right. He was a stranger who was also Emily's father.

"She'll come around. Give her time." Bob touched him on the arm. "You look like you need a drink."

"No, thanks." Mike felt lost, dislocated. He belonged with Chloe, but she was gone. He belonged with Emily, but she didn't know him. He found himself thinking about their cat, which was pathetic. "Bob, what happened to Jake, the cat?"

"Sara took him, and her boys love him already. We couldn't take him. Danielle hates cats."

"Sure." Mike hid his dismay. Sara was Chloe's best friend, and he'd never get the cat back now. "You know, I think I want to go home."

"To your house, now? Why?" Bob frowned, surprised. "Aren't you tired?"

"No." Mike was still on Afghanistan time, eight and a half hours ahead. "Can I borrow your car?"

"Don't go, it's not a pretty sight." Bob placed a firm hand on Mike's shoulder. "There was a lot of blood. Danielle cleaned up what she could, then she got professionals in, and even they couldn't get it all."

Mike blinked, horrified. He couldn't picture Chloe's blood, in their home, in her kitchen.

"I know, it's tough, and you'll need a good night's sleep tonight. There's a lot to do in the next few days. We didn't get a chance to talk schedule, but you have to pick out a casket tomorrow."

Mike couldn't listen, thinking of Chloe's loving heart, leaking blood until it stilled. He thought of Emily's tiny heart, beating down the hall, and his own heart, broken.

"The funeral is the day after tomorrow. It's the only day we could get the church, with the holidays. I know it's rushed, but we had no choice."

Mike felt a flicker of clarity. "Bob, I want to go *home.*"

Chapter Six

Mike felt stricken when he spotted his house toward the end of the quiet, snowy street. He'd dreamed of coming home to Chloe and the baby, but he never imagined the scenario without her. No soldier dreams of coming home to an empty house, and even the sight of the house, white clapboard colonial, reminded him of Chloe. She was the one who'd found it online, obsessively checking the MLS, getting the jump on the Realtors and falling in love with its thumbnail photo. She knew it would be perfect for them, and she had been right. He remembered the day they'd taken possession and celebrated by making love in the empty living room.

On the floor? Chloe had asked, laughing, but she was already pulling her shirt over her head.

No, on the sales agreement. Did you see how many copies they made? That's a mattress.

Then you're on the bottom! Chloe had unfastened her lacy bra and reached for him.

Mike shook off the memory, approaching the house. Christmas lights lined the porch roof, wound around the downspout, and ran along the side to the kitchen, in back. Chloe must have strung them by herself, for a holiday she wouldn't live to see.

I am so sorry, honey.

Mike reached the house, steered into his driveway, and pulled in behind her yellow VW Beetle, parked where it always was, since they kept his Grand Cherokee in the garage. His headlights blasted the vanity plate he'd bought her, which read RTEEST. Chloe had been confused by the plate, he remembered.

Thanks, but what does it mean? Rit-est?

No. Artiste. Isn't that French for artist?

Ha! You speak French now!

No, I speak license plate.

Chloe had laughed. She had a wonderful laugh, light and happy, and Mike loved to make her laugh. He was a quiet guy, but he tried to be funny for her. He cut the ignition, plunging RTEEST into shadow, then sat still a moment, trying to gather his composure before he went inside. His only shot was that he'd cried all his tears out, though he knew that wasn't medically possible. He pressed down the emergency brake, yanked the key out of the ignition, and climbed from the car.

The frozen air hit him in the face, and his breath turned to steam. He walked up the driveway to her Beetle, put his hand on the frigid handle, and pressed the button, which he knew would be unlocked. Chloe left everything unlocked, which drove him nuts, until now.

Honey, you should lock up!

In Wilberg? Are you kidding?

Mike got inside the car, sat in the front seat, and closed the door behind him, without knowing why. Because it was hers. Because she sat here last. Because she loved this car. He didn't readjust the seat, though his knees didn't fit under the wheel. He sat in darkness, feeling the seat behind him, the shape of her body, fitting his. He closed his eyes. He could have been in bed, with her spooning him, behind. She liked that.

Don't get any ideas, she would joke. *I'm just cuddling.*

Cuddling is permitted. No ideas at all.

Mike opened his eyes. The dashboard was deep and black, and he glanced around to see how she'd left it. The console held a Chap-Stick, a ballpoint, half a pack of gum, loose change, and other junk. He dug in the console, spotted a silvery tube of lip gloss, and picked it up. She didn't wear much makeup, but she was always reapplying this stuff.

Why do you do that? he asked her, once.

So I look kissable.

You look kissable right now. Want me to prove it?

Mike's chest tightened. He wished she were here, so she could leave everything unlocked and put on makeup she didn't need. He put the lip gloss in his pocket and was about to get out of the car when he saw the Dunkin' Donuts cup in the cupholder. Chloe was never without a cup of coffee.

I'm addicted, she would say.

Mike thought of Bob and Danielle saying she'd been drunk on vodka, which was impossible. Chloe didn't even drink vodka, much less to excess. He wondered if there would be police reports or a coroner's report. He didn't know the legalities, and it wasn't as if she'd been murdered. There would have been an autopsy. The thought made him physically sick.

He got out of the car and walked up the driveway to the house, where he climbed the few steps of the porch, then stopped short. Their welcome mat was covered with red roses in shiny foil, a poinsettia plant with a red-and-green ribbon, and a bouquet of red-and-white carnations, wrapped in transparent paper. A pile of sympathy cards sat wedged among the flowers, and there were handwritten cards from her former students. One read, WE MISS YOU, MS. VOULETTE.

Mike felt hit in the chest, as if he'd been shot. The flowers showed him how much Chloe was loved, and also that she was lost. They proved that she had lived and she had died. It was almost more than he could bear. He gathered them up tenderly, unlocked the door, and went inside.

Chapter Seven

Mike set the flowers on the console table, flicked on the light and surveyed the entrance hall. The house was foreign and familiar, both at once. It was the same entrance hall, but something was missing.

Chloe is missing.

Mike set aside the thought, then it struck him. The area rug was gone, an Oriental that Chloe had bought in Lambertville, and the oak floor showed the faintest square of lighter wood. Then he realized why the rug wasn't here. It must have been stained with blood. He worked his jaw, suppressing a wave of nausea. Chloe must have crawled from the kitchen to the entrance hall. She was trying to save herself. Because he wasn't there to save her.

He crouched on his haunches and ran his fingers along the hardwood, which was smooth and clean, with barely any grit or dirt. He placed his palm flat against one spot, the way he had on Emily's heart. He wondered crazily if he would feel Chloe's heart stop, the way he had felt Emily's beat. He felt nothing but cold wood, inanimate. It used to be alive, but it wasn't anymore.

Oh, honey. I'm so very very sorry.

He got down on his hands and knees, scrutinizing the grain of the hardwood, looking for some of her blood. The floorboards were of random width, and the aged oak was rich with browns, golds, and blackish gray. He ran his finger down one dark vein and realized how much it was like a human vein, narrowing to the tiniest of cracks, a wooden capillary. The floorboards were clean, which meant she hadn't bled through the rug. She must have lost too much blood before she'd even got this far.

Mike, she was drunk.

Mike didn't believe it, not a word. Bob and Danielle were mistaken. Maybe Chloe had a drink, or maybe a neighbor had stopped in, or Sara or her other teacher friends had come to see the baby. She might have gotten a bottle of vodka out for them. It was the holidays, after all. Mike felt driven to understand what had happened, to retrace the last moments of her life. Maybe if he knew the order of events, he could reverse everything, like hitting a button on a videotape. He would rewind it back to his deployment, then to his enlisting in the Reserves. He wanted to serve his country, but he didn't want it to cost him his wife. He would have paid the price, but not Chloe. Not her.

He found himself moving on his hands and knees toward the kitchen, the reverse of what Chloe had done in her final hours. He kept running his hands over the wood until he reached the threshold of the kitchen. He couldn't see the floorboards anymore because the entrance-hall light was behind him. The only light in the kitchen was the colored Christmas lights shining through the windows, so he stood up and flicked on the kitchen light.

Mike took a second to let himself absorb the sight. An unmistakable darkness stained the floor between the table and cabinets. He walked over to it slowly, his heavy boots creaking on the hardwood, profaning it somehow. His kitchen floor had become hallowed ground. He eyed the stain, reflexively estimating its size as if it were a flesh wound, which it was, in a way. The darkness was about four feet wide by five feet long, lethal by any measure.

Please. Please forgive me.

He looked around the kitchen, which had been decorated by Chloe, with her painterly sensibility and her attraction to the happy colors of her native Provence. The walls were a sunny yellow, the woodwork a crisp white, and the curtains had a flower pattern that was bright red, warm gold, and deep blue. Chloe's collection of Quimper plates ringed the room, each showing a French peasant in primitive dress. Mike remembered the day he had hung them, with her supervising.

Honey, they have to face each other, Chloe had said.

Why?

They're married.

Like I said.

He found his gaze returning to the stain. Chloe's blood had seeped into the floorboards, running from her veins into its veins, as if to bring it back to life. But it was only wood, not flesh or bone, and Mike knew firsthand that nothing dead ever revivified. He couldn't imagine her lying here, dying in her own kitchen, in a spreading pool of her own blood.

His thoughts defaulted to the doctor in him, trying to understand her final moments. People who bled to death didn't simply lose all their blood, as most laymen believed. When their blood level dropped, tissues went into oxygen deprivation, which triggered the metabolism to slow down. The body would lose its ability to stay warm, which in turn caused hypothermia, depressing the heart rate, circulation, and the blood's ability to clot, or coagulate, the last line of defense. Finally, the cells, starved for oxygen, would produce lactic acid, which dropped PH levels in the blood as the body began to crash. The heart would cease to contract and it would surrender, the vessels and fluids released in a slow process. Every step of the way, Chloe would have known she was dying.

Suddenly Mike felt his gorge rising. He rushed to the sink, where he vomited until he was dry heaving. He turned on the hot and cold water and the garbage disposal, waiting for his stomach to settle, resting his shaking hand on the counter. His mouth tasted disgusting, so he drank some water from the tap, then looked around for a paper towel. The rack on the wall was empty, leaving only the cardboard tube, which Chloe never could have done.

Mike, when you use the last paper towel, replace it, huh?

He went to the pantry and opened up the cabinet where they kept the paper towels, but there were none. Chloe always kept back-up, but Danielle or the cleaners must've used them. He wiped his mouth on his sleeve, then spotted something glinting in the back of the cabinet. He shoved his hand in and pulled it out. A bottle of Smirnoff vodka, half-full.

Mike held it, in astonishment. He twisted off the lid and took a whiff. Vodka. If the paper towels had been there, the bottle wouldn't have been visible. It was hidden, not even where they kept their liquor. He moved some cans aside, and there were no other bottles. It couldn't have been Chloe's vodka. Maybe the cleaners had left it when they cleaned.

He set the bottle down and went to the top cabinet, where they kept their liquor. Mid-priced merlot, chardonnay, and pinot bottles stood in front, with a few of hard liquor in the back. He took out each bottle, double-checking. The wine bottles remained sealed, and the only opened ones were a bottle of Tanqueray, a quart of Chivas, and Patron tequila, all from his deployment party. They'd invited his partners and their wives, and the staff. Mike drank beer, and Chloe drank wine, as usual.

He opened one cabinet after the next, relieved to find no more vodka bottles, then went back to the kitchen and looked in the first base cabinet, next to the sink. Nothing but frying pans, in a concentric stack. He went to the cabinet under the sink and spotted a tell-tale glint behind the bottle of Windex. He reached inside and pulled a bottle out by its neck, throttling it between his fingers. It was another bottle of Smirnoff, mostly full.

Mike shook his head in disbelief. He stood up with the bottle, cool and smooth in his hand. The cleaners must have left this, not Chloe. He wasn't in denial, it didn't make sense. She had no reason to hide vodka from herself. Maybe somebody was hiding the vodka *from* her. Maybe she didn't know it was there, or the other one, either. Just because it was here didn't mean she drank it.

He set down the bottle, left the kitchen, and went to the front door, then opened it and hustled to the Beetle in the frigid air. He tore open the car door, reached inside, and grabbed the coffee cup from the cupholder. There was still liquid left in the cup, of whatever was inside.

He held the coffee cup a second, examining it in the Christmas lights. The plastic lid bore traces of Chloe's pink lip gloss, and her lips imprinted around the tiny slot. He held the cup to his lips and put his lips where hers had been.

Kissing her one final time.

Chapter Eight

Mike hurled the bottle against the kitchen wall, where it shattered, spraying glass and vodka. He'd missed the Quimper plate. Alcohol poured down the wall, making the yellow paint slick. His chest heaved in fury and confusion. Chloe was a secret drunk. If she hadn't been loaded, she'd be alive today.

He threw another bottle, higher and harder. It exploded on the wall, an inch from the Quimper plate. Vodka and glass shards rained everywhere. It killed him to think that she drove while she drank vodka and coffee. It killed him that he didn't know why. It killed him that he thought she was okay. It killed him that she was dead.

He fired another bottle and hit the Quimper plate. It smashed on contact and fell off the wall in pieces. He crossed to the wall and yanked off every other plate, smashing the married couples on the floor. He looked around for something else to throw, his mind ablaze. Chloe could have killed Emily in that car, drinking and driving. She could've killed herself. She could've killed anybody.

Mike seized a kitchen chair and flung it across the room. He grabbed another chair and hurled it against the cabinets. He flipped the kitchen table and swept the toaster off the counter. He yanked out the microwave plug and flung the microwave into the air. He stormed to the pantry, tore open the liquor cabinet, and yanked out each bottle, smashing them on the floor. He reached the tequila, but spared it. He tugged out the cork and took a swig. Tequila burned down his throat. He stalked out of the kitchen, down the hall, and upstairs in a rage.

He stormed to their bedroom, lurched to Chloe's bureau, and straight-armed her perfume bottles onto the rug. He set down the tequila, picked up her jewelry box, and sent it spiraling toward her closet. He pulled out each one of her drawers and dumped them, and he was just getting started. He was going to destroy everything, the way Chloe had destroyed everything. Him. Their life. Their baby's life. Herself. He wouldn't rest until he laid to waste all he once knew, and loved.

Turns out he had to come home, to wage war.

Chapter Nine

Mike opened his eyes. It was light. His head pounded, his tongue felt dry. He didn't know where he was. The FST had to roll out. He had to get to the OR. Casualties were on the way in the medevac.

"Mike, wake up!" Bob was standing over him in his topcoat, shaking him.

"Okay, okay. I'm awake." Mike put his hands up. His brain started to function. It was all coming back to him, in a sickening blur. He was home in bed, and Chloe was a secret drunk. And even so, he mourned her with every beat of his heart.

"Come on, Mike, we gotta go. Didn't you hear your phone?" Bob stood over him. "What did you do? The house is a mess."

Mike's head hurt like hell. He caught a whiff of Bob's minty shaving cream, which nauseated him.

"Get up, we're gonna be late for the funeral director. We have to get a casket. We've been trying to call you. I have Danielle's car."

Mike rubbed his eyes, remembering. He still had his phone turned off.

"We have to pick out the casket and get them the dress, that's my marching orders." Bob shook his head. "After that, I have to go to the city, I have a pretrial conference that I couldn't get out of. Try telling a federal judge his schedule isn't the only schedule. If this case settles, I'm done with work until after the funeral. Sara's coming over to pick out the dress."

"Sara, here? When?"

"Around noon." Bob looked around, eyeing the debris. "She wanted to help out, so we decided that Danielle should stay home with the baby and Sara should come over and pick out the dress, but I didn't know it would look like this. Sheesh."

"I found the booze." Mike felt sick at heart. "She hides it, I don't know why. I found booze in the car, too, so she drives drunk. I don't understand, I just don't. It's not her, it just isn't her."

Bob sank onto the bed, deflated. "I didn't think she'd drink and drive. Don't tell Danielle. She doesn't need to know."

Mike didn't like secrets, but he let it go. A snowblower blared outside, and the patterned curtains hung open. Sun shone through the window, glittering on the jewelry strewn on the rug. "Sorry I freaked on you, when you told me."

"S'allright." Bob turned to him, his expression pained. His white collar was so sharp it cut into his neck. "My conference is at eleven, in the city. You can get ready fast, right?"

"Sure. I'll shower and wear clothes from here." Mike started to get up, but Bob stopped him, checking his watch.

"No, wait. Let's go to Plan B. You stay put. I'll go pick out a casket, and you clean yourself up and the house. Get ready for Sara."

"Thanks, but no. I should get the casket." Mike sat up, fighting queasiness.

"No, you meet Sara. She really wants to see you, and I'll buy a nice casket, I looked online. They have bronze, copper, and stainless steel, but I'd go with hardwood. Something simple, maybe cherry. The poplar looked ugly in the picture."

"Yes, fine, cherry." Mike felt mixed up, loving and hating Chloe. She deserved either the best casket, or cardboard. He wondered when he could see her body. "When is she, you know, going to be ready?"

"Not until the end of the day. I'll order flowers, too. The funeral home has a package deal. What was her favorite color?"

"Yellow." Mike thought of the kitchen walls, slick with vodka.

"I'll get lots of yellow. Mums, roses, right? Burial expenses are about fifteen grand, all told. Her burial expenses come out of her life insurance, under the will. You were her beneficiary."

Mike hadn't even thought of it. Bob had drafted their wills, powers of attorney, and their living wills. "Okay, whatever."

"I bought a burial plot, which fits two people, and I can be reimbursed by the estate. FYI, we ran an obit and a funeral notice, too."

"Thanks. I appreciate everything, really."

"I know." Bob touched him on the shoulder. "Clean up downstairs, so Sara doesn't see it like that. Don't tell her about the drinking. We didn't tell her."

"I don't like keeping secrets. I forget them." Mike's head thudded. "Anyway, haven't we had enough secrets?"

"So what are you saying?" Bob frowned. "You're gonna tell Sara, 'hey, your best friend was a drunk'? Why speak ill, and she'll tell Danielle. Keep it to yourself."

"But what does Sara think about how Chloe died? She won't understand why Chloe didn't call 911."

"Sara didn't question Chloe's death. Sara thinks Chloe hit her head so hard she died, which is completely possible. I told her, you know how many people die in household accidents each year?"

"You said that? You lied to her?"

"No, I didn't lie, I just didn't tell her everything. It's an omission, but it's not material." Bob rose, abruptly. "Chloe paid, okay? She paid enough. She paid with her life."

Mike didn't know what to say. Bob was right, and wrong, too.

"Wait." Bob hurried to a mound of clothes on the floor. "You know what? Forget Sara coming over, you can't clean up in time. We'll pick out the dress. I'm going to the funeral home. I'll take it over."

"Let me help." Mike got out of bed and crossed to the ransacked clothes. He recognized every outfit, feeling his grief and anger resurge. It was true that Chloe had paid, but he would pay, and Emily, too. The baby would grow up without her mother.

"Just pick one." Bob gestured at the clothes. "Which one would she like? Did she have a favorite dress?"

"The white." Mike pointed to a dress he knew Chloe loved, and Bob lifted the dress up by the hanger, a filmy sheath of ivory silk. The contours of the dress had been shaped by Chloe's body and it hung suspended in the air like her very ghost.

"Now we need shoes. What shoes go with the dress? What did she wear with it?" Bob shifted to the pile of overturned shoeboxes, and Mike spotted the sexy black stilettos Chloe adored. She'd worn them once when they made love, one of the few times they'd gotten kinky. He looked away from the stilettos.

"Take the brown ones."

"Done." Bob grabbed the shoes and straightened up. "Do you think we need underwear and all?"

"No. I'm not doing that, and neither are you." Mike didn't even want to think about somebody at the funeral home, dressing Chloe. It occurred to him there was so much he didn't know about what happened to her body. "Bob, did they autopsy her?"

"Yes, sorry." Bob glanced at his watch. "They had to, by law."

"Does that mean there's a police or a coroner's report?"

"I suppose so."

"Did a coroner come that night, too? Does Chester County even have a coroner?"

"Sure. Yes. Why do you ask?"

"I want to know." Mike tried to think through his hangover. "I assume if they had reports, they would show alcohol in her blood. A toxicology screen would show the levels, how drunk she was. Don't they have to do a tox screen for an accidental death? I don't know, you're the lawyer."

"I'm not a criminal lawyer, but I can follow up. Look, I gotta go. I'll keep Danielle's car, you keep mine. Take care. Clean up. Bye." Bob turned away and left the room, the sheath fluttering beside him, floating through the air.

"Thanks, bye." Mike surveyed the damage of their bedroom. He'd dumped her bureau drawers and emptied her armoire. The bedroom looked searched, and he realized that he had been looking for more bottles. He remembered finding one in Chloe's nightstand

and looked over. Her hand cream and hardback books lay on the floor, next to an uncapped Smirnoff's bottle. Some had spilled out, soaking the novel's pages.

Mike spotted a framed photo of Emily near the book, so he walked over and picked it up. He had taken the picture, and she was asleep in her carryall. He flashed on the soft, warm, and substantial bundle she'd made in his arms last night. He would spend time with her and remind her of who he was again. He wanted her to know that she still had a father who loved her very, very much.

His pity party was over.

It ended when he sipped from that cup.

Chapter Ten

"Anybody home?" Mike walked in the front door, having show-ered and changed into his old clothes, a black down parka, a white oxford shirt, navy V-neck sweater, tan Dockers, and loafers. He felt raw and horrible inside, but he had to move forward and there was a lot to do, for Emily.

"Mike, that you?" Danielle called from upstairs.

"Yes." Mike glanced around for his backpack, which was leaning beside the couch. He went over, unzipped it, and yanked out his lap-top and power cord.

"Hi, how are you?" Danielle came downstairs with a sympathetic frown, dressed in a maroon V-neck with khakis.

"Fine, thanks. Danielle, I'm sorry I was such a jerk last night."

"Don't say that, and you weren't, poor thing. Bob called and told me what happened at the house."

"I know." Mike slipped the laptop under his arm and kissed her cheek. "Is Emily awake?"

"No, she just went down."

"I keep missing her. When does she sleep? Does she have a schedule?"

"Yes. She naps twice a day, the first time around now, the second around four."

"Good to know. I won't wake her up again." Mike managed a smile, and Danielle smiled back, touching his elbow.

"When she wakes up, we'll reintroduce you, like you said. She'll get used to you. Don't worry." Danielle met his eye directly, her gaze a sharp blue, with an intelligence behind them. "Now, did you eat? I have turkey sandwiches, if you want one. I'm not going to work."

"Thanks, I'd like that."

"Good." Danielle led him into the kitchen, and Mike looked around for an outlet for the laptop.

"I need to check my email. Do you mind?"

"Not at all, make yourself at home. We have Wi-Fi, and the outlet's by the end of the table." Danielle went into their stainless steel Subzero. "We'd love for you to sleep here while you're home, in the guest room. It would be more comfortable for you and the baby, too."

"Thanks so much, I'd appreciate that." Mike plugged the laptop in, set it on the table, opened the lid, and fired it up.

"We're happy to have you." Danielle poured him a Coke and brought it to the table.

"Thanks, again." Mike let his laptop find the network, typed in the password, and logged into his email, skimming subject lines that read Condolences, Sympathy, So Sorry To Hear About Your Loss, and We're So Sorry until he got to PhillyNanny, AuPairinPA, Live-In Professionals, and Childcare Professionals. "As far as childcare for Emily, when I go back, I know you work during the day, but I know you'll want to help with her."

"Of course, I will." Danielle was opening the turkey. "It's only for a month, so we think she should stay here."

"I was hoping you'd say that. Thank you so much. I'd appreciate that." Mike's mouth went suddenly dry, because he didn't want to presume anything. "I know you love your job, and Bob needs you at the office, so I'm thinking that I should hire a nanny to take care of Emily during the day, or whenever you guys need a break or have something you need to do at night."

"I have a better idea." Danielle set down the plate with a thick turkey sandwich, then sat across from him, with a growing smile.

"How about I stop working for Bob and take care of Emily until you get back?"

"Really?" Mike asked, surprised. "How would that work? Can you take off for a month?"

"Yes. Look, I love my job, and I loved helping build the firm, but I also love Emily and I feel as if she needs me now, now that Chloe is gone." Danielle's expression darkened, falling into the sad lines of last night, and the folds around her mouth deepened. "The more I think about it, the more I think Emily should be with family, full-time, until you come home."

"That's such a kind offer, but I would never presume to ask you. It's a whole month you'd be out of the office."

"You're not asking me, and I adore that child. She's so much fun, and she's supersmart."

"What makes you say that? Love, bias, or both?" Mike took a bite of his sandwich, which was delicious.

"Besides her incredible genetics? I mean, her daddy's a doctor."

Mike smiled, flattered. "Does she say any words yet?"

"Not really, but she babbles. She picks things up so quickly, and she asks for information. At the zoo, she'll point at an animal, as if she's asking you to name it." Danielle's eyes lit up. "She loves giraffes, and we got her a stuffed giraffe that plays music. I think babies know more than we give them credit for."

"Ha! Everybody knows more than we give them credit for."

"And she's so active, and you can see she really wants to walk. She's unbelievably cute, isn't she? Apropos of nothing, but she is." Danielle's face shone with warmth. "I'd love to be home with her, all day. It's the least I can do for my sister. She'd do it for me, and I know she'd want it this way."

Mike felt a pang, knowing that was true. "But really, what does Bob say? Can he spare you at work?"

"Yes, and he's all for it. He wants what's best for Emily, too." Danielle nodded toward the toys in the family room. "We're all set up for her, and her crib is here. She loves us and she's used to being here. Why introduce a third party to her now, when she'll already have so much to adjust to? It's only until you come home." Danielle's eyes turned plaintive. "Let me do this, for Chloe, Emily, and for you."

"That's so amazing of you." Mike felt his heart ease. "You would have to let me pay you."

"I wouldn't hear of it."

"No, really. We'll fight over that later."

"You'll lose. I always get what I want."

Mike smiled. Danielle was funny and smart, but tougher than Chloe, with a logical mind. "Are you sure about this?"

"Yes, totally. You know, this is an impossible time for you, and for me, but most of all for Emily. She lost the best mother ever."

"Chloe was, you think?" Mike had never doubted Chloe as a mother, but his world turned upside-down last night. "I always thought she was, but now—"

"Stop." Danielle's mouth set firmly. "Chloe was a wonderful mother, even if she indulged a little, I know. She was devoted to Emily, and don't blow this drinking thing out of proportion. She wasn't with the baby the day she died, and I'm sure she didn't drink when Emily was with her."

Mike thought of the Dunkin' Donuts cup and the hidden vodka bottles, then remembered he wasn't supposed to say anything. "Why do you think she drank? Was she unhappy?"

"She didn't *drink*. She missed you, I know, and I'd understand if she had a drink or two. We grew up with wine at the table, and I have a glass or two, every night. It doesn't mean I'm an alcoholic, and Chloe wasn't either." Danielle shook her head. "She just had an accident while she was drinking, which was terrible, terrible luck."

Mike let it go. The sisters had been close, but Danielle was the conservative one, and Chloe might have edited what she told her, so Mike changed the subject. "Do you think Emily misses her?"

"I'm sure she does, and it breaks my heart. She doesn't say Mommy yet, but she tries." Danielle bit her lip. "But the good thing is, Emily's used to being with me. I used to go with them to music class on Saturdays, too. Chloe and the other moms would play recorders and xylophones for the babies, or shake maracas."

Mike thought of a photo that Chloe had emailed him, of Emily and the other moms and babies, wearing sombreros at music class. He didn't understand how such a good mother could be such a bad mother, both at once.

"I think Emily deserves that kind of attention, and you can't buy that. It's love. It's love of family." Danielle gestured at the laptop. "I know I sprung this on you, and you don't have to tell me now. Mull it over. It's a standing offer."

Mike felt reassured, and grateful. "You would've made one helluva lawyer."

"That's what Bob says." Danielle cocked her head. "Hold on. Did you hear that? The baby monitor. I think she's up."

"But she just went down." Mike heard a babbling sound coming from the monitor.

"It happens." Danielle rose, smoothing down her sweater, her eyes twinkling. "Shall we try again?"

Chapter Eleven

Emily wailed at the top of her lungs, clinging to Danielle as she stood at the entrance to the family room. The baby had burst into tears at the sight of Mike, who had walked over to her, holding out his arms.

"Danielle, what did I do wrong?" Mike stopped, his arms falling to his sides. "I was just happy to see her."

"She didn't expect to see you. You're new, and babies don't like new people, especially around this age."

"What about this age?"

"At seven months, their stranger anxiety is strongest, and she got introduced to you in the worst way, last night in the dark. Go back to the couch and give her time to get used to the idea that you're here."

Emily cried harder, her eyes as red as her holiday romper, which had an embroidered penguin in a Santa hat. Her hair looked damp at the scalp, under a headful of dark blonde curls.

"Okay." Mike backed up to the couch and kept smiling. "Hi, Emily, hello, Emily." He kept his voice soft and sweet. "It's Daddy, honey. How's my baby girl?" He didn't know whether to sit or stand, so he popped up and down like a suburban jack-in-the-box. "Did you have a nice nap?"

Danielle rocked the hysterical baby. "Aw, sweetie, it's okay, that's your Daddy, and he just wants to say hello."

"Don't be afraid, Emily." Mike looked around, picked up a toy dog, and gave it a kiss. "See the dog? You like dogs, don't you? I like dogs."

"Put that down. She hates that toy."

"Oops, sorry." Mike dropped the dog, flustered. "What toy does she like?"

"The bunny, the pink."

"A bunny, yay!" Mike picked up the bunny and stroked its fuzzy head. "Look, Emily, I'm a nice guy. I come in peace."

"Emily, see your bunny?" Danielle tried to put a pacifier in Emily's mouth, but she wouldn't take it, crying full bore. "Here, have your binky." Suddenly the doorbell rang, and Danielle looked over. "Hang on, I'll be right back."

"Sure." Mike flopped on the couch, hearing the wailing subside as soon as they left the room. He tossed the bunny aside and remembered how he used to hold Emily all the time. She would look up at him, sucking her pacifier. She even used to fall asleep on his chest.

"Mike, Sara's here!" Danielle called to him, and Mike stood up as she came back holding a teary Emily, sucking on her pacifier. They lingered at the threshold of the family room while a grief-stricken Sara entered the room and crossed to Mike, opening her arms in her thick wool coat.

"Oh, Mike, I'm so sorry about Chloe."

"I'm sorry, too, for you." Mike hugged her close, and Sara made a short, bulky bundle in his arms, sagging against him, drawing strength from him. She and Chloe had been best friends from their first year teaching, and Mike found himself in a solar system that revolved around Chloe, but the sun was missing.

"I still can't believe it, can you?" Sara released him, tears filling her large eyes, as brown as chocolate syrup. Her hair was almost the same color, cut at her chin, and her thin lips quivered with emotion. "She should be here. She would've been so happy to see you. It's good that you're safe, thank God."

"Thanks, but it's so strange, isn't it? You and me, but not her?"

"I know, I miss her, so much." Sara blinked her tears away and moved a strand of hair from her roundish cheek. "I'm not making this easier on you, am I?"

"You don't have to make it easy." Mike managed a smile for her. "It's not easy. It's impossible."

"That's how I feel, too. Chloe was my best friend, since forever. I knew her before Don. She even knew my parents." Sara wiped her eyes with her palm, like a little girl. "Nobody at school can believe it. They all loved her, and Sue, Allison, and Michelle are beside themselves."

"I bet." Mike winced at the names of Chloe's teacher friends. He liked them all, and there was no tighter-knit group than teachers, except soldiers.

"Don sends his love, too. He had to work, but he'll be at the wake. By the way, is it okay with you that we took Jake?" Sara brightened a little. "The boys always wanted a cat, and they fell in love with him. But don't worry, they know we have to give him back when you get home."

"Thanks so much for taking him," Mike said, wondering how he would ever take Jake away from her boys, but he'd deal with that later.

"Sara, would you like coffee?" Danielle asked, keeping her distance with the baby, who'd stopped crying, sucking wet-eyed on her pacifier.

"No, thanks." Sara took off her coat, revealing dark slacks and a silly red sweater with a huge candy cane, obviously one of the Ironic Holiday Sweaters that she and Chloe used to wear every Christmas, for a joke at school. Mike suppressed a stab of pain, and Sara grimaced, reading his expression. "Oh no, Mike, the sweater, I forgot."

"It's okay." Mike didn't want her to feel bad and changed the subject. "So if you're wondering why my daughter is hysterical, it's my fault. She hates me."

"No, she doesn't." Sara smiled, shakily. "She's just getting used to you again."

"That's a good way to think about it." Mike forced himself to smile back. "We're like those movies where the wife gets amnesia and forgets she loves the husband."

"She'll be fine, in time." Sara patted him on the back, and Mike always liked her easy manner, especially with kids. She had three sons and twenty-four students in her class, so nothing fazed her. "Here, maybe I can help. Danielle, can I have her?" Sara took Emily from Danielle, grinned at the baby, and held her up so that her tiny legs drooped together like an old-school clothespin. "How's baby Emily? How's the littlest angel?"

Mike marveled as Emily smiled down at Sara, then Sara cradled her and moved slowly toward him.

"Emily, you don't have to worry about a thing." Sara kissed her on the head. "So many people love you, and we're gonna take great care of you, aren't we?" Emily sucked harder, her blue eyes trained on Sara, and Mike noticed the baby's eyes were a pale blue, like bluets growing wild in a meadow. Sara moved closer to him with Emily, saying to her, "You know much I love you, and so does your Daddy, and he's here with us, right now. This big, hunky handsome guy belongs to you, did you know that?" Sara kissed Emily again. "Isn't that great? That you have a Daddy who loves you?"

Mike held his breath and stayed perfectly still, then Sara stopped. Emily was closer to him than she'd ever been in daylight, and her gaze met his directly. He felt the same wondrous connection as last night.

But in the next second, Emily burst into tears, spitting out her pacifier.

Later, Danielle went upstairs with the baby, while Mike stood at the kitchen counter with Sara, having coffee. They'd tried for a half an hour to calm Emily down, to no avail, and Sara patted him on the back.

"Don't worry, Mike. She was just tired. She woke up early from her nap."

"Right, I know." Mike wanted to talk about the vodka and understand why Chloe had been drinking, but he'd promised Bob to keep it a secret. "Sara, let me ask you, how was Chloe while I was away? Was she okay or what, emotionally?"

"She missed you, but she was happy with the baby."

"Really?" Mike didn't think it added up. "Could she have been depressed, like postpartum or anything?"

"No, not that." Sara hesitated. "To be honest with you, she was having a tough time. I think being on her own, with such a new baby, was hard. It's just the war, and the bad luck of the timing, with you being deployed when the baby was a newborn—" She stopped, abruptly, and Mike sensed she was protecting him.

"Tell me, Sara. I can handle it. She lived it, so the least I can do is hear about it."

"But it'll just make you feel bad."

"It doesn't matter how bad I feel, I want to understand. Tell me the truth."

"You know it's not your fault at all, you had to go, but I think it was hard on her, and it kind of caught her by surprise." Sara's face fell, her characteristic smile gone. "In the beginning, people dropped over from school, seeing the baby, saying hi, helping out, but then winter came on, and everybody got busy, and she was on her own. She worried about you all the time, watched TV news and checked online for the latest coverage of the war."

"She never told me she worried." Mike thought back to Chloe's emails, which he practically had memorized. "Her emails are all upbeat and happy, about the baby."

"She didn't want to worry you." Sara cocked her head. "I bet you did the same. You didn't tell her when you were down or in danger, did you?"

"No, of course not." Mike remembered editing his emails and Skype calls, because he couldn't tell Chloe the truth. "I didn't want to worry her, either."

"That's loving, really. She was trying to be brave, and I know she felt surprised at how hard it was, with a new baby. It's like labor. If we knew how hard it was in advance, nobody would do it." Sara smiled, sadly. "And just so you know, I was there a lot, checking on her and Emily. I only wish I'd been there that day, you know, the day she . . ."

"It's okay, really." Mike didn't make her finish the sentence, and

Sara swallowed hard, shaking her head slowly, with the bewilderment of grief.

"I know she felt alone, every new mother does, but she was so happy being an at-home mom." Sara sniffled. "She told me, all the time. I saw it, and she was a born mother. Why do you ask?"

Mike couldn't tell her, so he said the next thing that came to his mind. "I wonder if I can be as good a father."

"Of course you can."

"Can a father be as good as a mother?"

"Yes, Don is. He's great with the boys." Sara smiled, warmly. "It depends on the father. I hate to say it, but my father would not have been a good mother, but times were different back then. It was the generation when the father was happy to be the second-string, like an understudy."

Mike had felt that way, with Chloe. She had been so good with Emily that he was happy being her second banana, like the general practitioner to her specialist.

"I know that your dad left when you were little, right?"

"Yes, I was ten." Mike hated to go there. "I barely remember him."

"But your mom was great."

"Absolutely, the best." Mike still missed her, though she'd been gone fifteen years. She died of breast cancer, and her bravery inspired him every day, even in Afghanistan. She would have been so proud to see him graduate from podiatry school and go on to serve.

"And you loved her, and you turned out great, so there's proof. It's not about gender, it's all about love." Sara touched his arm. "You can be a great father and you will be."

Mike wished he were that sure. "If Emily were a boy, I'd have a better shot."

"That doesn't matter, either. Your mother was a woman who raised a great man. You'll be a man who raises a great woman. You'll see, it'll come naturally, it did for Chloe. She was also the most nurturing person on the planet. Didn't you think so? Didn't she take great care of things? The kids at school? Her art, all of us?" Tears filmed Sara's large, round eyes, again. "She made us all feel so loved, didn't she?"

Mike swallowed, remembering. He felt bathed in Chloe. She had brought him love, light, and colors. And now, pain. "Sara, let me ask your opinion about something. Danielle offered to take care of Emily, until I come back."

"I know. She already asked me what I thought about the idea."

"Okay." Mike went with the flow. These women had better intelligence than CENTCOM. "So what do you think?"

"I think it's an awesome idea." Sara showed a flicker of her typically cheery self. "Danielle loves Emily, and Emily loves her and Bob. I think it helps Emily to be with someone she loves, and they want to help."

"Right, they are amazing."

"I also think it's better for you. You can finish your deployment and not worry. If it's a stranger, you know you're going to worry, and so are Danielle and Bob." Sara opened her palms. "Besides, look at this house, and it's even better to have her live here, so she's not thinking about Chloe. If she's home, she'll be looking for Mommy. If she's here, she expects Danielle."

Mike felt a tug, wondering if Emily would forget Chloe. He knew it could happen, because Emily had forgotten him.

"What's the matter?" Sara asked, frowning slightly.

"Nothing." Mike couldn't say it without getting emotional.

"So, what do you think about Emily staying here? It's a no-brainer, right?" Sara shrugged. "What's better than family?"

Chapter Twelve

Mike walked down the carpeted hallway to his office. He wanted to stop by, since his group partners had been emailing him about changes in the practice, and he could see immediately what they meant. The sign at the glass entrance read:

SUBURBAN FOOT & ANKLE, LLC, SPECIALIZING IN FOOT & ANKLE RECONSTRUCTION

DR. JAMES D. HAGGERTY, DPM, FACFAS
DR. ANTHONY M. MAZZACARO, DPM, FACFAS
DR. MICHAEL J. SCANLON, DPM, FACFAS
DR. DAVID M. WATERMAN, DPM, FACFAS

But underneath was an addition:

LYON & HAGGERTY, LLC, SPORTS MEDICINE

DR. RICHARD A. LYON, DPM, FACFAS
DR. JAMES D. HAGGERTY, DPM, FACFAS

Mike opened the door, which led to an entrance hall that had been redecorated, even since he'd deployed. The walls had been painted bright orange and plastered with felt banners from Lower Merion, Haverford, and Great Valley High Schools. Underneath was a yellow ribbon that read, WE HONOR OUR ARMY RESERVIST, DR. MIKE! HOME SAFE SOON!

He walked through a new door into a reception area that had been completely reconfigured, almost half the size. The reception desk was still there, though he didn't recognize the receptionist, a young girl with a ponytail. "May I help you?" she asked, looking up attentively.

"I'm Mike Scanlon."

"And who do you have an appointment with today?" The receptionist started hitting keys on her keyboard, her attention shifting to the computer screen.

"I'm the Dr. Scanlon on the door. Call me Mike."

"Oh no, sorry. Awkward!" The receptionist grimaced, giggled, and covered her mouth with her hand. "I'm Julie Mura."

"Hi, Julie. Are Jim or the others around, or in surgery?"

"Dr. Haggerty's in. Let me get him or see if there's somebody over there that can help you."

"That's okay, I know where I'm going." Mike opened the door to the examining rooms, but he'd spoken too soon. The hallway used to lead to a circle of examining rooms, but only two were left, then there was a new wall, but he had no idea what was on the other side. The construction must have been recent because he could practically smell the drywall.

"Mike, is that you?" asked a voice behind him, and he turned around to see one of their nurses, Susie. "Mike, I'm so sorry about Chloe."

"Thanks." Mike gave her a brief hug, glad to see a familiar face. She looked like she'd lost weight, slimmer in scrubs covered with pink ribbons. "You got so skinny, didn't you?"

"Thirty pounds off, thanks." Susie released him with a teary smile. "I'll be there tomorrow night, with everybody."

"Thanks, I appreciate that." Mike didn't want to dwell. "What's going on here? Everything looks different."

"I know, right? It's a brave new world, now that we started with the sports. This is the great divide." Susie patted the new wall. "I call it West Berlin, but the new people are too young to know what I'm talking about."

"Where's my office? Where are any of the doctors' offices?"

"There's only one office now, and you share it. We boxed up your things carefully, don't worry, and you'll have your own file cabinet."

Mike shrugged it off. "I guess we don't really need our offices, anyway."

"That's what Jim said, and did you see the child at the reception desk? Tanika moved to Cleveland, and Jim had to let Marilyn and Lorene go. Welcome to the recession."

"That's too bad." Mike's partners had written about the diminishing caseload, with patients putting off elective surgeries because of the economy. He'd still gotten his base share though he hadn't known it came at the expense of the staff. "Where's Jim?"

"Follow me." Susie bustled ahead, and Mike fell into step beside her.

"How's Tony and Dave?"

"Good. Tony's in surgery, and Dave's in with a patient." Susie pressed through the wood door, and Mike slipped through behind her, surprised. The hallway emptied into a bustling space painted the same orange as the entrance hall and blanketed with team photographs. Susie rolled her eyes. "Smells like team spirit."

"We have new staff here, too?" Mike asked, as nurses hurried in and out of examining rooms. One rolled past a new portable x-ray machine, which had to cost a fortune.

"Dr. Lyon brought a lot of his people." Susie walked ahead. "Let's find Jumbo."

Suddenly the door to an examining room opened, and Jim stepped out, file in hand. He was a big blond bear of a man, in his late thirties, though his hair was thinning. His back was to Mike, and he was talking to his patients, a mom and a young son.

"Now stay off that foot, even though it's in the cast, you got me? Go Aces!" Jim shut the door, turned around, and opened his arms when he spotted Mike. "Oh, buddy, you're home. I'm so sorry about Chloe."

"Thanks." Mike hugged him back, trying not to choke up. They'd been in practice together for almost ten years, during which he and Chloe had become good friends with Jim and his wife, Laura.

"Laura's been on the phone with Danielle. We can't believe that Chloe's gone. I got a second, want to talk?"

"Sure, thanks." Mike felt his throat tighten. "If you're busy, I get it."

"No this is important, I want to see you. I got one case, then I get a break." Jim opened the door of an empty examining room and motioned him inside. "Here. Be right back."

Susie squeezed his arm. "Mike, I gotta get back to work. See you tomorrow. I'll say a prayer for you and the baby."

"Thanks." Mike went in, shut the door behind him, and sat down across from the examining table. Posters of young runners and soccer players lined the wall, and opposite him were glossy brochures titled Cleat Selection, Running Shoes and You, and Orthotics Aren't Those Things on Your Teeth. He tried to wrap his mind around the changes here. They didn't need his permission under their partnership agreement to rearrange the offices, and Jim knew how to pinch a construction penny, coming from a working-class upbringing like Mike. Still he wondered what Tony and Dave thought of the new sports-medicine practice, since they'd ended up on the outs.

Jim burst into the room. "Sorry about that, Mike. The kid's in X-ray so I'm good for a few minutes."

"No worries." Mike sat up, as Jim rolled over a stool, sat down, and looked at him with concern.

"So, I'm still in shock, man. How the hell are you doing?"

"Not so great."

"I believe it." Jim shook his head, stricken. "She's gone, just like that. I don't how you deal, I don't know how I would. It must feel like the rug got taken out from under you."

"And the baby, too."

"Right." Jim's eyes flared. They were large and wide-set, a pale blue set against his fair, ruddy skin. "What are you going to do about the baby? Laura said Danielle and Bob want to take her."

"They do, she just made the offer today. I think I'm saying yes."

"Hell yeah, I'd take them up on it, no question. How you gonna find anybody better?" Jim talked fast, in the flat accent of Northeast Philly. "I couldn't do half the things I'm doing here if I had to worry about childcare. You need that on autopilot. Otherwise, it's a hassle, your turn to pick up, my turn to pick up, is the nanny sick, is the nanny doing drugs, having guys over, whatever. Who needs that? Don't overthink it."

Jim's rap on Mike was that he thought too much, but Mike liked that in a surgeon. "Family is the short answer, isn't it?"

"Sure, need us to help with anything? We'll be there tomorrow night." Jim raked a hand through his hair, then patted it down. "Bob was the one who called us and told us the news. Laura answered and got hysterical, of course. I would think somebody would hear Chloe calling for help, or that she'd come to in time to call 911."

Mike wondered if he should tell Jim about the drinking, but let him keep talking.

"I'm like, she's *dead*? You have to be kidding me, this is impossible, this woman was perfectly healthy, so full of life, you know, we all loved her, even the kids. Remember she taught Courtney calligraphy and I had to buy that two-hundred-dollar calligraphy set from Tokyo or wherever?"

"Kyoto."

"Whatever." Jim rubbed his face, making faint marks. "Chloe was way too young to die, and it's just so weird the way it happened. I know this is hard to hear, but if I were you, I'd get ahold of that damn autopsy." He raised an unruly eyebrow, his reddish-gray hairs a tangle. "I'd want to know *exactly* how it happened. I swear, she musta had a hairline fracture, something pre-existing, for a knock on the counter to do her in. Maybe an earlier concussion, one she didn't know about, or even an aneurysm. What do you think?"

Mike needed a sounding board and he would swear Jim to secrecy, even from Laura. He was just about to tell him when Jim's phone rang.

"Hold on a sec." Jim slid his BlackBerry from the pocket of his lab coat and pressed the IGNORE button. "Sorry, day from hell. Go away." He looked back up at Mike. "Anyway, so, where were we, hey, what do you think about the place?"

Mike changed his mind about telling him, at least for now. The moment had passed. "What gives? So we renting to this Lyon guy or what?"

"Okay, so Rick Lyon, he's a good guy, outta D.C., I'd introduce you but he's giving a seminar, beating the bushes. Anyway, I met him a couple months ago at Parents' Night, his son's in Alex's class, and he starts telling me that kids' sports injuries are blowing up, especially with the travel teams and everybody wanting scholarship money in the economy, the girls, too. I'm like, how do we get in on that, because our business is dropping off."

Listening, Mike realized that Jim was just another Chatty, a superhero in charge, and he was the second banana here, too. The funny thing was, he didn't mind. Maybe that was why he felt comfortable being the understudy, as a father. He didn't like the spotlight. He didn't want to be the sun.

"And of course, I'm seeing a problem down the line, because my mama didn't raise no dummy, that people are putting off the bunionectomies because of the money." Jim barely took a breath. "Lyon's telling me he needs room in the western subs to expand, and I'm like, I got room and we can do that with our eyes closed, it's the same procedures in a sports-medicine wrapper. So now the cases are through the roof, and the system administrators in Philly are starting to take notice . . ."

Mike zoned out as Jim went through the metrics about how they made so much the past quarter, on top of base shares. He sensed that Jim was just trying to avoid any silences, and all of it used to be so important to Mike. It mattered less to him now, and maybe that was called perspective. Chloe had died because he wasn't here, and on the other side of the world, soldiers were dying because he wasn't *there.*

Jim touched his arm, in a final sort of way. "But you don't need to know all this now. We can talk about it when you get back."

"Okay, but why did you let Lorene and Marilyn go? If money's a problem, I won't take my base cut."

"Stop, St. Michael." Jim waved his meaty hand. "It wasn't the money. Marilyn was slacking, and Lorene asked for a raise, which so wasn't happening, then she gave me attitude."

"Are Tony and Dave on board, with all these changes? They emailed me that the practice is down."

"Sure, they're fine, both making bonuses over base. Now tell me you're safe over there."

"I'm safe." Mike thought of the yellow ribbon on the door. "What's with the sign, Dr. Mike, all that?"

"What? Why?" Jim recoiled. "We're proud of you, man."

Mike remembered that Jim found a way to let the media know when he was deployed and the local newspaper had done a feature on him. "And it's good for business."

"So, why not?" Jim shrugged it off jovially. "We are proud of you, really, but if you don't like it, I'll take it down."

"No, it's okay."

"So what's it like over there? You gotta take care of yourself. I mean it, you better come back in one piece, for my sake. I don't have a lot of friends. I'm straight-up annoying."

"I know." Mike rose, and so did Jim, touching him again on the back.

"You get to shoot anybody or they chain you to the table? I'd love to go over there and light up the Taliban. Hoo-ah!"

"The docs don't say hoo-ah, Jim."

"Why not, man? I would. I'd go over there like Rambo, saying hoo-ah all the time. Hoo-ah to my heart's content. Say it for me, soldier boy."

"Hoo-ah," Mike said, to humor him. "Last question. Why the orange?"

"You mean on the walls?" Jim smiled. "The orange was chosen because no local high school team has orange in its school colors. I figured that out myself. We can't play favorites, these kids take this seriously, and the parents do, too. One kid told me the worst part of the game is driving home in the car with his *mom*. Anyway, *orange*. It was my idea." Jim pointed to his chest proudly. "Not just another pretty face, this one."

"No, not at all," Mike said, and they laughed. It felt good to be silly for a minute.

Because Mike knew where he had to go, next.

Chapter Thirteen

"I'm Mike Scanlon," he said to the young funeral director, who materialized from a side door. The entrance hall was otherwise empty and quiet, with navy blue carpet and blue-and-gold-flecked wallpaper.

"Pleased to meet you, Dr. Scanlon. Scott Beeberman." The young man extended a slim hand. He was of slight build in a dark suit, with a patterned tie and jelled hair. "My father told me to expect you. My condolences on your loss."

"Thank you, and for your help with my wife."

"Of course, your brother-in-law was here today, selecting one of our caskets. The Embassy, a cherry model. He said you would be fine with that, but if there's a problem, please feel free to inform me. Here, come with me." Scott started walking, and Mike fell into step beside him, down a hallway lined with cushioned benches and tasteful landscapes. Scott kept talking, in a quiet tone. "We have set aside a room for you on the lower level, and you can stay as long as you like."

"Thank you." Mike realized that he and Chloe were under the same roof for the first time in six months.

"In addition, if you're unhappy in any way with your wife's appearance, please feel to let me know that, as well. We did use a photograph that your brother-in-law supplied to us, which was very helpful."

"Oh, I didn't know." Mike glanced over as they passed a podium with a padded guest book, next to a white pen molded to look like a quill.

"We find we get better results and our families are generally pleased. Do you have any questions?"

"Yes, a few." Mike swallowed hard. "She was autopsied, correct?"

"Yes." Scott didn't bat an eye. "But I think you'll be pleased with her appearance, and it's absolutely fine to have an open casket. You'll see what I mean."

"Can I get the results of the autopsy?"

"We don't have the report, but I can make you a copy of the death certificate."

"Thank you. Is there a police report, too?"

"There would be, for a fatality, but we don't have a copy of that, either."

"I see." They reached a landing and descended side-by-side, and Mike reached for the polished banister, suddenly weak in the knees. They reached the lower floor, which he realized was a euphemism for the basement.

"Please, this way." Scott walked him down a hallway lined with closed doors, stopped at the middle one, and gestured to a cushioned bench against the wall. "Please have a seat, and I'll get that information you requested. This way, I won't interrupt you, later. My office is on this level, and I won't be a moment." Scott glided off, and Mike tried to get his act together. He couldn't believe he was sitting outside the room where Chloe lay, in a casket. He felt oddly as if he were waiting for her, a sensation that wasn't unfamiliar.

Are you ready yet? Mike was in the bedroom, switching off the TV. Chloe was in the bathroom finishing her makeup, but they were late for dinner with his partners.

Chloe had come out finally. *Well? How do I look?*

Her eyes were as blue as forget-me-nots, and a light tan tinted her fine nose and high cheekbones. Her face was the shape of a heart, and her lips smiled a Cupid's bow, glossy pink. Her dark blonde hair hung wavy to her shoulders, and she had on her favorite white dress, which showed off slim, tan legs. She was the most naturally beautiful woman he had ever seen, like some wildflower.

"Dr. Scanlon, here we are." Scott reappeared and handed Mike an envelope. "Your wife's death certificate is inside, and so is her cell phone. Your brother-in-law must have left it. Shall we go in now or would you like a moment?"

"I'm ready," Mike answered, though he was anything but.

"Allow me." Scott opened the door into a medium-sized room with the same blue rug and wallpaper, and a walnut credenza. "There's a house phone and bottled water, for your convenience. I'll check on you in twenty minutes, but if you finish sooner or need me, please pick up the phone. Any other questions?"

"Yes." Mike faced the credenza, because it was easier than facing the front of the room with Chloe's casket. He still couldn't look over at her body. "I know there was a knife wound. Can you give me some details?"

"I think you'll be pleased with the repair. You shouldn't be able to see anything."

"I mean the details." Mike wasn't overly concerned with Chloe's appearance, but Scott lifted an eyebrow.

"Pardon me?"

"How deep was the wound, how long was it, how did you repair it? I want to know everything, as much as possible." Mike wanted to know what he could because there was so much he'd never know, like about the drinking. "Did you see any old injury on her head, by any chance?"

"I don't usually have a discussion like this with a surviving spouse, but if you feel it's appropriate, I will."

"I do. Please, I'm a doctor."

Scott pursed his lips. "The knife wound was about a quarter-inch deep, but approximately five inches in length. We sutured it closed with a baseball stitch, sealed it with PERMASEAL, then added a layer of cotton web roll towel."

"Why do you do that, the towel?"

Scott frowned, plainly uncomfortable. "To prevent leakage of embalming fluid or staining of her garment."

Mike swallowed hard. "She was exsanguinated when she came in, right?"

"Yes, but as you may know, exsanguination sufficient to cause death is incomplete. Unlike doctors like yourself, who measure blood in liters, we speak in terms of blood weight, and your wife had three pounds of blood when she came to us." Scott gestured at the coffin, but Mike didn't look over. "Your wife is lying in repose, and since the wound was interior, we positioned her arm against the body, so the sleeve of the dress would hide the towel."

Mike thought of the white dress, then oddly, the underwear. "I'm sorry that we didn't give you any, uh, underwear."

"That was no problem. We keep a supply of fresh packs in that event. Now, if you have no other questions, I'll give you some privacy. Again, my deepest condolences." Scott left the room silently.

Mike walked over to a chair, sat down, braced himself, then made a conscious effort to raise his eyes to the casket. At the sight, his chest tightened with anguish, and tears came to his eyes. He heard a gasping sob and realized it came from him. He covered his mouth, holding in whatever he could. Crying, shouting, emotion. He looked at Chloe's body, making himself see her.

Her face was an inanimate mask of the memory he'd just had, a mannequin of herself. Her hair had been brushed in soft waves, her eyes were closed, and her eyelids lightly lined. Her lovely mouth was a glossy pink and curved into a sweet, natural smile, evidence of the mortician's skill. She had on the white dress and brown shoes he'd picked out this morning. Profound sadness swept over him, and he hung his head, slumping in the chair.

He had no idea how long he sat that way, collapsed. The envelope sat in his lap, and he opened it, mechanically. Inside was a white paper, and he pulled it out. It read DEATH CERTIFICATE, and he scanned the information: Decedent, Chloe Voulette. Sex, F. Date of Death, December 15. Age, 32. Date of Birth, July 13. Marital Status,

Married. Surviving Spouse, Michael Scanlon. It sickened him to see his own name on Chloe's death certificate. He felt horrified to be a Surviving Spouse.

He read the Time of Death, between 5:30 P.M. and 6:00 P.M., and realized that he had been asleep when she died, half a world away. He didn't wake up the moment she passed, like in the movies. He didn't know she was gone. He didn't even know she drank vodka. He didn't know anything, anymore.

He slid the certificate into the envelope and took out Chloe's phone. It was a BlackBerry, and it was turned off. He pressed the ON button, and the phone came to life. The photo on her home screen caught him by the throat. It was of him, and he remembered the day she had taken it, a Sunday afternoon in early June, a week before his deployment. He'd been working in the yard with his shirt off while Chloe sat in the sun and Emily slept in her carryall, in the shade. Mike hadn't realized Chloe was taking his picture until he happened to look up and ask her.

What are you doing?

What's it look like I'm doing? Chloe snapped the photo. *You're hot, for a Dad. Nice smile, nice shoulders, nice abs. And that butt, break me off a piece of that!*

Stop it, lady. I'm married.

Who cares? I'm more fun than your wife.

I bet you are, but I love my wife.

Mike looked at himself in the photo, because he was looking at her, with love. Chloe always said he was handsome, but he thought he looked regular, like a million other guys, straight nose, long face, brown hair, brown eyes. He didn't know she had made him her backdrop photo, because when he left for Afghanistan, it was the baby. It touched him so deeply that she'd switched the photo, consciously choosing his picture, as if it were proof that she loved him, above all.

His thumb scrolled over to the phone log, where he noticed the last call she'd received was from Danielle. He felt a pang when he saw that it came in on 12/15, the day she had died, at 4:28 P.M. Chloe couldn't have answered the call, near death. He pressed Call Voicemail, then through to hear the message. Danielle's voice was incongruously cheery, and she said: "Hey honey, hope you're having a nice day. Emily and I are having a wonderful time at the mall. Just wondering if you wanted Chinese or Thai for dinner. If I don't hear from you, I'll surprise you. See you at five o'clock. Love you, honey."

Mike pressed END, agonized. He wished he had been there to save Chloe's life, but he wasn't even on the same continent, and Danielle was at the mall with Emily, happy and shopping, while Chloe lay bleeding to death. Then he realized something. Chloe had died between five thirty and six, and Danielle was due home at five. So Danielle must have come home late, by an hour. If she hadn't been late, Chloe would still be alive. If she hadn't stopped for takeout, Chloe would still be alive. There were a million what-ifs, and his what-if was the worst of all.

Mike couldn't take it anymore. He set the phone down, rose, crossed to the casket, and knelt stiffly on the cushioned pad. He gazed at Chloe's body, breathing in the air around her, Febreezed rather than perfumed. His eyes found the towel covering her wound, a faint outline through her dress, but he didn't have the heart to look closer. He wasn't her doctor, he was her husband.

And now, her Surviving Spouse.

He placed his hands over hers, but they felt hard and so cold that his grief swallowed him up.

Mike put his head down, and cried his heart out.

Chapter Fourteen

Mike slumped behind the wheel of Bob's Mercedes, sitting in traffic on Lancaster Avenue. Exhaust floated between the cars in chalky plumes, and the dashboard clock read 5:45 P.M., as if to plague him. Less than a week ago tonight, at about this time, his wife was dying, which only raised more what-ifs. What if it hadn't been the holidays, a Sunday, what if, what if, what if?

The light turned green, and Mike cruised forward, then came to another stop, preoccupied. He'd driven this trip so many times after he'd picked up Thai takeout. Chloe liked the vegetarian red curry, with brown rice. He found himself wondering whether Danielle had picked up Thai food or Chinese that night. Thai would have gotten her home on time, but Chinese not.

Mike fed the car some gas, then braked again. Up ahead he spotted a white-and-gold Wilberg Police cruiser, stuck in the same traffic. There had to be an official report about Chloe's death. Suddenly his cell phone rang, and he dug in his jacket and retrieved it. The display read BOB RIDGEWAY, and he pressed ANSWER. "Hi, Bob."

"Mike, how you doing? I just called the funeral home, and they said you left."

"Yeah, I'm stuck in traffic."

"How was it? Does she look okay? The guy there, Scott, said she looked good."

"She looks fine" was all Mike could say.

"Did you like the casket?"

"Yes, Bob, thanks. Everything is all good."

"What time do you think you'll be home? Danielle wants to know, she's making dinner."

"I may be late, so don't wait." Mike hit the gas and traveled half a block until he had to brake again. "I'm thinking of stopping by the police station."

"Why?"

"To see what their file looks like, on Chloe."

"Really?" Bob's tone turned disapproving. "Why do you want to put yourself through that?"

"I'm curious, I guess." Mike didn't know how to explain. More wanting to know everything.

"There's no point to it, Mike. What're you gonna find out from the cops? Come home. Hold on, Danielle's saying something." Bob must've covered the phone with his hand because Mike couldn't make out what they were saying, though he could hear some back-and-forth between Bob and Danielle. "Mike, Danielle says, please come straight home. Dinner's almost ready, and the baby's awake. Danielle says you could spend time with her."

But Mike had his eye on the cruiser, which was turning left, toward the station.

Chapter Fifteen

Mike walked up the pathway to the Wilberg police station, in a historic house that was typical of Chester County, long and narrow with white clapboard siding, a double-wide entrance door, and shutters painted a black enamel. Its front porch was lined with all-white holiday lights, and its roof covered with snow, as austere and lovely as if painted by Andrew Wyeth, whose family farm was only ten minutes south.

Mike ascended the stairs and went to the door, where a sign read OFFICE HOURS, 9:00 A.M.–4:00 P.M. He wasn't completely surprised that their small suburban town didn't have a full-time police force, in this economy. Still, he could see that there was a light on inside, so he opened the door. It led to a carpeted, rectangular reception area with modern chairs, and an open reception window above a ledge held a call bell, like an old-time hotel.

Mike walked to the window, where we could see a few uniformed policemen stuffing trash into a garbage bag. "Can you help me? My name is Mike Scanlon, I live on Foster Road."

"Hold on." A cop in a dark blue uniform came to the window, smiling in a professional way. He wore a gold badge and a thick utility belt with his service revolver. "I'm Officer Ketrube. We're not usually open this late, but a few of us got stuck cleaning up after the holiday party. What can I do for you?"

"My wife Chloe Voulette died last Sunday, in an accident in our home. My sister-in-law found her and called 911. I was wondering if there was a police report."

"Of course, my condolences." Officer Ketrube slid a form from behind him and set it on the ledge. "Just fill this out, and we can get you a copy of the report."

"Thank you." Mike took the form, which read Right-To-Know Request Form.

"Under Request Submitted By, check the box for In Person. Here's a pen." Officer Ketrube passed him a blue ballpoint, and Mike filled out the form.

"So when there's a 911 call, you make a report of what happened?"

"Yes. We call it an incident report or a blotter. It's a computer-generated form, filled out by the patrol officer who responded to the call. It states generally what took place. Date, time, event, like that."

"Here we go." Mike finished the form and pushed it back across the desk.

"Thank you. May I see your driver's license?"

"Sure." Mike slid his wallet from his back pocket, extracted his driver's license and military ID, and handed it over. "Can I wait for the report?"

"No. It takes five days. My lieutenant reviews all request forms, and by law we don't have to produce it for five days."

"Damn." Mike didn't hide his disappointment. "I'm on funeral leave from Afghanistan, and I have to go back. Can't you help me out? I'd appreciate anything you can do."

"Sometimes we can make an exception for emergency circumstances, but that's up to the lieutenant. Hang tight." Officer Ketrube left the window, and Mike glanced around. On the wall hung six framed portraits of uniformed police officers, their hands folded in her lap, next to an American flag and the blue flag of the Commonwealth of Pennsylvania. In the next minute, Officer Ketrube reappeared at the window, accompanied by an older officer, who wore a suit and tie.

"Dr. Scanlon, I'm Lieutenant Ashe. My sympathies on the loss of your wife. I understand it's a difficult situation, with your being home such a short time. My brother's on his third tour in Iraq. He got stop-lossed."

"I know how that goes. They don't do that to the docs. So what do you think, Lieutenant? Can you help me out with the report?"

"Yes, of course." Lieutenant Ashe nodded, with a tight smile. "Given the situation, and your serving our country, I'm not going to make you wait."

"Thanks so much."

"Here we go." Lieutenant Ashe slid a paper across the counter, and Mike looked down. The top read Incident Report Form, WBT, 12–00746, and all of the blocks were filled in: under Reporting Person/Caller was typed Danielle Voulette Ridgeway, with her birthday, age, race, sex, Social Security number, and driver's license number. Under Responding Units, it read Vehicle Number 746, Patrol Officers deHill and Gerard. Below that was a short narrative, a few lines that described his nightmare:

Victim CHLOE VOULETTE, Caucasian female, age 32, resides 637 Foster Road, Wilberg, PA, found at residence, apparently deceased of a single, self-inflicted knife wound to left arm, from household accident. Victim found by DANIELLE RIDGEWAY, relationship to victim, sister. DANIELLE RIDGEWAY called 911 upon arrival and discovery, 6:32 pm. Patrol Officer deHill called coroner, victim pronounced dead on scene, 6:50 pm.

"This says 911 was called at 6:32 P.M." Mike thought it seemed strange that Danielle got home that late, especially given the baby's schedule and the dinner hour, and she hadn't called Chloe to say she'd be late.

"Correct." Lieutenant Ashe tilted his head to read the form. "That time is accurate. That's the time we received the call in the radio room. Each call gets logged when it comes in. The tape of the calls are at County. If you want to hear the tape, you can fill out another form, but that will take three days and I can't waive it."

"No, that's okay." Mike didn't want to hear Danielle in her worst moment. He hated those 911 recordings, even on TV.

"Okay, then. Take this." Lieutenant Ashe slid another form across the counter. "It's a letter from me, saying your request was formally granted."

"Thank you." Mike folded the papers in thirds and put them in his coat pocket.

"You're welcome." Lieutenant Ashe nodded again. "I'd wish you happy holidays, but I can't imagine this will be an easy time for you."

"No, but thanks, anyway." Mike forced a smile, left the window, and walked out, wondering if he could find a way to understand why Danielle had been late that night.

Chapter Sixteen

Mike felt the tension as soon as he stepped into the living room. Danielle looked up from a floral needlepoint she'd been stitching, under a high-intensity lamp with a magnifying glass attached to its stem, and Bob glanced over from a wing chair, with his laptop. Its screen cast white squares of light onto his reading glasses, and he'd changed into a blue fleece pullover and jeans. A big TV played a *30 Rock* rerun on mute, and the gas fireplace flickered behind smoked glass.

Mike didn't know what was wrong. "Hi everybody, sorry I'm late."

"You're not late." Danielle set aside her needlepoint, rose, and came over. She seemed tired, and her lips tilted down at the corners. "So what did the police say?"

"Nothing really new." Mike avoided her troubled gaze. "How's the baby? Did she go to sleep already?"

"Yes, she went down, sorry. We tried to keep her up, but it's not good for her, you understand."

"Sure, totally." Mike realized that it was around 7:30 now. "What time does she go to bed?"

"She eats at five thirty, gets a bath, and is in bed by seven, usually."

Mike didn't understand. It confirmed his sense that Danielle had gotten home oddly late the night Chloe died. He glanced at Bob, who had returned to his laptop. "Hey Bob, how was court, or your conference?"

"Annoying. The damn case didn't settle, so I have a ton of work to do."

"Too bad." Mike figured that explained his bad mood. "By the way, the funeral director gave me Chloe's cell phone. They said you'd left it."

"I totally forgot." Bob didn't look over. "So you got it, good."

"Yeah, no worries." Mike took off his coat, but his papers fell out of his jacket pocket onto the rug, and Danielle bent over to pick them up, frowning.

"What's this?"

"Oh, whoops." Mike was kicking himself. "It's the police report. They gave it to me at the station."

"Oh no, no." Danielle flushed as she glanced at the papers, stricken. "I don't want to see this, please, Mike. Take it away."

"Sorry." Mike felt a wave of guilt at her anguish, and Bob looked over, frowning.

"What is it the police told you? Anything?"

"Nothing, really." Mike lost the will to suck Danielle into his what-if vortex, and she took his arm, gently.

"No need to apologize, but let's not talk about this anymore, please. You must be starved."

"Thanks." Mike went with her into the kitchen, where a place setting waited for him, and he sat down.

"Mike, if you want my advice, this is exhausting and only going to get worse, so you should eat, watch a little TV, and get yourself to bed."

"Sounds like a plan." Mike sipped some water, and Danielle went to the stove and ladled rice and beef stew onto a plate, its rich aroma filling the air. She carried the bowl over and set it down.

"Here you go."

"Thanks." Mike picked up his fork and tasted a piece of meat, which was probably delicious, but he didn't feel like eating.

"I can't wait until Emily gets old enough for real food. She's still on baby food, and Chloe makes her own—" Danielle stopped abruptly, her skin flushing. "I mean, made her own baby food. You know, boiling organic vegetables herself, then processing them."

"That's probably the best thing, huh?"

Bob entered the kitchen, catching the end of the conversation. "Of course it is, and we bought a gourmet food processor. Danielle's been making baby food by the ton." He leaned against the cabinet, crossing his arms. "So Mike, what did you decide about whether we should take the baby? Danielle told me that she made you the offer, but you had to think about it."

Mike finished his mouthful of beef stew, dismayed. It was impossible to miss the offense in his tone, and he realized that he was the source of Bob's unhappiness. "I hope you don't feel hurt or anything. It just came as a surprise, and I wouldn't have presumed Danielle could make such a big sacrifice."

Danielle interjected, "It's not a sacrifice, Mike. I really want to do it. I think it's best for Emily, too."

Mike turned to Bob. "Danielle runs your office, doesn't she? How do you feel about her taking a month off?"

Bob's arms stayed folded, and his lips formed a businesslike line. "I can work around her, and I admire her for stepping up for Emily the way she is. It's the right thing to do."

"Yes, totally, it was, it is. I mean, it's great and I appreciate both of you. The only reason I hesitated was because I didn't want to impose. Do you really want a baby around, when it's not your own?" Mike realized he'd said the wrong thing when Bob and Danielle looked at each other. He remembered too late that Danielle couldn't have children, which was a sore spot. "Guys, I'm sorry. I didn't mean it that way. I meant it's a huge burden to take on, that's all."

Danielle reached across the table and patted his hand. "I know that's what you meant."

Bob unfolded his arms, softening. "You're not pushing the burden on us, we're happy to assume it. Don't you think it would be best for Emily if she stayed with us? What more do you need to know to make your decision?"

"Nothing, really," Mike answered, defensive. "There's been so much to deal with, I feel like I haven't had a second to focus on it."

"So, focus now." Bob's tone softened. "What do you think?"

"Okay, then, Bob and Danielle, you're on." Mike felt put on the spot, but there was no point in delay. "I think it's a wonderful offer you've made, and I accept with gratitude. I appreciate you both more than I can say."

"Oh, Mike." Danielle came around the table and hugged his shoulders. "Thank you so much. We appreciate your confidence and trust. You know we'll take the best possible care of her. We love her more than life itself."

"We sure will." Bob smiled with relief. "You had me worried. I don't want to see my niece taken out of this family. You never know what you're getting with agencies. Danielle wouldn't sleep a wink."

"It's what Chloe would want, too." Mike reached for his water, taking a sip.

"Then we're all agreed." Bob clapped his hands together, as if to dispel the tension between them.

"We're all agreed." Mike nodded, and Danielle went back to her seat.

"I promise you, I will always do what's best for that child, no matter what." Danielle looked him in the eye, and Mike returned her gaze, touched.

"I know you will, and I thank you for it. She's a lucky baby to have you both, and so am I."

Bob sat down noisily. "Well then, there's some papers you should sign, if we're going to take care of the baby until you get back."

"Like what?" Mike asked, chewing his stew.

"A temporary guardianship, in case she has to be taken to the hospital, God forbid, while you're away." Bob went into lawyer mode, his manner official. "We don't want to be in a position where we can't get her the medical care she needs because we're not the parents."

"Okay, how do we get those papers? Can you draft them, like you did the wills?"

"Of course. I didn't want to push the button until you had decided. I'll email one of my associates and get her started, so we get them signed before you go back."

"Sounds good." Mike's heart eased for a brief moment. He knew he was doing the right thing for Emily, and the baby would be happy here. He took another bite of stew, telling himself he didn't need to know why Danielle was so late that night.

Chapter Seventeen

Mike tossed and turned, sleepless. The mattress felt so wide and cushy, and he'd grown accustomed to this skinny, unforgiving rack in Afghanistan. He closed his eyes, trying not to think. It seemed impossible that Chloe was lying apart from him, somewhere else, not even of this world. The only part of life left for him was the baby, sleeping down the hall. On impulse, he got out of bed and padded to the door. He had on his boxers and undershirt, so he didn't bother with the robe that Danielle had hung on the hook for him. He went down the hall, keeping his footsteps light.

He reached her room, put his hand on the knob, and turned it as slowly and quietly as possible, then crept inside, tiptoed to a rocking chair in the corner, and sat down carefully. He didn't want to terrify her or bring Danielle running; he just wanted to be with his daughter. It didn't matter that she wasn't awake; it mattered only that she was breathing, and he could hear that, her soft little puffs of respiration, one after the other. It made him smile because it was louder than he'd expected. He wondered if Emily would grow up to snore, like Chloe.

I don't snore, she had said.

Honey, face it. You snore.

How dare you? Girls don't snore.

I know one who does.

Mike smiled at the memory. He leaned his head back in the rocking chair and found himself rocking, silently. The chair didn't squeak, and the rug was thick. It soothed him on some primal level, the rhythmic motion and the regular breathing of his child, not six feet away.

He wished he could go over and pick her up, but even that wish ebbed away with the rocking of the chair. It was his need to hold her, not her need to be held by him. He was her father, but he was also a stranger, and in a few days he would be gone. It would be selfish to barge his way into her life, temporarily, insisting. Much better to stay in the chair, being in her tiny presence.

His gaze wandered around the dim room, taking in the crib, the changing table, the chest of drawers, the baby monitor with the glowing button, and the diaper pail, all of which he had bought with Chloe. It was an odd sensation, to be sitting in the room he knew, but in a completely different house, and to have Danielle, an almost-Chloe, now in Chloe's place.

He felt dislocated and strange again, as if he existed betwixt and between, a life in the interstices of time and space, not on earth but somehow suspended in the air, one of a haphazard family of leftover people. There was no mother to hold them altogether, nothing to keep them in orbit, no sun at all. It was cold and dark as outer space, and they floated aimlessly in the void, holding onto each other's hands, pulling each other's fingers and arms, stretching each other's limbs like taffy, moving in blackness without path or direction, seeking a gravitational pull to order them and give them something they could safely encircle, like a center, or a home.

Later, Mike woke up in the rocking chair, at the sound of a tiny cough. The chintz curtains were light from the morning sun behind them, but there was no clock and he didn't have a watch. He didn't want to disturb the baby, so he stayed still.

"Bbb," Emily said, like a little motorboat in her crib.

Mike felt charmed. It sounded ridiculously cute.

"BBbbbb bha."

Mike smiled as Emily kept making happy little sounds in her crib, all of which seemed to start with B. He tried to figure out what she was saying. Ball? Box? Boy? Baby? *Bob?*

Mike felt a tug in his chest. It better not be Bob. He put it out of his mind; it wouldn't help to be jealous of Bob or anybody else.

"Bbb BAH!" Emily raised her voice, and it sounded more like a cry, as if she wanted to get up.

Mike straightened up in the rocking chair, slowly. He couldn't get out in time and he didn't want to escape, anyway. He wanted to try again.

"Bah! BAH!" Emily said again, loudly. She had a strong voice for a little baby. She was something, this kid, he could tell. Made of sterner stuff.

"BAHHHHH!" Emily seemed to be calling out, and Mike saw his chance. He got up, walked to the crib, and peeked over the rail, ducking down so he didn't seem so imposing.

"Hi, honey," Mike whispered. "How's my little baby?"

Emily looked at him. Her eyes flared, then widened, and her little arms flew backwards. Her tiny chest heaved once or twice, and she began to cry.

"Aw, Emily, it's okay." Mike picked her up and held her close, against his chest, rocking her the way Danielle had the other night. "Emily, Emily, it's okay. Everything is okay. I love you, and you don't have to worry."

Emily only wailed.

"It's okay, baby." Mike spotted a pacifier in the crib, scooped it up, and tried to put it in Emily's mouth, but she turned her head this way and that. "Emily, take your pacifier, it's okay."

Suddenly the bedroom door opened, and Danielle appeared in a chenille robe covered with cartoon coffee cups. "Mike, I could get her, I was just coming in to get her."

"I know, but I want to try." Mike cuddled the crying baby. "Let me just give it a try. I'm supporting her head, I got it."

"All right, sure." Danielle smiled, uncertainly. "She always wakes up cranky, but she likes the pacifier."

"The pacifier is my friend."

"Right." Danielle ducked out of the bedroom. "Good luck," she said, closing the door softly behind her.

Emily wailed louder, twisting her head. She seemed to be

looking for Danielle, but Mike walked away with her, to the window.

"It's okay, Emily, it's okay." Mike cradled her, trying to get the pacifier into her mouth, but she turned her head back and forth, then raised her hand and almost batted it away.

"Wow." Mike felt almost proud. "I didn't know you could do that, honey. What a good arm. You'll be a great little pitcher someday."

Still she cried.

"Here you go, honey. Here's your pacifier." Mike watched her twist her head back and forth, then predicted when she'd turn to the left, so he took the pacifier and plugged it in her mouth, then he held it there, fighting the sensation that he was going to suffocate her. "Don't you want your pacifier?"

Emily cried and tried to push the pacifier out of her mouth with her tongue, while she twisted her head back and forth. Mike started to sweat, not wanting to force the pacifier on her, so he took it out, giving her a break.

Emily bawled, full-bore. Tears streamed down her soft cheeks. Snot leaked from her nose.

"Honey, it's okay," Mike soothed, but it wasn't working. His mouth went dry. He felt unreasonably nervous. He couldn't believe how hard this was. He was amazed that mothers did this every day. He just didn't know what to do.

Emily cried at the top of her lungs. Her little face burned bright red. Her chest heaved, and she began to make hiccupping sounds, like she was entering a baby danger zone.

"Mike?" Danielle opened the door. "Can I help?"

Emily burst into new tears, reaching for Danielle, hiccupping and heaving.

"Danielle, what do I do? What am I doing wrong? She won't take the pacifier."

"Give her to me." Danielle took the howling baby from Mike's arms. "If she keeps going like this, she'll throw up."

"She'll what?" Mike asked, but in the next second, he had his answer.

Chapter Eighteen

"Good morning, Bob." Mike came downstairs, showered and shaved as Bob was leaving, slipping a topcoat over his suit.

"Morning. Unfortunately, I'm off to work." Bob grabbed his laptop and slid it into a messenger bag that read THE RIDGEWAY GROUP. "I'll be home by three, and the wake's not 'til seven. We'll go over a little early, at six."

"Bob, don't be late," Danielle called out from the kitchen. "Mike, come have some eggs."

"Be right in," Mike called back. "I owe you a new bathrobe."

Danielle chuckled. "Stop, I'm christened, is all."

Bob winked. "She has other bathrobes, believe me. I've gotta meet a client, but I could be finished at noon if you wanted to go over and clean the house. I'd be happy to help."

"Clean my house? Why?" Mike hadn't been planning to go back home. He wanted to stay here and try to make progress with Emily.

"I'm just saying, because of, you know, the way it was left." Bob lowered his voice, glancing toward the kitchen.

"Oh, okay. I guess you're right, but you don't need to come back. Maybe I'll go over there myself, I'll see."

"If you want me to go with you, gimme a call. If not, I'll stay at the office and finish up. I'm taking Danielle's car, so you can keep mine. I don't think we need to get yours out of the garage. By the way, I put those documents for the temporary guardianship in the living room." Bob gestured at the coffee table, and Mike looked over, surprised to see a thick stack of papers.

"That was fast."

"Thanks." Bob went to the front door and opened it, letting in some cold air, despite the storm door. It looked cold and gray outside. "All you have to do is sign them, but don't date them. My notary will take care of that. They're self-explanatory, but if you don't understand something, make a note and we'll talk about it. I gotta go." Bob called back to the kitchen, "See you, honey, love you."

"Love you, too," Danielle called back.

"See you, Bob, and thanks," Mike said, as Bob left, then he walked to the coffee table, sat down on the couch, and skimmed the first page.

"Mike?" Danielle called from the kitchen. "Are you coming in?"

"After I see these, okay?" Mike started to read the papers, and the one on top read TEMPORARY GUARDIANSHIP AGREEMENT:

I, Michael Patrick Scanlon, of 637 Foster Ave., Wilberg, PA, as custodial parent of my minor child, Emily Voulette Scanlon, do hereby grant temporary plenary custody of the abovementioned minor child to Robert and Danielle Ridgeway, the uncle and aunt of the abovementioned minor child.

Mike wasn't sure what plenary meant, but it didn't seem like it mattered, so he read on:

I, Michael Patrick Scanlon, believe that it is in the best interest of the aforementioned minor child that she remain in the physical and legal custody of her uncle and aunt, the aforementioned Robert and Danielle Voulette, and that they be granted full and plenary powers of temporary guardianship, including but not limited to the following . . .

Mike scanned the list, which seemed to cover every conceivable situation:

In the event of an emergency or nonemergency situation requiring medical treatment, I hereby grant permission for any and all medical and/or dental attention to be administered to the aforementioned minor child.

In the event of an accidental injury or illness, I hereby grant permission for any and all medical attention to be administered to my minor child.

This permission includes, but is not limited to, the administration of first aid, ambulance, and the administration of anesthesia and/or surgery under the recommendation of qualified medical personnel . . .

Mike read to the next page, under a section that was titled Finances:

The parties have jointly agreed that such guardianship shall be provided by Robert and Danielle Ridgeway to me, Michael Scanlon, completely gratis and free of charge, and that all reasonable expenses of care of the minor child shall be borne by the guardians, Robert and Danielle Ridgeway. In the event of extraordinary medical, legal, or other expenses relating to her care, the parties agree to discuss reimbursement of same, and will use best efforts to arrive at a mutually agreeable reimbursement and settlement.

Mike felt amazed by their generosity, but he didn't expect Bob and Danielle to pay Emily's bills and would leave a lump sum for them to draw from for the next three months. He knew how to fix it in the contract, because Bob himself had told him when he'd reviewed the partnership agreement for Suburban Foot & Ankle. Mike picked up the pen, drew a line through the section, initialed his change, then read to the bottom:

This agreement is effective upon signature of all parties, and will extend as long as necessary, beginning on the date of execution.

He thought that sounded right, and a red flag had been affixed next to his signature line, SIGN HERE. Bob and Danielle had already signed on their signature lines, and he picked up the pen, but paused, feeling strange. He couldn't shake the sensation he was giving Emily up, and the papers made Chloe's death so real, even before her wake. He wondered what would happen if he was killed in Afghanistan, then realized this agreement would probably remain in place.

"Mike?" Danielle called from the kitchen. "Your eggs are ready."

"Be right in." Mike stared at the signature line, holding the pen. He felt the weight of the world, but the opposite was true. If he signed, he was completely unencumbered. He had signed away his child and he had no wife. He didn't even have a cat anymore. If he died in Afghanistan, it would be as if he didn't exist at all and never had. Emily wouldn't remember him, but he hoped they would explain to her who her father was and why he had signed these papers.

For her.

Chapter Nineteen

Pewter clouds concealed the sun as Mike cruised down his old street, relieved to see that none of his neighbors was out, undoubtedly because it was twenty degrees. He pulled into the driveway, cut the ignition, and got out of the car. He avoided looking at Chloe's Beetle, hustled up the porch steps, unlocked the front door, and went inside. His gaze went automatically down the hall to the kitchen, but he caught himself. His pity party was supposed to be over.

He glanced at the family room, relieved that he hadn't messed it up. The couch and chairs were a cheerful paisley pattern that Chloe had loved, and they looked good next to an end table she'd bought at an auction.

Isn't that the cutest table ever? It's Sheridan.

Sheraton like the hotel? Mike had been half-joking.

Please, you're embarrassing yourself. It's an antique.

It's not antique, it's secondhand.

Stop. Now you're embarrassing me, because I married you.

Mike tried not to think about Chloe, but it was impossible. He walked into the family room, aching inside. She'd picked out most of the furniture, and he'd been happy to let her do it, not only because she loved to go antiquing but because she could put different things together and make them look like they belonged that way.

He crossed to a pine chest they used as a coffee table, which held last week's newspapers. The entertainment section lay on top, because she'd always read the gallery openings, circle some, and never have time to go. To test himself, he picked up the paper, turned to the gallery openings, and sure enough, there were three ballpoint circles. He stared at the circles, imagining Chloe making them. He wondered if there had been a mug on the table beside her and whether it held coffee or vodka. He wondered why she drank, and if it was because she was unhappy that she didn't get to go to art shows, or had quit teaching when the baby came. Or simply because she missed him, or all of the above. His chest constricted, and he dropped the newspaper.

He left the family room for the sunroom, which Chloe had made into a studio of sorts. Her artwork was everywhere, lying propped against the walls, and there was an easel set up with a half-finished watercolor of the cat. Coffee cans of brushes sat on a shelf, and trays of paints were stowed in their own special area. Chloe had told him that she didn't miss painting, because creating a baby was the most fulfilling thing she had ever done. He had believed her until he found the bottles. Now he didn't know what to believe.

He turned away, walked to the kitchen, and stopped at the threshold. The bloodstain was still there, and even if he replaced the floorboards, he would always know it had been there. He had seen her standing at that spot a thousand times, rinsing a glass, getting water for a recipe, or filling a vase of roses from their garden. Chloe had died in her own kitchen, and Mike realized all of a sudden that he could never live in this house again. He'd price the house to sell and take the first offer that came along.

He turned his back on the kitchen, walked to the front door, and twisted the knob. He said a mental good-bye, and the front door closed behind him.

Chapter Twenty

Mike held open the door to the funeral home, letting Bob and Danielle go inside with Emily, bundled up in her puffy pink jacket. The baby had stopped crying at the sight of him, but he was keeping his distance to play it safe. He let the door close behind them and shook off the cold.

"Welcome." Scott Beeberman strode toward them, in his dark suit. "Hello, Dr. Scanlon, Mr. and Mrs. Ridgeway."

Mike gestured at Danielle. "Scott, I don't think you met Chloe's sister Danielle or our daughter, Emily."

"No, I haven't." Scott smiled sympathetically at Danielle. "Please accept my condolences on the loss of your sister. The baby is adorable."

"Thank you." Danielle hoisted Emily higher, cradling her.

"Please, walk with me, and you can spend some time together, privately." Scott led them down the hall, stopped at a small sign that read VOULETTE, and opened a set of curtained French doors. "Would you like me to take your coats?"

"We'll keep them, thanks," Mike answered for Bob and Danielle, whose attention had turned to the front of the room, where Chloe lay in her casket. He realized that they hadn't seen her yet, and they looked stricken. Their foreheads buckled, their eyes filmed, and their lips parted at almost the same time, their expressions matching so perfectly it almost looked rehearsed.

Danielle hiccupped a sob, turned to Bob, and handed him the baby. "Bob, take her out of here. Go."

Mike stepped over. "Here, let me," he said, but Emily started to whimper, and Bob took the baby.

"Mike, I got her. You go with Danielle to the casket."

"Okay," Mike said, because Danielle was already walking toward the casket, beginning to cry.

"Oh no, Chloe. This can't be. This can't be true." Danielle knelt on the pad in front of the casket, her hands clutching its polished side. "I'm so sorry, I'm so sorry, Chloe. I should've been there, I should've been there."

Mike put his arm around Danielle's shoulder, anguished. He thought he'd saved her from the what-ifs, but he hadn't.

"I should've been there, Chloe. If we'd been together, this wouldn't have happened."

"Danielle, no." Mike reached for her as she burst into hoarse, choking sobs that wracked her small frame, coming from deep within. He couldn't bring himself to look at Chloe's body again. The scent of refrigerated flowers filled his nose.

"I never should've left her alone." Danielle pulled some Kleenexes from her coat pocket and cried into them. "What kind of sister am I?"

"It was an accident. Don't blame yourself."

"No, Mike, you don't understand. It *is* my fault. I did this. She's dead because of me. I killed my own sister."

"No, don't say that." Mike rubbed Danielle's back in the thick tweed coat. "You didn't do this. Nobody did this, it was an accident."

"Mike, no. You don't know everything. You don't know the truth, not all of it." Danielle looked up at him, her eyes flooded with tears and her cheeks streaked with mascara. "I was supposed to be home earlier, but I was late. I picked up Thai food, and I should've gone straight home, but I didn't get home until late."

Mike listened, agonized. Now it would come out, about why she got home late the night that Chloe died.

"I was supposed to be home at five, we agreed. But on the way home, I was driving down Lancaster Avenue, and I saw this antique store in Paoli, you know that one, near the Rita's?"

"Yes, I know."

"Well, I saw they had this hutch in their window, and I wanted to get it, but I couldn't decide." Tears flowed down her cheeks into the Kleenex. Her words and the sobs seemed to run together. "I went and looked at it, then the baby had to be changed and fed, and I didn't want to make her wait until we got home, you know I like to keep the schedule. I was so wrong, I was late, and I'm never late. The one day I'm late, my sister . . . my sister . . ."

"It's okay, I understand." Mike hugged her around the shoulders, trying to calm her down. "What's done is done. It's not your fault, it just isn't."

"Yes, it is, Mike. I was being selfish. It wasn't even for her. It was for me. I was going to ask Bob to give it to me for Christmas." Danielle held the soggy Kleenex to her nose, and Mike could see she was heartbroken.

"Danielle, don't blame yourself, people are late every day, it happens."

"You have her phone, and if you listen to her messages, you can hear me calling her. I even said I was coming home at five." Danielle wiped her nose with the Kleenex. "I didn't even bother calling to say I'd be late. I figured we'd have to microwave the food anyway, and I thought it didn't really matter what time I got home, but it did, it did."

"I understand, you don't have to explain it to me." Mike gentled her to her feet. "Don't blame yourself, you have to stop this now."

"I can't, I can't. I did this. I'm so selfish. She's my sister. My little sister." Danielle took a final sniffle. "Oh, no, I'm a mess, I need to go to the ladies room."

"I'll help." Mike steered Danielle out of the room and into the hallway, where Scott joined them, taking her other arm.

"The lounge is this way."

"Lead us, please." Mike kept Danielle on her feet and going forward down the hall as she sagged between him and Scott.

"I never should've done it, I never should've done it." Danielle sobbed, sniffling. "I wish I could take it all back. I wish I could take everything back."

"Right this way." Scott led them to a paneled door that read LA-DIES LOUNGE. "Dr. Scanlon, it's empty, so if you would like to go in with her, you may. I'll stay here in case any guests come early."

"No, don't." Danielle sobbed, shaking her head. "I want to be alone. I need to be alone."

"Okay, just take it easy, we have plenty of time." Mike let Danielle go, and she pushed open the door and went inside. He spotted Bob in the hallway and crossed to him. The baby was on his shoulder, but turned away. "Oh boy, she's really upset."

"I know." Bob nodded sadly. "She's been beating herself up since it happened."

For the next few hours, Mike greeted a teary blur of mourners, hugging him, telling him they were sorry, saying they were praying for him, and he felt awash in the comfort and love of so many people. "Sara, Don," Mike said, hugging them both. "Thank you for coming, I really appreciate it."

"You know we love you, Mike." Sara wiped her eyes, grief-stricken. "We'll be praying for you."

"Thank you." Mike felt relieved he hadn't told Sara about the vodka. It wasn't the way he wanted her to remember Chloe. The reception line shifted, and Jim appeared with his wife Laura, throwing open his arms in his dark topcoat, his eyes pained and his face ruddy from the cold.

"Mike, we're so sorry, we both are."

"Thanks." Mike released him, then Laura hugged him, too.

"Oh, Mike, we're just beside ourselves. Please accept our deepest sympathies. We can't imagine how awful this is for you, and we love you."

"Thanks so much." Mike managed a smile, then hugged the next person and the next, until he caught sight of his partners Tony and Dave, with their wives.

"Mike, we're so sorry." Tony gave him a hug, and so did his wife Jill, then so did Dave and Bonnie, then all four stood around him in a teary circle.

"It was so nice of you guys to come." Mike hadn't realized how much he missed them, and it was surreal to be among them without Chloe. He felt suddenly shaky. "Is it hot in here, or is it me?"

"Mike, you okay?" Tony took his arm, his brown eyes filled with concern. He had thick black hair and a large nose. "You want to sit down, man?"

"Let's go outside, get some air." Mike glanced at the reception line, which was basically over.

"Sure, good idea." Tony, Dave, and Mike left the room while their wives went to talk to Danielle and see the baby. The three men made their way down the hall and to a screened-in porch outside, with patio chairs around a table.

"Great, that feels better." Mike eased into a chair at the table.

"You needed the break. That's a lot of people in there." Tony sat down, plunging his hands into his pockets and drawing his coat around his compact frame. "We're so sorry about Chloe."

Dave sat down next to him, nodding. "Yeah, Mike, if there's anything we can do, let us know."

"Thanks." Mike liked them both, so much. Dave was tall, skinny, and African-American, and Tony was short, dark, and Italian. They couldn't have looked more different, but they called themselves brothers-from-another-mother.

"Sorry I missed you yesterday." Dave frowned behind his wire-rimmed glasses. "I heard you came in."

"Yeah, sorry I missed you, too. I was surprised by the changes in the office, though. It was more than I thought from the emails. How are you guys working with that?"

"Let's not talk about that now."

"It's okay, I want to. What's going on? Fill me in."

"No, don't worry about it tonight." Dave shook his head, his expression pinched. "The last thing you need now is shop talk. We can talk another time."

"No, I might not have another time, and I want to know. I wish you had told me already."

"We didn't want to worry you over there. We figured you had enough on your plate."

"I get that, and thanks." Mike knew they were being considerate by not telling him, just like Chloe had been, but he felt better knowing the facts. He appealed to Tony, the more talkative of the two. "What's going on? I want to know."

"Fine." Tony's dark eyes flashed with anger. "Our business fell off, but Jim's using that for an excuse to start a new practice. It's all about sports medicine for him, and our side is like a ghost town. We're both looking to get out."

"Leave the group?" Mike shook his head, incredulous. "We've been together almost a decade."

"I know, I'm sorry, but I'm out. I'm hoping I can join a group in Bryn Mawr."

"But why break up? Why don't you join Jim and Lyon? They'll take you, won't they?"

"In a word, no." Tony shook his head, his feathered hair blowing in the wind. "We asked him, and he said no."

"No way," Mike said, appalled. "He's not just gonna ditch us."

Tony snorted. "Mike, you're the nicest guy in the world. This is why I miss you, man."

Dave smiled sadly. "Mike, we'll keep our eyes open for you, but I doubt there will be a practice when you get back."

"Why throw it away?" Mike wanted to change their minds. "We're making money, and I love working with you guys. If we make less, we make less. It's still enough, right? Jim said you're getting bonuses over base, and I'll be home in no time."

"Sorry, but no." Tony's lips buckled. "It's not only the money, Mike. I refuse to be treated like dirt in my *own* practice."

Dave shook his head, resigned. "I found a new group of orthopedists who left Rothman. They're in East Goshen, out of the system."

"Out of the system?"

"I know, I'm going to find life beyond this galaxy." Dave smiled tightly. "I'm boldly going where no black man has ever gone before."

Mike reeled. "I figured you were unhappy, but not this unhappy."

Tony interjected, "I'm not unhappy, I'm homicidal."

Dave squinted against the cold. "Look, I'm really sorry, Mike. If room opens up for you, I'll let you know. We'll stay in touch, I have your email."

Mike tried to keep it together. All he felt was loss, on top of loss.

"Hell, we'll always be friends." Tony smiled, gesturing at Dave. "We'll still golf. We're going to Pebble next month."

Mike didn't golf. They must've forgotten.

"I'll teach you to play," Dave offered, reading his mind.

"Okay." Mike rose stiffly, forcing a smile. "I should go inside," he said, chilled to the bone.

Chapter Twenty-one

Mike rested in the rocking chair, sitting in the darkened bedroom while Emily slept. Bob and Danielle had gone to bed, and he'd sneaked in, in his borrowed bathrobe. He closed his eyes, trying not to think of the wake and the news from his partners. There came a snuffling sound from the crib, but he didn't think Emily would wake up and he wanted to be in her presence.

He eased out of the rocking chair, crossed to the crib, and peeked inside. Emily was lying on her back again, her head to the side. She was sucking a pacifier, and he stood as still as he could, his eyes taking in every detail. He was trying to memorize the way she looked, so he could carry the image back with him. It hadn't worked when he deployed the first time, and Chloe had told him he was silly to try.

I'll send you a picture, every day. You won't have to remember, you'll have the real thing.

Mike had disagreed. The picture wasn't the real thing, even the memory wasn't the real thing. He was in the presence of the real thing, this baby who didn't want any part of him but who *was* a part of him, and all that he had left in the world. It would be so hard to leave her, and he couldn't imagine letting her go without having held her. He'd kept checking on her at the wake, and she'd fallen asleep on Tony's shoulder, whom she barely knew.

Mike saw himself flunking as a father, the proverbial slow-motion wreck that he was powerless to stop or derail. Maybe he didn't have what it took. If he was naturally good at surgery, then he could be naturally bad at parenting. He wondered if his father had felt that way or never realized it. He didn't know if lousy fathers knew they were lousy, or whether they were spared by their own selfishness. His father hadn't stayed long enough to answer these questions.

He remembered the morning his father had left for work, on the day he never came back. Mike had watched him walk down the street, his bearing characteristically erect, heading to the train station to catch the 7:15, his newspaper under his arm. Mike had replayed that scene so many times since then, not only as a child, but even, embarrassingly, as an adult, hoping it would come out a different way. And each time, he'd say the same thing, like a secret prayer.

Don't go.

Chapter Twenty-two

The funeral procession began, and Mike walked with Danielle behind the polished casket, which was being rolled down the center of the church on an elevated metal gurney. He still couldn't believe that Chloe was sealed inside, but he had seen it with his own eyes, when he'd said good-bye, one last time. He'd cried himself out, leaving him with an emotional exhaustion and an agonized love for his wife.

Danielle walked next to him, numb and teary, carrying Emily, precious in a little red coat, white tights, and pretend shoes. Bob was one of the pallbearers and he looked stricken beside her casket, at the back, and the other pallbearers were Jim, Tony, and Dave, Sara's husband Don, and Scott from the funeral home. Even Father Hernandez, their elderly priest whom Chloe liked, looked teary-eyed as he swung an ornate brass censer on a clanking chain, trailing thick black smoke and wreathing the air with burning incense.

Mike focused on putting one foot in front of the other, the smoke filling his nostrils and his head pounding with the powerful notes of the organ. The congregation turned as he walked by, and he spotted Laura, Jill, Bonnie, and Sara, so distraught on his behalf. He saw himself through their eyes, objectified, a father left alone to raise a little girl. He vowed to himself before God that he would be better than his own father, and it struck him that there was no better place to start than here, in the presence of the holiest of fathers.

Mike stopped abruptly in the middle of the church and turned to face Danielle. "Danielle, please let me have the baby. I should be the one holding her at her mother's funeral. It's okay if she cries."

Danielle looked as if she didn't know what to say, her glistening eyes widening at this spontaneous moment. Bob, the other pallbearers, and Father Hernandez looked back, frowning and halting the procession.

Mike held out his arms. "Don't worry, Danielle. I'm her father."

"Here, take her." Danielle, shaken, offered him Emily.

"Thanks." Mike reached for the baby, cradled her against his suit and tie, and looked into her bottomless blue eyes, his heart swelling, full and complete. He felt as if he were finally doing right by her and Chloe, the three of them together as family, for one last time.

A murmur of approval rippled through the congregation, and a wave of loud sniffling. Emily burst into tears, but Mike had expected as much. He held her close, faced front, and the procession started moving again. Her crying reverberated in the lofty church, a heartbreaking sound against the organ.

"It's okay, honey," Mike whispered into her soft ear. He held Emily close, even as she began to scream louder, squirming and twisting her head. He kept walking down the aisle, and the heels of his dress shoes clicked on the marble floor. Father Hernandez swung the censer as he processed, his white-and-gold robes swaying back and forth.

Suddenly Emily stiffened, arched her back, and launched herself out of Mike's arms, heading for the marble floor.

"No!" Mike shouted in horror. It startled him so badly that he lost his balance and began to fall backward.

Danielle screamed. The congregation leapt to its feet. Father Hernandez whirled around, his robes swirling. The organ music stopped. Everyone gasped.

Emily was about to hit the floor when Bob stepped backward, reached out, and grabbed her by the coat. "I got her!" he shouted, collecting the bawling baby.

"Thank God!" Danielle rushed to Emily. People craned their necks or jumped to their feet, saying, "He dropped her!" "What happened?" "Is the baby okay?"

Father Hernandez peered down at Mike, his hooded eyes wide. "Son, are you all right?"

Mike looked up at Christ on the Cross, then closed his eyes, in hell.

Chapter Twenty-three

Mike hadn't wanted to relive the funeral, but they'd gotten the story out of him as soon as he got back to the 556th that night. Chatty, Oldstein, Phat Phil, and Joe Segundo were sitting on racks and supply boxes in their tent, which was as messy as a frat house with stinky socks, free weights, paperbacks, and old DVDs. An illegal space heater cast a warm, orange glow on their grizzled faces, all of which looked at Mike in disbelief.

"You did what?" Chatty asked, shaking his head. He had on his garbage-bag Batman cape, and for some reason, had taken to wearing night-vision goggles pushed up on his scrub cap like designer sunglasses. It would be pure Chatty to wear what the Army considered a sensitive item in the least Army way possible. "Scholl's, you're telling me you dropped your baby?"

"Mike, are you serious?" Oldstein chimed in, incredulous. His forehead wrinkled deeply under his watchcap, and he blinked behind his wire-rimmed glasses, which were on the thick side, making his sharp brown eyes look smaller. Phat Phil exchanged glances with Joe Segundo, and they both stopped eating their Snickers bars.

"What can I say?" Mike swallowed, hard. He felt empty, raw, and exhausted. "She's strong, for a baby. I didn't know. She just popped out of my arms." He groped for words to describe what had happened. He had replayed the scene so many times. "It was like she launched herself, like a rocket."

Joe Segundo frowned. "So what happened?"

"She was fine, thank God."

Chatty kept shaking his head. "Wait, wait, wait. What? I don't understand. Scholl's, you can't tell a story to save your life. How could she be fine if you dropped her on the floor?"

"She didn't hit the ground. It was a marble floor. If she hit the ground, she could've fractured her skull." The very thought made Mike sick to his stomach. "My brother-in-law caught her."

Everyone exchanged glances for a minute, and Chatty rose, hitching up his ACU pants, his cape wrinkled. "Hold on, Scholl's. Are you telling us that you dropped your baby at your wife's funeral? And your brother-in-law caught her? Like a football?"

"Yes." Mike felt so ashamed, heartsick. He had avoided Emily for the rest of his leave, and she cried every time she saw him. He worried Emily would never warm up to him, much less love him.

"That's the funniest thing I ever heard!" Chatty erupted in laughter. "You fumbled your own daughter!" Phil, Joe, and Oldstein looked at each other, then they burst into laughter, too.

Mike blinked, astonished. He felt jarred that they could laugh at such a thing. His only daughter could have been killed, at his wife's funeral.

"Oh, no, no, no! You're killing me! It's too funny!" Chatty threw himself backwards onto his rack, laughing and kicking his feet. "She launched herself like a rocket? A *rocket*?"

Phat Phil guffawed. "A *baby* rocket!"

Oldstein shouted, "No, a missile! A baby missile! A shoulder-to-air baby missile!"

Mike didn't know how to react, then he realized he was back in Helmand, at the end of a never-ending war. He'd had reentry issues going home, and now he was having reentry issues coming back. He remembered that the only way the 556th survived was through gallows humor, and they all laughed at their darkest moments, including him. He also knew that they were only trying to distract him, bringing him out of his misery, the only way they knew how. He started to smile because Chatty looked so funny, rolling back and forth in hysterics, then Mike started laughing, and soon the tent was filled with the sound of insanely sad laughter.

"Scholl's, catch!" Chatty tore off his goggles and threw them at Mike, who dodged them.

"Yeah, catch, Scholl's!" Phat Phil joined in, laughing and throwing the Snickers bar. "Can't you catch, butterfingers? Get it? Butterfingers!"

"Scholl's, go long!" Joe hurled a paperback.

Mike ducked and raising his arms to shield himself from the things they started throwing, and he felt good for the first time in forever, the laughter momentarily releasing his pain, dispelling his shame, guilt, and grief. They'd cured him, if only for now, as they threw everything they could at him, and when Mike was on the ground, they buried him under their clothes, books, boots, blankets, and a lamp, then jumped onto the top of the pile with the abandon of much younger men.

Leaving Mike underneath, laughing and feeling that he belonged here, at war. Because he was finally, and for only a brief moment, at peace.

But that night, Mike tossed and turned in his rack. His sleep cycle was completely flipped. His thoughts were full of Emily and Chloe. Their tent was frigid and drafty, and the space heater illuminated the others, sleeping. He heard a snuffle from Oldstein, and Phat Phil turned over, making his rack squeak. No sound came from Chatty, and Mike didn't know if he was sleeping. Typically he slept the least of the docs, always the first one running to the OR, a heavy burden even for a superhero.

Mike gathered his blanket around him, stuck his stocking feet in his boots, and made his way across the cluttered tent, stepping over the junk they'd left on the floor like sloppy frat boys. He went outside, where the cold air hit him full in the face and neck. He trundled to one of the beach chairs in front of the tent, which was usually the first thing they set up at camp, to make it homey.

He sat down and looked into the darkness, past the tents for the nurses, the Tactical Operations Center, and the soldiers who guarded them. He could see the soldier at post by the red tip of his cigarette, and beyond him lay the desert southwest of Kandahar, on the road to Lashkar Gah, near the Pakistan border. The night was still, the sky broken neither by ordnance nor stars, and clouds obscured the horizon, obliterating the division between heaven and earth. He found himself looking up, wondering if Chloe's soul was there, somewhere.

"Hey," said a voice, and Mike turned to see Chatty, in his blanket, cape, and boxers, his night goggles still on his scrub cap.

"Did I wake you?"

"Nah." Chatty clumped over, eased into the chair, and crossed his legs, revealing a hairy calf. He sighed, wreathing them both in chalky breath. "I wonder how long this is gonna last."

"The quiet?"

"Yes."

"Maybe they went south." Mike knew the Taliban didn't like fighting in the cold, preferring to hide in Pakistan, in the lawless Federated Tribal Areas.

"I know, but I hate it." Chatty shook his head.

"Me, too." Mike also knew that Army communications being what they were, the FST hadn't been told when or if the brigade would strike, and nobody knew when or if the enemy would attack. It was a life lived on tenterhooks, and the docs took it into consideration when they analyzed vitals, because nobody's blood pressure was normal, ever.

"Silent night, holy night, eh?"

"Oh, right." Mike had almost forgotten about Christmas. He had been en route at the time, and the gift shops had been decorated at the base in Kuwait. "How was Christmas? What did you do?"

"We were at Bagram, so the usual." Chatty looked into the distance. "Strippers and pizza."

Mike smiled. Bagram was the nearest base, about twenty-five miles north of Kabul. The FST was entitled to chill when they were at base, but lately they'd had to assist in the hospital, called Camp Lacy, because it was shorthanded. "Was it bad?"

"Not too. I drained some mighty heinous abscesses, and I&D."

Chatty meant irrigation and debridement, or cleaning out the wounds, trimming away the dead tissue, and packing them, without closing. Most soldiers endured multiple surgeries on the same wound, but Mike never heard a single one complain.

Chatty looked over. "So how you doing?"

"Fine."

"That why you're out here? Because you're so fine?"

Mike couldn't smile. "Okay, my practice is imploding, and my wife bled to death because she was drunk when she cut herself."

Chatty blinked. "You need cheering up. How do you hide money from a surgeon?"

"Tape it to his children."

"How do you hide money from a plastic surgeon?"

Mike had heard that one, too. "You can't."

"How do you hide money from an orthopod?"

"How?"

"Put it in a book. Did you know the one about the two podiatrists? They were arch rivals."

Mike groaned. "Please stop."

Chatty's expression grew serious. "So tell me. Start with your partners, we'll ease into it. What happened?"

Mike sighed, then told him the story.

Chatty nodded, considering it. "My judgment? Haggerty's a jerk."

"You can't blame him. He saw an opportunity and he took it."

"I do blame him. He should've lifted you all up, invited you all to join, especially you. You can pin fractures with your eyes closed. When you go back, find a new group." Chatty turned to the black horizon. "Now, what happened with Chloe?"

Mike told him, not finishing until it was almost dawn and the sky had lightened to purplish, but was still opaque, like a lid on a pressure cooker. "Hell, I don't even know when she started drinking."

"It sounds like she started after you left, which makes sense."

"I think she drank with Emily in the car."

"You don't know that. Cut her some slack." Chatty drew his cape around him. "Give her the benefit of the doubt. You'll make yourself crazy. You'll start doubting everything you know."

"That's what I'm doing."

"So don't. You know what you know. She probably started after you left and it got the best of her. It's the war." Chatty threw up his hands. "She's only human. Don't judge her. Just love her."

Mike felt it resonate in his chest. He eyed the horizon, beginning to show itself, and squinted against the light of a new day.

"Don't worry, the baby will get easier. They're not real until they talk, and once they start talking, they never stop."

Mike smiled. Chatty had three daughters.

"You'll be fine." Chatty chucked him on the arm. "Come on, Scholl's. Let's see that studly smile."

Mike didn't have a chance, because there was a commotion at the Tactical Operations Center, as Joe Segundo burst from the front flap.

"Wake up, everybody!" he shouted. "There's four in the air and more to come! It's *on!*"

Chapter Twenty-four

Mike came out of the OR tent, squinting against the sun. The brigade had sustained heavy casualties in the attack last night, and the 556th had operated for thirteen hours straight. All cases were expected to return to duty, though two were injured severely enough to be transported to Landstuhl. Mike's last patient was in recovery, The Kid With The Dragon Tattoo. The soldier had survived the fragment wounds, but his tattoo was KIA.

Mike inhaled, and the cold air carried traces of smoke and ordnance. The sky was cobalt blue, and the Registan Desert packed in frozen ridges. A dust devil whirled in the distance, a cyclonc of sand spiraling upward on unseen currents. Mike looked around camp, which was calm after the chaos of last night. Chatty, Oldstein, and Phat Phil stood outside their tent, talking with two soldiers. Oddly, from their group came the sound of a child crying.

Mike walked over, and in the middle of the group stood a boy about six years old, holding a spotted puppy with a cut leg. Tears streaked down the child's dirty face, and fabric wrapped around the dog was soaked with blood. Mike looked over at Chatty. "You gonna fix it, or am I?"

Chatty frowned. "Colonel Mustard says we're not allowed."

Mike sighed. Colonel Mustard was Chatty's name for Lieutenant

Colonel Colin Davy, the Deputy Commander of Clinical Services. Mike turned to the soldier, named Jacobs, whose eyes were bloodshot after fighting all night. "Jacobs, what's the deal?"

"I don't like it, either, but I got orders." Jacobs shrugged, his cheeks dotted with acne. The soldier behind him, Tipton, looked grim. "Davy says you can't do anything for the dog. It's against regs."

Chatty scoffed. "Jacobs, kindly tell Field Marshal Numbnuts he's not the boss of me. This is my FST, and I don't take orders from him or anybody else."

"Aw, come on, Jacobs." Mike knew the Army didn't advertise it, but FSTs and Combat Support Hospitals routinely provided medical care to host nationals, coalition forces, Afghan army and police, even enemy detainees, because the Afghan hospitals were horrendous. "We're supposed to help the host nationals."

"I feel you, but Davy says the dog is not a host national."

"We're helping the kid, not the dog." Mike's heart went out to the boy, who gazed up at him, big dark eyes fringed with long eyelashes.

"Sorry." Jacobs shook his head. "The kid shouldn't even be here. I was taking him out of camp, but he saw the Red Cross and ran in."

"Where's his parents? How'd he even get here?"

"His village isn't far, due north, where it gets scrubby." Jacobs waved beyond the camp perimeter, marked with Humvees. "His grandfather brought him. He's one of the elders. We checked him out."

"Where's your terp?" Mike meant the brigade's interpreter. The boy could have spoken Pashtun, Dari, or Urdu, or any dialect thereof. The FST had English and Spanish, though Mike's Latin was useless everywhere.

"He's with the detainees. We got two. The grandfather's waiting." Jacobs nodded toward the gate, and Mike craned his head to see a frail old man in a *shalwar kameez*, or a white turban, and a brown *patu*, a shawl the men wore over their long traditional smocks, leading a donkey on a rope.

"If the grandfather's an elder, doesn't he have pull?"

Chatty scoffed, impatient. "We're spending more time talking about it than it would take to fix. The dog's gonna die."

Phat Phil looked over, squinting. "We're not vets."

Oldstein snorted. "I taught at Johns Hopkins. I can duct-tape a puppy."

"And I'm Batman," Chatty added, and they all smiled.

Mike crouched and held out his hand, and the boy took a step forward, which touched him. "Aha! I see the problem, don't you, Dr. Chatty?"

"Yes, I do, Dr. Scholl's," Chatty answered, playing along. "What is it?"

"This child is injured." Mike pointed to the boy's pants, covered with the dog's blood. "That's major blood loss, don't you agree?"

"Agree, Major Blood Loss. Have you met my colleagues, Major Pain In The Ass and Major Faux Pas?" Chatty turned to Jacobs. "Soldier, we have to treat this host national. Please inform Colonel Mustard. He's in the conservatory, with a pipe."

Jacobs rolled his eyes. "Doc, that's dog blood, and you know it."

"Wrong. Dog blood is a lighter red, more cerise, less vermillion."

"Let me have your puppy, buddy." Mike held out his arms, but the boy took another step closer. "Does he want me to pick him up?"

"Obviously, Scholl's. Just don't drop him." Chatty chuckled, and the others joined in.

"Here we go, honey." Mike scooped up the boy and puppy, and they rose and walked toward the OR tent. The boy felt surprisingly light, and his timid gaze shifted toward Mike, then away. "Don't be afraid. We're gonna take care of your doggie."

"Wait. Oh, hell, no." Chatty glanced over his shoulder, then stopped. The grandfather was walking into camp with the donkey, motioning to the little boy, and the guards were talking to him.

Mike halted. "Looks like he didn't expect us to take the boy. He probably thought we'd just take the puppy."

"They should call the terp." Chatty shook his head, watching with his hands on his hips.

All of a sudden, Mike didn't understand what the grandfather was doing with the donkey, and in that split second, he sensed something was wrong. "Chatty, look," he said, but Chatty's eyes widened with horror.

"No!" he screamed, just as the grandfather pulled a grenade from a saddlebag, yanked the pin, and hurled it at Phat Phil, Oldstein, Jacobs, and Tipton.

KABAAM! A white-hot orange blast exploded in the middle of the men. The tent went up in flames, *whoomp*. The beach chairs flew into the air. A percussive wave knocked Mike backwards. He hit the ground. The boy and puppy went flying. Chatty fell beside him, his mouth open, screaming or saying something.

Mike couldn't hear, deafened. He scrambled to his feet, reeling. The boy lay on his back on the dirty ground, his head to the side. The puppy was nowhere in sight. Mike rushed to the boy and felt his pulse. It was beating. He was unconscious.

Chatty staggered to his feet, his face covered with soot. He lurched toward Mike and grabbed his arm. His eyes were agonized, his lips moving, saying something Mike couldn't hear.

"Oldstein!" Mike yelled, though he couldn't hear himself. "Phil! Phil!" He tried to get to his feet, but fell down and Chatty yanked him up. They ran together to the explosion and threw themselves on the ground, looking for bodies on the scorched and smoking ground. Smoke enveloped them, stinging their eyes and filling their nostrils.

Mike couldn't believe what he was seeing. A horrific nightmare, visions of hell. Body parts. A bloodied helmet. Oakley sunglasses. Bone fragments. A lid from a Copenhagen can. Soggy hunks of yellow fat. Skull shards. Brain matter, with its chemical odor. Donkey. Scraps of their tent, DVDs, a rifle, an ACU sleeve, the twisted beach chair.

Soldiers and vehicles raced to the blast from all directions. Flames flew skyward, superheating Mike's face and body. He and Chatty coughed and frantically crawled around, looking for anything they could stitch back together, but they knew their friends were gone.

"Oldstein!" Mike screamed anyway. "Phil!"

Joe Segundo came running through the smoke, clamped his hands on Mike, and pulled him away from the fire. A soldier grabbed

Chatty, but he fought him off, trying to get back, and it took another soldier to yank him away.

Mike broke free and ran for the OR, to check on The Kid With The Dragon Tattoo.

Please let me do one thing right. Just one.

Chapter Twenty-five

Mike hustled from one bay to the next, dragging the lone working lamp with him, treating nurses, soldiers, and staff for lacerations, smoke inhalation, and burns, while The Kid With The Dragon Tattoo rested in the recovery area. Soot streaked the air, and the stench of burned flesh clung to Mike's hair and ACUs. The 556th had lost Oldstein and Phat Phil, and the brigade had lost Jacobs and Tipton.

Nurses and staff wept as they cleaned up the debris of the OR. The explosion had knocked over the sonogram, ventilator, and a laptop, but they were still working. IV stalks had blown over, and medical supplies and equipment lay broken on the floor. Saline, antibiotics, and packed red blood cells came in plastic bags, but blood had to be refrigerated and the generator was out. Soldiers were reattaching a replacement to power it back up.

Mike's final patient was his nurse Linda, who had broken her ankle and sat on his table, her hair and face grayish with soot. He had already wrapped her foot and ankle, but he had to make a cast. His head hurt, and his ears were still ringing. He felt his jaw working to hold back his emotions. He poured sterile water into a bowl and began to bathe her bandages with his gloved hands. Outside, soldiers shouted to each other, trying to contain the fire. Chatty and Joe were with them, collecting and bagging the remains.

Linda sniffled. "One of the soldiers told me that we're the only FST he knows of that's been the subject of a direct attack. There have been FST docs killed in action, but never during a direct attack on a camp."

"Really." Mike didn't feel like talking, and Linda had worked with him long enough to know as much. He kept smoothing the bandages, sculpting as he went, so the cast dried comfortably.

"There was a doc from Wisconsin who was killed when his Humvee exploded, but this might be a new thing, attacking the FSTs."

Mike felt the cast start to harden, forming a nice, protective shell.

"The soldiers can't figure out what was up with the old man. He checked out. They radioed it into the brigade. He was even at the *shura* last week."

Mike nodded. A *shura* was a meeting with the village elders, to hear their grievances and have Civil Affairs pay them for any damage the Army might have caused. Money was the dirty little secret of the hearts-and-minds campaign, but Mike didn't think you could pay people not to kill you.

"They searched him and even the boy, but they didn't check the donkey. They think the Taliban planned the attack for today, knowing we'd be standing down after last night."

Mike used the side of his hand to squeegee the water from the bandages, so it wouldn't take too long to dry.

"I doubt very much that the boy was even his grandson. I think they just used him, and they didn't care if he lived or died."

Mike had heard that the boy had been taken to brigade command. He didn't know what had happened to the puppy. Oddly, it mattered. He still wanted his cat back, too.

"I bet they picked the cutest kid and used him as bait, and they knew we'd feel sorry for him." Linda's voice trembled. "You *know* they cut that puppy's leg. That's sick. *Sick.*"

Mike took off his gloves, finished. He was thinking about how the boy looked over at him, so timidly. He had assumed the boy had been afraid of him, but maybe he had been afraid of what was going to happen. He wondered if the boy knew.

"What kind of people will sacrifice a child? How many times have we helped villagers? Even detainees?" Linda slumped in her bloodied T-shirt. "We may not be perfect, but we're good, and good people can't imagine evil. It catches us by surprise, and it always will. We don't know the first thing about the kind of evil that would sacrifice a child."

"It's okay." Mike gave her a hug around the shoulders. "It's going to be okay."

"No, it's not." Linda broke down, and Mike held her, rubbing her back. He had to admit to himself that she was right.

He didn't think it was going to be okay, ever again.

Chapter Twenty-six

The Afghan night fell hard and moonless, the black sky as dense as onyx, making an impenetrable backdrop for the Chinook that lifted off, carrying the remains of Oldstein, Phat Phil, Jacobs, and Tipton. Mike was next to Chatty, choking back tears. All of the soldiers and the 556th FST stood at attention and saluted, crisply and in unison.

The Chinook ascended, catching up with its Apache escort. Mike couldn't see it anymore and neither could anybody else, but none of them looked away. They faced the engine noise until it vanished and the outline of the transport disintegrated, the blackness swallowing all four men, like death itself.

Mike looked over at Chatty, but couldn't make out his expression. The lamps were behind them at the blast site, running on generators to help with the cleanup, and all he could see of Chatty was a silhouette and his hair, blowing crazily. He worried Chatty was in trouble by the bizarrely stooped way he was standing. "Chatty, you all right?"

Chatty swung his head toward Mike, and the light caught the wetness on his cheeks. "You believe this, Scholl's? This cannot happen. This is just unacceptable."

"I know."

"Oldstein, Phil, those kids. Did you see Jacobs, after?" Chatty's words sped up. "I saw his boots, I saw his face, I saw him *shredded*. So I say no."

"I know," Mike said, to soothe him. Linda and Joe Segundo looked over, frowning. Soldiers craned their heads as they fell out to resume cleanup. Mike caught Joe's eye and made a motion for a syringe, behind Chatty's back, then Joe took off.

"No, no." Chatty clutched Mike's arm, squeezing tight. "I want to ask you a question, what's worse, what you see or what you don't? Tell me, because I didn't see this coming, I didn't see that the old man was gonna kill us, I didn't see any of that, not any."

"Neither did I," Mike said, stricken.

"I'll tell you what I see. Oldstein's glasses, don't ask me why they survived, because Oldstein sure didn't. I cannot live with this, I cannot."

"Chatty, we'll deal with it, we can—"

"No. No. I don't know what to do, I don't know what we're gonna do or how we're gonna help these kids. I can't believe I let this happen, I can't believe I made this mistake." Chatty kept squeezing Mike's arm. "I made the biggest mistake of my life, and I made the biggest mistake of *their* lives, I *cost* them their lives, Scholl's."

"No, we both did it. We both let him through."

"No, I did," Chatty raised his voice. "*I* did it, *I* told Jacobs to back off, I *bullied* him, you saw it, I told him, it's my command. He went against orders and now he's dead, because of *me*."

"Come on, don't do this." Mike tried to force Chatty to the ground, instinctively wanting to settle him. "Sit, sit down."

Joe Segundo hurried over, discreetly passed Mike the syringe, and grabbed Chatty's other arm. "Sit down, chill. Sit down and we'll talk about it."

"No, no, no." Chatty went to the ground, so that the two men ended up sitting down opposite each other, with Joe kneeling beside Chatty, pressing down on his shoulder, talking into his ear, his accent more pronounced under stress.

"*Jefe*, you gotta keep it together. You the chief. You can't lose it now. We need you now."

"I didn't see it coming, I didn't." Chatty dropped his face into his hands and rubbed it hard with open palms, up and down. "What a colossal, *colossal*, blunder. I was so wrong, so wrong, I didn't think."

"That's not true, Chatty." Mike put a hand on his other shoulder. He wouldn't use the syringe unless necessary. "They checked him out, he checked out. We had no reason to suspect—"

"Not we, not we, not we, *me, I*. I'm the one responsible." Chatty started to rake his cheeks with his fingernails. "No, no, no. This cannot be. I will not accept this, I cannot."

"Chatty, stop." Mike caught his hand in alarm, but Chatty pulled it away. "You're gonna hurt yourself—"

"Stop!" Joe tried to catch Chatty's hands.

"No!" Chatty clawed his face, leaving welts on his cheeks, dangerously close to his eyes.

"Stop, Chatty!" Mike fought to stop him. The only thing a surgeon worried about more than his hands was his eyes. Soldiers and nurses came running over to help, and Mike knew it was go time. He took the syringe, tore off the cap with his teeth, and pinned Chatty's right arm to the ground with his knee, while Joe knelt on top of his left. "Count of three, hold him down. One, two, three!" Joe, the soldiers, and two nurses bore down on the struggling Chatty, and Mike yanked Chatty's sleeve up, plunged the syringe into a bulging vein, and depressed the plunger.

"No!" Chatty kept saying, blood bubbling from the scratches on his cheeks, but Mike succeeded in injecting him. They didn't let go until Chatty's head had fallen to the side and he had passed into merciful oblivion.

"Hurry, let's get him inside," Mike said, pocketing the syringe. It was a violation, but it was also an emergency.

Chapter Twenty-seven

Mike was back in the OR, treating Chatty's eyes as he lay sedated on the table. He wouldn't have expected Chatty to melt down, but he was starting to let go of any expectations. After all, he'd expected to be part of a four-man FST until he went home to his loving wife and baby.

"How's his eyes?" Joe Segundo approached the table, hooking a mask over his ears. Soot dulled his hair on the sides, under his scrub cap.

"They're fine." Mike put a drop of ophthalmic wash in Chatty's bloodied right eye, then closed the lid. He couldn't tell if the lens or cornea was unscratched without eye drops and a special light that the FST didn't have, but as far as he could tell from his examination, the only ocular injury was some broken capillaries.

"Thank you, Jesus." Joe crossed himself.

Mike didn't realize Joe was religious, but he didn't know him as well as Chatty did. He expected that was going to change, then he reminded himself to stop expecting things. Goldstein and DeMaria had expected things, too, and so had Chloe.

"We gotta get him up and running, so he can be *El Jefe* again."

Mike scanned Chatty's face. Long scratches scored his cheeks, oozing blood and raising welts, but none required stitches. Still he couldn't imagine Chatty would be wearing his cape, anytime soon. "Joe, I don't think he's going to be feeling like *El Jefe* for a long time."

"No way, he can handle it, yo." Joe frowned, his face dusted with silt, plugging the pores on his nose.

"It's not going to be easy for him." Mike crossed to the restocked shelves and fetched antiseptic wash, sterile water, and gauze, then brought them back, ripped open the gauze pads, and made a nice stack. "They're going to investigate, talk to him and me, too. He already feels responsible and he's only gonna feel worse. I feel it, too."

"But you did the right thing. I was there when they radioed it in and got clearance." Joe blinked. "He's Batman, no question, no *doubt*. He don't do it for himself, any of it. He does it for us, to keep us going."

"I guess that's true." Mike had never thought of it that way. He squirted solution and water on the gauze.

"The 556th can't do it without him, and he can't do it without you. You gotta stay, Doc."

"What?" Mike wasn't sure he'd heard him right.

"Will you volunteer for another tour?" Joe's eyes were a plaintive brown over his mask. "Give us a year. He won't ask you, but I will, for him, for all of us and the brigade."

Mike couldn't believe the turn the conversation had taken. Water from the soggy gauze dripped through his fingers. "Joe, I'm out in a month. I have to go home. I have a baby. My wife just died. I just buried her."

"I feel you, but we need you. *Jefe's* done two tours, and this is my fourth. Once you're here, you're here. I already called about replacing Oldstein and Phat Phil."

"Already?" Mike asked, aghast. "We just put them on a bird."

"It's my job." Joe opened his palms. "We could get a call anytime. Taliban could kick us while were down. We can't sit aroun' with our thumbs up our asses."

Mike knew he was right. War didn't stop for the dead. War didn't stop for anything or anybody. He wiped the blood from Chatty's cheeks.

"They got no docs to send us now, not even a general trauma surgeon. They won't have nobody outta training for a month, and he's a general trauma surgeon. They don't even have another bone doc they can transfer us, much less a foot doc."

"You're sure?" Mike's mouth went dry as he cleaned the wound. He tossed the bloodied gauze on the tray and reached for a new piece.

"Sure I'm sure. It's a long-ass war, Doc, and we're tapped out. There's only, like, fourteen FSTs left. They could shut us down."

"Then who'll support the brigade?" Mike asked, appalled.

"Ain't nobody but medics and buddy care." Joe frowned. "They'll medevac 'em out to Bagram or another base hospital. You need the stats? Sixty percent of wounds here are orthopedic. Sixty percent of those are lower extremities. That's *you*. And now it's heating up."

Mike thought of Jacobs and the rest. Their faces, their acne, their water bottles for spitting chew, their American flag tattoos.

"Even if they replace you with a rook, when we got two other rooks, it'll be a disaster." Joe lowered his voice, so the staff didn't hear. "Experience makes a difference, yo. We all got better from the beginning of the deployment. Our DOW rate down to 2 percent."

Mike didn't have to ask. DOW meant Dead of Wounds, and he knew death now. He knew what loss felt like, and the families left behind.

"If we add in the very severe injury, or ISS that's greater than twenty-four, and severe injuries, or ISS between sixteen and twenty-four, our DOW rate only goes up to 9 percent."

Mike knew that ISS meant Injury Severity Score, but these kids weren't numbers to him, anyway.

"Our transfusion rate went from 18 percent to 10 percent."

Mike didn't have to ask why that mattered. The FST only carried twenty units of packed blood cells, or PRBCs. If they could conserve it, they could stay out longer and treat more causalities.

"That's better than any hospital in theater, even Bagram." Joe's tone gained urgency. "They can't make you extend, it's up to you. They know you're non-mission after the tour."

Mike felt non-mission, which was Army jargon for burnt out.

"Do a year. You can do it, Doc." Joe's eyes grew animated, and his heavy eyebrows flew upward. "I watched you, I seen you. You never get tired. You don't even talk. You keep your head down and you do your thing. You're like a surgery machine, yo."

"When do I have to decide by?" Mike reached for a tube of anti-bacterial ointment, uncapped it, and smoothed a glistening layer onto Chatty's scratches, like a father fixing a playground boo-boo. He'd never thought of Chatty as needing him and if he didn't re-up, he'd be leaving not only the brigade, he'd be leaving Chatty.

"ASAP. I want to get the jump."

"I'll think about it," Mike answered, spent. All he wanted to do was rest, then he remembered that their tent had gone up in flames. "I'm finished here. Let's get him to recovery, and he'll sleep it off, then we can help outside."

"Sure." Joe nodded. "Hey, you know what I just realized? It's New Year's."

Mike met his eye, and neither one of them said anything.

Chapter Twenty-eight

Mike combed through the charred items from their tent, strewn on a scorched crater about thirty feet in diameter. He didn't care about his own things, but he'd already found Phil's blackened iPod and Oldstein's glasses, which, miraculously, had only a stem missing. Mike wanted to find anything of theirs and return it to their families. It was the worst New Year's of his life, as it would be of theirs.

Mike toed the Ripped Fuel bottles, burned paperbacks, *Sex and the City* DVDs, and a Madden video game. He didn't want to think about whether he would re-up now, while the air still reeked. He didn't expect to find any family photos, because all the FST docs carried them in their Velcro ammo pockets. He kept his Emily photo with Chloe's silver crucifix, and he remembered Phil showing him a photo of his sons.

Heah's my hooligans, Phil had said, in his New England accent. His sons smiled side-by-side, dressed in bowties and navy-blue jackets. *They look just like their mutha, thank Gawd.*

Mike kept searching on the ground. He'd found Phil's and Oldstein's boots for the memorial service, and the soldiers had found Jacobs's and Tipton's, which had their names and blood types written on the toe, typical for a combat brigade. Mike could tell Oldstein's boots because he knew Oldstein was a size thirteen, from treating his plantar's warts.

These warts are disgusting, Oldstein had said. *Why won't they go away for good?*

Nothing goes away for good, Mike had answered, but he'd been wrong.

"Heads up!" a soldier called out, and three Humvees pulled up, then their massive engines shuddered into silence. Lieutenant Colonel Colin Davy and his aides emerged from one and were met by Chatty and Joe Segundo. It was time for the memorial service.

Mike, the FST nurses and staff, and the soldiers fell in at the makeshift memorial site. A battered American flag tied to the defunct generator served as a poignant backdrop for four Soldiers Crosses, one for each of the fallen, their rifles driven into the ground upside-down, their bayonets in the frigid Afghan soil. On the butt of each rifle rested a soldier's helmet, and four pairs of combat boots sat in a row before them.

The 556th stood in a ragged phalanx compared with the neat rows of the soldiers, and when Lieutenant Colonel Davy strode to the front, Mike could see why the man inspired both bravery and fear. Davy was in his forties, well-built, about six feet tall, with a craggy face, a flinty eye and a wide jaw that jutted forward, almost level with his helmet.

"Good morning," Davy began, in a voice that was commanding, yet carried the genteel lilt of someplace softer. "We gather to remember four of our best soldiers and medical personnel. I will keep this brief, as we're in theatre."

Mike's fingers closed around Oldstein's glasses.

"I'd like to say a few words in memorial to Private First Class John Jacobs and Private First Class William Tipton." Davy scanned the soldiers, and each young face was a mask of muted pain, every mouth a somber line. "Private Jacobs was a first-class soldier and the most lovable doofus you'd ever want to meet. Jacobs memorized *Scent of a Woman* and thought he could do the tango. Ladies and gentlemen, Jacobs was no Al Pacino."

The soldiers chuckled hoarsely, the nurses sniffled, and Mike felt his chest constrict. Chatty hung his head, sucking in his lower lip.

"You will recall the time I caught Private Jacobs dancing with Private Kefauver, at an undisclosed location. It was not a pretty sight. In fact, it was the ugliest thing I've ever seen, including that skittles-and-hotdog cake you made for my birthday."

Mike couldn't listen to the rest about Tipton, who was such a Green Bay Packers fan that he wore his cheesehead into combat one day, instead of his helmet.

Davy gestured at Chatty. "Now I'd like to turn the program over to FST Commander Chatham, who will say some words about Majors DeMaria and Goldstein."

Chatty raised his head, but the whites of his eyes were blood-red and his scratches looked like crayoned tear tracks. He took a moment to collect himself, and the only sound was the thrumming of the blowers ventilating the OR and the shrill whistle of the wind through the Registan.

"Lieutenant Colonel Davy, thank you," Chatty began, his voice rasping with raw emotion. "The first thing I need to say, before I talk about my dear friends, is that I am sorry. I took an oath before I came here, not only to serve my country, but to do no harm. In both, I have failed."

Oh no, Mike thought to himself. A nurse sniffled, and soldiers exchanged glances, but Davy stared ahead, as if Chatty weren't saying anything.

"I take full responsibility for the deaths of these four fine soldiers, and I will bear that responsibility to my own grave. I apologize to each and every one of you."

Davy didn't blink, but some of the soldiers sniffled.

"Now let me tell you about Phat Phil DeMaria. Phattie had the manual dexterity every surgeon prays for, but his trade secret was a voodoo doll of Eli Manning, on which he used to practice his suturing."

Mike winced at the memory of Phil's voodoo doll. Tears came to his eyes, and he realized he was losing his family, slipping through his fingers like blood in the OR.

"Those of you who know Phil learned the difference between a Providence accent and a Boston accent, or you pretended that you did, because he would not shut up until you admitted that there was a difference." Chatty recovered his composure, though his eyes glistened. "Major Phil DeMaria and Major Adam Goldstein came into this war as doctors, but they left as soldiers."

Mike hung his head, too sad to hear Chatty talk about Oldstein, then Chatty finished and Davy gave the Final Roll Call, in which all of their names were called and each man or woman responded, so that when he called "Major Scanlon," it was all Mike could do to reply:

"Here."

Mike bowed his head as the Final Roll Call finished and Davy called the name of each fallen soldier three times, ending with his full name and rank. A heartbreaking silence followed each time, and by the end of the ceremony, Mike had squeezed Oldstein's glasses so tight they made an impression in his palm. They all fell out, and Chatty made a beeline for Mike, took him by the arm, and walked him from the crowd.

"Scholl's, we need to talk. Joe told me he asked you to extend. Don't even think about it. You *cannot* do another tour, much less a year."

Mike should've known Joe would talk to Chatty. "What are you going to do without me?"

"Not your concern, I'll get by. You're finished, done. Go tell Joe, now." Chatty squeezed his arm, and Mike didn't think he'd gotten his act together, completely.

"Now? Why?"

"You can't let this get a life of its own. The next thing you know, you'll spend your freaking life in Helmand Province."

"I didn't say yes."

"You didn't say no. Go to Joe and tell him, so he can tell Davy. The train is leaving the station. You don't know how Davy operates."

"No, I'm trying to make up my mind." Mike glanced over Chatty's shoulder, and Joe and the nurses were looking back, curious.

"You can't say yes." Chatty frowned. "You just lost your wife. You have a baby. You want to make her an orphan?"

Mike felt the power of the argument. "I know, but what will happen here? They don't have anybody to send you now, much less two docs."

"I'll manage." Chatty's tone remained firm. "Your tour is almost up and you're shipping out. If I could order you, I would."

"What if they shut down the 556th? Who's going to treat the brigade? I don't want that blood on my hands, Chatty. I've got enough."

Chatty grimaced, his scratches buckling. "I have blood on my hands, too, and if you get your ass shot off because you re-upped, I can't live with that. They won't shut us down. Davy has clout."

Davy was already barreling toward them, with two officers in tow. Mike and Chatty turned, and when Davy reached them, he extended a large hand to Mike. "Dr. Scanlon, good to meet you."

"Yes, you too." Mike shook his hand. "My condolences on the loss of Jacobs and Tipton."

"Thank you," Davy said quickly. "While I appreciate Commander Chatham's apology, it is my opinion that your and Chatham's actions were reasonable in the circumstances. I'm prepared to tell same to Central Command. They're not starting the investigation yet because we're about to launch a new offensive, Operation Viper. We have excellent intel on insurgency locations related to the attack. That commands first priority, which is as it should be."

Chatty's lips parted in dismay. "When does Viper begin? We need to get ready."

"You'll be told as soon as I have further details, but that's not what we need to discuss." Davy turned to Mike. "Dr. Scanlon, it's my understanding that you are extending for another year."

"No," Chatty interjected. "He's not, I can run this FST with new docs, no problem."

Davy ignored Chatty, his flinty gray eyes boring into Mike. "Dr. Scanlon, I hope that you will extend, given the needs of my brigade."

"I'm thinking it over," Mike answered, but Chatty seized Davy's arm, startling the aides.

"Dr. Scanlon just lost his wife and he has a new baby at home. Don't pressure him."

"Pardon me." Davy shed Chatty's hand with a deft motion. "The health and safety of my brigade is my highest responsibility. I need the 556th to remain operational."

Chatty's eyes flashed. "You have the juice to tell them not to shut us down."

"I won't dignify that with a response, and I won't risk having my brigade go without medical care because Dr. Scanlon wants to go home to his baby." Davy swiveled his head around to Mike. "Dr. Scanlon, I have children, and all my men have children, and most of us are on third and fourth tours, away from home for five and six years now. I don't think a year is too much to ask of a man who is partly responsible, as you are, for the fact that two of your unit were KIA."

Mike's head was spinning. "I don't understand. You just said we acted reasonably."

"There's more than one way to view the same set of facts. If you extend, the investigation will go easier."

Chatty's eyes narrowed. "Don't threaten him. I don't care what they do to me, I deserve it. If there's a punishment coming, I'll take it."

Davy scoffed. "Chatham, if you go down, Scanlon goes with you. You did it together, and you just admitted your guilt in front of witnesses."

"Screw you!" Chatty shouted, outraged.

"Chatty, please." Mike didn't want Chatty to get himself in trouble, so he faced Davy. "I'd like to talk it over with my family, first."

"Done." Lieutenant Colonel Davy motioned to Joe Segundo. "Sergeant!"

"Yes, sir!" Joe hustled over.

"Major Scanlon needs to speak to his family. Hook him up for a videochat on your network. I'm authorizing it for this purpose." Davy gestured to one of his aides. "We'll give you our codes, for this one-time use."

"Yes, sir." Joe saluted, then left with the aide.

Davy turned to Mike, his jaw set with grim purpose. "Talk to your family. I'll await your answer at the Humvees."

"No, hold on." Mike had to put on the brakes. "After I speak to my family, I'd like time to think it over. I'll get back to you with my decision as soon as I can."

"Make the right choice, Scanlon." Lieutenant Colonel Davy turned away, followed by his aide, without another word.

Chatty turned to Mike. "He's railroading you. Don't let him."

"I won't," Mike told him, meaning it. "It'll be my decision. Not his, and not yours either."

"Okay, okay." Chatty seemed to stand down, his face falling, a bizarre sight with his blood-red eyes and long scratches, like a scary clown.

"Catch you later." Mike patted him on the arm and walked alone to the Tactical Operations Center.

Feeling for the first time, more soldier than doctor.

Chapter Twenty-nine

Mike waited in a folding chair, and Joe tapped the keys of a heavy-duty laptop in a black Pelican case, on a folding table that served as his desk, blanketed with dusty papers, records, maps, and supplies.

"Doc, sorry, I didn't mean to get Davy on your ass." Joe glanced over, with regret. "I jus' gotta take care of the 556th, yo."

"I know, Joe. No worries." Mike was trying to imagine how Danielle and Bob would react to keeping Emily another year. Then he had to figure out how he would react to being without her that long.

"When was the last time you ate? Here, take this." Joe passed him an MRE, or Meals Ready to Eat, from some stacked on the table. "That's the cheeseburger, number six. I score us the best. The spaghetti with meat sauce, number twenty. The Southwest beef and black beans, number fifteen. They try to stick us with that nasty pot roast, I toss it out. Phat Phil said it tasted like mouse."

Mike sensed Joe was trying to make it up to him, for getting him in trouble with Davy. He dug in his pocket for the iPod and glasses, then set them on the table. "You want to send these back?"

"Sure." Joe put them quickly in a box under the table. "Thanks."

Mike felt a sudden hunger, out of nowhere. He ripped open the MRE box and slid out the plastic packs, tearing open a cold beef patty, which came with a packet of barbeque sauce. He squirted it on the patty and took a bite.

"Ain't you gonna heat that up?"

"No." Mike never bothered with the flameless heater that came with the MREs.

"I always do." Joe leaned under the table, rummaged around in a box, and pulled out a can of Red Bull. "Here, take it. Okay, your videochat's up. I'll give you some privacy. Remember OPSEC."

"Got it." OPSEC meant operational security, and Mike didn't know how he'd explain why he'd been asked to re-up. "Can I say we're shorthanded?"

"Negative. How do you get shorthanded in war? What if they figure it out, put it on Facebook?"

"Okay." Mike slid over just as the laptop screen changed to a picture of Danielle in their lovely kitchen, and the disconnect between here and there was impossibly strong. Her hair looked shiny and blonde, her blue eyes were bright with makeup, and she had on a glittery black V-neck. She looked so pretty, safe, and American, as if she were from a different planet, one consisting entirely of leafy suburbs.

"Mike, what a surprise!" Danielle beamed. "Happy New Year!"

"To you, too." Mike forced a smile. "How are you?"

"Fine, how nice to hear from you!" Danielle looked down, watching his picture on the screen, but she tried to look up, too, to meet his eyes. "I feel so cool, doing this technology thing! And here comes Bob!"

"Great." Mike could hear jostling over the microphone as Bob wedged his way into the screen. He had on a white turtleneck with a navy blazer with shiny gold buttons.

Bob grinned. "Happy New Year!"

"Back at you, buddy. Did you guys go out?"

Danielle answered, "No, too many drunks on the road. We had some people over, Bob's clients and the neighbors. We let Emily stay up late, saying hi to everybody. You should have seen her work the room."

"Aw, what a good girl." Mike felt a deep pang, dreading not seeing her for a full year. Meanwhile, he wondered why Emily would go to everyone but him. "How is she?"

"Adorable," Danielle answered. "How are you? Are you safe?"

No. "Yes."

Bob nudged Danielle. "He can't answer that, dear."

"Sorry." Danielle turned to Mike. "You look so tired. How are you feeling? You can tell us that much, can't you?"

I'm awful. "I'm fine."

"Are you getting enough sleep?"

Of course not. "Yes, sure."

"Are you eating well?"

"Yes." Mike held up the nut raisin mix that came in the MRE. "Snacks aplenty."

Danielle brightened. "And is that Red Bull? I didn't know you had Red Bull."

"Yes." Mike hoisted it like a glass of beer. He didn't want them to worry. "All the comforts of home."

Bob smiled. "Hoo-ah!"

Mike braced himself to pose the question. "I'm calling for a reason, and it's going to come as a surprise. I've been asked to volunteer for a year here. I wanted to know if that was even possible, and if you could take care of the baby."

"Of course we could!" Danielle's eyes lit up, but Bob frowned.

"Mike, if you're asking that, the powers-that-be better have a damn good reason."

"I can't explain more. I haven't made up my mind, but I have to decide soon. I wanted to know what you thought about Emily, and your job."

"She'll be fine!" Danielle gestured so excitedly her fingers blurred the webcam. "I'd be happy to keep her for as long as it takes. I *love* having her, and I love being home with her. We can work it out at the office. No problem."

Bob was still frowning. "You'd stay until a year from now?"

"Yes." Mike's heart ached. "I'd miss her first steps."

Danielle waved him off, blurry again. "Aw, don't worry, Mike. I'll film it all for you. I bought a new digital camera and it has a video function. I've been taking movies like crazy."

Bob rolled his eyes. "She thinks she's Steven Spielberg."

Mike thought of the other firsts he'd be missing. First words. First . . . whatever else. He didn't even know what the other firsts were, that's how bad a father he was. "Bob, can you really do without Danielle at the office for a year?"

"Yes, I'll figure it out." Bob shifted forward, leaning on his elbows. "I don't know why the Army still needs you, but if it does, then I say, God bless."

Danielle nodded. "I'll keep praying for you. But the one thing you won't have to worry about is Emily. We'd love to keep her."

Mike swallowed hard. It was wonderful, and awful, to hear. "If I do stay, I'll figure out how to wire you money for her expenses."

Bob waved him off, his hand blurring. "Don't worry about it. We can settle it when you come home. It's not like we're paying college tuition."

"And the cat, you know, we'll have to decide about him."

"What cat?"

"Our cat, remember? Jake." Mike didn't know why nobody counted the cat. He loved that damn cat. "If the boys want to keep him, they can. Sara said they loved him, and I won't ask for him back. Thank her and Don for me."

"Will do. Oh, and guess what, we might be getting an offer on your house. Somebody who lives around the block from you wants to buy it for their daughter."

"Sell it." Mike didn't care about the house. He was preoccupied with Emily and his decision.

"The Realtor's asking 425. The comps are 420. I wouldn't go below that. I can handle it for you. The power of attorney covers it."

"Handle it, thanks. 420 is great."

"What about the cars? Want me to try and sell Chloe's?"

"Yes, fine." Mike didn't know how he'd get back into Emily's life, a year from now. "Danielle, do you think that Emily will forget about me if I stay? Or do you think she'll, maybe, like me better when she's older?"

"She'll love you whenever you come home." Danielle smiled, sympathetically. "Mike, do what you need to do, and we'll take care of her for you. We love her and we love you."

Mike felt the words touch his heart, already tender. The memorial service, the deaths, Chloe, it was all too much, which told him it was time to sign off. "Thanks, I'd better go. I'll stay in touch and let you know what I decide."

"Yes, of course. Be safe, Mike."

Bob put his arm around Danielle. "Right, take care."

"Bye, thanks." Mike hit the END SESSION button, and the laptop screen turned black. Suddenly, his radio/walkie-talkie started to crackle at his waist, alerting they had incoming casualties. He heard shouting outside, and a frantic Joe Segundo ducked into the Tactical Operations Center.

"Doc! Davy's brigade hit an IED on the way back, and they took fire. Four wounded. They have no medic, so we don't know how many urgent. The bird's already in the air. We got customers!"

Mike leapt to his feet, his adrenaline surging. It was a worst-case scenario come true. The Taliban was kicking them when they were down. "Two docs and four wounded. I don't like those odds."

"Me, neither."

Chapter Thirty

Mike and Chatty triaged the casualties, then hustled to the sink to scrub up, where Chatty turned to Mike, his long red scratches distorting his cheeks.

"Scholl's, what'd your in-laws say?"

"They're fine with the baby." Mike scrubbed up. "Now's not the time to discuss it, right?"

"Fair enough, let's review. The first urgent is the gunner and he's the most critical." Chatty finished scrubbing up and dried his hands. "Gunshot to the chest, entrance through the armpit, transmediastinal. Losing blood fast."

"Got it." Mike dried his hands and grabbed a packaged gown, his thoughts racing. A soldier with a transmediastinal gunshot wound, or TMGSW, was shot through the chest, crosswise. The bullet would have done grievous damage, and the IED blast was a double whammy, because it sent shockwaves that rattled brains, shattered bones, and caused internal bleeding.

"The second urgent is a driver. Neck and face wounds, and his left arm is severely injured but still intact."

"Right." Mike gowned up with the help of a nurse who came over, assisting him silently. He knew that the driver's neck and arm would have glass and metal fragments from the explosion. Humvees had armored windows, but they couldn't withstand an IED blast within ten feet.

"The third urgent is Davy's aide." Chatty gowned up with an assist from the same nurse, who left when she was finished. "Soft-tissue damage in the right thigh from fragments or bullets."

Mike grabbed a package of gloves and opened it, remembering Davy's aide, who had just set up his videochat. He didn't know which one got wounded.

"I'm happy Davy wasn't hit. Nobody takes him out but me." Chatty flashed a wicked grin, and Mike cheered to see a glimmer of his old self.

"Number four is a GSW to his right foot and leg. He's calling my name."

"Right, so what's the game plan?" Chatty gloved up. "How do we run an offense with only two of us?"

Michael blinked. Chatty had never asked him for a game plan before, and he felt the relationship turn topsy-turvy. "You're going to need me to assist on the gunner, so I say you start on him while I start on the driver. Once the driver's started, I move on to the aide, and we put the sarge on ice."

"I'm worried about the gunner. His color's bad." Chatty's face fell. "He shoulda gone to Bagram, but we're closer. They coulda worked him up, they have the toys."

Mike knew the old Chatty never would have said anything like that. "We can get it done. Our DOW rate's as good as theirs."

"You don't realize what a monster that case is gonna be." Chatty shook his head. "If we miss any bleeders in his chest, he's a goner."

"We won't miss any." Mike tried to convey confidence to Chatty, which was backwards. They had to get going. "We're gonna need fresh whole, don't you think?"

"Yes."

"So let's get Joe started." The 556th had a pre-screened blood-donor system to get fresh whole blood from the nurses, staff, and brigade. It was an order Chatty would have given, but Mike spotted Joe and motioned him over. "Are we good to go on the walking blood drive?"

"Sure. We got the Form 572s and lab confirmations of blood

type. You want me to tell the nurses to start drawing?" Joe looked from Mike to Chatty and back again, awaiting instructions.

"Yes," Mike answered. "Tell them to get ready to transfuse it, too. How are we fixed for plasma?"

"We got four units, fresh frozen."

"Thaw it out."

"Will do." Joe turned around and took off.

"We're back in business, Chatty." Mike clapped him on the arm. "Let's do this. You're still Batman."

"No, I'm not." Chatty didn't move. "He doesn't make mistakes."

"Yes he does. Ever see Catwoman? He shoulda put a ring on it."

Chatty emitted a burst of laughter, but it sounded hollow, then he leaned over. "I can't stop thinking about them. I can't believe they're gone. They should be here. They would want to be here."

"They wouldn't want us to get distracted, not now. Why don't we get this done, for them? We'll dedicate it to them. Let's go!"

The next few hours were a bloody blur, as he and Chatty swung into action. Chatty and his team got busy on the gunner, and Mike took the driver. He said his homemade prayer, staunched the bleeding, and extracted fragments at speed, then left Linda to finish. The driver became The First Guy After Phil And Oldstein.

Mike changed his blood-soaked gloves and gown, then rushed over to the aide, whose femur had been shattered, so he'd have to use binders, which would take longer than he'd expected. "How you doing, Chatty?" Mike called out. "I'm gonna be a little late."

"No worries, honey. Dinner will be ready."

"Keep it warm." Mike felt reassured by Chatty's joking, so he sent up another prayer, cleaned out the bone splinters, and finished with The Second Guy After DeMaria And Goldstein. He sent Joe to call them a transport, then checked Chatty's bay. "Chatty, I'm free. You need me?"

"I love you, Scholl's, but I don't need you," Chatty called back, and a few of the nurses smiled.

"Okay." Mike hustled to the sergeant, whose left foot needed a few pins.

"Scholl's, which little piggy went to market?" Chatty called out, to some chuckling.

"*This* one!" Mike called back, and everybody laughed. He shifted into another gear, finished The Third Guy After Phil And Oldstein, changed his gown and gloves, and hurried to Chatty's bay, which was crowded with nurses who parted for him, revealing a sight that required a strong stomach. The gunner's chest cavity showed a massive incision from left to right, splitting the torso like a huge and bloody grin.

"Don't barf, Scholl's." Chatty sutured a bleeder, his fingers nimble and his technique flawless. "To catch you up, the bullet entered the left chest along the anterior axillary line just above the nipple. The bullet exited the torso through the right midaxillary line, at the nipple. It was a 7.62 mm round, not deformed."

Mike glanced at the bullet, which lay bloodied on the side tray, a coppery missile as long as a dog tag. The fact that it wasn't deformed meant that it hadn't damaged as much tissue as it tore across the gunner's chest.

"I performed a bilateral tube thoracostomy and evacuated a large hemopneumothorax from the left chest." Chatty kept working. "I found a large laceration of the upper lobe, hemorrhaging from segmental pulmonary vessels . . ."

Mike translated. The gunner had been a living hemorrhage, and the evidence was everywhere. Blood drenched Chatty's gown, gloves, and Kerlix bandages on the tray. Empty bags of PRBCs and plasma lay on the floor. "So what do I do?"

"Make sure I didn't miss any bleeders."

"In other words, he's good to go?" Mike asked, code for *is he going to live?*

"Sure as you're born, Scholl's." Chatty smiled behind his mask, his bloodshot eyes wrinkling at the corners. "Four up and four down. We did it. Way to go, everybody. I think we made them proud today." He acknowledged everyone with a nod, and there were wet eyes around the table, because they were all thinking of Phil and Oldstein.

Mike's smile faded when he noticed Davy in the triage bay, supporting his men or waiting for Mike's answer.

Either way, it didn't matter.

Mike had made his decision.

Chapter Thirty-one

Mike felt satisfied with his decision, which he'd told Davy when they had a private moment, and he stood with the others in the blowing snow, watching the helicopter take off with the last cases, tilting forward like a top-heavy firefly. Davy, Chatty, Joe, and the soldiers ducked to clear the rotors, then the soldiers piled into the Humvees, closing the doors behind them.

He watched the Humvees turn, fall into a line, and drive off. Even that was dangerous because the brigade didn't have any of the new MAPS, or Mine-Resistant Ambush Protected Vehicles, which withstood IEDs better than the older Humvees. Mike couldn't help feeling that combat infantrymen never got the respect they deserved. They were called grunts, but there had to be a better word for somebody driving a vehicle that could be blown up, to an outpost directly in harm's way, to serve his country and protect each other. A better word would be *hero*.

Mike wondered if he could have been one of them, living in utmost danger, protected only by Heskos, walls of lined wire baskets about eight feet high, made by the soldiers themselves, who filled them up with rocks and sand. They'd shape their Heskos like a U or a hook, facing the enemy, and they'd use plywood and sandbags to build bunkers. They'd name their outpost whether the Army liked it or not, scrawling slogans on the sides, making it their own, a home.

Mike doubted he could live the way they did, for months on end. They'd lose weight and get acne, stomach issues, and ringworm. They'd have no electricity or running water and no hot food. They'd pee in PVC tubes stuck in the ground and they'd defecate in common pots, having almost constant diarrhea. The Taliban paid teenagers five dollars a day to shoot at them, a fortune in a country with an average yearly income of four hundred dollars. The Taliban also paid in heroin, or they would attack when they were high, making them even more dangerous.

Mike came out of his reverie when he noticed Chatty and Joe walking toward him, their heads down and their hands shoved into their pockets. He knew that only one of them was going to be happy about his decision, and he walked to meet them, ready to take the heat.

Chatty's expression went grim. "Why'd you extend? I begged you not to, man."

Joe extended a hand to Mike. "Doc, I jus' want to say thank you. The 556th needs you. You doin' the right thing."

"Thanks." Mike shook Joe's hand, then turned to Chatty. "Think about what we did in that OR. That made the decision for me."

"So you want to be a hero, is that it?"

"Maybe, yes, or maybe I just don't want to be a jerk. I can't turn my back. I don't want to be the guy who abandons them. Or you."

"Don't do it for me, man." Chatty groaned, shaking his head and looking down, over his red scratches. "Please, don't."

"I did it for me. I don't want to be the guy sitting safe at home on the couch, knowing I left you all. I couldn't live with myself. You did two tours, Joe did three. There's a reason those kids write their blood type on their boots. They need *docs*."

"What about your family?"

"I know." Mike felt a deep pang. "But it won't cost the baby, it'll cost me. I'll be home in a year, and I'll still be her father, and we'll be a family again."

Joe nudged Chatty. "It's done, *Jefe*. It's over. He made his decision, and we gotta respect it."

Mike chucked Chatty on the arm. "Right. You're stuck with me for a year. We'll leave together, you and me. We'll turn out the lights. Bye, see ya, Afghanistan."

"You piss me off." Chatty smiled, begrudgingly. "It's like you saw a burning building and ran in. This has to be the dumbest move in the history of dumb moves."

"Thank you," Mike said, and Joe laughed, but Chatty remained incredulous.

"Scholl's, this has to be the dumbest thing you have ever done. In fact, it might be the dumbest thing *any* podiatrist has ever done and they do the dumbest things in the history of dumb things."

Mike gave him a playful shove. "Come on, you didn't think I was going to let you stay by yourself, looking pretty for some other guy, did you?"

Chatty pushed Mike back. "I told you to get out, but you had to do it your way."

"Yes, I did." Mike shook it off and started walking toward the OR, and they fell into step beside him. "You need me here, Chatty. Who else can you get to do three procedures while you do just the one?"

"Oh, salt!" Joe erupted into merry laughter, clapping his hands. "Doc, you did *not* just say that!"

Chatty's red eyes flared. "For real? For *real?*"

"You heard me, slacker. Race you to the OR." Mike took off running, bolting past the nurses.

Chatty gave chase, then Joe joined in and all the nurses, even Linda on her crutches, the entire 556th taking leave of its senses and tearing like demented children toward the bloody OR.

Chapter Thirty-two

Mike sat with Joe at his desk, reading the forms to renew his contract. He flashed on the custody agreement, but he tried not to think about that and picked up the pen. "Last one?" he asked, signing.

"One more, Doc." Joe took the signed form and replaced it with another.

"Don't do it, Scholl's!" Chatty called out from his rack, in back of the tent. They'd had to move into the Tactical Operations Center since the fire.

"Thanks for the support!" Mike called back, then signed the last form.

"Thanks." Joe took the signed paper and started scanning them into the computer. "Don't listen to him. We'll get it done, yo."

Chatty hollered, "No we won't, yo! Scholl's, I'm changing your name to Bonehead. What do you think?"

Mike smiled. "Joe, I should email home and let my in-laws know that I extended. Can't we consider this official business and use your email?"

Joe nodded. "Gimme a minute, and I'll lend you the laptop."

"Thanks." Mike sat down, trying to compose an email in his mind. He'd email his practice later, assuming there was still a practice to email, and he'd stop taking his base share, too.

"Here we go." Joe slid him the laptop, which was logged onto the military server. "Don't be long, okay? We'll be in Bagram soon to resupply, and you can Skype then. Also, remember OPSEC. I'm reminding you because of Operation Viper. The last thing I heard, they were delaying the offensive because of our staffing issues."

"I understand."

Chatty hollered out, "Explain it again, Joe. Talk slow. He's a bonehead, remember?"

"Chatty, go to sleep!" Mike started typing, keeping it short and sweet, because he could explain more later, when they were in Bagram:

Dear Bob and Danielle, I have decided to stay here so I would appreciate you taking care of Emily. I would write more but I can't now. I'll call as soon as I can. Thanks so much. Kiss Emily for me. Love, Mike

Mike pressed SEND and passed the laptop back to Joe, managing a smile. "Thanks."

"You're welcome, Doc. You'd better get some sleep, too. By the way, here's your mail."

"Thanks." Mike glanced at the mail wrapped around a *Journal of the American Podiatric Medical Association*. He'd put in a forwarding order online and it hurt to see the home bills, like gas, electric, phone, and water, from when Chloe was alive.

"Wait, hold on. I have one more thing for you." Joe ducked under the table, rooted around, and popped up again, holding a silvery tin heart, with flames coming from the top. "It's a *milagro*, a good-luck charm."

"Really?" Mike accepted it, touched

"I asked you to stay, and you agreed. This keeps you safe from harm, keeps you healthy."

"Where did you get it?"

"My girlfrien' gave it to me."

"No, I can't take it then." Mike tried to give it back, but Joe put up his hand like a wall.

"Please, she gave me two others, and I got one from my mom and my aunt, too. Trust me, every Tejano in the Army has a stash."

Chatty hollered out, "Joe, why don't you kiss him and get it over with?"

Joe laughed. "*Jefe*, you just jealous I didn't give you one."

"The hell I am!"

Mike smiled. "He's jealous."

"I know." Joe winked.

"Thanks, Joe. Good night." Mike tucked the milagro in the pocket of his ACU jacket with the crucifix and the Emily photo, picked up the packet of mail, and made his way to the back of the tent. Supply boxes had been stacked to form a makeshift wall between Joe's office and their sleeping area, which consisted of two cots placed end-to-end against the tent wall.

Chatty lay in his cot, with his night-vision goggles on his watchcap, which was pulled over his eyes. "I'm not jealous."

"Are too." Mike stretched out on his rack, putting his mail on his chest. It struck him that this was their first night without Phil and Oldstein, but the glasses and iPod were still under Joe's table, so they were under the same roof, after all.

"This truly sucks, does it not?"

"Yes, it does." Mike didn't have to ask Chatty what he meant. He stared at the ceiling, which billowed in the wind. Six inches of snow had fallen, and they'd had to brush off the top so the tent wouldn't collapse.

"Here's my problem, Bonehead. I find what's transpired completely unacceptable, yet it keeps happening. One unacceptable event after another. It's a slippery slope, my addle-pated friend, and before you know it, you're accepting the unacceptable."

Mike smiled, not because it was funny, but because it was true. "Which is, in itself, unacceptable."

"Ha! You're not so dumb after all. And if things weren't bad enough, our porn cache burned up. War is hell."

Mike groaned, not ready for gallows humor. "Too soon, Chatty."

"I can't sleep," Chatty said, after a minute, and Mike picked up his mail, set aside the bills, and opened up his podiatric journal.

"Would you like me to read you a bedtime story?"

"Does it involve women kissing? I love those stories at bedtime."

"No." Mike opened his podiatric journal. "It involves the consequences of pediatric obesity on the foot-and-ankle complex."

"Read on, it will put me to sleep."

"Once upon a time, there were ten obese children and ten children of average weight, and they were recruited for a cross-sectional research study." Mike paraphrased the abstract of the article. "Anthropometric parameters were measured to evaluate active ankle dorsiflexion, arch height—"

"Enough. Tell me a story where the pizza boy comes in and meets the two girls and they start kissing."

Mike set the magazine down, moved aside the household bills, and flipped through his junk mail. "All I have is a class reunion reminder, a Valpak, and a discount card from a guy who wants to plow my driveway." He stopped at an unfamiliar envelope that wasn't junk mail, with a return address from the Coroner's Office of Chester County, Pennsylvania.

"Come on, tell me a story. Start with the pizza. What kind of pizza do they get? I like mushroom."

Mike couldn't speak. The envelope must contain Chloe's autopsy report and toxicology screen, which would show the alcohol levels in her system.

"I also like pepperoni. Can't you just taste a pepperoni pizza right now? Real New York pizza. Thin crust with gooey mozzarella and that yellow cornmeal on the bottom."

"*Jefe!*" Joe hollered from the office area. "Please stop talking about pizza! Noise discipline!"

Chatty called back, "Your problem is that you think MREs are food!"

Joe yelled out, "I'm responsible for your nutrition! I keep my family well fed!"

Chatty yelled back, "Then get me a New York pizza! Bonehead, you ever have John's, in the Village? Or Bleeker's?"

"No." Mike got up stiffly, folding the autopsy report in with the other mail. "I have to go to the bathroom. Be right back."

Chatty rolled his watchcap up, so he could see. "Scholl's, it's twenty degrees out there. You can't hold it in?"

"Nah." Mike stuck the mail under his arm.

Chapter Thirty-three

Mike sat on one of the supply boxes in the freezing latrine, stuck his high-intensity flashlight between his teeth, and opened the envelope. The report was four pages, and it read at the top, Office of the Chester County Coroner. There was a grid with the coroner's and his assistant's name, and the box was checked Full Autopsy Performed, with the date and exact hour. Under the name, it read Chloe Voulette, and it had her date of birth, age, race, and sex, as well as Body Identified By, and in that blank was filled in Danielle Voulette Ridgeway. The case number was #2013–770.

Mike read the first few lines:

The autopsy is begun at 8:16 p.m. on December 15. The body was presented in a black body bag. The subject was wearing a blue cotton sweater and jeans. Jewelry included two smooth-textured gold hoop pierced earrings, one-inch diameter, one in each ear, one gold watch on left wrist, and one gold and diamond engagement and wedding ring.

Mike read on, to the section under General Appearance:

The body is that of a well-developed, well-nourished, adult white female who appears to be the stated age of 32 years. Body height is 66 inches. Body weight is 129 pounds. Rigor mortis is generalized to late. Livor mortis is anterior. The body is cold to the touch. Artifacts of decomposition are absent and evidence of medical and postmortem care is absent. There is obvious evidence of a single knife wound to the left forearm.

Mike wasn't sure if he could go on, but he wanted to know the alcohol content of her blood. He skimmed the report, concerning identification, then the other parts of the external examination, including head and neck, trunk, and extremities. There was a section on injuries, which described the length and depth of the wound, and below that was a section on internal examination, which began:

Internally, there is almost no blood present in the heart and great vessels and tissues, due to exsanguination from the wound.

Mike skipped ahead to the internal examination section, which described the Head–Central Nervous System, Skeletal System, Respiratory System, Throat Structures, as "unremarkable." He knew it was a term of art, but nothing about Chloe was unremarkable, to him. The internal examination continued with the Cardiovascular System, Gastrointestinal System, Urinary System, and at the bottom, the Female Genital System. It killed Mike to think that anyone, even a doctor, was intruding on Chloe's privacy in such an intimate way. Still, he read the paragraph:

Female Genital System: The structures are within normal limits. There is no evidence of recent sexual activity. Examination of the pelvic area indicates that the subject was pregnant at the time of death. The uterine walls reveal swelling and mucosa consistent with healthy pregnancy. The fetus was approximately four (4) weeks gestation. Fetuses under twenty (20) weeks gestation are not considered viable and therefore the fetus was not autopsied.

Mike felt stunned. He must've read it wrong. That was impossible. He shined the flashlight on the report and read it again; **Examination of the pelvic area indicates that the subject was pregnant at the time of death**. He didn't know what to do. He didn't know how to react. It wasn't possible. There had to be some mistake. He flipped back to the first page of the report, to double-check that this was Chloe's autopsy. The coroner could've confused her with somebody else, but the first page was clearly marked and her case number was at the top of the page. The coroner could have been wrong about her being pregnant, maybe she had some kind of uterine tumor or cyst that he had mistaken for a fetus.

Mike tore through the rest of the report, reading to see if there was any other mention of a pregnancy, but there wasn't. There was no toxicology report either, and under Toxicology, it stated, cryptically: "blood, bile, urine, ocular fluid, nasal swabs." He understood that to mean that those fluids had been taken, but that the report would follow later, so he didn't have any answers about the vodka. But that didn't seem important anymore. Nothing seemed important anymore.

Mike sat in the freezing latrine, lost in the fog of his own breath. It didn't make sense. It couldn't be. Chloe had been faithful to him. They were in love. He rubbed his eyes, then his face. He told himself that this wasn't happening, that it couldn't be happening. He wanted to scream but the others would hear him, unless they thought it was a monkey, howling. Maybe the howling at night wasn't monkeys at all, but men trapped in war, ceaseless, brutal, and far from home.

Mike felt tears come to his eyes. He couldn't stop them and didn't try. Everything he loved and believed in was gone. He could barely deal with losing Chloe, and now he had lost the knowledge that she loved him and was true to him. He dropped the papers and the flashlight, then doubled over and wept from the depth of his very soul.

Chapter Thirty-four

Almost a full year later, Mike could not get past the fact that Chloe had gotten pregnant by another man. He didn't tell Chatty or anybody else, and the knowledge changed him, inside. He stopped saying his homemade prayer, though he couldn't bring himself to throw away the crucifix Chloe had given him. He kept it in his Velcro pocket with the Emily picture and the milagro, and lately, found himself patting his pocket like a nervous tic, to make sure they were safe.

His stomach bothered him, and his weight dropped. He couldn't sleep for wondering who Chloe's lover was, when the affair started, when it ended, where they did it, when they did it, how they did it. He went online at base and tried to get into her Gmail, but it was password-protected. He'd even emailed Google at Decedent's Accounts to see if they'd let him into her account, but they wouldn't unless he sent them a death certificate and jumped through a bunch of other hoops, too difficult to do from Afghanistan. Still, he did his job and didn't lose a single soldier, not even The First Woman Soldier After Chloe Died And Got Pregnant. The only person who could make him laugh was Chatty, but he'd changed, too. He became *El Jefe* again, but he never wore his new Batman cape, and he told Mike something that struck him as weird, but true:

Scholl's, this war's no fun anymore.

The 556th was on its way to a new posting, a brigade to the north in the mountains, and Mike was crammed in the backseat of the Humvee, on a night too frigid to be warmed even by the body heat from Chatty, Joe, and the driver, Dermot. The engine noise filled his ears and the vibration rattled his teeth as the Humvee traveled along the dirt road behind the others, spaced the standard-operating-procedure distance apart, because if one Humvee ran over an IED, the others wouldn't be affected.

Mike patted his jacket pocket and fought the impulse to take out Emily's picture. He felt more distant from her than ever, and in their Skype sessions, when Emily sat in Danielle's lap, it was like a TV show. And then there was the time she'd called Danielle "Mommy."

She calls you Mommy? Mike had asked.

I think it's easier to say than Danielle, and when we go to Mommy & Me classes, I want her to feel like the other kids.

Sure, right. Mike wondered how he'd feel the day that Emily called Bob Daddy.

Mike sat in the back next to Chatty, who was looking out the tiny window with his night-vision goggles. On any other night, he'd be stargazing, but he was scanning the terrain for the Taliban. It was mountainous, with dips, goat trails, and wadi to hide in, and holly oaks to use for cover. Everybody startled when they bumped over a rock, but nobody said anything. They were all thinking the same thing and the engine was too noisy, anyway.

Mike's gut tensed. He knew Chatty worried about him, tacitly accepting the responsibility for his renewing his contract, which had the effect of making him turn more inward, because he kept his regrets about renewing to himself. Still he and Chatty were forever joined, like parents in a family that had lost a child, linked by shared grief.

Mike felt the Humvee slow its speed, as the ones ahead of them stopped. They were guarded forward and rear by up-armored Humvees, with turret gunners on top, and the Humvee behind theirs contained two new general trauma surgeons they'd finally gotten,

Pat Freznick from Chino, California, and Peter Sullivan from Dallas, who was in his early fifties. Sullivan was typical of the end-stage wave of older docs who left successful practices to serve, and MED-COM needed them so desperately that it age-waived them, even if they couldn't make the fitness qualifications. Chatty teased Sullivan about it all the time, nicknaming him Gramps.

Gramps, it's a war, not a retirement village.

Mike looked out the window, but it was all black outside, a void in the middle of nowhere. He didn't know if the upcoming operation, Operation Rattlesnake, would be a success, and if it was, whether it would matter. Their old brigade had become infected with a nihilism, and the soldiers groused more about the Fobbits stationed at FOB Kandahar, or POGs, Persons Other Than Grunts, or worse, REMFs, which stood for Rear Echelon MFers. Mike had heard that the GMOs, or general medical officers, were prescribing more anti-depressants and sleep meds than ever before, and he had no reason to believe that the new brigade would be any happier.

BAM! Suddenly an earsplitting explosion rocked the Humvee. A blinding white flash went off. The front of the five-ton vehicle flew into the air and crashed to the ground with an earthshaking jolt.

Mike whipped wildly around in his shoulder harness. He fought terror to think. They'd hit an IED. It scored a direct hit under their front bumper. Rock and earth thundered onto the Humvee roof. The windows exploded. Hot shrapnel and glass flew everywhere. Mike screamed but couldn't hear himself. Chatty slumped in his seat, his window cracked.

"Chatty!" Mike unlatched his harness and reached for Chatty. The Humvee engine burst into flames. Black smoke flooded the interior. Joe and Dermot became frantic shadows trying to get out of the vehicle. Flames licked under the dashboard, superheating Mike's face, searing his lungs. He gasped for breath. They'd burn alive if they didn't get out.

"Joe, Joe, you okay?" Mike couldn't hear it if they replied. He unlatched Chatty and grabbed him by his jacket but his head flopped over. Flames erupted on the hood of the car, flooding the interior with light and heat.

Mike reached across Chatty to grab the door handle. He wrenched it down but it jammed. He lifted his leg and kicked the door open. The sudden blast of cold air made the smoke thicker, billowing everywhere.

Mike coughed, his lungs choked. He climbed over Chatty, grabbed him by the jacket, and yanked him from the Humvee. He dragged him through the snow, struggling with his weight. Horrific orange flames lit up the black night. Mike saw Joe and Dermot trapped in the burning Humvee. The doors on older models jammed, so buttons had been installed, to be pulled open from the outside.

Mike left Chatty by the side of the road and dashed back to the Humvee. Heat seared Mike's face and smoke filled his lungs. He kicked the button on the door. It flew open.

Joe fell out coughing and hacking, engulfed by heat and smoke.

"Hurry, go!" Mike yanked him out of the way, and Dermot scrambled from the Humvee, coughing and spitting. Suddenly all hell broke loose.

Pop pop pop! A barrage of gunfire echoed, loud enough to burst through Mike's ringing ears. He spun around, reeling in a cloud of smoke. Red muzzles flashed from both sides of the road.

Dermot, Mike, and Joe threw themselves on the frozen ground. Dermot and Joe fired back, and Mike drew his weapon for the first time ever, then saw Chatty lying unconscious in the snow, exposed to enemy fire.

"Cover me!" Mike raced over to Chatty in a crouch and threw his body on top of him. He kept firing, his head down, his small caliber weapon a peashooter compared with the AK-47s. He felt the sizzle of their big bullets flying past him, their percussive waves rippling through the air.

Joe and Dermot returned fire. The brigade fought back, the gunners blasted their massive .50 caliber weapons, wheeling right and left in turrets, lighting up the night. Behind them, flames from the Humvee shot into the sky. Smoke billowed heavenward. Finally the Taliban stopped shooting, but the brigade didn't let up, laying down suppressive fire.

Mike had emptied his gun and so had Joe, but both men remained prone, their heads down. Every sense stayed on alert. Adrenaline flooded their systems. Their hearts pounded against the inside of their body armor. In minutes, the firing ceased. Soldiers chased the fleeing Taliban or raced to grab fire extinguishers from their Humvees.

Joe looked over, eyes wide under his helmet. His face was blackened with smoke, and his head was silhouetted against the orangey fire. He was saying something, his lips were moving, but Mike couldn't hear a word.

"Go see if there's any casualties!" Mike told him, still adrenalized. "I'll see about Chatty!"

Joe scrambled to his feet, and Mike rolled off Chatty, felt his neck for his pulse, and felt his heart lift when he found it blessedly strong. "Chatty!"

Chatty struggled to sit up.

"You okay? You feel okay?" Mike scanned Chatty's body but there was no evidence of injury, though a concussion was always possible. "Chatty, who's the president?"

Chatty's lips were moving, and he wrenched off his goggles, leaving whitish rings on his sooty face. His eyes went wide with disbelief when he saw the fire.

"You missed the fight!" Mike laughed, finally understanding the rush of combat. He couldn't hear a thing, but he was so happy they all had lived that he couldn't stop talking. "We made it! I shot my gun like a big boy!"

Chatty was saying something, but Mike rose unsteadily, his thoughts racing to the others.

"Chatty, we have to get back to the Humvees! We need to see if there's wounded!"

Chatty grabbed him, reached for the medical pack at his belt, and flipped open the Velcro pouch. He was saying something, looking down, so Mike looked down, too, but didn't understand what he was seeing. It must have been a trick of the light, from the fire. Something was lying in the snow, in the dark.

Then, suddenly, he collapsed.

Chapter Thirty-five

Mike opened his eyes, groggy, and looked around a familiar recovery room, with fluorescent lighting and walls lined with shelves of medical supplies. He realized, dimly, that he was at Camp Lacy, Bagram's Combat Support Hospital. He'd assisted here and checked on soldiers in this very bed. His world had gone topsy-turvy, and the doctor had become the patient.

He was snowed under, anesthetized. He hurt all over, in a vague, achy way. His could feel in his throat that he'd been intubated, but he didn't know how he'd been injured. He must've caught a bullet, but he could see and hear. He moved his legs and they responded. He closed his eyes and was about to drift back into sleep when an Afghan doctor-in-training passed through the room, carrying a rattling tray of instruments.

Mike felt agitated under the morphine. He knew that Bagram trained local doctors, but now it disturbed him. He wondered if the doc knew the Taliban who had ambushed them. They lived in the same area and probably spoke the same dialect. He heard voices nearby, speaking English and Dari, the most common language around Bagram. He drifted back into a restless, anxious sleep.

"Dr. Scanlon?" said a voice, and Mike woke up to see a doctor in a scrub cap, his goggles still on. He had a five o'clock shadow, probably from a night in the OR, and he looked to be about Mike's age, with crow's feet around brown eyes. "I'm Scott Peddie. How are you feeling?"

"Yes, hi." Mike felt his brain waking up slowly. His body hurt more than before.

"Do you feel comfortable?"

"I'm fine." Mike shifted under the covers to shake Peddie's hand, but felt an excruciating pain in his left arm. "Oh, that *hurts*."

"No, please, don't move it." Peddie guided Mike's arm down.

"What? Why?" Mike looked down at his arm, which lay under the covers but was grotesquely short. He shifted over to withdraw it, feeling a pain he'd never known. His elbow and lower arm were gone, and there was a massive bulb wrapped around his upper arm. He gasped. "What is this?"

"Relax, please."

"What did you do?" Mike flashed on last night, with horror. He'd looked down to see his sleeve and arm blown off. He hadn't felt anything, he'd been so adrenalized. "Where's my arm? Where's my *hand*?"

"Let me get you something to calm you." Peddie looked toward the OR. "Jamie? Jamie?"

"No, I don't want that." Mike kept shaking his head, his mouth agape. "You didn't take my arm, did you? I need my hand!"

"I'll explain everything—"

"What happened? This can't be." Mike looked over as the nurse hustled in with the Afghan doctor. "Get him out of here! I don't want him near me!"

"Okay, calm down." Peddie waved the nurse and doctor away, then looked down at Mike, pursing his lips. "I'm sorry, and I can imagine how you feel."

"No, you can't!" Mike couldn't believe this was happening. "What did you *do*? Are you *insane*?"

"If there was any way to avoid it, we would have. Please, try to remain calm. I'll strongly suggest you take a—"

"I said, I don't want a *pill*!"

"Okay, you don't have to take one then. We won't do anything you don't want us to do."

"Except take my arm, my *hand*?" Mike couldn't stop shaking his head. "This *can't* be! What did you do? Tell me exactly!"

"I'm sorry, but it was necessary to perform a transhumeral amputation to the left arm above the elbow, taking your non-dominant hand. We left as much as we could for your prosthesis, including your shoulder—"

"No!" Mike cried in anguish. "Didn't you know I'm a surgeon? Didn't they tell you? What were you *thinking*?"

"I did know, but we had no choice."

"Who's *we*? You and who else? *Who?* Nobody asked me. Nobody asked *me*!"

"That was impossible. You were losing blood and we had to act quickly to save your life. You took two units, immediately."

"So why not ask me after I'm transfused? You had the tourniquet on, didn't you? Chatty did that." Mike remembered that much.

"We did. In fact, Commander Chatham assisted me in the OR. Your administrator was here, too—"

"No, no!" Mike felt crazy. "I don't believe you! They wouldn't let you do this!"

"The gunfire strafed your elbow, essentially shearing it off. The soft tissue had been blown off."

"No, no." Mike couldn't bear it. "What about the *bones*? You couldn't save *anything*? You couldn't pin *anything*? You can do anything with a halo! I've done it, on the foot and ankle!"

"No, your bones were splintered. We always salvage if we can, to preserve functionality." Peddie's tone remained calm. "There's no way I would ever take the hand of another surgeon if I had an alternative, but I didn't. By amputating just below the shoulder, we were able to salvage a significant skin flap, which, as you know, will aid significantly the primary closure."

Mike felt sick. It was real. It sounded real. He could visualize the procedure. He'd seen it done. "What was my MESS score?"

"Nine."

"What about a reattachment? Did you have the hand?"

"Yes, Chatham brought it, but we're not equipped to do a reattachment here, and even if we could, we didn't have sufficient soft tissue. You'll be going to Landstuhl in an hour, where you'll have a revision, then you'll be going home."

"I want to see it!"

"What?" Peddie blanched under his stubble. "Dr. Scanlon, Mike—"

"I want to see my hand! I know you haven't thrown it out yet! I want it back! It's mine!"

"Nobody's ever asked—"

"Go get it, *now*!"

"Okay, please, stay calm." Peddie turned away and left the recovery room.

"And I want my jacket, too! I want the things in my pocket! I want everything that belongs to me, *right now*!" Mike fought to regain control. His gaze fell on his bandaged stump, which suddenly was killing him, his traumatized nerves burning all the way up to his neck.

"Here we go, and those items, too." Peddie returned with a stainless steel tray covered with a blue surgical drape and a plastic baggie that held Emily's picture, the crucifix, and the milagro.

Mike accepted the baggie and put it on his chest, then reached for the tray. Every movement jostled his left arm, sending pain shooting through his nerves, like electricity running along a live wire. "I'll take that."

"Here." Peddie handed him the tray, and Mike set it down on his belly, appalled at its lightness, as if it held thin air. He didn't want to take off the drape with Peddie watching. He wanted to be alone with his arm, a thought that struck him as completely nuts. Maybe he could hold his own hand.

"Please go and give me some privacy."

"First, I'll elevate you." Peddie cranked up the bed, and Mike realized he'd been in Peddie's position before, but he never knew how it felt from the other side.

"Listen, I'm sorry. I know you're just doing your job. I guess you saved my life, so thank you."

"You're welcome. I'm sorry about what happened, and I understand." Peddie stepped away, his mouth a grim line. "Call for me or Jamie if you have any questions. Your morphine is on a drip, and the button's on your right. You know how it works."

"I do, thanks," Mike said, as Peddie left the room. He eyed the drape, but wasn't ready to remove it. The tang of alcohol, iodine, and blood emanated from the tray, and reality began to set in. He contemplated the fact that he was sitting apart from his arm, which was no longer attached to his body.

On impulse, Mike picked up the tray and moved it onto his chest, so that it met the end of his compression bandage, crudely completing his arm, the way he was born and always assumed he'd die. He pressed the button on the morphine drip, then pushed it again and again, though it was pointless. The drip had a governor, so it was like pressing an elevator button once you'd already called the elevator.

In time, he felt a pleasant snow begin to cloud his brain, so he removed the drape.

Chapter Thirty-six

Mike was waiting to be transported to Landstuhl when Chatty and Joe entered the recovery room, and his throat caught with surprise. He hadn't thought he'd get a chance to say good-bye to them. Chatty walked over, putting on a brave face, and Joe had a raw, reddish burn on his left cheek, glistening under Neosporin.

Mike managed a smile. "Doesn't anybody check the security around here?"

"Shut up." Chatty rested his hand on the bed rail. "How are you?"

"Fine, not bad. How did you get away?"

"If we told you, we'd have to kill you."

"They tried that already," Mike said, and they all chuckled, hollowly.

"How're they treating you? Peddie's a good guy."

"Yeah." Mike gestured at Joe's burn. "You got a souvenir, huh?"

Joe forced a smile. "Gonna get a tattoo over it, yo."

Chatty interrupted, "I told him, get a tattoo of me. Put my face on your face, then you'll be pretty." They chuckled again, but it died down quickly.

Mike fell suddenly silent. There was everything to say, but he didn't know where to start. He felt so off-balance, and now he was leaving them, when things were hot. He felt afraid for them and tried not to choke up. "I hate to leave you in the lurch."

"Don't say that. We'll be fine." Chatty's lower lip puckered. "Scholl's, about your arm, you have to know Peddie did everything he could. I assisted, I was right there and so was Joe." His blue eyes filmed. "I don't know if that makes you feel better or worse."

"Better." Mike nodded, gritting his teeth not to cry.

"Peddie tried to save it, and so did I. Really."

"I know, thanks." Mike didn't want to lose it, especially seeing them for the last time.

"Thank you for saving my life. You got me and Joe out of that Humvee."

"Right," Joe chimed in, his thickish Adam's apple moving up and down. "Thank you, Doc. Dermot says it, too."

Mike cleared his throat. "You would've gotten out just fine."

"Not true." Chatty shook his head. "Anyway, I owe you, so here's what. I'll be home in the summer, and Joe's out a month before that, and we're all gonna work together."

"What?"

"My buddies are foot guys and they said they'll put you to work, in the same building as me. We don't even have to break up. Our love abides." Chatty forced a smile, his eyes shiny. "Joe's in too, with my group. The 556th is moving to a better location, under much better management."

"Chatty, how?" Mike didn't want to say out loud that he couldn't be a surgeon again. That he didn't know how he'd earn a living. He couldn't even freeze a wart.

"Scholl's, what happened to you is unacceptable." Chatty gestured at Mike's arm. "I'm not going to accept it and neither are you. You're going to go through rehab and get your prosthesis, and if you can't do surgery anymore, you'll work with my foot guys without doing surgery. We'll figure it out. We can do it. You'll see."

There was a commotion at the threshold of the recovery room, and they turned to see Lieutenant Colonel Davy entering the room with his aides. Joe straightened up as Davy strode to Mike's bed. "Major Scanlon, I trust you're recovering well."

"Fine, thanks," Mike answered, having nothing else to say. Chatty looked daggers at Davy, who ignored him.

"Major Scanlon, the Army appreciates your service and your sacrifice. You acted with unparalleled bravery during the ambush, and I have submitted a recommendation that you be awarded the Purple Heart and the Bronze Star. Until that is approved and can be awarded with the appropriate air of formality, I would like to present you with this coin." Davy shook his hand and gave him a gold coin.

"Thank you." Mike accepted the coin, surprised. He never thought he'd get a medal and he never wanted one. He wanted his arm back.

"Major Scanlon, we wish you safe travels to Landstuhl and on your trip home. Best of luck in future endeavors. Thank you again for your service." Davy turned to Joe. "When will you be getting a replacement for Dr. Scanlon?"

Chatty's eyes flared with outrage. "Who the *hell* do you think you are? He's right here."

"Pardon me?" Davy arched an eyebrow, and his aides exchanged looks.

"You try and replace him when he's right *here*? You drop a coin on his chest, like a *tip*? You put in for a medal? Is that all you got after you *blackmailed* him into renewing?"

"That's enough, Chatham," Davy shot back.

"Oh you don't like that? Then you're really not gonna like this." Chatty pulled back his arm and punched Davy solidly in the jaw.

And then it was *on*.

Part Two

Chapter Thirty-seven

"Welcome home, Mike!" everybody said, smiling hard. A small crowd greeted him in Bob and Danielle's elegant living room, which smelled like perfume, roast beef, and fresh gin. "Welcome home!"

"Wow, hi!" Mike felt touched, if caught off-balance, and backed against the front door next to Bob.

"Welcome, Mike!" Danielle beamed, next to Sara and her husband Don, Jim and his wife Laura, and a few of Bob and Danielle's friends.

"Thanks." Mike set his backpack down and stood so that his left arm was slightly behind him. He was trying to hide his empty sleeve, though he knew they had to see it, sooner or later. Evidently, sooner.

"Mike, we love you." Danielle hugged him, and Mike kept his left arm out of the way. He'd had revision surgery a month and a half ago, and his incision had healed, though it throbbed under its compression bandage, which told him it was time for another Oxycontin. Danielle released him, her eyes shining. "I hope you're not overwhelmed by the welcoming committee, but we wanted you to know how happy we are that you're home."

"Thanks so much." Mike kept up his smile, trying to process everything. Danielle's hair was longer, uncharacteristically loose to her shoulders, and she had on an artsy dress, even more almost-but-not-quite-Chloe than a year ago. It bollixed up his emotions, given his confused feelings for Chloe. "This is so nice of you, and everybody."

"It's our pleasure." Danielle smiled back. "We're so proud and happy."

"To Mike!" Jim raised his glass, and Laura and the others followed suit, chiming in, "To Mike!" "We love you!" "Welcome home!" "To our hero!"

"Thanks so much." Mike took in all the wet eyes, and everyone looked happy to see him, even if they felt sorry for him. "Where's Emily?"

"Here she is!" Sara stepped forward with Emily, who had on a blue velvet dress that brought out the cornflower hue of her eyes, so much like Chloe's that Mike felt a deep pang of love and grief, knotted together. Emily was only a year and eight months old, but she had grown so much bigger, her body long and on the wiry side. Her face was wider, her cheeks were chubby, but her nose and lips still retained the soft, unformed contours of a baby's.

"Hi, Emily." Mike couldn't help but reach for her little hand, just to make contact with her, to reassure himself that she was real and they were both alive.

Emily turned away, biting her knuckle, and Sara smiled, tolerantly. "Emily, turn around, it's Daddy. Say hi." She handed Emily over. "Mike, here, don't worry, take her."

"Emily, come to Daddy, honey." Mike held out his right arm, and Emily rested in the crook of his elbow, her diaper crinkling. "You got so big! What a big girl!" She still didn't face him, a bout of shyness, but at least she didn't start crying or launch herself from his embrace, however defective. "Hi Emily, how are you, sweetie?"

Emily stayed turned away, her knuckle in her mouth, and Sara patted her arm. "Emily, say hello to Daddy. That's your Daddy."

"Emily, hi." Mike caught a whiff of a strawberry shampoo that clung to her wispy blonde curls. "Can't you say hi?" He wanted to hear her voice, how she spoke, and which words she knew. He tried to think of a way to get her to talk and noticed she had on shiny patent shoes. "What pretty shoes. Are they new?" Emily kept her head turned, but Mike wanted to try again. "Emily, are your shoes new? Do you want to talk to Daddy? Girls like shoes, right?"

Emily turned back. "Mommy, I want Mommy!"

Jim called out, "Welcome to fatherhood, pal!"

Everybody laughed but Mike, who felt disturbed, though not on his own behalf. Chloe was Mommy, but he seemed to be the only one who remembered that, because Danielle was already stepping forward, holding out her arms for Emily.

"I'll take her, Mike." Danielle accepted Emily, kissed her on her smooth cheek, and cuddled her close.

"Excuse me a minute," Mike said, trying to get his bearings. He retrieved his backpack and turned toward the stairwell. "I'm just going to run upstairs and change. Be right back."

"Of course." Danielle nuzzled Emily, who buried her face in her neck. "You don't need help, do you?"

"No, thanks," Mike answered, forcing a smile. He hustled up the stairs, hit the landing, and hurried down the hallway to the guest room where he'd stayed before. He flicked on the light, closed the door behind him, and fished out his bottle of Oxycontin from his backpack. He went into the bathroom and gulped one with water, then put the bottle back in his backpack. He was supposed to be weaning himself off the higher dosages, but he was in pain.

He crossed to the bureau and opened the drawer, and Chloe's cell phone was where he'd left it. He was dying to know who she was sleeping with. He picked it up and pressed the ON button, but the battery had lost power. He went back to his backpack and got his own charger, because he had the same phone. He plugged it into the outlet and phone, pressed On, and Chloe's phone came to life.

He thumbed to the phone function, pressed Menu, and looked up her call logs. The calls were to and from Sara's mobile phone, Danielle's mobile phone, and Bob's office phone, in an almost alternating rotation. Then he noticed a number he didn't recognize with no name attached, a 999 exchange in the 610 area code, which was local. Mike thought a minute. Nine nine nine was a common cell-phone exchange. He pressed to the most recent time he saw the 999 phone number, and it gave him pause. The date was December 14, at 9:26 P.M., and the call was from Chloe to the number. If it was her lover, she'd called him the night before she died.

Mike's mouth went dry. He scrolled back and saw a call from the same 999 phone number a day prior, at 8:32 P.M., and then the day before that, at 10:45 P.M. There was no identification of the caller in the phone, so he highlighted the phone number and pressed CALL. The phone rang, and his heart thundered against his chest. The ringing stopped, and a mechanical voice said, "This number is no longer in service."

"Damn!" Mike said, momentarily stumped. He scrolled to the text function, but it was completely wiped clean. If there had been any texts between Chloe and her lover, she had erased them, in an abundance of caution.

"Mike?" called a voice, and he turned around to see Danielle, eyeing him with concern. "I knocked, but there was no answer. You're looking at Chloe's phone?"

"Oh, yes."

"I'm so sorry." Danielle crossed to the bed, deflating in her flowy dress. "Having people over was a bad idea, wasn't it? I was only trying to make you happy, and we're all so proud of you. Truly proud."

"No, it's wonderful, it's great." Mike slipped the cell phone in the pocket of his ACUs. "It's so thoughtful of you, and everyone."

"But my timing is off, it's too soon. You must miss her, so much. I bet coming home and seeing Emily brings it all back to you. Now you're looking at her phone. I miss her too, all the time."

"No, it's fine." Mike tasted bitterness in his mouth. He wished his Oxy would kick in.

"You practically ran out of the room. I'm so sorry." Danielle rubbed her forehead, leaving little pink trails. "I should've waited. Bob says I try too hard, and he's right."

"No, not at all." Mike felt a stab of guilt. He sat down beside her on the foot of the bed and put an arm around her. "I'm happy to see everyone."

"Then why did you run up and look at Chloe's phone? You're missing her."

"It's not that, honestly." Mike both did and didn't want to tell

Danielle, but he was dying to know if she knew whom Chloe was having an affair with. He suspected that Danielle or Sara knew, or maybe both, because they were Chloe's kitchen cabinet.

"You're just trying to make me feel better."

"No, I'm not." Mike decided to go for it. "I'm looking at Chloe's phone because I know that she was cheating on me. I know that she was pregnant when she died. What I don't know is who got her pregnant. Do you know who she was with?"

"*What?*" Danielle recoiled, astonished. "If this is a joke, it's not funny."

"No, it's no joke. It's driving me nuts. Did you really not know? I don't blame you for not telling me before, but tell me now, please. It's been driving me crazy, for a year."

"Chloe would never cheat on you." Danielle shook her head, adamant. "She loved you. You were happy."

Mike didn't know whether to believe her. "That's what I thought, but I was wrong. Did you know she was having an affair? Do you know who it was with?"

"No, of course not! This can't be."

"Hold on." Mike started to believe her. He opened the phone with his thumb and scrolled down to highlight the 999 number. "Do you recognize this phone number? This could be the guy."

Danielle looked at the number, nonplussed. "No, I don't. Is this real?"

"Yes. I called, but it's out of service. He called her the day before she died. Maybe they had plans to meet." Mike turned to her, intent, and Danielle did seem genuinely shocked. "Think back to last year, the day she died. You were taking the baby to the mall. Did you plan that? It wasn't spontaneous, was it?"

"I hate to think about that day." Danielle winced, and Mike felt guilty all over again. He'd had a year to get used to this idea, but he'd surprised Danielle with it, upsetting her. It showed him how obsessed he'd gotten, but he didn't care, thanks to the Oxys. He had all the same emotions, but they just didn't matter.

"I'm sorry, forget it."

"No, wait, it was planned."

"So she knew she'd have the day to herself."

"Yes." Danielle nodded, pained. "She asked for it. It was her idea. She wanted to stay home. She said she wanted the break."

"Maybe she was meeting him."

"Meeting who? I don't believe you. This is crazy." Danielle was shaking her head, and a strand of hair fell into her eyes, so she tucked it behind her ear. "Was she really *pregnant*? How do you know?"

Mike told her quickly about the autopsy report, and when he was finished, Danielle was reeling.

"So what are you going to do now?" she asked, miserably.

"I'm going to find out who the 999 number is. I'm going to start with Sara. Chloe told her everything." Mike realized he'd said the wrong thing when he saw Danielle look stricken. "She probably didn't tell you because she didn't want you to think badly of her. You're her big sister."

"Right." Danielle's mouth flattened to a disapproving line. "If I knew she was cheating on you, I would've killed her."

Mike managed a smile. "Don't you have any idea who it could be? There weren't that many men around her. Did she ever mention anyone?"

"No."

"No name? Not even a friend or a casual encounter, in the food store or anywhere?"

"No. I can't even imagine."

"Was there a daddy in any of the groups you used to take Emily to, like music?"

"No, and I still take her. There's only moms and nannies." Danielle shook her head, bewildered. "Let's not tell Bob about this, okay? I don't want him to think Chloe was, well, you know."

Mike let it go. "After our old house sold, on Foster Road, you had the stuff boxed and stored, right?"

"Yes."

"Where is the storage place?"

"It's the one on Lancaster Avenue. Why?"

"Is her laptop there?"

"I assume so."

"I want to look through it." Mike raked his hair back with his fingers, a nervous gesture he did too often, lately. "I want to check her email, and I think she had a password file in the computer. She would have gotten email from this guy or she could have met him online. Who knows what she was up to?"

The hubbub from the party swelled, and Danielle stood up, smoothing her dress. Her fingers went to her cheeks, and she seemed to smooth them out, too. "This is a such a shocker. Why didn't you tell me earlier?"

"I didn't want to do it in email."

Danielle nodded. "Okay, we'll talk about this later. They're all down there. I should go. You stay here, and I'll tell them you're tired. They'll understand."

"No, let me change, and I'll be right down." Mike stood up and met her eye, sharing the uneasy bond of a terrible secret. "I'm sorry, I know this wasn't easy for you."

"You, either." Danielle gave him a hug. "Put it out of your mind for now."

"Will do." Mike felt the Oxys work their magic, even as he wondered if Chloe's lover could be downstairs, among the guests.

Chapter Thirty-eight

Mike changed into a navy blue V-neck, Dockers, and loafers, and floated through the evening, thanks to two beers and the Oxycontin. He greeted everyone, but kept his eye on Sara, who was talking with Danielle's friends in the dining room. Sara had to know whom Chloe was sleeping with, and he wondered if he could get her alone.

Mike sidled over to the dining room table, which held dips, raw vegetables, and cheese cubes, as well as scalloped potatoes and a carve-it-yourself roast beef, which looked great. He picked up a plate to get some, then realized he couldn't carve it with one hand. They'd taught him in rehab to cut food with a rocking motion, but it wouldn't work with a slab of beef. He was about to abandon the plate and join in Sara's conversation when Jim materialized at his side.

"Let me assist, I know you're a carnivore." Jim picked up the carving knife and stabbed the beef with the fork, then set the meat on Mike's plate. "Here, *mangia.*"

"Thanks." Mike realized he had no way to cut the meat. Luckily, Jim didn't seem to notice, instead meeting his eye, his face falling.

"Joking aside, I feel for you. Don't think I don't."

"I know." Mike flushed, hoping it didn't show. "I appreciate it."

"How's your pain?"

"Manageable. I'm weaning off of Oxy."

"Good. Swelling's down when? Three months or so?"

"Maybe more." Mike could feel eyes on them.

"You didn't get fitted for your prosthesis yet, did you?"

"No, not yet. I'm in that in-between stage. The flap's pretty much healed, but the swelling hasn't gone down enough for an initial fitting." Mike wanted to change the subject. "How's it going with Lyon and the new practice? You guys taking over the world, or at least the Main Line?"

"We're doing great. Prosperity agrees with me." Jim brightened, patting his stomach, which hung over his belt slightly. He had on the blazer and khaki pants he used to wear to their continuing education classes. "But listen, I have plans for you. You free to meet with me and Lyon tomorrow morning?"

Mike turned, surprised. He had to complete rehab before he could work, but wanted to know his options. "Sure thing. What time?"

"Come by around noon. We can talk about it."

"Thanks, will do." Mike thought of Tony and Dave, who weren't here tonight. They'd emailed him when the practice broke up and sent partnership dissolution papers he had to sign. Last he'd heard, they'd moved and were joining new practices. "How are Tony and Dave? Do you know?"

"Nah, I'm sure they're fine, though. Take care. Gotta go find Laura."

"Go." Mike spotted Sara in the family room, playing on the floor with Emily. He left his plate, threaded his way through the crowd, and sat down cross-legged on the rug with them. "This looks like fun. What are you guys up to?"

Sara looked over, grinning. "Emily, look, how nice! Daddy came to play with us."

"I'd love to play with you." Mike adopted her sing-song tone. "Emily, what are you playing?"

"Beep beep!" Emily said, driving a school bus on the rug.

"Emily, is that bus going to school?" Mike picked up a toy that was shaped like an egg with a face. "Don't forget this kid. She wants to go to school, too."

"No."

"Oh, sorry about that." Mike smiled, even if all he got was a no. It was a thrill to hear her cute little voice, and he caught a flash of teeth, nice and even. "Emily, look at all those teeth! I wonder if you can smile. Can you smile?"

"No," Emily answered, looking down, and Mike couldn't help but laugh.

Sara grinned. "She's entering the terrible twos. Get ready for a rough ride."

Mike saw his opening. "Sara, by the way, are you free tomorrow after school? I'd like to stop by, to catch up."

"Totally. Come by at three thirty, okay? Same classroom."

"Great, thanks."

"Beep beep!" Emily drove the bus to Mike's loafer, then pointed at his sweater sleeve, which hung empty. "Where is dat?"

"My arm?" Mike hadn't realized that Emily would notice, so he wasn't ready for the question.

Sara answered quickly, "Emily, Daddy only has one arm. Daddy lost his other arm."

Emily turned her curly head to Sara. "He find it?"

Mike decided to give it a shot. "Emily, my arm got a boo-boo, and the doctors couldn't fix it, so they took it off. I don't need it because I have another one. Here's my hand." He held up his right hand. "You have your right hand, too. Want to hold up your hand with me?"

Emily blinked, confused, so Mike reached for her little hand and placed it against his large one. Hers felt warm and vaguely sticky against his palm, but he was so charmed he would have held it forever.

"Emily, see? We both have a right hand."

"Where dat hand?" Emily pointed again, still not understanding.

"I don't have it anymore. It's gone." Mike showed her his left side, and his sweater sleeve dangled like a molted snakeskin. Out of the corner of his eye, he spotted Jim and Laura looking over, with sympathy.

"I see it?" Emily scooted forward with the bus, tucking her leg underneath her, her white tights dirty at the knee.

"There's nothing inside. Just a big Band-Aid."

Sara caught Mike's eye. "I don't think that's a good idea."

Emily rose, but wobbled, fell forward, and whacked Mike's left arm with the toy bus.

"No!" Mike sprang backwards in pain, and everyone turned at the sound.

"I sorry! I sorry!" Emily dropped the bus and burst into tears.

"Honey, it's okay!" Mike reached for Emily, but it was too late.

"Mommy!" Emily ran away, crying. "Mommy!"

Chapter Thirty-nine

The next morning, Mike showered, dried off, then braced himself to shave, because he still wasn't used to seeing his amputation in the mirror. He went to the sink and confronted his reflection, using his coping mechanism, which was to see his body through a doctor's eyes, pretending he was his own patient, The Podiatric Surgeon With Only One Arm. Otherwise, Mike had no way to deal with the fact that his left arm just stopped in thin air, grotesquely shorter than it used to be, leaving him feeling deformed, inferior, like half a man, though he never acknowledged those feelings, even to himself. He tucked them away each time he tucked his empty sleeve into his pocket, pretending he was whole, normal, and himself again.

So in the mirror, Mike noted that the left arm had been amputated the standard ten centimeters below the shoulder joint and six above the elbow joint, and that the fifty-odd crude, healed stitches over the skin flap on the distal end of his arm formed a raised scar in an upside-down U, or aptly, a frown. There wasn't much swelling, and the skin color was normal, which meant circulation was good, and bottom line, Mike had what his doctor at Landstuhl had called "a good stump."

He'd been taken aback, though it wasn't the first time he'd heard the term "stump" and he'd even used it himself in the OR. But it was jarring to hear it applied to his own arm, though he got used even to that, because everybody called his left arm a stump. They gave him a "a stump sock" or a "stump shrinker," a compression bandage he used to keep the swelling down, and the nurses taught him how to wash his stump, palpate his stump, and tap or massage his stump, to help with the pain. In time, Mike learned to be grateful he had a good stump, not one with redundant soft tissue, which produced a larger, oddly bulbous or irregular deformity, or the opposite problem, an excessive retraction of the soft tissue, which produced a narrowing to the flesh almost to the bone, in which the stump had a more pointy appearance.

Mike twisted on the faucet and picked up his plastic razor, thinking back to his month at Landstuhl, which showed him that no matter how awful he secretly felt about his stump, he was one of the lucky ones, having an upper-limb amputation, only one at that, and to the non-dominant hand. He didn't have to learn to walk again like the lower-limb amputees, or face the challenges of multiple-limb amputees. The courage of those soldiers made him feel ashamed for having any self-pity at all, so he kept it to himself during adaptive rehab, where they told him to get a buttonhook if you can't button your shirts or buy pullovers, and taught him cross-body and shoulder-elevation stretches to avoid contracture of his remaining muscles. This morning he would skip his exercises because he had to get going. He finished shaving, dressed, and went downstairs.

"Good morning, everybody." Mike walked into the kitchen, where Bob was finishing his eggs and Danielle was at the sink. Emily was in the family room, playing with her toys. "Hi, Emily," Mike called out, but she didn't turn around.

"Good morning." Danielle smiled, already dressed in jeans and a colorful peasant top. Her style had definitely gotten more like Chloe's, maybe because she was home full-time, more relaxed than he'd ever seen her.

"I'm late." Bob rubbed his face, clean-shaven. "Gotta go."

"Thanks again for last night. It was good to see everyone." Mike crossed to the coffee machine, slid out the glass pot, and poured himself a mug.

"How do you feel this morning?" Danielle turned from the sink, with a smile.

"Pretty good, thanks."

Bob brought his dish to the sink. "I can't believe you slept through that racket."

"What racket?" Mike asked, sipping hot coffee.

Danielle rolled her eyes. "Bob, don't be that way."

Bob picked up his wallet and tucked it inside his dark suit. "Emily was up most of the night. You really didn't hear?"

"No, sorry." Mike didn't explain that he slept soundly because of the sleeping pill, on top of another Oxy. "What happened with her?"

"She woke up twice, talking about your arm." Danielle twisted the water off. "I think it shook her up to see it."

"Oh, I'm sorry." Mike felt a guilty stab and eyed Emily. "What can I do? Should I go in there and try to talk to her?"

"No, don't. She's tired. Let's not set it up to fail." Danielle dried her hands on a dishtowel. "Do you want some eggs? I've got scrambled ready."

"I'd love some, but you don't have to do that. I can get my own breakfast, honestly."

"I know, but I like to do it." Danielle bustled over, took a plate from the cabinet, and spooned two mounds of fluffy scrambled eggs. "Say when."

"When, thanks."

Bob cleared his throat. "Mike, Danielle said that you wanted to go through your things at the storage unit, to see if there was anything you needed."

"That's right." Mike figured that Danielle had made up some story about why he wanted to go to the unit. He avoided Bob's eye, picked up his fork, and took a bite of his eggs, which were deliciously buttery. "Danielle, these are awesome, thank you."

"Okay, your car's in our garage, so feel free, but you should check the closet in my home office first. I put some boxes up there, Chloe's valuables and letters, both of your wills, and other things I didn't trust to storage."

"Oh. Is her laptop up there, too?"

"You were looking for Chloe's laptop? I should've mentioned this, but I threw it out."

Mike couldn't hide his surprise. "You threw out Chloe's laptop?"

"Yes, I'm sorry. It got so damaged that day, it crashed."

Danielle looked at Mike, pursing her lips. "I'm sorry, too. I didn't know. I thought it was in the storage unit, but evidently not. It had all her photos and everything. It kills me that we don't have it anymore."

Mike wouldn't be able to find Chloe's password file without her laptop. "Bob, I don't understand. Was it broken or what?"

Bob's upper lip curled in distaste. "Frankly, there was blood all over it. I tried to wipe it clean, but it wouldn't turn on. I found it on the kitchen floor."

"Could we not talk about this? Please?" Danielle shuddered. "Mike, when does your rehab begin? I remember you mentioned that, in one of your emails."

"I should call to set up some appointments, but I want to see about a job today." Mike was thinking about Chloe's laptop, wondering how else he could get into her email.

"What do they do, in rehab?"

"Flexibility exercises, but I can do them on my own." Mike swallowed his eggs. He was stalling on rehab because he was in no hurry to account for his increased Oxy use. In fact, he was already wondering how he could resupply.

Bob put his dirty glass in the sink. "Well, in the good news department, we wanted to talk to you about your living arrangements."

Mike held up a hand, with his fork. "Let me beat you to the punch. I appreciate everything you've done for me and Emily, but the first thing I'm doing this morning is to go to a Realtor's office and get him started on finding us a place, at least to rent, until I can buy."

Bob smiled. "We appreciate that, but you're welcome to stay here as long as you like. We love having you and we want what's best for you and Emily. The longer you stay with us, the more we can ease her transition. What do you say?"

Danielle smiled. "If you have to start your rehab, it doesn't make sense for you to get a babysitter while you go to your appointments or whatever. This way, you can come and go as you please. Doesn't that make sense?"

Mike looked from Danielle to Bob, feeling a warm rush of gratitude. "You guys don't have to do this, really. I'm a big boy, and I have the money, and I'm ready to move away from home."

Bob chuckled. "If I were you, I'd take us up on our offer. Start looking for a house if you want to, but staying here takes the pressure off. You don't have to find one right away, in winter. It snowed again last night, four more inches." He gestured at the backyard, which was covered with newfallen snow, its crusty surface reflecting the frigid sun. "Stay here, focus on your rehab, and get your feet back on the ground. There'll be better listings in March."

Danielle nodded, from the counter. "What job are you talking about?"

"Jim says he has something for me, and I'd love to get in with his new partner, if I can still practice."

"How wonderful!" Danielle beamed.

"I know, right? I'm so lucky on the job front. So many ampu—" Mike caught himself—"*vets* don't get these opportunities, and I have two. My buddy from Afghanistan said he'd give me a job, too, in Greenwich."

"Greenwich, Connecticut?" Danielle frowned. "You'd move away?"

Bob seemed to stiffen in the threshold. "You wouldn't want to move. There's no need for that."

Mike realized he'd said the wrong thing. "No, right, I'd much rather stay here and work with Jim. I'm just saying I have a Plan B. I don't want you to think you have to take care of Emily and me, like a mooch."

Bob's expression softened, and he picked up his messenger bag. "We never think you're mooching, Mike. So, will you stay with us, here?"

Danielle made praying hands. "Please, Mike? Stay with us?"

Mike felt vaguely pressured, but they were only trying to help him and Emily. "Thanks for the offer, and yes, of course."

"Wonderful." Danielle smiled.

"That's settled." Bob leaned over and kissed Danielle on the cheek. "Now I gotta go. Love you."

"You, too." Danielle smiled. "Bye."

"See you," Bob said, leaving. "Bye, Emily!"

"Bye, Daddy!" Emily called back.

Chapter Forty

Mike went up to his bedroom with a coffee, unpacked his laptop, fired it up, then sat down in the desk chair. He was going to crack Chloe's email if it killed him. The screen came to life, and the laptop found the wireless Internet, which wasn't password-protected, so he got online and went directly to Gmail. The screen popped into view, and on the right, it read SIGN IN and underneath that USERNAME and PASSWORD.

Mike typed in her username, hunting and pecking with one hand, and paused at password. Back in Afghanistan, he had tried emily1000, their go-to-password for most sites, the other variations of their birthdays, and their old street name and house number, but they didn't work. He thought of Jake the cat, typed in Jake, then tried to guess at which numbers Chloe would pick. Then he realized something. Chloe didn't have Jake or Emily when they'd met, so the password wouldn't be anything relating to them.

Mike remembered the address of Chloe's old apartment, 2-C, which was in a house at 101 Maple Avenue. He typed in Maple2C101, but it didn't work. He tried MapleAve101, but that didn't work either. He typed in CV10210, Chloe's initials and her house number, but he was wrong again. He drank some coffee, trying to get his brain in gear. He was still on Landstuhl time, and his stump began to throb.

"Mike?" came Danielle's voice, with a knock at the door.

"Come in. How's Emily?'

"Down for her nap."

"Good. I'm on your wireless, hope you don't mind. I'm trying to get in to Chloe's Gmail but I don't know her password."

"Oh, I see." Danielle entered the room, pulled up a chair, and glanced at the screen. "It feels intrusive, trying to break into her email."

Mike looked over. He had passed that stage a long time ago. "I understand how you feel, but now I just want to know who the guy was. You don't have to be here. She didn't cheat on you, after all."

"No, that's okay." Danielle eyed the screen, biting her lip. "You need her password? Try Lucie, spelled the French way."

"Who's Lucie?"

"Lucie was our first dog, a big red golden retriever. I use her for all of my accounts and I bet Chloe did, too."

"Really?" Mike typed in Lucie, then stopped. "What would the numbers be? Do you know? You need to have numbers."

"Try 214."

"Where'd you get *that* from?" Mike shook his head, surprised. "I've been racking my brain for a year."

"You would never have guessed it, you didn't know about Lucie. We got her on Valentine's Day. That was a big thing for Chloe, and she always made us have a birthday party for her."

Mike added 214 and pressed ENTER. The screen changed instantly. "Great!"

"Voila," Danielle said, but she didn't sound as happy.

Mike watched as a blue bar appeared on the screen, filling up quickly while Chloe's email loaded, then it changed to the brown background of a standard Gmail account. He avoided glancing over at Danielle, who had fallen quiet, and scanned the senders. There was a slew of junk mail that kept coming after Chloe's death, and he scrolled to December 15 of last year. Most of the senders were Sara, other women, and Facebook notices, but there was an email address he didn't recognize: Mac702@wahoo.com.

"Mac702?" Mike read aloud, turning to Danielle. "Do you know who that could be?"

"No idea."

"Did she know anybody with the first or last name Mac Something?"

"Not that I remember." Danielle shook her head, mystified. "Are you going to open it?"

"I want to and I don't want to. Is that possible?"

"Yes, it's exactly how I feel."

"You can go, if you want to. You don't need to know who he was, or read this. If there's one thing I've learned, it's that you can't unknow what you know. You can't unsee what you saw. I wish I didn't know about her cheating. But now that I do, I can't ignore it." Mike looked over, meeting her eye, evenly. "This is your chance. You want to go outside and I'll fill you in later, or not? Up to you."

Danielle eyed the screen, emitting a small sigh. "I'd like to know," she answered, with a firmness that surprised him.

"Okay." Mike clicked OPEN, and the email popped onto the screen. It read:

Can't wait to see you tomorrow. Just let me hold you and make love to you. Everything will be all right, you'll see. I love you.

Mike clenched his jaw, involuntarily. He could feel Danielle waiting for his reaction and he didn't want to look over. He tried to get past the moment. "Be careful what you wish, right?"

"No," Danielle answered, gently. "You didn't wish for this. You didn't wish for this at all."

Mike didn't want to go there, not now. "So obviously the guy isn't signing his name, which I get. Do you know who this could be?"

"No, not in the least."

Mike looked back at the screen and there were only six emails from Mac702. They started on November 7 and ended on December 14. "So it looks like the affair lasted a month." His chest felt tight, his emotions bleeding through the Oxycontin, and he wished he could take another pill. He slid the chair back and got up.

"Excuse me, I forgot to take my pill this morning, and my arm is hurting."

"Of course." Danielle's mouth turned down at the corners, in sympathy. "Is there a lot of pain?"

"Yes."

"What are you taking?"

"Steroids for swelling, something for edema, antibiotic in case of infection, and a few others." Mike went to his backpack, got his Oxy bottle, and brought it back to the desk. He uncapped the bottle with his thumb and shook one out, but all the capsules rolled onto the desk. "Oops!" Mike felt his face go hot. A million things were harder with one hand, but he remembered he wasn't supposed to feel sorry for himself.

"Let me help," Danielle said quickly, pushing the pills into a pile. "You take your pill, and I'll put these away."

"Thanks." Mike's mouth was too dry to swallow the pill, so he slugged some coffee, and Danielle put the pills back in the bottle and handed it to him.

"Here we go."

"Thanks." Mike sat down, returned his attention to the email, and realized he could chart the chronology of the affair, so he scrolled to the oldest email from Mac702, and clicked OPEN. It read:

It was great just talking to you. As I mentioned, if you could use a hand at the house, I'm free to come over, anytime. Call on my cell. It's better and quicker than email. Text is also fine.

"So the 999 cell number was Mac702's, but he didn't sign his name. Damn!"

"Wonder where he works." Danielle puckered her lips.

"So do I. His identity isn't obvious from his email address, so it suggests that it was somebody she knew." Mike thought aloud. "She obviously just had a conversation with someone about needing some help around the house, or something like that, so she wasn't surprised when she got his email."

"Could be."

Mike clicked to the SENT file to see how Chloe had responded, which was:

I would love that! I'm afraid of heights and the last time it snowed, it almost broke the gutter out back. Yikes! Thanks so much for your help!

Mike felt a pang, reading her words. It was just how she talked, open and friendly, and seeing it in print was like being in her presence. He got lost a minute, remembering her. He'd be crying if not for the Oxys.

"It's not like she was looking to cheat."

"She didn't say no, either." Mike clicked on the next email from Mac702, which read:

I never had so much fun in my life. You're an amazing mother and amazing artist. I didn't mean to open up so much but you brought that out in me. Can't wait to see you again. Please make those muffins?

"You jerk," Mike said to the screen, starting to see red.

"Still no name. Go to the one on November 11."

"Veteran's Day. How ironic." Mike opened the next email from Mac702, which read:

That was the best day ever. You have only yourself to blame that I overstayed my welcome. You're simply the most beautiful, fascinating woman I have ever met.

Mike had to look away, out the window. The sun was blindingly bright, making golden streaks on the snow's crust, not strong enough to melt it. He wished he could be like that, so that none of this got to him, not the emails, Emily's tears, the loss of his arm, or Phat Phil and Oldstein. He wished he had a heart made of Kevlar. He returned his attention to the laptop and scrolled over to the SENT file, to see how Chloe had replied:

Your words are way too kind. I have to admit I opened up a lot, too, but I think that's part of being alone so much and worried about Mike. Please forgive.

Mike read her email again. It made him feel better, seeing that she had at least mentioned him and was missing him. "I wonder whether Mac702 was married, too. It's possible, and that could be why he's using the screen name instead of his real name."

"It's certainly possible." Danielle lifted an eyebrow. "I've heard stories about husbands with secret email accounts and phone numbers. I have a friend whose husband used drop phones, for talking to his mistress."

"That could be why the cell phone was out of service, like those calling cards we used at base. Maybe it was a phone nobody knew about, not even his wife, assuming he was married." Mike scrolled to the next email, which came the next day, on November 12:

I know we just hung up, but I can't stop thinking about you. I know you didn't mean things to go so far, but I couldn't help myself. I know you regret it, but I'm hoping I changed your mind on the phone. This is the beginning of something amazing and you deserve to have the love you need. You can't blame yourself for needing to be held. I'm falling in love. Say that you are, too.

"Oh, man," Mike said, but it came out like a long, slow moan. He could read between the lines. They had slept together. He raked his hair, wanting to tear it out by the root.

"I'm so sorry, Mike."

"This makes me sick." Mike couldn't look over at Danielle, and he realized that he couldn't read in front of her. "Danielle, I changed my mind. Would you mind if I read these alone? I don't think Mac702 is going to mention his name, if he hasn't already."

"I understand, sure." Danielle sighed, meeting his eye. "I'm sorry about this, but I believe in Chloe. She didn't love him, she loved you."

"Thanks."

"Let me know if you need anything, or if you find out who he is." Danielle got up, left the room, and closed the door behind her. "See you later."

Mike confronted the screen, bracing himself. He went to the SENT file, found Chloe's email to Mac702, and clicked OPEN:

You almost changed my mind on the phone, but I admit I'm not thinking straight. What happened between us was wonderful, but it was also wrong and I don't want you to be misled. I feel horrible today, guilty. I appreciate the comfort and affection and closeness we shared, but it can never be more than that and it should never happen again.

Mike swallowed hard. He scrolled down, noticing that there were no emails the weeks of November 18, November 25, December 2, and December 9. If Chloe died December 15, when she was about a month pregnant, the child would've been conceived sometime the week of November 11, early in the affair. He clicked to the last email to Chloe from Mac702, which read:

I can't begin to tell you what these times we had together have meant to me, and I think you know anyway. I heard what you said today, but I can't end this so easily, and I don't believe you want to, deep inside. You're not answering my texts or calls, so I had to resort to email, but please just see me one more time, to talk about this. I don't want to throw us away.

His blood started boiling again. Chloe had tried to break off the affair, but this guy wasn't taking no for an answer. Mike clicked ahead to the SENT file to read her last email to him:

I've listened to your messages but you have to respect my wishes. Please don't come over or drop in again. This relationship was wrong when it started, and continuing it only makes it more wrong. I know that you are not the answer to my loneliness or depression. I have to get back on my feet. Please respect that, and I wish you all the best. Good-bye.

Mike felt the his love for Chloe coming back. He began to understand why she'd done what she'd done, because she'd been lonely
and worried about him. It wasn't because she didn't love him, it was
because she'd needed him more than he realized, maybe even more
than she'd realized. Chloe was a casualty of war, too. He no longer
judged her, he forgave her, and the very notion eased his heart.

His anger went immediately to her lover, who had insinuated
himself into her life, their marriage, and even their bed. She'd been
vulnerable and weak, and he'd taken advantage of her. He logged
out of her email and into Facebook as Chloe, because he knew her
password was Emily1000. He hadn't had the heart to deactivate
her account and he'd been hoping it would help him find out who
her lover was, someday.

Chloe's Facebook page popped onto the screen, and he scanned
the sad RIP postings, which he had read when he was in Afghanistan. He double-checked to see if any had been posted by someone
named Mac or a guy who had Mac in his first or last name, but there
weren't any. He clicked over to her Facebook Friends and scanned
them, too. There were two Mac names, one MacGonigle and another MacTeer, but they were women. Still, he wasn't giving up that
easy.

He logged out, went back to Chloe's email account, opened the
last email from Mac702, and hit REPLY, then wrote to him:

This is Chloe's husband, Mike. I'm back. I don't know who you are, but
I'm going to find out and I'm coming after you. If you're married, I'm telling
your wife. I'm bringing the war home. To you.

Mike hit SEND, then got up, a man on a mission.

Chapter Forty-one

Mike parked his Grand Cherokee at the end of his old street, cut the ignition, and eyed his house, which had been bought by a couple with a baby girl. There was a white minivan where Chloe's VW had been, and he pictured the family sleeping in his bedroom, with their child in a crib like Emily's, then he shooed those thoughts away. He was here because one of the neighbors might have seen a strange man or unusual car at the house, which could give him a lead on Mac702.

He tucked his left sleeve into his jacket pocket, pocketed the keys, got out of the car, and walked down the street, toward Neil and Malika Gustin's house, a stone colonial with a slate roof. Neil's maroon Lexus was in the driveway, and the sidewalk had been shoveled, which was no surprise. Neil was always the first to shovel, and Chloe used to tease him.

Neil's making you look bad again. Get your butt out there! Use the Backsaver!

Mike knocked on the door, which was opened after a moment by Neil, who broke into a wide grin when he recognized him.

"Mike, come in, we heard you were home." Neil was tall, thin, and African-American, and he had on jeans and a Penn sweatshirt because he was on the faculty. "So good to see you."

"Good to see you, too." Mike came inside, shaking off the cold, and Neil shut the door behind them. The family room was snug and warm, and his sons Jason and Luke flopped on the plaid couch, watching cartoons in their pajamas. Mike was surprised at how much they'd grown. "Hi guys, how are you doing?"

"Boys, say hello to Dr. Scanlon." Neil gestured to Mike. "You remember, he used to live across the street, then he went into the Army. You should thank him for his service to this country."

"Thank you, Dr. Scanlon," the boys said in unison. Luke, who was younger, piped up, "I play Call of Duty. I'm on level four."

"Way to go!" Mike smiled, and Neil put a hand on Mike's back. "I'm so sorry about Chloe. It still seems so hard to believe."

"Thanks. I feel the same way."

"It's good you're home safe. Malika will be sorry she missed you. She's running errands with the baby." Neil's eyes were a soft brown, and he had more crow's feet than last year. "I heard you got a medal. Congratulations!"

"Thanks." Mike guessed Neil had heard about his arm, too, but he kept his sleeve in his pocket anyway.

"You want some coffee or something? I'm supposed to be fixing the sump pump and I need a break."

"No, thanks, I won't bother you. I was just wondering if you saw any strange cars or anything around the house, the month before Chloe died. Like any strange men, or anything like that, helping her around the house."

Neal frowned. "I don't think so, but I'm in town all day. Malika would know, and I'll ask her."

"Great. It could've been on the weekend, too."

"No. I didn't notice anything or anyone new." Neil ran a palm over his hair, which he kept short and natural, with new silver strands at his temples. "Why do you ask?"

"Some cash that went missing." Mike was improvising. "I figure maybe it was a workman or someone helping her around the house. Did Malika mention anything like that, like some new guy helping her with the house?"

"No, not that I know of, or remember." Neil shook his head.

"I'll ask Malika when she gets home. Maybe Douglas or Susan saw something?"

"I'm about to ask them. Well, I'd better go, thanks a lot. Have her call me, my number's the same. Thanks again, Neil. Stay well."

"You, too. Stop in anytime, especially if you can fix a sump pump."

"Sorry, I'm only a surgeon," Mike shot back, until he remembered he wasn't anymore. He left the house and hustled across the street to Douglas and Susan Steingard, who'd come out to shovel. Susan was sweeping off her Toyota 4Runner and she turned with a big smile when she recognized Mike.

"Mike, what a surprise!" Susan rested the broom against the car and gave him a warm hug. She was a small woman in a puffy blue parka, with a knit cap pulled down to her round blue eyes. Freckles dotted her nose, red at the tip from the cold. "I was just thinking of you the other day, because I heard you came home. Thank God! How are you?"

"I'm fine, thanks. How have you guys been?"

"Terrific. The girls keep me busier than when I was a lawyer. They're in fifth grade now." Susan gestured at their daughters, who were playing in the snow in the front yard. "They're making an iPad. They're lobbying."

Mike laughed as Douglas made his way down the driveway in an orange parka and Sorrel boots, holding a windshield scraper. His red ski cap made a crooked cone on his head, and his glasses were steamed up at the bottom rim, nearest his cheeks.

"Mike, good to have you home!" Douglas grinned. "All hail the conquering hero."

"Hardly, sir." Mike always liked Douglas, a tax lawyer at a big firm in Philly. "How are you?"

"Same old, same old." Douglas was on the short side and wiry. "I entered my first Iron Man and finished by nightfall."

"Of the same day, even," Susan added with a sly smile.

"Congratulations." Mike cut to the chase. "Here's what I came to ask. Some cash went missing from the house before Chloe died, and I'm thinking maybe a workman took it or someone helping her out.

Do you remember seeing any workmen or new guys around during that time? Like a car in the driveway, one you hadn't seen before?"

Susan frowned, in thought. "No, not really, I don't."

"It would have been around Thanksgiving or the holidays."

"No, I don't remember anybody unusual. Your brother-in-law was there, but nobody new or strange." Susan's fair skin flushed. "I wish I had seen her more often around that time, but the holidays get so busy. That's why it was so shocking when she . . . ." Her voice trailed off, and her pretty face fell. "I always wish I had been around that day, but I was shopping."

Douglas put an arm around Susan, looking at Mike. "I'm so sorry for your loss, too."

"Thanks, maybe I'll go see the Kulls, on the off-chance that they saw something."

"They're not home. They went to Jackson Hole. I think they're coming back next week."

"Oh, too bad."

"Oh, wait a minute." Susan brightened. "I don't remember anybody strange, but the new kid used to help her out, from time to time."

"What new kid?"

"From down the street." Susan pointed down the street. "A new family moved in next to the Kulls while you were away. Chloe did mention him, now that I think about it. His name is Pat. The parents are nice, but he's kind of entitled."

"What's his last name?"

"MacFarland."

Mike felt it like an electric shock. Mac could be short for Mac-Farland. "You said he's a kid. How old is he?"

"I'd say he's in his mid-twenties. That's a kid to me."

"Me, too," Mike said idly, but he eyed the house down the street, his anger rising. It was possible that Pat MacFarland was Mac702, because Susan hadn't seen a strange car in the driveway and Pat wouldn't have driven over.

Mike's heart beat harder, like a fist pounding on a door.

Chapter Forty-two

Mike knocked on the MacFarlands' door, trying to stay calm. He felt a cramped twisting in the arm that wasn't there anymore, his characteristic phantom pain. In the next moment, the door was opened by a heavyset, middle-aged man in a flannel shirt that wasn't tucked in, over baggy jeans.

"Can I help you?" the man asked, frowning behind his bifocals.

"Yes, hello. My name is Mike Scanlon, and I used to live two doors down, with my wife Chloe and our new baby."

"Oh, right, I'm John MacFarland." John's eyes flickered with recognition, a cloudy gray. "I recall the name. You were in Afghanistan, right?"

"Yes."

"Thank you for your service. How can I help you?"

"I thought I'd come by to talk to your son. He was helpful to my late wife while I was away, and I wanted to say thanks."

"Right, come in. My condolences." John stepped aside, and Mike entered the well-appointed entrance hall. "Hang on a sec, I'll get Pat. I think he's awake." He went to the base of the stair and hollered up, "Pat, can you come down? Someone's here to see you."

"What does Pat do for a living?" Mike tried to keep his tone casual, though his heart hammered away.

"He's in between jobs." John frowned. "He graduated a few years ago, but he got laid off. He's a graphic designer, websites, all that. Fortunately, he can freelance."

Mike remembered one of the emails from Mac702 had flattered Chloe and her paintings. "And he lives here?"

"Yes, for the time being. My wife loves having him home. She's up in the shower, or I'd have her meet you." They both looked up to the stairwell as a huge mastiff bounded down, its wide pink tongue lolling out of its mouth. John shook his head, indulgently. "Here's Gigi, Pat's dog. Gigi stands for gentle giant, so don't worry."

"Good to know." Mike edged backwards as the mastiff hit the rug with a *thump,* and John moved to grab its collar, but missed, chuckling.

"Gang way. She jumps up."

"Hi, Gigi." Mike caught the mastiff as she jumped on his chest with her front paws, drooling and panting. He moved his stump away, wincing. "Whoa, she's a horse."

"Weighs 150 pounds. No, Gigi, down." John tugged the dog to the rug, where she plopped on her butt and her hind legs flopped apart. "She needs obedience, that's for sure."

Mike felt a start when he spotted Pat, coming downstairs. He was handsome, about six foot two, with thick dark hair, brown eyes, and a relaxed smile. He had on a black T-shirt with loose-fitting blue athletic pants, and when he reached the foot of the stairwell, he gulped a spoonful of cereal from a bowl he was carrying.

John turned to his son. "Pat, you remember that woman down the block, in 637? You used to help her out when we first moved here."

"No, not really." Pat shrugged.

"Sure you do. You were over there."

"What was her name again?" Pat took another spoonful of cereal.

"Chloe Voulette," Mike interjected, wondering if Pat was lying. If he was, it would've been because of the email.

"Chloe, you say?" Pat crunched away, and John shook his head in disapproval.

"Pat, why don't you put the cereal down and talk to the man? This is her husband."

"Dad, what? I'm eating."

Mike simmered, his jealousy glaring. Pat had good looks, a young and able body, and his entire life rolling out in front of him, like a red carpet. "Pat, our house was two doors down, and I heard you helped her with heavy lifting and things like that. This would be around Christmas of last year. Remember now? Is it coming back to you?"

"Not really, but why?" Pat set down the bowl on a side table, sucking cereal out of his teeth.

"She had dark blonde hair, she was really pretty? A new mom, with a baby girl?" Mike felt madder by the minute, losing control of his temper. "You have to remember her. You remember her."

John looked over at Mike, blinking. "Well, to be fair to Pat, it was a while ago, and you know how kids are—"

"He's no kid," Mike shot back. "Men his age are fighting and dying this very minute." He turned to Pat. "I have one question for you. Is your email address Mac702?"

"What's your problem, bro?" Pat snorted, tossing his bangs from his forehead.

"I'm not your *bro*. My *bros* aren't here. My *bros* are in Afghanistan." Mike angered at the thought of troops dying so this kid could slack. "Why don't you man up? I'd like to know what you did for my *wife*. I'd like to know *exactly* what kind of help you gave her last year."

John raised a hand, frowning. "Now, wait just a minute, you said you wanted to thank him."

Pat scoffed. "I offered to help her move some boxes."

"You telling me you didn't do more?" Mike shouted, beyond reason. "You didn't take advantage of her? You didn't comfort her in her hour of need?"

"What the hell—" Pat started to say, but Mike exploded, punching Pat in the face.

All hell broke loose. Pat staggered backwards. John rushed to help him. Gigi lunged at Mike, knocked him to the floor, and planted her paws on his chest, barking frantically. Mike shouted and raised his arm, but Gigi clamped down on his right shoulder, then shook him back and forth.

"No, no!" Mike felt the mastiff's teeth, and his stump seared from being jostled. Tears of rage sprung to his eyes. "You *preyed* on my wife, you bastard! You preyed on my wife! I'll kill you!"

"Mom, help!" Pat hollered. "Dad, get Gigi!"

"Gigi, drop it, drop it!" John yanked the mastiff backwards, and Gigi opened her jaw, releasing Mike.

"Why couldn't you leave her alone? Why?" Mike scrambled to his feet and crazily threw another punch, but didn't connect. "She didn't love you, she loved *me!*"

"Get out!" Pat seized Mike by his jacket, and a tall, dark-haired woman appeared at the top of the stairwell, her eyes widening in fear.

"John, Pat!" she screamed, terrified, in a robe. "Oh no! Help! Help!"

"Karen, stay upstairs!" John yelled. "Don't come down!"

"Mom, call 911!" Pat hollered, but Mike punched wildly and caught him under the chin.

"She was my *wife, my wife!*"

Pat shook off the punch, grabbed him by the stump, flung open the door, and whipsawed him onto the porch. "Get the hell out!" he yelled, slamming the door closed with a *bang!*

Mike stumbled off the porch, holding his stump and staggering down the steps. Blood dripped onto the snow from his nose. He raised his hand to catch the flow, but pain from the bite arced to his shoulder. His adrenaline ebbed away, leaving him aching all over.

He hustled down the sidewalk, crunching over ice and salt crystals. He kept his head down, passing his old house without looking over. He had made such a fool of himself. He couldn't defend his home, his marriage, or his wife.

He had almost reached his car when he heard the blare of approaching police sirens.

Chapter Forty-three

The sirens shook Mike to the bone, a reminder of Helmand Province, but he remained acutely aware that he was standing across from his old house, sniffling his own blood, having just had his ass kicked by the stud who probably impregnated his wife. The police cruiser tore around the corner, its tires spraying clotted snow. He leaned against his car and pinched the bridge of his nose to stop the bleeding, hoping the Gustins and Steingards weren't watching.

The police cruiser lurched to a stop behind his Grand Cherokee, and its sirens silenced abruptly, leaving an echo vibrating in the air. The cruiser doors flew open, and two cops sprang out and hustled toward him, one tall and the other short, in uniforms with thick insulated jackets.

"Mr. Scanlon?" The tall cop motioned to Mike. His nametag read Officer Joseph Torno, and his jacket bore the embroidered patch of the Wilberg Police. "Place your hands against the vehicle, sir."

"I'm Mike Scanlon. Sorry you guys were called. This is hardly a police matter." Mike placed his hand against his car, and Officer Torno patted him down.

"Other hand, too, Mr. Scanlon." Officer Torno reached for the empty sleeve. "What the hell?"

"I have one arm."

"Sorry." Officer Torno took his arm and turned him around. He looked young, and his eyes were a bright blue under the patent bill of his cap. "I suppose I can't cuff you."

"There's always a silver lining." Mike forced a smile.

"You'll have to come with me, Mr. Scanlon." Officer Torno led him to the cruiser. "Is this your vehicle?"

"Yes," Mike answered, as the short cop came around his right side.

"You have the right to remain silent," he began. "Anything you say can and will be used against you in court. If you don't have a lawyer, one will be appointed for you . . ."

"Miranda warnings?" Mike groaned, as the short cop continued. "Am I being arrested, Officer Torno?"

"Yes, sir, for assault. You'll be booked after we take you to the hospital. You need to see a doctor."

"Are you kidding?" Mike felt disgusted with himself. "I don't need a doctor, I am a doctor, and it's just a nosebleed. I'm fine, and so is he. I hardly got in a punch."

"You mind telling me what happened, Mr. Scanlon?" Officer Torno opened the cruiser's back door, while the short cop guided Mike into the backseat, palmed Mike's head, and buckled him into the safety harness.

"It's a private matter, between me and Pat." Mike didn't want to explain. It was humiliating enough that he had been arrested in front of his neighbors. He wondered how he'd gone from being a respected doctor to an anger-management case, with a prescription-drug problem and a criminal record. He slid over in the seat, which was black plastic and smelled like Armor All. A plastic window separated him from the front seat.

"Mr. Scanlon, would you mind if we searched your vehicle?"

"Go ahead. It's open."

"Thank you. Please remain seated, Mr. Scanlon." The short cop closed the back door, then jogged to Mike's car, while Officer Torno opened the front door of the cruiser and climbed into the driver's seat. He shut the door behind him and eyed Mike in the rearview. "You need a Kleenex for that nose?"

"No, thanks." Mike tilted his head back, and the nosebleed was finally slowing.

"I understand you were bitten by their dog. FYI, its rabies shots are up to date. Is the wound bleeding?"

"It's fine." Mike's right arm hurt, but it was nothing compared with his stump. He hoped he hadn't reinjured himself, because the local ER wouldn't have a doc who could repair a complex upper-limb amputation. "So Pat's charging me with assault?"

"You're referring to the complainant, Patrick MacFarland?"

"Is complainant a fancy word for jerk?"

Officer Torno didn't smile. "He says you hit him in the ear and the chin. Is that correct?"

"Well, yes."

"Did he hit you first?"

"No." Mike conceded the obvious. "Your basic assault, right?"

"Yes, sir." Officer Torno pursed his lips. "He's claiming you dam-aged his ear, and his front teeth are loose."

Mike looked out the window. So much for do no harm.

"Are you under the influence of drugs or alcohol, Mr. Scanlon?"

"A prescription for pain." Mike doubted he should be answering any questions. "Do I need a lawyer?"

"You'll need somebody to bail you out."

Mike dreaded calling Bob and he'd wait. It wasn't an emergency, and he might be in the ER a long time.

"The complainant says you're a returning vet, sir. Is that cor-rect?"

"Yes."

Officer Torno glanced at him in the rearview. "Are you under psychiatric treatment?"

"Of course not," Mike answered, then realized the cop had no way of knowing that he wasn't a battle-crazed war vet who went around bashing heads. Or maybe he was, considering that he had one arm and he'd picked a fight with a man almost twice his size and almost half his age, plus a dog as big as a Humvee.

"Here's my partner." Officer Torno watched through the windshield as the short cop jogged back to the cruiser, opened the door, got inside, rubbing his hands together.

"His car's clean."

"Good, then we're outta here." Officer Torno clipped his harness on, steered around the Cherokee, then lurched off. The cruiser rumbled down Foster Road, and Mike watched his house pass by, then the MacFarlands', feeling a wave of shame. The cruiser turned onto Paoli Pike and accelerated past houses and stores, and Mike realized he wouldn't be able to meet Sara at three thirty. Now more than ever, he wanted to see her and confirm his suspicions about Pat.

"Okay if I text somebody I was supposed to meet?" Mike called to Officer Torno.

"Is it your lawyer?"

"No. But it's important, and she'll be waiting for me."

"Make it fast, and then no more. I'm cutting you a break."

"Thanks." Mike slid his cell phone from his pocket, wincing. He thumbed to the text function and scrolled to find Sara's name. He highlighted her name, pressed it, then typed with his thumb, **cant make it today, sorry, will call tonight.** He pressed SEND and was about to put the phone back when the text alert chimed. It was a reply from Sara, which read, **No worries! Call whenever! Xoxox!** He slipped the phone back in his pocket and looked out the window, but he hardly saw anything at all.

Three hours later, Mike was sitting in the examining room at Wilberg Memorial's Emergency Department, gingerly putting his jacket on over his new compression bandage, finally ready to go. He'd gotten a tetanus shot for the bite, and his stump didn't need a flap repair, though he'd gotten a lecture about doing his exercises and elevating his upper body, to prevent edema.

"Here we go, Dr. Scanlon," said a young nurse, entering the room with discharge papers. "Will you sign these for me?"

"Yes, thanks." Mike took the papers and signed them at the bottom.

"Don't you want to read them? It's directions for wound care."

"I'm up to speed." Mike handed her back the papers, and the nurse handed him a flurry of prescriptions.

"These are the scripts for antibiotics, steroids, diuretic, a stool softener, and pain."

"Great, thanks." Mike folded them and tucked them in his back pocket, happy to have the refill on Oxy. He'd already taken a capsule, but it hadn't helped much. He zipped up his jacket just as Officer Torno appeared at the curtain, his eyes a worn blue under his cap.

"Dr. Scanlon, are you ready to leave?"

"Yes, thanks." Mike checked the wall clock, which read 6:45. "Sorry it was such a long wait."

"It's all right. Let's go." Officer Torno motioned to him, and the nurse stepped aside.

"Thanks," Mike said to the nurse, who smiled back.

Officer Torno took Mike's arm and walked him past the doctors' station, and they passed together through the exit doors, which let in a blast of freezing air. Darkness had fallen outside, and the sky was black ice.

Mike shuddered against the cold. "So what happens now? We're going to the world's prettiest precinct house?"

"Oh, you've been?" Officer Torno led Mike to the cruiser, which idled in a parking spot nearest the door.

"Yes, last year, when my wife died."

"Oh. Sorry." Officer Torno opened the back door of the cruiser, and the short cop was a silhouette in the front passenger seat. "Please get in, Dr. Scanlon."

"Thanks." Mike slid into the backseat, which was warm. "Okay if I call a lawyer now?"

"Yes." Officer Torno shut the door, went to the front seat, and climbed inside. The cruiser steered out of the parking lot while Mike turned on his phone, which came to life with a red star of a Missed Call. He scrolled down and saw it was from Danielle, so he highlighted the number and called back. He realized that the last thing Danielle knew, he was meeting Sara at school and would be on his way home for dinner.

"Danielle?" Mike said, when she picked up. "How—"

"Oh Mike! Oh no!" Danielle wailed. "I've been calling and calling! I have terrible news!"

"What is it?" Mike asked, alarmed. "Is Emily okay?"

"She's fine, but—" Danielle burst into sobs—"it's Sara."

"What about her?"

"Mike, Sara's dead."

Chapter Forty-four

The news hit Mike like a body blow. "What happened?"

"She was mugged on the way to her car. Stabbed."

Mike gasped. "Where? How?"

"In the parking lot at the Acme. Don called here for you, he didn't have your cell."

Mike felt stunned. "Sara texted me a few hours ago."

"Where are you? Are you on your way home?"

Mike couldn't speak for a moment, knowing firsthand the agony Don would be feeling, to lose the wife he loved, the mother of his sons, so horribly. Tears came to Mike's eyes, and his hand throbbed as if it were still there, a phantom pain burning to the end of finger-tips that were gone.

"Mike? Where are you?"

"I'm on my way to the Wilberg police station. I'm sorry, but I need Bob to bail me out. Is he home yet?"

"*What?*"

"It's nothing serious. I'll explain later."

"How could it not be serious? You, in jail? I'll be right there."

"No, you stay home with the baby." Mike didn't want Emily dragged into a police station, however picturesque. "Please, I'd rather that Bob came. I need a lawyer."

"I'll call him right back. We just hung up."

"Good, thanks, and don't worry. Bye." Mike pressed END, working his jaw to stay in control. Sara was such a loving presence, so grounded and constant, the one everybody counted on, even Chloe. He just couldn't believe she was gone and he wanted to understand how she had died. He shifted forward in the seat, toward the perforated screen. "Officers, did you hear about a stabbing at the Acme, a woman named Sara Hambera?"

"Yes." Officer Torno's gaze shifted to the rearview.

"So it's true." Mike felt sick to his stomach. "I know her. She's my wife's best friend. She had three kids. She was a wonderful person, a teacher."

"Sorry. It's a crying shame."

"Do you know what happened?"

"No more than what you said. We don't have the details."

"My sister-in-law said she was mugged." Mike struggled with his emotions to process the information. "The Acme isn't in Wilberg, is it?"

"No. Clifton. It's on the border."

"How often does that happen in Clifton, violent crime like that?"

"Not a lot, but we're not immune. A woman was killed last year at the Granite Run Mall."

"But this wasn't at a mall." Mike couldn't wrap his mind around it. "It's not like she'd have packages or valuables. It was at a grocery store."

Officer Torno returned his attention to the road, and they hit traffic, a line of red lights. "Did she drive a nice car?"

"No, she had an old Honda. It's about seven o'clock now, so somebody had to see something." Mike checked the full parking lot of a strip mall on the right, which only confirmed his confusion. "Do you know if they caught the guy? Or if they have any suspects?"

"Don't know that either." Officer Torno fed the cruiser some gas when the traffic started moving again, then he steered to the right, onto the road that led to the precinct house. The strip malls gave way to stone houses, covered with snow.

Mike slid back on the seat, in a sort of numb shock, as the cruiser rumbled past Christmas lights, twinkling in the dark night. He couldn't believe Sara was gone, when she'd just texted him, and he opened his phone, scrolled to the text function, and reread her text: **No worries! Call whenever! Xoxox!** The text had come in only hours ago. He flashed on the day Phat Phil and Oldstein died. They'd been there one minute, gone the next. It happened every day in war, but not in the suburbs.

Mike felt his gut twist. Chloe was gone, and so was her best friend. It would have broken Chloe's heart to know what had happened to Sara, just as it had broken Sara's to know what happened to Chloe. There had been so much death, and all of the bodies weighed on his heart. He couldn't leave any of them behind, nor did he want to.

He looked out the window, trying to keep it together. He realized that he wouldn't be able to confirm that Pat MacFarland had been Chloe's lover, but that didn't matter right now.

His left arm hurt like hell.

Even though it was gone.

Chapter Forty-five

Mike paced his cell, a closet-sized room of white tile that contained a stainless steel bench and sink next to an open toilet. The cell had no bars, and a door with a Plexiglas window overlooked a narrow hallway. He'd been here over an hour, trying to process the fact that Sara had been murdered, and his thoughts kept turning to Don, their sons, then Chloe, DeMaria, and Oldstein, as if the losses were linked, on a continuous loop. His stump throbbed mightily, and he could feel the Oxycontin wearing off.

The sound of talking came from the hallway, and a police officer was unlocking the door to admit Bob, in a rumpled suit and striped tie. "Hi, Mike."

"Bob, thanks so much for coming."

"No problem," Bob replied, falling silent until the police officer had left, locking them both inside. "Don't look so upset. We got this."

"It's about Sara. It's a shock."

"I know, of course, it's horrible. I feel for Don and the boys." Bob's expression was tense, and he had a five o'clock shadow. "But as for you, I met with the assistant district attorney, who might be twelve years old. They sent the B-team. The varsity is in Clifton."

"Because of Sara's murder?"

"Yes, that's why the judge is on call tonight. Otherwise you'd have to stew in here until tomorrow."

Mike lowered himself onto the steel bench, and his gaze fell to his hand, where fingerprint ink covered his fingerpads. "I can't believe she's gone. The two of them, now. Her and Chloe."

"I feel the same way, but you need to focus. Your arraignment begins any minute. So what the hell happened? I read the information, but it didn't have any detail." Bob leaned against the tile wall, and Mike struggled to switch mental gears.

"I found out that Chloe had an affair while I was away, and I think it was with Pat MacFarland, so I hit him, or tried to."

Bob's mouth dropped open. "Are you *serious*?"

"Yes."

"Does Danielle know?"

"Yes."

Bob's eyes flared. "Okay. We'll discuss that later. To stay on point, were there any witnesses to what happened with you and MacFarland?"

"Yes, I cold-cocked the guy in front of his father, and I told the cops that I did it. There's no way for me to weasel out of it, so don't try."

Bob pursed his lips. "The defenses to assault are self-defense, defense of others, and consent, as in an altercation. You sure it wasn't an altercation?"

"No, I attacked the guy. I'll take the punishment they give me, but I can't believe that they'd put me in prison for my first offense."

"No, and it's only a misdemeanor, though the sentence is two years. They're agreeing to bail, so that's good."

"How much was it? I'll reimburse you."

"I know you will. Now, in the arraignment, don't say anything unless the judge asks you a question. Let me do the talking, and when the judge asks, plead not guilty."

"Why?" Mike's stump throbbed. "I did it, Bob. I hit the guy and I'm guilty. Why would I plead not guilty?"

"We have to make the Commonwealth prove its case. Right now

they're not offering you a deal to reduce your charge, and until they do, we go with not guilty."

"I can't swear that I'm not guilty."

"They don't swear you in at these things." Bob scoffed. "Can't you work with me on this? Everybody who's guilty says he's not guilty. That's the system."

"It's still a court. It's still a judge. It's still my word."

"Mike, please. I don't have time to fight with you about it. I'm trying to preserve your legal rights down the line."

They both looked over as the police officer returned, unlocked the door, and stood in the threshold. "Folks, we're set up for the arraignment now. Please, come with me."

Bob left the room, and Mike followed him, with the officer gripping him by the arm. They walked down a carpeted hallway that had offices on the right side, and the officer opened a door onto a tiny room that was only slightly larger than Mike's cell. He assumed it was the anteroom to the courtroom, because it held no furniture except a television on a metal stand, with a camera mounted on top. The TV was on, though its screen had no picture, layered with multicolored static.

The police officer turned to Mike and Bob. "The Assistant District Attorney will be here in a minute, and District Judge Griffiths will appear momentarily."

Suddenly, a slight young man with short red hair slipped into the room and nodded to them both, and at the same time, the TV flickered. Onto its screen popped a female judge in a black robe, and it took Mike a moment to realize that this was the courtroom and the woman was an actual judge. She bore an uncanny resemblance to Judge Judy, though he could have imagined that, since she was on TV.

"I am District Judge Griffiths and we're here for the preliminary arraignment of Defendant Michael Scanlon." Judge Griffiths peered at them over black reading glasses. "Good evening, gentlemen."

The Assistant District Attorney stepped forward, in an oversized dark suit with a skinny black tie. "Judge Griffiths, I am Robin Durant, representing the Commonwealth."

"Thank you, counsel." Judge Griffiths turned to Mike. "Dr. Scanlon, you are represented by counsel, is that correct?"

"Yes," Mike answered, though it felt strange to be talking to a television, like justice on Skype.

Bob cleared his throat. "Your Honor, my name is Robert Ridgeway, and I'm here on behalf of Dr. Scanlon."

"Fine, thank you." Judge Griffith's gaze shifted to the Assistant District Attorney. "Mr. Durant, it is my understanding that the Commonwealth does not oppose bail in this matter."

"That is correct, Your Honor."

"Fine, thank you." Judge Griffith took off her glasses and focused on Mike. "Defendant Scanlon, the purpose of a preliminary arraignment is to make sure that you understand the charges against you. Are you currently under the influence of alcohol or drugs?"

"I'm taking medications for a recent surgery, but they do not affect my answers, if that's the point of the question."

"What are those medications?" Judge Griffith checked some papers on her desk.

"Antibiotics, steroids, and a prescription painkiller. I've come directly from the hospital, Your Honor."

"Fine, thank you. Let's begin. You are charged with a single count of violation of Title 18 of the Pennsylvania Crimes Code, Chapter 27, Section 2701, which defines simple assault as when someone 'attempts to cause or intentionally, knowingly or recklessly causes bodily injury to another.' Do you understand the charge?"

"Yes, I do." Mike reddened to think that the statute was the exact opposite of his Hippocratic oath.

"How do you plead?"

"Not guilty," Mike answered, because he had caused Bob enough trouble.

"You are charged with one count of making terroristic threats in violation of Title 18 of the Pennsylvania Crimes Code, Chapter 27, section 2706(a), which provides that a person commits the crime of terroristic threats if the person communicates, either directly or indirectly, a threat to: (1) commit any crime of violence with intent to terrorize another. Do you understand the charge against you?"

"Yes."

"How do you plead?"

"Not guilty."

"Defendant Scanlon, this concludes your arraignment. Your preliminary hearing will be held within ten days, at which time the Commonwealth will present its evidence against you. You are released on bail and you will be free as soon as your bill is paid. You must come back and appear at your preliminary hearing. Please sign the subpoena regarding your next court appearance, which will be provided you by the Assistant District Attorney. Thank you."

Later, Mike found himself in the heated passenger seat of Bob's Mercedes, being driven back to Foster Road to pick up his car. He was lost in his own thoughts while Bob took a business phone call, broadcasting the conversation through the car's sound system.

Bob was saying, "They'll go higher, I know it. He has authority for fifty under the insurance, so we should get at least that much . . ."

Mike turned his face to the window. Sara occupied his thoughts, and he had so many memories of her with Chloe that it was almost impossible to conjure one woman without the other. They turned onto Foster Street, which was still, dark, and quiet.

Bob was saying, "Why the hell are you even calling me with this, at this hour? You're not gonna make partner if you can't . . ."

Mike glanced ahead to his old house, which still had its Christmas lights up, probably using the eyehooks he had screwed inside the porch fascia, which had made Chloe and Sara laugh when they'd come home from the mall, with their Ironic Holiday Sweaters.

Chloe had said, *Babe, cupholders, really? It doesn't have to be perfect.*

Sara had said, *Leave him alone. They're surgically correct Christmas lights.*

Mike blinked away the memory. It had been the first year of the Ironic Holiday Sweater, and this past one would be the last. Pain lanced through his stump, and he couldn't wait to get to his car so he could take a pill.

Bob pulled over behind it, still on the phone. "Okay, fine, gotta go," he said, hanging up.

"Thanks for the ride and the help." Mike opened the car door. "I want to get over to Don's. I'll be home as soon as I can. Tell Danielle not to worry."

"I'll go with you."

"You don't have to." Mike was jonesing for the Oxy. "Go home to Danielle and the baby."

"They're fine. I'll call her and follow you to Don's."

"Okay, good." Mike closed the door, hustled to his car, and shook a pill out onto his lap.

He swallowed it dry, but it went down easy.

Chapter Forty-six

Mike sat in a kitchen chair at Don and Sara's, surrounded by a homey clutter. Bookbags lay on the floor like suburban tripping hazards, and the table was piled with skinny *Wimpy Kid* paperbacks, permission slips that somebody had to bring back to school, and reusable nylon lunch bags. Flat Stanley pictures and aging report cards blanketed the refrigerator, and multicolored magnetic letters on the freezer spelled, FOOD HAS CALORIES, DUMMY.

"I'm so sorry," Mike said again, as Don slumped opposite him. He had round brown eyes that were puffy tonight, a largish nose, and lips on the heavy side, which fit with his overall build, a teddy bear of a guy.

"I know you know how I feel, brother." Don's wet eye met his, a grim connection. "You're the only one who really knows. This isn't supposed to happen, is it?"

"No, not at all." Mike felt a wave of deep grief. "A buddy of mine in the Army would say this is unacceptable."

"It sure is." Don nodded, with a final sniffle. Light from the overhead fixture shone on his dark wavy hair, illuminating a nascent bald spot. He sat hunched over his beer in a forest green fleece from his company, Hambera Construction.

"How are the kids doing?"

"They cried, you can imagine." Don rubbed his beefy face. "They're finally asleep, and my parents are upstairs. Thank God for grandparents, huh?"

"Totally," Mike said, though Emily had none, which was one of the reasons he felt so lucky in Bob and Danielle. Bob was to his right, leaning against the counter with a beer. "You're gonna get through this."

"I am?"

"Yes. For the kids."

"Did you, for Emily?"

"Not yet." Mike didn't want to talk about himself. He hadn't told Don about his arrest when he saw how upset he was, at the front door. "Do they have any suspects? They must have. The Acme, after work, couldn't be busier."

"That's why I'm staying optimistic, and it's early." Don shook his head. "No weapon turned up yet. They're looking for witnesses, but nobody saw anything."

"How is that possible?"

"They didn't find her right away. The coroner hasn't come back with the time of death yet, but they told me how they think it went down."

Bob stepped to the table. "You don't have to talk about this, Don. We're friends, here to see if we can help."

"No, it's okay. I need a sounding board." Don waved him off. "Think about the timing. Sara called me about three thirty, when she was leaving school. She told me she had to run some errands, then she had to stop by the Acme."

"Did they find food shopping bags in the car? Had she gone shopping already?"

"No, she was attacked as she left the car to go into the store." Don winced. "Her purse was taken, but no jewelry. She still had her watch and earrings, which weren't expensive. But her wedding and engagement rings were, and she still had those."

"I'm trying to understand the motive. A purse? It doesn't figure."

"I know. We're not the richest people in this neighborhood and we don't look like we are, either. You know how many BMWs are in that lot, at any given time?"

"So assume it was random, a purse snatching. Do you think she would have fought him over it?"

"No way. She was smarter than that and she never had much cash on her, unless she was going by Staples for school supplies, on our dime."

Mike knew how that went. Chloe used to spend their money on classroom supplies all the time, like most teachers.

"Anyway, the police found one single knife wound, to the heart." Don took a slug of bottled beer. "It would have . . . done it, right?"

"Yes." Mike felt awful at the agony on Dan's expression, his forehead collapsed into lines. "She wouldn't have felt any pain, if that comforts you."

"It does." Don's heavy lower lip trembled. "The cops say he took her purse, sat her back in the driver's seat, shut the door behind her, then took off."

Mike tried to visualize it. "She would look like she was sitting in a car, maybe taking a nap."

"Right. An old man noticed that she was in the same position during all of his errands and he called the cops."

"What time was that?"

"About six thirty."

"Don't they have any surveillance tape? They must have cameras in that lot."

"They do, but snow covered them."

"Oh no." Mike let it sink in. "I wonder if it was someone she knew. She let them approach."

"Yeah, but she'd let anybody approach. She was so friendly." Don's eyes filmed, but he blinked tears away. "If somebody asked her what time it was, she would have told them, and it would have been too late."

"You're right." Mike could envision someone getting Sara's attention, then surprising her. He thought about what Linda had said, after DeMaria and Oldstein were killed. *Good people can't imagine evil. It catches us by surprise, and it always will.*

"It doesn't make sense to me, any of it." Don shook his head in bewilderment. "Why her? The cops asked me if she had any enemies, and I almost laughed. It couldn't be that it was targeted at her, could it?"

Suddenly Mike had an answer to the question. Now that Sara was dead, he wouldn't have any way of finding out the identity of Chloe's lover, so, if he reasoned backwards, maybe it was possible that Sara had been killed to prevent her from telling him. It sickened him to think he might have played a part in Sara's being murdered, but he had to own it, and he looked Don in the eye. "Don, this might be crazy. But I might know a reason that Sara was killed."

"What?"

"Chloe had an affair, when I was away. It lasted a month, then she shut it down. She was actually pregnant when she died."

Don's eyes widened. "Are you kidding?"

Suddenly Bob started coughing, his hand going to his chest. The veins in his neck bulged over the starchiness of his cutaway collar.

Mike looked over. "You okay?"

Don began to rise. "Need water?"

"No, I'm fine," Bob choked out, waving them off. He straightened up and crossed to the paper-towel dispenser. "It just went down the wrong way. Excuse me."

Mike figured that the news of Chloe's pregnancy shocked him. "Sorry, Bob, I should have told you, but we didn't get a chance. I told Danielle today, too."

"Was she upset?" Bob wiped his eyes over the sink, then turned on the water and leaned over to slurp some.

"Yes, but not as upset as I am." Mike turned back to Don. "To make a long story short, I went into Chloe's email and found the email address of her lover, which is Mac702@wahoo.com. I got into a fight today with a young guy who lives on my street, Pat MacFarland, because I thought it was him."

"A fight?" Don leaned forward, urgent. "You fought this Pat MacFarland?"

"Yes, I had sent Mac702 an email that said, I'm coming after you. So that means that Chloe's lover could have been on the lookout for me today, whether he's Pat MacFarland or not. Whoever he is, he could have been worried he was going to be exposed and he went after Sara."

"I'm not following you. Why would he go after Sara?"

"To keep her from telling me who Chloe had an affair with. He would have known that Sara was Chloe's best friend, and most men would figure that a woman would tell her best friend if she was having an affair."

"Of course." Don blinked. "They told each other everything. I heard about it when you and Chloe had a fight. I know what you fought about. You work too hard, and it drives her crazy."

"Right, I heard you don't stand up enough for yourself with your employees." Mike had never spoken so openly to Don before, and it struck him as sad that it had come too late. "You're too nice a boss. They take advantage of you."

"Exactly." Don paused. "But I didn't know Chloe was having an affair. Sara never told me that, and I'm not really surprised. I'm sure they had things they kept between them, and I get that."

"Me, too. It would make you think badly of Chloe, and Sara wouldn't want that." Mike nodded. "All right, so we know that Sara didn't tell you, but I think she knew. That's why I wanted to talk to her today."

"You were going to talk to her today?"

"Yes, I texted her. I was supposed to meet her today."

"She didn't mention that. Maybe she guessed you were going to talk to her about the affair. So she didn't tell me about the text because she hadn't told me about the affair. That means that Sara's killer could have been Chloe's boyfriend." Don's eyes widened. "You think Pat MacFarland killed Sara?"

"Possibly."

"Who is he, where does he live?" Don jumped to his work boots. "I'll go there, right now."

Bob stepped over, waving a hand. "Slow down. We don't have all the facts yet, and it's for the police to follow up."

Mike had to agree. "Right, let me explain. We're not sure it's him, all we know is the killer *could* be Mac702 and we don't know if Pat is Mac702. But we know that Mac702@wahoo.com is the email address of Chloe's lover, which gives us two new leads. The host site has to have the identity of whoever has registered that email address, and every computer has its own ISP address. We should tell the police and they can follow up."

"Wait, first, I could go check Sara's email to see if they talked about Pat MacFarland, or the affair, on her email. They probably did. You know how they were, texting and emailing all the time. The computer's upstairs." Don hurried to the threshold. "I could have the name of my wife's killer in her email."

Mike rose, too, his heartbeat quickening. "I should've searched Chloe's other email, but I went half-cocked this morning."

"When did you say they had the affair? I'll search by date."

"Last year, from Thanksgiving to Christmas. Want me to come with you?"

"No, stay here. I don't want to upset the kids."

Bob stopped Don with a hand motion. "Don, if this is too much to do tonight—"

"No, it's fine. Wait here." Don left the kitchen, and Bob crossed back to Mike.

"Listen, Mike, I want to find out who killed Sara as much as anybody, but I think you're speculating wildly. And no, I don't think running to the police like chickens with your heads cut off is prudent."

"Why?"

"You're all over the map. This afternoon you went to MacFarland's house and punched him in the face. You were convinced he was Chloe's lover, correct?"

"Yes."

"You still think that?" Bob lifted an eyebrow, skeptical. "Why would he kill somebody to keep it a secret he was having an affair? Or even that he got someone pregnant?"

"It's possible, I don't know." Mike felt himself waver, and his mind flipped through the possibilities. "Still I'd like to know where Pat was at the time Sara was killed, wouldn't you?"

"Be realistic. He was probably at a dentist's office or a lawyer's. I fully expect him to sue you for damages, on top of the criminal case."

Mike wasn't worried about himself, right now. "But what we're saying about Sara's murder is at least possible, isn't it? We should go to the police with it and let them figure it out. There's no downside, and it might lead to Sara's killer."

"There's a downside for you, after what you did today." Bob's frown deepened. "Are you going in there to accuse Pat of killing Sara? You could be adding a harassment charge to any litigation against you, and your credibility is at an all-time low tonight."

"Then I won't accuse him outright because I don't know for sure anyway, and I won't mention the assault charge unless they ask me."

"Still." Bob shook his head. "I don't think the police are in the habit of taking statements from people who were charged with assault the very same day. Why don't you sleep on it and see how you feel tomorrow?"

"I don't agree." Mike felt as if he was right, even after a day when his every instinct was proving wrong. "You don't defeat the enemy by sitting around, thinking about things. You act."

"Mike, there is no enemy." Bob stiffened. "You're not at war. You're home. You need to realize that, and with due respect, it's not your call. Sara is Don's wife, and it's his call."

"Then I'll ask him."

"What's the rush? He's been through the mill today, and now you got him riled up, thinking he's on the trail of his wife's killer." They both turned to the sound of heavy footsteps hurrying down the stairs, and Don entered the kitchen with a paper, his lips pursed in disappointment.

"Turns out Sara did know about the affair, and they talked about it in email, but they didn't say his name and it was only one time. You can see why." Don held out a printed copy of an email from Sara to Chloe.

"Thanks." Mike read, with Bob beside him:

C, You dropped a bomb on me last night. I love you and I know this is a hard time for you, but I have to say, I think you're making a big

mistake. Call me at lunch today and let's talk. Love you, no matter what.
S xoxoxo

PS From now on, don't put anything in print. Don and the boys use my computer.

"Damn." Mike felt a stab of regret, wishing Chloe had listened to Sara. "Your wife was a great friend."

"I know, right?" Don nodded, frustrated. "Still, go to the cops with what we know. I would go with you, but I don't want to leave the kids. I'll call the District Attorney and tell them you're coming. His name is Sanford James, he told me his assistants would be at the Clifton precinct house tonight. Okay?"

"Yes." Mike folded the email to bring as evidence, but Bob stepped over to Don.

"Don," he said, "I've told Mike that I'm not sure this is the best idea for him, at this time. I think his credibility is hurt because of his assault on Pat MacFarland today. It would look like harassment and could impair his case when it goes forward."

"No, it won't. I'm good to go." Mike appealed to Don, turning to him like a judge. "I might not be the most credible guy in the world, but if you pave the way with your phone call, they'll know what to expect. I don't want to sit on it overnight while some killer gets his ducks in a row. It's your call, but I'd move on it right now."

Chapter Forty-seven

Mike hurried with Bob to the Clifton Township Administration Building, an institutional box of gray stone, three stories tall, which housed the local police and other township agencies. The media clustered out front on the sidewalk, talking in groups and posing TV reporters in klieglights. Boxy newsvans lined the curb, and traffic slowed to gape or honk for fun.

Mike kept his sleeve tucked in his pocket as they approached. "I wonder when was the last time Clifton had a murder case."

"Three years ago, there was a murder after a domestic dispute." Bob strode along, his topcoat flying open. "This neighborhood has a higher per capita income than Wilberg, and the school district's better, but we didn't buy here because I wanted new construction."

Mike felt as if he needed to reestablish a rapport, since the disagreement at Don's. "I appreciate your help tonight."

"Happy to do it. But let me do the talking in there, okay?"

"All right," Mike answered reluctantly, as they hurried past the reporters, climbed the steps to the entrance, and went through the glass door, which led to a rectangular anteroom ringed by blue chairs. Two township employees in ID badges sat in the corner drinking coffee, but Mike crossed to the Plexiglas window on the right, which was staffed by a female police officer. He was about to speak to her when Bob cut in front.

"Excuse me," he said in a low tone, glancing over his shoulder. He introduced himself and Mike, then added, "I'm an attorney with The Ridgeway Group. District Attorney Sanford James is expecting us."

"Excuse me, Mr. Ridgeway." The officer rose, vanished from the window, then returned after a moment. "Sir, the door to your right will buzz. Come in and I'll meet you."

"Thanks." Bob and Mike were admitted into a spacious, well-lit squad room that contained a honeycomb of gray cubicles, their walls plastered with kids' school pictures, peewee football leagues, calendars, and official notices. A white dry-erase board hung between two windows in the back, with black Sharpie scribbles: Jim S. On call 2/7 through 3/4. Dave E. On call 3/5 through 2/11. They followed the officer down a hallway with doors marked INTERVIEW ROOM A, B, and C. The door to Interview Room C hung open, and the officer showed them inside.

"Here we go," she said, gesturing to a compact young woman in a slate gray pantsuit, who stood up, flashed a professional smile, and extended her hand.

"Hello, gentlemen, I'm Jane Marcinko, an Assistant District Attorney working on the Sara Hambera case." Jane was attractive, with hazel eyes and strawberry blonde hair, cut short. Freckles covered her small nose, and the only flashy part of her generally conservative demeanor were glasses with a cherry red bridge and stems. "I was asked by District Attorney James to meet with you, as he had to leave. I also spoke with Don Hambera on the phone, so I know the situation."

"Excellent." Bob paused. "Wait, didn't you go to law school with Mary Trestlemenn?"

"Yes, we were at Villanova together."

"I thought so." Bob smiled. "Mary works for me. I met you at her wedding last month. You played a sonata on the piano, right? An original composition?"

"Right! I remember you, now." Jane's eyes lit up behind her colorful glasses. "Oh no, my playing was off that night."

"Not at all." Bob grinned. "You clerked for the Third Circuit, as I recall. Did you enjoy your clerkship?"

"Loved it." Jane smiled, and Mike hid his impatience with the small talk, though Bob was only warming up.

"Clerking is such a valuable experience. Everybody should do it."

"I agree." Jane nodded. "Did you?"

"No, I had to work, but I regret it, one of my two regrets in life. One, that I didn't clerk and, two, that I don't play jazz piano."

"Ha! Then I'm two for two."

"You play jazz piano, too?"

Mike couldn't take it another minute. "To cut to the chase, I have the email—"

"Mike, please." Bob glanced at Mike with a stiff smile, then turned back to Jane. "Jane, Dr. Scanlon is my brother-in-law, and he just returned from Afghanistan, where he served as an Army doctor."

Jane turned to Mike. "It's an honor to meet you, though I'm sorry about these circumstances. Don told me why you're here, on the phone."

Bob interjected, "Then you know that we have the email of a man who was having an affair with Dr. Scanlon's late wife, and Dr. Scanlon believes there's a possibility that whoever murdered Sara Hambera did so because she knew about the affair and wanted to keep it quiet."

Mike shook his head. "Wait, no, I think it's more than a possibility, it seems likely to me. These women were best friends, and the email shows that Sara knew and disapproved of the affair. Here, take a look." He pulled the email from his inside pocket and handed it over, and Jane's eyes went back and forth as she read it, her lips flattening, then she looked up.

"Do you have any evidence to support this theory, Dr. Scanlon?"

"It's common sense, and it provides a motive for an apparently random crime. I'm hoping that you can find out who is registered to the email address of Mac702@wahoo.com or trace the ISP address to find the identity."

"We could find that ISP address without a problem, but that

would take us only to a private network, business, or large private service provider, like Comcast."

"That's a start, isn't it?" Mike asked, encouraged.

"It's a start that doesn't lead anywhere. Once we find out the ISP address, then we have to penetrate the private company, or Comcast, to find out to whom in the company or network the ISP address belonged. To do that we would need a court order."

"Okay, so get one."

"The court will deny any request for such an order, in this case. The same goes for trying to subpoena the information from the host site. We'd lose."

"Why?"

"Think about the logic of the request, and you'll understand." Jane eased her glasses up higher onto her nose. "You're asking me to find out the identity of Mac702, because you believe that he murdered Sara so that the affair would remain a secret. You have no factual basis for that, only your speculation."

"But the murder occurred right after I sent him an email, saying I was coming after him." Mike caught Bob's eye and didn't mention the assault case. "So he knew the jig was up."

"That establishes a temporal connection between the sending of your email and the murder, but not a logical connection. That's not proof, in other words."

"I can't get the proof if I can't get the information." Mike thought hers was a circular argument. "Once we find out who Mac702 is, then we know if there's a connection."

"It doesn't work that way under the Constitution. There's a privacy interest that needs to be protected."

"The privacy of a killer?"

"You're putting the rabbit in the hat. We don't have any evidence that Mac702 is a killer." Jane cocked her head. "If your wife had been murdered, that would be a different case. Then I might have a factual basis for believing that Mac702 was a suspect. But that's not the case we're positing. This is the murder of a friend of hers, which is too tenuous a connection." Jane opened her hands, palms up. "I wouldn't even ask for an order in this case."

"What's the harm in asking? Why not go to court and see if the judge grants it?"

"If we go to court and ask for an order without a factual basis, we undermine our office."

Mike bristled. "Aren't you supposed to be thinking about Sara? And justice?"

Bob shot him a warning glance, but Mike ignored it, and Jane seemed undaunted anyway, continuing her argument.

"We are thinking about Sara and we're mindful of our duty to represent all of the citizens of the Commonwealth. We serve none of them if we run into court and lose."

Mike didn't get it. "Do you only fight battles you can win? Don't you sometimes fight a battle because it's the right thing to do?"

"Mike." Bob waved him off. "Enough."

"Enough what?" Mike couldn't let it go. "Sara matters. She had a family, she taught middle school. She was a person, a mother. This theory gives you a motive when there doesn't seem to be any at all. Isn't that worth investigating?"

Bob interjected, "Jane didn't say she wasn't investigating. She said she's not going to court with the email."

Jane rose, nodding in Bob's direction. "That's right. Please rest assured that we are investigating."

"What are you doing to investigate?"

Bob turned to Mike, his expression tense. "Mike, they're doing what they need to do."

"Bob, I'm allowed to ask a question." Mike controlled his temper. "She's a public servant. She's supposed to account to us. It's her job."

"Gentlemen." Jane raised her hands like a referee, then turned to Mike with a stern gaze. "Dr. Scanlon, you're incorrect. It's my job *not* to discuss this case or this investigation with you, the reporters outside, or a hotdog seller on the street. All of that information is confidential from third parties, who have no association with the case."

"I'm not a hotdog seller. Sara and Don are friends of mine, and Sara was my wife's best friend. Don sent me here."

"Nevertheless, you're not immediate family. We wouldn't discuss our investigation in any depth, even with Don." Jane set the email on the table. "Tell you what, I'll meet with District Attorney James and discuss this information with him. He or I will get back to you, if need be. Thank you for coming in."

"Thank you, Jane." Bob flashed a smile, then went to the door. "Mike, we have to go."

"Thanks." Mike turned and left the room, but Bob stormed ahead of him and out the door. They hustled past the reporters, and Mike didn't bother to chase Bob, who stalked ahead, climbed into his Mercedes, and drove out of the lot.

"See you at home," Mike said, to himself. He'd struck out with Bob, but it was Sara who mattered to him.

One was having a hissy fit, and the other was dead.

Chapter Forty-eight

"Hi, everybody." Mike walked in the front door, and Bob was already standing in the living room, evidently giving Danielle an earful.

"Mike, are you okay?" Danielle looked up worried, her mouth open slightly. She was already dressed for bed in a red cashmere robe, and she'd been stitching her floral needlepoint under her magnifying lamp.

"I'm fine, thanks." Mike shed his coat and went to the closet to hang it up.

"But you *assaulted* someone?" Danielle rolled up her needlepoint, set it aside, and rose. "That's not like you."

"He could be the one, Danielle." Mike closed the closet door and faced them. "He could be Mac702."

"Then you made a scene at the police station? That isn't like you, either, not at all."

"I didn't make a scene."

Bob snorted. "You certainly did. You embarrassed the both of us."

"I asked a few questions. I pressed her."

"No, you were belligerent. Her friend works for me. They'll be gossiping about us all night."

"So what? Sara was murdered."

"I like to maintain some decorum as boss. I like my associates to think well of me and my family, and I don't need them to hear that you acted out with an Assistant District Attorney." Bob flushed, angrily. "And it's not because of Sara, it's really because of Chloe. You want to find out who she was sleeping with."

"Okay, that, too. I'll cop to that. It's both. I want to get to the bottom of it. Don't you?"

"The police are investigating, and so is the Assistant District Attorney. What more do you want?"

Mike gave up. He wanted to make peace, but he only knew how to make war. "Look, let's not try and talk it over now. Sara was murdered today, and we're all on edge."

Danielle's forehead creased, and she tugged her robe around her. "But I feel like something's happening to you, Mike. Please don't take this the wrong way, but I think you might want to see a therapist."

"I don't need a shrink, thanks." Mike felt a sharp cramp travel up his missing arm.

"What about at rehab? I saw online, at the VA website, that they have a support group there. You can call and set up the appointments, or see a professional on your own."

"I know, I will. I just got home." Mike tried to stay calm. "How's the baby?"

Bob scowled. "Don't dismiss my wife. She loves you. She asked you a question."

"And I asked her one, and I love her, too." Mike wanted to hear about the one good thing in his life, Emily. "I just want to know how the baby is. Is that a crime?"

Bob threw his topcoat on the chair, piqued. "What the hell, Mike?"

"The baby's fine," Danielle answered. Her lower lip trembled, but Mike couldn't tell if she was hurt or angry, or both.

"Look, I'm sorry, Danielle. I appreciate everything you're doing. Don't think I don't, because I do."

"I understand, but you need help and you're not getting it. Don't you think you should have done that today, instead of going to that boy's house?"

"That boy is a man." Mike grimaced at the pain, or maybe at having to account for his time.

"But you're making matters worse for yourself, don't you think?"

Bob interjected, "That's *exactly* what's happening. I tell him to plead not guilty, he gives me a hard time. I tell him to let me do the talking to the Assistant District Attorney, and he picks a fight with her." He pointed at Mike. "You're worried about the enemy, Mike? You're your own worst enemy."

Danielle recoiled. "Don't be that way, honey."

"What way?" Bob threw up his hands. "We have to get on the right foot here." He faced Mike again. "It only takes a second to get a criminal record, then what are you gonna do? Who's gonna hire you then?"

Danielle placed a hand on Bob's arm. "Honey, don't pressure him. He's not himself." She turned to Mike. "Mike, we have to be honest with each other. Bob is right, we're getting off on the wrong foot, but I know it's not you, it's the painkillers. The Oxycontin. You're taking ten pills a day, when you're supposed to be cutting back and taking half that."

"How do you know how many I'm taking?" Mike recoiled, surprised.

"I saw the discharge instructions."

"The ones on my dresser?" Mike felt his temper flicker.

"Yes, I had to clean in there, and I saw the papers, so I read them, because I'm worried about you. I'm trying to help you."

Bob interjected, "We both are, but you're fighting us."

Danielle nodded, frowning. "I admit, I counted the pills. I had seen on the bottle that there were thirty when they were prescribed, and if you were taking one every twelve hours, as prescribed, you should have had a lot more left."

Mike reddened, defensive. "Danielle, it's one thing to see papers on my dresser and another to go in my medicine chest."

Bob scoffed. "May I remind you that *your* medicine chest is in *our* house?"

Danielle's eyes widened, plaintive. "Mike, I didn't go in your medicine chest. I saw the pill bottle when you dropped the pills this morning. Remember, when we were on the computer? I respected your privacy, I did."

Bob shook his head. "Neither of you have any business talking about privacy when you were hacking into Chloe's email. That's what started this whole thing."

"We weren't *hacking*." Danielle glared at Bob, and he scowled back.

"You were, too. You shouldn't have. You should have let it lie. You're only adding fuel to his fire."

Mike raised his hand. He didn't want them fighting because of him. "Please, don't fuss. I'm sorry I started this, and you're right. Mea culpa."

Danielle's eyes shone wetly. "It's okay."

Bob faced him, but his forehead remained knit. "Apology accepted."

"Good, thanks." Mike wanted to move on. "Now, if somebody tells me where those things are from my old house, I'll leave you both alone, so you can get to bed."

"What things?" Danielle asked.

Bob cocked his head. "You mean in the storage unit?"

"No, you said you kept our personal things in the house, didn't you?" Mike had thought about it on the ride home. "When you told me how Chloe's laptop got broken."

"Oh, right, there are a few boxes in the closet of my home office."

"Can I look through them? Just tell me where. The office is next to my room, isn't it?"

"Now? It's so late." Bob frowned, and so did Danielle, their foreheads like his-and-her masks of malcontent.

"Mike," Danielle said, her tone gentle. "Don't you want to get some sleep?"

"No, thanks. I don't feel tired at all. It's almost morning in Landstuhl."

"But you're home now."

"I'm aware of that, but I'm still in its time zone."

"Why do you want to look through the boxes?"

Mike was so tired of explaining himself. "Because Sara was murdered, and I want to know who did it, and I have a theory that Chloe's lover killed Sara. If that's true, it's on me because I sent him an email, threatening him. So I'm going to look in every box upstairs and go through every single picture, credit card receipt, and old telephone bill to see if I can figure out who Mac702 is, because he got my wife pregnant and killed her best friend."

Danielle shook her head. "Don't you think the police will do that?"

"I don't know what they'll do, and there's no reason I can't help out. If I don't find anything that helps in the boxes from the closet, I'll drive over to the storage unit and look there. I won't sleep until I know I've done all I can do. It's all I can think about."

"Can I just say that I'm worried that you're, kind of, losing it? Getting obsessed, out of jealousy, with this Mac702?"

"If I am, I don't care." Mike flashed on Afghanistan, lying awake in his rack, night after night. "Chloe was all I used to think about and that was taken away when I found out she was pregnant, but this isn't about me anymore. Now I want to know if Mac702 killed Sara. So I'm obsessed, it's true, because I loved my wife and I loved her best friend, yes, I'm obsessed, completely."

Danielle blinked, and Bob had gone quiet.

Mike realized they thought he was crazy, but so be it.

Maybe he was.

Chapter Forty-nine

Mike closed the lid of the third and last box, having gone through wedding photos, passports, old pictures, sketches, their marriage license, recent bills, their new wills, life-insurance policies, an old deed, an old house-insurance policy, and three baby albums that Chloe had made while he was deployed. None of it had contained anything that related to the identity of Mac702.

Mike sat cross-legged on the rug, sad and exhausted. Every task was made more difficult with one arm, and his stump was killing him, swelling from the activity, but he still wanted to look through Chloe's black-lacquered jewelry box. She used to put receipts, bills, and anything she thought was important inside, and he lifted the lid. The jewelry glittered in the light of the desk lamp, a tangled pile of gold chains, earrings, and necklaces along with old photos, some receipts, and some sea-glass beads.

Mike's throat caught at the sight. He had given her a lot of the jewelry and remembered it on her. The delicate rose gold chain that rested on her collarbones, the long garnet earrings that got tangled in her hair, the string of silvery Tibetan bells that jingled when she moved. He looked away, to the pile of wrinkly receipts on top of the rings. He checked each one, but they were from the bookstore, the dry cleaners, and a shoe repair. He was about to close the lid when he spotted an ornate gold bangle he hadn't seen before. The gold had scrolled etching, gleaming with a richness that was unmistakably eighteen-karat.

Mike's mouth went dry. He'd never seen the bracelet before and he hadn't given it to her, and she certainly hadn't bought it for herself. She didn't shop much since Emily was born, and even so, this looked too expensive for her to have bought herself, or for Sara to have bought for her. At eighteen-karat gold, it could've cost a grand. He realized with a start that Mac702 must have given it to her.

Mike got up, grabbed a Kleenex, and wrapped it around the bracelet. The police might be able to get fingerprints from it, or they could go to jewelry stores in the area and ask if they sold any bracelets like it in November or December of last year, and to whom. It seemed like a great lead, and he'd bring the bracelet to the police tomorrow. He went to the door, buoyed by his success and getting his second wind.

He'd go through that storage unit, if it took him all night.

Chapter Fifty

Mike didn't get home until early the next morning, but the kitchen lights were on, so he knew the household was already awake. "I'm home," he said, hanging up his coat, and even that simple act set nerves jangling through his chest, shoulders, and neck. His stump needed to be rested and elevated, but that wasn't happening anytime soon. He headed into the kitchen.

"Hi, Mike." Bob sat at the table in his plaid robe, catty-corner to Emily in her high chair, and Danielle was on the baby's other side, in her robe too, looking at him with concern.

"You poor thing, were you in that storage shed all night? Did you find anything?"

"Not there, no. Hi, Emily." Mike smiled at Emily, who squirmed at the sight of him. She looked adorable in a fuzzy yellow sleeper with an embroidered giraffe, and her amber curls were flattened on one side, as if she'd slept on them.

"Aw, Emily." Danielle leaned over to her. "Emily, it's just Daddy. Daddy's home. Say, hi Daddy."

Emily's eyes were a confused blue, as if she couldn't decide whether to laugh or cry, and Mike remembered the boxes of her baby pictures from last night. There were so many photos he hadn't seen before, and looking through them, he felt as if he'd vicariously experienced her growing from baby to toddler.

"Emily, it's Daddy. I'm happy to see you. How are you?"

Emily blinked, puckering her lips and drawing backwards, so that her soft chin vanished into the folds of her neck. Her hands were slick with butter from scrambled eggs on her plate. "No," she said, pointing at the window.

"No?" Mike asked, not understanding.

"She said 'snow.'" Danielle gestured at the windows, where another few inches had fallen, clumping on the shrubs and filling in the deer tracks. "It's hard to understand her if you're not around her. You'll get the hang of it."

Bob chuckled. "Danielle's the family interpreter."

"Right, snow," Mike said, but Emily was looking away. He crossed to the coffeemaker, slid out the pot, and poured himself a mug. An under-cabinet TV played the local news on low volume, and a weatherman in a bowtie stuck a yardstick into a snowdrift. Mike had practically frozen in the storage unit last night. "So how are you all?"

"Great," Danielle answered, beginning to rise. "You want eggs or pancakes? Bob had both."

"No, please sit. I ate at a diner." Mike waved Danielle back into her seat. "Again, I'm sorry about last night."

"We are, too." Danielle smiled in a reassuring way. "It's over. Families fuss, it's normal."

Bob sipped his coffee. "Perfectly normal."

"Thanks," Mike said, relieved. "Did you hear anything from Don or the police?"

"No."

"I did find something in Chloe's jewelry box, a bangle that I think she was given by Mac702." Mike sipped his coffee. "I'm going to turn it over to the police today."

"A bangle?" Danielle lifted an eyebrow.

"Really?" Bob brought his mug and plate to the sink. "What does that tell you?"

"I figure the police can go to the jewelry stores and ask if they

236 | Lisa Scottoline

sold any bracelets like it in November or December of last year, or maybe they can get fingerprints from it."

"They can do that on *Castle*." Danielle watched Emily, who was pressing scrambled eggs into her mouth. "The police can do so much, nowadays. They can get latent prints and even partial prints. They can even get fingerprints from paper, did you know that?"

Bob rolled his eyes, turning from the sink. "Nancy Drew, reporting in."

"Hmph," Danielle said lightly, smiling at Emily. "Emily, you finished your breakfast? Did you like that?"

"No," Emily answered, then laughed.

Mike smiled. "Was that a no or a snow?"

"I think it was a no." Danielle wiggled Emily's foot in its non-skid footie. "You little sillyhead."

Mike winked at Emily impulsively, and she tried to wink back, scrunching up her nose and squinting both eyes. It was so great and unexpected, he almost laughed. He winked again, and Emily winked back again.

Danielle looked over with a smile. "Emily, Daddy's flirting with you. Can you wink? Wink back at your Daddy." She winked in an exaggerated way. "Like this, see? Wink your eye."

"I do it." Emily scrunched up her nose and squinted both eyes, and they all laughed.

"Good job!" Mike said, completely charmed.

Bob kissed the baby on her head. "I gotta go grab a shower. I have to go to the office today, after church. Self-employment is a trip, isn't it? You always have a job, but you *always* have a job. Tell me how the Eagles do, will you?"

"I can't, I'm going to see about work, too." Mike had been trading emails with Jim. "I'm meeting with Jim and Lyon at the office today."

Bob smiled, pleasantly. "Good. Back in the saddle, eh?"

Danielle smiled, too. "Oh, that's wonderful, Mike."

"Thanks." Mike sensed they were all on their best behavior. "I'll know more after rehab about what I can and can't do, but I want to understand my options."

Bob patted his shoulder. "I hear that. You'll come with us to church, right?"

Mike flashed on the church where he'd fallen, trying to hold Emily. He thought of Chloe's casket. Phat Phil, Oldstein, and now Sara. "Uh, I don't know. I haven't been in so long."

"So what?" Bob frowned. "You're welcome, you know that."

"What about Emily? Do you get a sitter?"

"No, we take her."

"Emily goes to church?" Mike kept the surprise from his tone. Chloe would have approved, but he was getting a better idea. "Guys, why don't you two go to church and leave Emily home with me? I'll take care of her."

"Really?" Bob asked.

"Sure, why not? It gives you guys a break."

"Don't be silly." Danielle rose, tying her bathrobe tighter, but it wasn't loose. "We don't need a break, and we like to take her. Everyone loves to see her, even Father Hernandez."

Mike was about to give in, to make them happy, but he noticed Emily's gaze fixed on him, and in the next second, she scrunched up her nose in another Emily-wink. It was so cute he felt his heart jump, which he knew wasn't medically possible. "No, really, I'd like to stay here with her. I've hardly seen her."

"You sure?" Danielle lingered beside the high chair, resting her hand protectively on the plastic tray. "She'll have separation anxiety. I don't leave her very often."

"It's only for an hour or so." Mike wanted to be closer to Emily and he had to start somewhere.

"It's not easy, you know."

"Nobody's shooting at us, are they?" Mike smiled more confidently than he truly felt. "What's the worst that could happen?"

Chapter Fifty-one

Mike had expected Emily to be upset after Danielle and Bob left, but not *this* upset. He sat cross-legged on the floor, and she stood in her yellow sleeper at the front door, pounding it with her little fists, as if she could break it down and run after them. She cried hysterically, her face turning red, her eyes pouring tears, and her nose streaming.

"Mommy!" Emily sobbed. "Daddy!"

"It's okay, Emily. They'll be back soon, you'll see." Mike kept his tone soothing, though she couldn't hear him anyway. She'd burst into tears the moment they closed the door, twenty minutes ago, and showed no signs of flagging. Mike had no idea how to calm her down and had never felt more useless in his life.

"Mommy! Daddy!"

"Don't cry, Emily. Want to read a book, honey?" Mike picked up a book called *Spot Goes to School,* from a pile on the floor. "Look, sweetheart, here's a book about Spot the dog. The teacher wants to sing, but where's Spot? Look, open the flap and here's Spot. Aw, Spot is sad because he can't sing." Mike rejected that as unhelpful, picked up another book, and held it up.

"Here's one about Spot at school. What did you bring, Spot?" Mike lifted the flap. "Look, Emily. Spot brought his bone!" He held the book high, but she didn't turn around, so he turned the page. "Here's Spot on the playground. Where's Spot, Emily?" He opened the flap. "There's Spot, in the tree!"

Emily bawled harder.

Mike gave up on Spot, found a book about cats, and held it up, shifting into her field of vision. "Emily, look at the cats. Don't cry." He opened to the first page. "Here's a picture of a cat and a lion. See?"

Emily hiccupped tears, inconsolable, and Mike was sad, for her. He could see that she thought her parents had just walked out on her, never to come back, and he couldn't imagine how awful that felt, until he remembered that his father had done just that. He never wanted Emily to feel that desolate, ever.

"Aw, honey, don't be sad, I'm here, Daddy's here, and we can read books and have fun. Just give it a chance." Mike heard himself begging, but that was fine, if it worked. He turned a page in the cat book. "Look, Emily, here's cats cleaning themselves. They lick their feet to make sure they're nice and clean." He spotted a Maine Coon Cat that looked exactly like Jake. "Look, Emily, here's Jake the cat. Remember Jake, our cat?"

Emily looked over miserably, resting her hands on the front door. She didn't stop crying, but Mike could see he had gotten her attention. Last night, he'd seen plenty of photos of Emily with Jake, and it was possible that she remembered him.

"Hi, Jake the cat. I love you, Jake. Jake was a great cat." Mike turned the page, and there was a picture of a calico cat playing with a mouse toy. "Look at the cat with his toy! I love cats. Do you like cats, Emily?"

Emily sniffled, but her sobs slowed, and Mike sensed the cat book was doing the trick. He turned the next page. "Emily, look at the kitten. There's two baby kittens. This is an Abyssinian cat and kittens." He eyed the photo of a mother cat with two kittens and edited it on the fly. "There's two kittens with their daddy. Look at the kittens with their daddy. They love each other. Isn't that so nice?"

Emily looked over, heaving a final sniffle. Tears wet her cheeks and mucus leaked from her nose, but her crying fit was ending.

Mike wanted to jump for joy, but he was learning that he did better if he stayed calm. He didn't want to jinx himself, like a pitcher on a lucky streak.

"Emily, look at the cat, rubbing on the person's leg. Jake did that. I love cats." Mike turned the page, which showed a picture of a lion. Emily had only one hand on the door now and was trying to see the book, so he turned the page. "Here's the lion, king of the jungle." He worked the propaganda angle. "He's the daddy lion, and he takes care of his family. The daddy lion loves his family."

Emily toddled over, keeping her distance but focusing on the book with teary eyes, and Mike felt so relieved that she was finally relaxing around him, and he turned the page. "This shows a leopard. It says that leopards live in Africa. Wow, I love leopards." He kept his voice warm and happy. "Look at all the spots on this leopard. It's just like Jake. All the cats are alike, whether they're big or little. I love them all."

Emily stood silently beside him, wavering slightly, her arms hanging loosely at her sides and her eyes brimming, though no new tears were flowing. Mike flipped to the next page. "Here we go. These are cats that live in the forest. Aren't they cute? Here's one who lives in South America. He sleeps in the trees during the day."

Emily pointed a goopy finger at the page. "Big."

"Right, big." Mike realized she had spoken to him, for the third time in her life, after "no" and "snow." He wanted to keep his streak going. "He's a big cat. This is a whole book about big cats. Isn't that so nice? I love big cats." He turned the page, skipped the scary cheetah, and went ahead. "Oh look at this. Here's a Scottish wildcat, an African wildcat, and an Indian Desert cat. There are so many different kinds of big cats in the world."

Emily kept her glistening eyes on the page, but plopped down, tucking her legs under her, and Mike couldn't believe it. She sat right next to him, but he acted natural and turned to a picture of an orange Persian cat. "Look at this cat. He has eyes that are nice and orange, aren't they? I think he's beautiful. Don't you?"

Suddenly, Emily got up, toddled over to the book pile, and started to paw through them. "I want metamin."

"Which one, honey?" Mike asked, but Emily found a small white book and was having trouble with the pages. He shifted toward her and saw its cover. "Oh, *The Tale of Benjamin Bunny*." He realized she'd been saying Benjamin. "I like Benjamin, too. Would you like me to read that book to you?"

"Yes." Emily handed him the book, and Mike wanted to cheer. He was up to four words. They were actually talking to each other.

"I would love to read it to you, honey. Let's read about Benjamin." Mike shifted over, rested his back against the couch, and opened the first page. "Oh, look at this little brown bunny rabbit. That's Benjamin, I bet." He began to read, and by the third sentence, Emily was standing beside him, looking down at the book, listening. He continued, and Emily sat down beside him, quietly, but he didn't show any reaction. He merely kept on, and it struck him that he was reading to Emily for the first time, his first "first." There were tears in his eyes when he read, The End.

"Again!" Emily said suddenly, and Mike smiled, delighted.

"You want me to read it again?"

"Yes." Emily looked up at him with shiny blue eyes, and Mike's throat caught.

"Great, let's read it again." He went to the beginning of the book and started to read, this time showing her different things in the illustrations. He noticed her eyelids getting heavy, so he pulled a big pillow from the couch onto the floor, leaned back, and rested his head, leaving room for her. "Honey, let's lie down. Put your head here, and we'll finish reading about Benjamin, okay?"

Mike held his breath, fearing he'd pushed his luck, but Emily scooted down, stretched out her little legs, and plopped her curly head beside him on the pillow, an act so trusting and tender that he fell completely in love with her. His heart filled with a happiness he'd never known.

Mike read until Emily fell asleep, her miniature chest rising and falling, then he closed the book and let his gaze travel over her beautiful face, taking in her features as if he were memorizing them, like the curl of her eyelashes, the hillock of her nose, and the gentle curve of her cheeks, where her tears had dried. She really did look like some sort of angel, a golden child with a halo of blonde curls. He felt so blessed to have her, and he understood as an epiphany that the state of fatherhood was a state of grace. He vowed silently, then and there, that he would love Emily, take care of her, and always put her first, until his very last breath.

He drifted off with peace in his heart and a smile on his face, feeling that, in a way, he had gone to church, after all.

But he woke up to the sound of screaming.

Chapter Fifty-two

"No!" someone shrieked, and Mike shot up from the floor, with a thousand panicked thoughts. Insurgents. IEDs. Gunfire. Wounded. He came to his senses in a flash. Bob and Danielle were charging up the stairs, toward the sound of crying.

"Emily!" Mike yelled, running up the stairs after them. He didn't know what was going on.

"Thank God, thank God!" Danielle dropped to her knees on the landing, holding a crying Emily. "Thank God she didn't fall, thank God."

"She's all right." Bob stood panting on the stairwell, his hand resting on the banister. His chest heaved up and down in his suit. "Everything's all right."

"I must've fallen asleep." Mike sank to the step in the middle of the stairwell, against the wall, his stump aching. "We were on the floor, side-by-side, reading—"

"You can't *do* that!" Bob shouted, whipping his head around to glare down at Mike. "You can't *fall asleep* on her. When we came home, she was at the top of the stairs, crying. She could have fallen down the stairs. She could have broken her neck!"

"Oh my God, I'm so sorry." Mike swooned with the horror of what could have happened. "I'm so sorry, I should've realized—"

"What happened?" Bob shouted. "Did you *nod out*? Was it the drugs? What? Are you a freaking *addict now*?"

"No, it wasn't the drugs," Mike said, defensive. "I was tired and I fell asleep. I shouldn't have, but I'm not a drug addict."

"I don't know what your problem is!" Bob's upper lip curled with scorn. "You begged us to leave her with you and you fell asleep on her. You're with her for two hours and you can't even stay awake? What's the *matter* with you?"

Danielle held Emily close as Emily wailed, full-bore. "Bob, you're making it worse, stop it." She turned to Mike, with frightened tears. "Mike, you can't fall asleep when you're babysitting, if she's not in her crib. I told you, you have to keep an eye on her. Why do you think we babyproofed everything? She's an active child."

"I know, I know." Mike sighed, miserably. "It was a mistake, and it won't happen again."

Bob scoffed. "You're damn right it won't! We'll think long and hard before we leave you alone with her again!"

Mike recoiled. "She's my child, Bob. I know I made a mistake—"

"A mistake that could have *killed* her!"

"I know that—"

"So don't let yourself off the hook so easy!"

"I'm not." Mike wanted to go to Emily, but she was crying too hard. "Emily, it's all right. Everything is all right. Daddy's here. Daddy loves you."

Bob snorted. "What a joke."

"Bob!" Danielle's eyes flared. "That's enough. Go cool down. I don't want you to say anything you'll regret."

"I won't regret any of it." Bob stormed up the stairs past Danielle and Emily, and the tension went down in the stairwell. The only sounds were Emily's sobs and Mike's heart, beating in his own ears.

"I really am sorry, Danielle," Mike softened his tone. "We had fun, we read. She fell asleep, I fell asleep. I assumed she'd stay asleep, but that was the wrong assumption."

"Was that the painkillers? Tell me the truth."

"No, absolutely not," Mike answered, then a wave of guilt washed over him. "I don't know—" he added, without finishing the sentence.

"You don't know what?" Danielle rubbed Emily's back. "Talk to me. We need to be honest with each other."

"Okay, the meds could have been a factor, but I didn't sleep at all last night, and I just felt so peaceful after she fell asleep that I just conked out myself." Mike looked at Emily, who was looking down at him. Her frightened eyes told him that her trust in him had vanished, which killed him. "Emily, I love you and I'm sorry. I took a nap and that was not a good thing for Daddy to do."

Emily twisted away, and Danielle held her tighter. "Her diaper smells. Did you change it?"

"No, she was fine when we fell asleep."

"Oh." Danielle stood up, her lips an unhappy line. "What time are you going to the office? I thought you said one o'clock, and it's almost eleven."

"Oh, right." Mike checked his watch. "I better get going, if I'm going to stop at the police station."

"That's what I thought. I'm going to change her diaper. See you later." Danielle walked down the hallway with Emily, and Mike felt as if his heart had been torn from his chest.

"See you later, Emily!" he called after her.

Chapter Fifty-three

Mike sat in his car, stricken, having parked a few blocks away from Bob and Danielle's. The street was cold, sunny, and lined with brick McMansions. The sidewalks were blown, the driveways plowed, and the cars snug in their garages, with fake windows. His head was pounding, his stump throbbing. He would have taken another pill, but it was risky to go to the police station in an altered state, and he didn't have that many left.

Are you a freaking addict now?

Mike had to call Don about the bangle. He could have called from the house, but he had practically fled. He reached for his Black-Berry, but he didn't start the car because he couldn't negotiate driving and dialing with one hand. He pressed in Don's number and composed himself while the call connected. "Don, how are you doing, buddy?"

"Hanging in." Don sounded better than last night. "How're you?"

"Fine, thanks. Did you hear anything new from the cops?"

"No, or the ADA either. I called twice about MacFarland, and they said they'll look into it."

"Good. Listen, I found something else that could help." Mike told him about the bangle, which was in its Kleenex inside his parka. "I don't want to get your hopes up, but it's possible there's fingerprints on it, or they can investigate stores that sell them."

"Great job." Don perked up. "Call me and tell me what they say about it."

"Will do. You need anything? I'm out and about."

"No, thanks, I'm about to leave. My sister's in from Switzerland, and we're going to buy a casket. You know how that goes."

"Sure, it's good you have family with you."

"It is?" Don chuckled, sadly. "I can't pee without someone asking me how I am. Plus there's reporters out front."

"Jerks." Mike felt terrible for him, especially with the kids. "Want me to come run 'em over? The cops can put it on my tab."

Don snorted. "Well, I gotta go. Stay in touch, buddy."

"You too. Take care. Let me know if you need anything."

"Thanks," Don said, and Mike hung up.

Later, Mike hurried up the walkway to Clifton Police Administration Building with his head down, passing the media camped out on the sidewalk. He reached the entrance and went inside the lobby, where two young girls in sweats texted away on iPhones. He went to the window on the right, where a police officer was reading the newspaper.

"May I help you?" the officer asked, looking up. He had dark hair, a strong nose, and round brown eyes with dark circles underneath. His nameplate read Ofc. Garabedian.

"Yes, my name is Mike Scanlon and I have some information about the Sara Hambera murder. I was here last night, meeting with Jane Marcinko, and I'd like to see her or someone else about it."

"So you have a tip?"

"No, I have evidence. Is Ms. Marcinko here?"

"Their offices are in the municipal building. Are you claiming the reward?"

"No, I don't want any reward." Mike hadn't realized there was one. "I want to turn in the evidence and talk to whoever's on the case about it. Can I come in?"

"Hold on a sec, be right back. I gotta see who's assigned."

"Thanks." Mike watched as the officer left the window. The

squad room looked almost empty, with two officers at their cubicles. One was on the telephone, and the other was looking toward the reception window. In the next moment, Mike recognized him. "Officer Torno?"

"Dr. Scanlon." Officer Torno rose from his desk chair, hitching up his thick utility belt, heavy with a radio, gun holster, and black baton. He walked to the window with a slight smile. "You feeling better today?"

"Yes, thanks." Mike wasn't sure what he meant, but took it at face value. "Aren't you with the Wilberg police? How come you're in Clifton?"

"This is my home department. I'm only there part-time. Most of the smaller districts around here share police, if they can't justify the expense of a full-time force." Officer Torno cocked his head. He wasn't wearing his hat, and his hair was in a brush cut. "So what brings you here today?"

"It's about Sara Hambera's murder. I was here with Bob Ridgeway, my lawyer, last night. We met with Jane Marcinko, the Assistant District Attorney, about the case."

Officer Torno looked surprised. "You met with her here, after you were booked?"

"Yes, and now I found something I think might be evidence."

"Really." Officer Torno moderated his tone, as if Mike were a nutcase.

"Yes, I wanted to turn it in, talk to somebody about the case. Do you know who's assigned?"

"We don't give out that sort of information, Dr. Scanlon, sorry."

"Officer Garabedian went to find them, I think." Mike was starting to worry about time. He didn't want to be late for Jim. "Unfortunately, I have to get going. I have an appointment."

"How about I receive the evidence? I'll give it to the assigned officers and have one of them call you."

"Thanks so much. Want to buzz me in?" Mike went to the door, pushed it open when it buzzed, and took the bracelet out of his jacket pocket. Officer Torno fished through one of the desk drawers, found a large manila envelope and a white slip, then met him at the desk.

"Okay, what do you have?" Officer Torno opened the manila envelope, and Mike handed him the bangle in its Kleenex.

"It's an eighteen-karat gold bracelet that I found in my wife's jewelry box. I'm hoping that it could be evidence, if it was given to her by the man who killed Sara Hambera."

"I see." Officer Torno picked up the bracelet by the Kleenex, put it in the envelope, and sealed it then gave him a form and a pen. "Please sign the slip to establish the chain of custody and write down your contact information. Include your operator's number from your driver's license and your cell number."

"Will do." Mike dug in his pocket, produced his wallet, and copied his operator's number from his ID, then flipped the wallet closed and put it away. He handed the completed form to Officer Torno. "Here we go. I'll expect a call from the assigning officers."

"Take care, Doc."

"Thanks." Mike left the squad room, walked out of the waiting room, and pressed through the glass exit door, where reporters and cameramen swarmed him, holding videocameras to their shoulders, the black lenses pointed at him.

"Dr. Scanlon, Dr. Scanlon!" they shouted, all trying to get his attention at once. "Dr. Scanlon, what is the evidence you just turned in on the Hambera murder? Is it the murder weapon? What information do you have? Are you claiming the reward?"

"What? Huh?" Mike stepped back, confused. He had no idea how they had this information, much less knew his name. Klieglights went on behind the videocameras, and he put up his hand to shield his eyes.

"Dr. Scanlon, why did you talk to the police? What is your involvement in the Hambera case? It was the knife, wasn't it? Where did you find it? How did you find it?"

"No comment, I have no comment." Mike edged back from the throng, and his mouth went dry when he spotted two young girls at the fringe. They were the ones who'd been in the waiting room, texting on their iPhones. He had assumed they were teenagers, but they must've been freelancers or stringers.

"Dr. Scanlon, where do you live? Who are you? What is your involvement in this case? What evidence do you have?"

"Please, move." Mike tried to press his way through the crowd, but they blocked his path, surrounding him. A panic he couldn't explain tightened his chest. "Excuse me, I have to go. You're in my way."

"Dr. Scanlon, was it the knife or something else?" The reporters closed in. "You have information about the Hambera murder? Please, it would just take a minute!"

"Move, please!" Mike felt trapped, and his heart beat faster. He broke a sweat despite the cold. Cameras zoomed only inches from his face. "Hey, watch it. Move!"

"Dr. Scanlon, where do you work? Where do you live? Did you know Sara Hambera? Do you have any leads in the case?"

"Let me go!" Mike turned to try to go forward, but somebody shoved a camera in his face and he batted it away. "Get the camera out of my face. I said I have no comment. No comment!"

"Dr. Scanlon, look this way! Just a minute, please!"

Mike charged forward, putting his hand ahead of him. His heart thudded in his chest. He was having a full-blown panic attack. He barreled down the sidewalk, but the reporters ran backwards, filming him and shouting questions.

"Dr. Scanlon, what evidence do you have in the Sara Hambera murder? Please, a comment!" A photographer jostled Mike's left side, and agony arced through his stump, reverberating all the way to his neck.

"Get away from me!" Mike swung back reflexively, knocking a camera to the snow. He broke free of the crowd and raced down the sidewalk, his empty sleeve flying.

Chapter Fifty-four

Mike headed for the back door of his office building, which they left unlocked when they worked on weekends. The drive had given him time to compose himself, though his shirt felt clammy from flop sweat under his parka. He'd taken an Oxy, which helped. He entered the building, expecting a hallway, but it was gone. In its place was a large door with gold lettering that read LYON & HAGGERTY, SPECIALISTS IN ADOLESCENT SPORTS MEDICINE. Above was a laser-printed sign, **WELCOME HOME, MEDAL-WINNER DR. MIKE! WE SALUTE YOUR COURAGE AND SERVICE!** Mike twisted the doorknob and went inside, where even the half-sized waiting room for Suburban Foot & Ankle had disappeared. The new one was spacious and sparkling, its peach-colored walls lined with team photos.

"Hi, I'm Carly. May I help you, sir?" asked a youngish receptionist.

"I'm Mike Scanlon, and Jim is expecting me. You're working on a Sunday?"

"I come in to catch up, and so do the docs. It's the only time we get anything done." Carly smiled. "Hang on a sec, I'll take you to Jim's office."

"Thank you." Mike went to the door and followed Carly past walls blanketed with team photos from Pop Warner, peewee football, and travel soccer. "Hitting the youth market, huh?"

"Pardon?" Carly turned her head around, and her ponytail swung.

"Nothing," Mike answered, as she led him to the door at the end of the hall.

"Jim?" Carly knocked on the door. "Dr. Scanlon is here."

"Come in!" Jim called out, and the door opened quickly, "Mike, welcome! Carly, this is the famous Mike Scanlon, who worked here before his deployment. He's a genuine war hero, did you realize that?"

"Oh no!" Carly grimaced. "I'm so sorry. I thought you were just a friend."

"Stop with the hero stuff, Jim." Mike never felt less of a hero than now, after he'd fallen asleep on Emily and gotten spooked by a couple of reporters.

"Come on, you got two medals!" Jim steered him into the office and gestured at a cushy blue chair across from his new desk, a glistening slab of glass atop a walnut pedestal.

"So you got your office back. Way to go." Mike took a seat and unzipped his jacket, but didn't unstick his sleeve from the pocket.

"Right, so how're you doing?" Jim crossed in front of a wall of diplomas and an array of commendations, above bookshelves crowded with medical journals and plastic models. He flopped into his desk chair, opened a drawer, and produced a bottle of Scotch with an elegant black-framed label. "Here's my new hobby. The Macallan Estate Reserve, a limited edition bottling, notes of citrus and wood, with a spicy finish. Guess how much it cost. Two hundred bucks a bottle."

"What?" Mike scoffed. "Macallan's like fifty bucks."

"That's not the good stuff. I'm a collector now, I don't drink anything else, and it's *The* Macallan. You have to say the *The*. And you sip it, you don't guzzle it." Jim took a glass tumbler from the drawer, blew in it, then uncapped the bottle. "Join me. Lyon will be late, he's always late."

"No thanks. I'm on meds, and I wouldn't taste the difference anyway."

"You would, too." Jim poured himself some, sipped it, and smiled with satisfaction. "Mmm, that's so good. I want to go to Scotland, see where it's brewed, in the Highlands." His expression changed, growing serious. "I heard about Sara's murder and I couldn't believe it. I was like, in Clifton? That's the safest place ever."

"I know, it's awful."

"What do the police say? Do they have any suspects?"

"Not yet."

"It's a helluva thing to come home to, as if you didn't have enough on your plate. Sheesh." Jim sipped his Scotch. "So what's going on? You okay, after Chloe, or is it tough? Laura's dying to fix you up."

"You want to know the truth?" Mike realized he needed to confide in someone. "While I was away, I found out Chloe was cheating on me. She was even pregnant when she died."

"*What?*" Jim's eyes flared, and Mike told him about the autopsy report, the Mac702 emails, Pat MacFarland, and his own arrest.

"They *booked* you? You can't hit a guy for sleeping with your wife? What's this country coming to?"

Mike couldn't manage a smile. "So what do you think? Do you think Sara's murder and Chloe's affair are connected? Do you think Sara was killed to keep her quiet? I think I'm onto something, with that bangle."

"I'd leave it to the police, if I were you. You got your own problems. I can't believe that about Chloe. Man, you must be sick over it."

"I was, but now I know why she did it. She was depressed because I was away."

"I was over there when they did the article, and she seemed fine."

"What article?"

"There was an article we ran to promote the practice, talking you up. We had a freelancer interview Chloe and take some pictures. Didn't she mention it?"

"No, not that I remember."

"Anyway, I didn't see any liquor around and I never heard about any guy, other than Bob." Jim paused. "Don't take this the wrong way, but is it possible that Bob was her, uh, boyfriend?"

"My brother-in-law?" Mike recoiled, incredulous.

"Why not? He's still a guy. Chloe was the pretty one, and he's not blind."

"You think Chloe would sleep with her sister's *husband*?"

"Look don't get all bent out of shape." Jim leaned back, putting up his hands. "Stranger things have happened. It's the suburbs."

Suddenly there was a knock at the door, and Jim rose as Rick Lyon came in, extending a hand to Mike.

"Hi, you must be Mike Scanlon. Welcome back, and thank you for your service to our country." Lyon was short and stocky, with wire-rimmed glasses, dark brown eyes, and a head of thick black curls. "I'm proud to meet a real war hero."

"You still haven't." Mike could feel his face aflame, and Lyon turned to Jim with a smile.

"Jumbo, he's just like you said. Look at him, blushing. He's like Captain America or something."

Jim grinned. "You better believe, as soon as he joins the practice, we'll press-release it."

Mike groaned. "Again, you're going to pimp me out?"

"No, we're going to *support* you."

"Ah, the sound of one hand clapping." Mike chuckled, and so did Lyon and Jim. It felt good to be around people who didn't feel sorry for him.

"Okay, let's get down to business." Jim clapped his hands together. "Mike, as you see, we've narrowed the focus of the practice to adolescent sports medicine. You're a regular font of knowledge about foot and ankle injuries, and we're going to put you to work."

"Thank you." Mike felt a rush of gratitude. "I appreciate your faith in me, but I haven't even started rehab yet. I'm not ready to start work until I know more about what I can and can't do."

"Sure, but here's where we see you fitting in. The most common sports injuries aren't new to you. Plantar fasciitis, shin splints, peroneal tendinitis, stress fractures"—Jim counted off his thick fingers—"Achilles ruptures, and Achilles tendinitis. Injuries you've treated before, in a non-sport context. You with me?"

"Yes." Mike nodded, intrigued.

"We're all about marketing and expansion, trying to generate new business, and a couple of months ago, Lyon and I put our heads together and we said, you know, after most surgeries, we're prescribing a walking boot, your basic cam walker. A no-frills, ugly boot, comes in black or gray. You remember at Suburban Foot & Ankle, we sold the HomeHealth boot for 350 bucks, after markup."

"Sure." Mike nodded again. It was illegal to receive any kickback from prescribing DME, or durable medical equipment, but it was legit to buy it and prescribe or sell it to patients, which was what they used to do with the HomeHealth boot.

"So, Lyon and me, we noticed that the kids' boots they make aren't great, and we should develop our own boot, anyway." Jim leaned forward over his desk, and the shiny glass reflected the crisp white of his polo shirt. "There's nothing special about the cam walker, and we had ideas to improve it, for kids. Okay?"

"Okay."

"So we designed a kid's boot where some parts were inflatable to customize the fit, we found a manufacturer who made a prototype and now we have an official Lyon & Haggerty walking boot for children and adolescents."

"Good idea." Mike shrugged. "Why not?"

"*Exactly!* Why not?" Jim's blue eyes lit up. "It's better designed for younger sizes, less well-developed muscles, shorter bone lengths, etc., and it can be customized, not just for fit. You can get it in school colors or *team* colors. You can get your *school's* name or *your* name on it." Jim talked faster as he got more excited. "All the kids in Pop Warner get it in their team colors. Varsity athletes in high school get the varsity model, with different piping for JV. It's a fully customizable boot, and we charge 425 bucks."

Lyon added, "The orthotics come in matching colors, too."

Mike saw the possibilities. "Insurance covers it?"

"Yes. We pitch it as designed for kids' sports injuries. It even gets them back in the game faster, because they wear it." Jim opened his hands, palms up. "It's a no-brainer. Why sell HomeHealth's boot when we can sell our own?"

Lyon interjected, "Kids customize everything, nowadays. My eleven-year-old, when he gets his braces adjusted, gets red bands like the Phillies. My thirteen-year-old gets maroon for the Haverford School."

"Here. This is the prototype." Jim reached to the credenza behind his desk, rolled open a drawer, and fished out a black walking boot with a hard plastic back and a soft inflatable front. He pointed at three Velcro straps over the ankle. "This is where you customize the straps and the inflatable buttons. It's fully weight-bearing, has arch support, and we sell extra supports, also customizable."

Lyon gestured at the boot, grinning. "Maybe you could get them for returning vets, in red, white, and blue."

"Hoo-ah!" Jim saluted.

Mike cringed, inwardly. "So where do I come in? What does this have to do with me?"

"There's a sports-medicine conference every week, somewhere. I've done a few, and Lyon's done one, but we need somebody to work them, who also knows what he's talking about." Jim set the boot on his desk with a *clunk*. "We need a podiatrist who can market this boot and sell it to these doctors."

"So you want me to take a turn at conferences, selling this thing?"

"Yes, the way I see it, this is a new business for you. Of course we cut you in on the net revenue, a full third after costs, exclusive of royalties. You can take this and run with it."

Mike's mouth went dry. He'd been expecting to be a podiatrist again.

"You can go to as many trade shows and conferences as you like, after the required minimum. They're all over the country. We could expand to the High Risk Diabetic Foot Conference and State-of-the-Art Lower Extremity, or any kind of sports conference, like the trainers' conferences, and they have a slew of those everywhere."

Mike didn't know how he'd travel so much, with Emily at home.

"You have the expertise and personality to grow it out the wazoo. Not to mention the fact that you're a vet. What do you say?"

Mike fumbled for words. "Thanks, I appreciate it, but to be honest, it's not what I was thinking. I wanted to practice. I mean, maybe I can't do surgery, but I can examine patients, wrap ankles, everything short of surgery. I can be a podiatrist again, in some capacity."

Jim's face fell. "I thought you might feel that way. Maybe we'll leave that door open, but we can't know—"

"Mike," Lyon interrupted. "We talked to our lawyers about you, and they advised us not to employ you in any clinical capacity. Our malpractice insurance will go up, and there's too great a potential for litigation if you see patients, hands-on." Lyon cringed. "Poor choice of words. You don't fit in, in a clinical capacity, as a full partner."

Mike blinked. "But I don't expect to be a full partner, if my work-load is less. It's not about the money. I just want to be a podiatrist again."

"Without performing surgery? Not possible, with us." Lyon frowned. "Surgery is three-quarters of our time. The case gets handled by the same doc, from exam to surgery to post. In fact, we need to do more surgery to make up for the shortfalls on the allowables."

Jim sighed. "Mike, you know how we work. When we see the mom and the kid, they want to talk to the man with the knife. The best route for you is selling the boot."

"So practice isn't a possibility here, in any form?"

"Not really," Jim answered.

"No." Lyon shot Jim a cool look. "Practice is *not* a possibility, and we're not doing you any favors to let you think it is. To be clear, we would like you to join us to grow our customized boot and orthotic business."

Mike looked over at Jim, who met his eye, pained. "I know you're doing everything you can for me, and I appreciate it."

"I am, pal." Jim's forehead relaxed, his relief evident. "I wish I could do more, but you know how it goes with lawyers, and this boot business can be a goldmine."

"Let me think it over and get back to you." Mike rose stiffly.

"Take this." Jim put the boot prototype in an open cardboard box on the floor. "Also, here's your personal items, from your old office. I keep forgetting to get them over to you."

"Thanks." Mike took the box, trying to act like he could hold it with ease in one arm.

"Listen, one last thing, there's a PAPSM conference tomorrow in King of Prussia."

"What's that?"

"Pennsylvania Academy of Podiatric Sports Medicine. You remember the conference drill, they give CME credits? We're vendors. We have staff there now, setting up the booth. I was gonna man it, and you should do it with me. Give it a dry run and see how you feel after that. What do you say?"

Mike tried to look on the bright side. At least he had a job, when so many didn't. "Great," he said, forcing a smile.

Chapter Fifty-five

Mike drove down the street and pulled into an empty parking lot, for visitors to Haverford College. He wanted to make a call and find out what other options he had, before he went forward with Jim and Lyon. He still had Chatty's offer in Greenwich, but he didn't know if that was real. He cut the ignition, slid out his BlackBerry, scrolled to his email function, and found Chatty's email with the phone number of his colleague Sean Carver. When the call connected, and Mike introduced himself and said, "You don't know me, but I'm a friend of—"

"I know who you are. You're Mike Scanlon, Chatty's buddy from Afghanistan. I've been expecting to hear from you. Chatty sings your praises. You guys got a real bromance."

Mike chuckled. "You call him Chatty, too?"

"Of course." Sean laughed. "Anyway, we need the help, we're busy as hell. Chatty said you have to do rehab first, but you can do that here, can't you?"

"I assume so," Mike answered, surprised. "Your business is doing well, in this economy?"

"We don't take credit. It's location, location, location." Sean chuckled. "This practice is in one of the wealthiest parts of the country, so nobody has any problem getting or paying for medical insurance. If there's discretionary procedures, they can pay for it out of pocket, if need be."

"But I'm not sure the extent to which I can do surgery."

"I know you're an amputee, and you can practice with us without doing surgery. We have plenty of nonsurgical patients, and if we run into a dry spell, we don't have a problem with you doing the initial intake on a surgical patient. It's not efficient or economic to take a surgeon's time to answer a million questions." Sean snorted. "And you know how much surgeons love questions."

"Great," Mike said, encouraged. "So when would I start?"

"As soon as you want, and Chatty already negotiated that we pay you what you were making before, which is fine. I can email you a copy of our employment agreement and bonus structure, which is excellent. Our clients are used to Manhattan prices because that's where most of them work."

Mike thought it was almost too good to be true. "But I need to relocate to Greenwich."

"Ha! You couldn't afford Greenwich, but you might have a shot at the surrounding suburbs." Sean laughed at his own joke. "I'm sure we can work out some advance for a down payment, if you find yourself in a bind."

"So I have a decision to make. When do you need to know by?"

"Two weeks, at the outside. Fair enough?"

"That's more than fair. I can't thank you enough."

"You're welcome, good-bye."

"Thanks again." Mike pressed END, torn. He was thrilled to think he could practice again, but he hated to move Emily away from Bob and Danielle. She loved them, and it would kill them to lose her. He wondered if he had any options closer to home, and he still had Tony and Dave on speed dial, so he pressed T and the call connected after two rings. "Tony! How the hell are you?"

"Mike!" Tony said warmly. "Is that you? Are you back? About damn time! How are you?"

"I'm fine. How are you?"

"We're all fine. I'm in South Jersey now. The Bryn Mawr practice didn't work out, and we moved. Her parents live here and they help with the kids."

"Where do you work?"

"A two-man group."

"You got any openings?" Mike asked, but he didn't add, *for a one-armed podiatrist?* It was embarrassing enough.

"Sorry, no, I'm hardly busy, but I'll keep you in mind, for sure. What, did Jim screw you over, like I predicted?"

"Not really." Mike didn't want to elaborate. "What's up with Dave?"

"Dave's semi-retired."

"What? How'd he pull that off?"

"Bonnie got a great job with one of the hospitals, and he consults for med mal trials. He's an expert witness, does exams and then testifies."

"Think I can get in?"

"Give him a call. Stay in touch, and I'll keep my ears open. We gotta get together, man."

"We will, after the thaw. Talk to you later. Stay well, pal. Say hi to Jill for me."

"See you."

"Bye." Mike hung up, pressed D for Dave on his speed dial, and waited for the call to connect.

"Yo!" Dave boomed, jubilant. "This really you, soldier boy?"

"Sure enough." Mike warmed to the sound. "There's nothing like an old friend."

"That's the truth. So, you're back? Thank God!"

"Yeah, and you're semi-retired. How about *that?*"

"I know, right?" Dave laughed. "I sort of fell into it."

"Tony said you're an expert witness. Think they have room for another? How do I get into that?"

"Oh man, to tell the truth, semi-retired means I can't get five full days of work. I was out of work for six months, and it puts a good face on it."

Mike felt for him. "I hear you, and I'm hoping it works out for you."

"It wouldn't have, but for Bonnie. She got a big job at Siemens."

"What a woman." Mike felt a twinge that told him his Oxy was wearing off. "Give her my love, will you?"

"Sure thing. If I hear of anything, I'll let you know."

"Thanks. We gotta get together," Mike told him, meaning it.

"We will. Call you. See you."

"You, too." Mike pressed END, then looked down at his phone, and his directory was a list of his podiatrist friends, all of whom were local. One of them could have an opening or put him in touch with somebody who did. He scrolled to the first name and got busy. Six calls later, he had no new leads on jobs. None of his friends knew of any openings, and most were worried about their own practices.

Mike looked out the windshield without really seeing anything. The sky was a blanket of steel wool, and everything seemed gray. Bottom line, he had a great option in Connecticut, but it wasn't one he could take without hurting Emily, Danielle, and Bob. He was about to start the car when his gaze fell on the cardboard box on the passenger seat. He found it depressing that his entire professional life could be contained in one box.

He scanned the contents. His lab coat was folded next to his wedding photo and a heart-shaped picture of Chloe and Emily. Then he thought of something. He reached in the box, pulled out his lab coat, and stuck his hand in the pocket. Inside was his prescription pad, which he kept there, per procedure. They never used to leave their pads in the examining room, as a security matter, but went with them from room to room.

Mike read his old pad. Under Suburban Foot & Ankle, it said Dr. Michael J. Scanlon, then ID Number 83736 and DEA Number 35242, for dispensing controlled substances.

He eyed the pad, tempted.

Chapter Fifty-six

Mike hurried to the drugstore, in a strip mall a few towns west of Wilberg, where he wouldn't be recognized. He entered with his head down, avoiding seeing his own image in the security monitor, ashamed of himself. He'd never done anything like this before, and it could cost him his license.

He passed customers browsing racks of leftover holiday cards and headed to the pharmacy, which would be in the back to the left, because all the stores in the chain had the same layout. He went to the drop-off window, next to shelves with an array of pregnancy kits. There was no line, unlike the pick-up window, which was eight people deep. "Hello," Mike said to the young female pharmacist.

"Hi, how can I help you?" she asked, fresh-faced, with dark hair, an earnest smile, and a crisp lab coat. Her red nametag read Erin.

"I'd like to fill this." Mike passed her the script, which was for Oxycontin, ten milligrams every twelve hours, quantity thirty. He knew she'd be looking for red flags, like thirty milligrams or higher dosage and a quantity of sixty pills, and he'd avoided them. He wished he could have called in the script, but he had to present in person for controlled substances.

"Date of birth?"

Mike told her his real birthday, then tried to act casual as she started hitting keys on the computer. He told himself that there was no way the pharmacist would suspect anything. The only way he could get caught was if she called Suburban Foot & Ankle to verify the script, but she'd only do that if she had reason to be suspicious of him. He didn't tuck his empty sleeve into his jacket, because it showed his bona fides.

"Phone number?"

Mike gave her his real cell.

"Where do you live?"

"Wilberg, on Foster Road." Mike knew it would be another red flag if he came from the city to fill the script.

"Oh, we have a store there, a new drive-thru." Erin's gaze fell to his empty sleeve, then her eyelids fluttered nervously. "Have you used us there?"

"No, I use the mom-and-pop store. Leed's." Mike had to have an answer, but not say too much, which was another red flag.

"Okay." Erin hit a few more keys, recovering. "May I have your insurance card?"

"I'll just pay cash." Mike hid his jitters. Cash was a red flag, but he knew his arm was his ticket.

"Do you have any allergies?"

"No."

"Would you like to wait for it? It might be half an hour. We're kind of busy."

"I'll wait, thanks."

"Sorry it takes so long." Erin smiled sympathetically. "We have a waiting area over there."

"Great, thanks." Mike stepped away from the drop-off window, grabbed a copy of *People* magazine, and went to a row of red bucket seats, next to a blood-pressure machine. He sat down and buried his face in the magazine, turning the pages and sweating under his parka until they'd finally gotten his script ready and one of the pharmacists called out:

"Mr. DeMaria? Phil DeMaria?"

"Here!" Mike called out, rising. By law, he couldn't prescribe opiates to himself, so he had written the scripts for the first few names that had come to him. DeMaria, Goldstein, and Jacobs were always on his mind, in a compartment that refused to stay closed. He'd fill the second script as Goldstein and the third as Jacobs, at two different drugstores in neighboring towns. The licensing agencies kept an eye out for pill mills, but these numbers wouldn't be high enough to trigger any investigations, even if somebody connected the dots.

Mike joined the pick-up line, in shame.

Chapter Fifty-seven

"I'm home!" Mike entered the empty living room, carrying the box from the office, with his new stockpile of pills tucked away inside.

"Mike?" Danielle called out, from the kitchen.

"Gotta run up to the bathroom." Mike hurried to the stairwell. "Be right back."

Bob hollered, "Don't be long."

Mike hustled upstairs to his room, set down the box, and dug out the three pill bottles. He stuffed the bottles between the mattress and box spring, which would do as a hiding place for now. He hurried downstairs, hung up his jacket, and went to the kitchen, filled with the aroma of roast chicken. "Dinner smells great!"

"Where were you?" Bob asked, folding his arms. The table had been set, but he stood behind Danielle, who was sitting in front of an open laptop.

"I met with Jim about a job, then ran some errands." Mike smiled, which came easily, given that he had taken an Oxy on the way home. "Where's the baby?"

"She went down for a nap," Danielle answered, her forehead knit.

"Is something the matter?" Mike asked, puzzled.

Bob shot him a look. "I would say so, as your lawyer. I'm trying to keep my temper, but I don't know what you're thinking. I got calls this afternoon from clients of mine, Jason Tilley and Marc Rubin. Imagine their surprise when they saw you on the news."

"I was on the news?"

"Here, come see." Bob edged Danielle out of the way and pressed the mousepad.

Mike came over, and the screen showed the Clifton Administration Building, with him coming down the steps. The voiceover said, "We have breaking news in the Sara Hambera murder case. Dr. Michael Scanlon was seen leaving the Clifton police station today, having turned in evidence in the case, though he declined comment for this reporter."

Mike watched with dismay as the next few shots showed him crowded by the press and hitting the camera, but the angle made it look as if were trying to hit the photographers. The voiceover continued, "Dr. Scanlon has just returned from two tours of duty in Afghanistan, and we have learned that he was arrested last night for assault on a former neighbor."

Mike looked up, meeting Bob's angry eye. "Obviously, that isn't the way it happened."

"All that matters is you look like you hit a photographer and you have a pending assault case. I already have a call into Jane, but I haven't heard back from her." Bob scowled. "How do they even know about the evidence? You didn't give an interview, did you?"

"No, they planted some freelancers in the waiting room, who overheard me."

"Why would you discuss confidential business in the waiting room? I didn't do it that way when I took you last night."

Danielle rose, pursing her lips. "Bob, please watch your tone."

Mike tried to defuse the situation. "Look, I'm sorry, but I wasn't trying to hurt anybody. The police aren't going to look at that when the assault case goes to trial, are they? Are they even allowed to use it in court?"

"No, but you know who is? Pat MacFarland, when he sues you. That's completely allowable evidence in a civil case." Bob shook his head. "The point is, from now on, you need to stay out of this murder investigation."

"Why? If they investigate that bangle, they could find the killer and Chloe's lover, and if they don't investigate it, I will. I have a picture of the bangle in my phone."

"Mike, you will do no such thing." Bob motioned at the laptop. "This is bad for me and my business. I've done nothing but good for you. I've taken you in and taken care of Emily. I'm representing you for free, and my thanks is that you ruin me?"

"Bob, I can't stop—"

"You can and you will." Bob stuck a finger in Mike's face. "You will not take me down with you. You will not take my law firm down with you. I will not let you interfere with my revenue stream. You've gone from my brother-in-law the hero to my brother-in-law, the thug. Two assaults in two days. You need anger management!"

Danielle turned to Mike, anguished. "You know we love you, and Bob is only concerned for your well-being. Instead of this murder business, we think it would be better if you focused on getting yourself into rehab. Look at this article." She gestured at a magazine that lay open on the table. "It's about wounded military who compete in shot put, wheelchair racing, and wheelchair basketball. This is so inspiring, and these men are so much less fortunate than you."

Mike looked at the magazine, with its glossy vets in black Army singlets, who were missing arms, feet, legs below the knee, and a lower body. He'd performed those amputations, he'd hacked those human beings into pieces. Guilt tore through his Oxycontin haze.

"I know, it's so moving, isn't it?" Danielle asked, softly. "I felt the same way. Each one of these men has overcome so many odds."

Bob harrumphed. "This is what you need to be doing, Mike. You need to get your head straight. Get back on track."

Mike edged backwards, away from the magazine. The men in the photos morphed into his patients, all of the soldiers swirling into a horrific vortex of blood and camo, all of the wounds becoming a single giant fleshy maw, gulping down muscles, eyeglasses, iPods, and men.

Bob said, "Mike? What's the matter with you? Where are you going?"

"Upstairs," Mike answered, in a waking nightmare.

Danielle asked, "What about dinner?"

"I'm not hungry," Mike murmured in horror.

Chapter Fifty-eight

The next morning, Mike hurried toward the convention hall, wearing his best suit and an ID badge on a red lanyard, with a fluttery red Vendor ribbon. He slid out of his wet raincoat on the fly, threw it over his arm with his dripping umbrella, and hustled past the doctors swarming to their seminar rooms. He remembered when he used to be one of them. He'd taken Chloe to the last conference he'd gone to, in San Diego.

I'm here for the vacation sex, she had said.

Mike looked away from the doctors, who were greeting each other, joking around, and catching up over buffet tables laden with fresh-squeezed orange juice, hot coffee, doughnuts, Danish, and fruit trays. They were dressed casually because they didn't have to sell anything, and their ID badges sported blue Attendee ribbons, as if they had won first prize, at life. If he moved to Greenwich, he could be one of them.

He chugged past, his stump aching and his head down. He had barely slept, but he hoped that today would go well, making it easier to stay home. He reached the exhibitor hall, showed his badge, and went inside, ducking other vendors in logo ballcaps, polo shirts, and jackets, buying bad coffee at the snack bar, carrying large grease boards, and rolling handcarts.

The crowd hurried around him, this way and that, and Mike began to feel closed in again. His pulse picked up, his mouth went dry. He'd taken a pill before he left the car, but one wasn't enough anymore. He tried not to panic and threaded his way through the crowd, passing all the company names he used to know; Amerigel, Advanced Skin and Wound Care, Gill Podiatry Supply and Equipment Company, and OsteoMed. He reached Row L, turned down an aisle lined with booths, and spotted Jim, in suit and tie. He was talking to Carly, who was dressed in an orange polo shirt with skimpy athletic shorts. Evidently, Jim had more than M&Ms to attract doctors to the booth.

Mike flagged him down, with a forced smile. "Reporting for duty, sir."

Jim saluted. "You know Carly."

Carly grinned. "Hey, Dr. Mike. Okay if I call you that?"

"Sure, hi." Mike held his umbrella and raincoat, awkwardly. "Is there a place I can stow these?"

"Let me." Carly took Mike's things, crossed to the back of the booth, and shoved them under the draped table.

"So what do you think?" Jim gestured, and Mike surveyed the booth. The front counter held samples of the boot, and a sign at the back read LYON & HAGGERTY, WALKING BOOT FOR ADOLESCENTS AND CHILDREN, in bright orange letters. Glossy action photos showed middle-schoolers playing soccer, tennis, and basketball, interspersed with the same models as they opened their school locker, strolled around the mall, and applauded on the sidelines, wearing their color-coordinated boots.

"Looks awesome." Mike kept his mood up. "So what do I do? Put me in, Coach."

"Check this out." Jim grabbed some literature from the table and opened it to head shots of Jim and Lyon, posing in lab coats. "Three pages full-color, with our bios and CVs. I had that article about you photocopied and stuffed in there, too, so you're officially on the team."

"Thanks." Mike pocketed the brochure, ignoring the headline about Military Medicine because underneath was a photo of Chloe, smiling hard as she held up a photo of Mike.

"We'll be swamped in fifteen minutes. Watch me for the first couple of guys, then jump in. Tell any doc you can about the boot. Remind him that their practice gets 5 percent if they prescribe us. Got it?"

"Yes."

"You probably know some of these docs, so target them. If you don't know them, lead with your being a vet."

"Can't we soft-pedal that?" Mike had tucked his suit sleeve into his pocket, but any orthopod would know he was an amputee.

"Look around you, at the other booths. They're kids, straight out of college." Jim made a sweeping motion at the universe, in general. "None of them has your life experience. None of them has your medical expertise. None of them has been where you have. *You* can help us distinguish our product. Am I right, or am I right?"

"Okay." Mike noticed a group of doctors coming down the aisle, laughing and joking, a flurry of blue ribbons.

"Showtime," Jim said under his breath. "See that guy in front, Josh Haber? Has a six-man practice in Jenkintown that serves four school districts. Watch and learn." He put on a big smile, lifted his chin, and waved at Josh. "Joshua, as I live and breathe! Here comes trouble!"

Haber looked up, surprised over his rimless glasses. He stopped his conversation as Jim strode to him, shook his hand heartily, and steered him and his colleagues back to the booth.

"Josh, meet my partner." Jim presented Mike with a flourish. "Mike Scanlon, just back from Afghanistan. You're looking at a real live combat surgeon."

"Wow!" Josh's smile broadened, and he tugged off his reading glasses. "What an honor to meet you. Jim told me so much about you." His expression sobered. "Sorry to hear about the loss of your wife, too."

Mike felt his cheeks burn. "Thanks, good to meet you."

Jim picked up a boot. "We're putting Mike to work, helping get the word out about our boot. This is what I was telling you about, at the wedding. Fully customizable, and they can get it in Cheltenham High colors."

"You're *shameless*." Josh's eyes twinkled, amused.

"Of course I am!" Jim burst into laughter. "You know why? I believe in this product. You should, too. Kids never put up a fight about wearing it, and your practice gets a percentage."

"How much?"

"Five."

"Excuse me, did you say ten?" Josh smiled slyly, and Jim laughed.

"Please. What are you getting from HomeHealth? They send you a fruitcake for Christmas?"

"Ha! You got that right." Josh checked his watch. "I'll give you a call. I gotta meet with some reps." He turned to Mike. "Nice meeting you, and stay away from this character. He'll corrupt you."

"That's what I'm hoping for," Mike said, and they all laughed. Josh and his colleagues moved on, and Jim turned to Mike with a grin.

"You're a natural! You did great! See how easy it is?"

"It's the percentage that does it."

"Of course. Rather, that's part of it, but the boot still delivers." Jim looked away, distracted as a trio of doctors came down the row. Carly met them, bouncing over with brochures, and Jim said under his breath, "Give Carly a second. They like her."

"Is she our secret weapon?"

Jim winked. "My momma didn't raise no dummy."

"Don't you think it's a little cheesy?"

"Why? She majored in physical therapy at Penn State and has the best ass in sports medicine. Watch me do my thing." Jim flagged down the threesome. "Dr. Sam Bertold, is that you? Up this early?"

"Very funny." Sam rolled his eyes, an intense brown behind thickish wire-rims. He was a chubby man in his late forties, and his dark suit strained at the middle button. "Show some respect, Haggerty. I'm the midmorning keynote speaker."

"Working your way up to lunchtime keynote?"

"Ha!" Sam laughed. "I'll let you know when I hit dinner."

"Playing for varsity, then!" Jim laughed, and so did Sam and his colleagues, grouping around and blocking Mike, who noticed a well-dressed woman at the periphery, picking up the boot and trying to fasten the Velcro.

"May I help you with that?" he asked.

"Yes, thanks." The woman looked up with a smile. She had curly brown hair and colorful reading glasses on a beaded lorgnette. "My son is thirteen and runs track, but he broke his ankle on the ice in our driveway. Our podiatrist says he can't run for four more weeks, but then he won't be able to go to the regionals in winter track, because he missed too many practices."

"That's too bad."

The woman cocked her head. "Can you can settle a family feud? My husband says he can run in two weeks, not four. He's an orthopedist, too, but he specializes in tennis elbow."

"What do you think?"

"I'm just the mom, but I think we should wait."

"The mom matters." Mike was thinking about Chloe and Sara.

"So what do you think, about my son? Two weeks or four?"

"Of course, I haven't examined your son, but I'm with his podiatrist. You can't hurry the healing process, not at that age." Mike slipped into his old role like a comfy pair of jeans. "The last thing you want is a thirteen-year-old running before he's not healed. If he damages a growth plate, he could end up with one leg shorter than the other."

"Oh no." Her eyes flared in alarm. "Can that really happen?"

"Yes. It must hurt him, too."

"He says it doesn't."

"He's downplaying it. They all do."

"I knew it!"

Jim looked over with a caffeinated smile. His friend Sam Bertold was taking a cell phone call, leaving his friends to stand around, waiting. Jim said to the woman, "Excuse me, if your son is a runner, we also make custom orthotics that can be used with or without our boot, and placed in any shoes or sneakers. Running is a repetitive-motion sport that requires a rigid orthotic. Soccer, tennis, basketball, or gymnastics require a more flexible orthotic device, because they're start-stop, complex motion, or cutting sports."

The woman frowned. "That isn't what we were talking about."

"Oh, I see." Jim blinked. "How can I help you then? Where is your practice?"

"I'm not a doctor, my husband is. I know what orthotics are, and my son doesn't need them."

Jim dialed his smile down. "Well, thank you very much for stopping by."

"You're welcome." The woman eyed Mike, knowingly. "I gather I should be going. Thanks again."

"Bye now." Mike smiled, and Jim watched the woman walk away, then turned to Mike.

"Why did you spend so much time with her? She's not buying anything, she's not even a doc."

"No one was waiting, and she asked me a question, so I answered it."

"Mike, these aren't patients, they're customers. Don't be an altar boy. Push the boot." Jim looked away as Sam Berthold hung up. "Sam, meet my partner, back from two tours in Afghanistan. This is Mike Scanlon."

"That name sounds familiar." Sam frowned. "Aren't you the guy that had a fight? With a news photographer?"

Jim scoffed. "No, that's not him. It must've been a different guy."

Mike tried to shrug it off. "It was me, but it wasn't a fight. It might look that way on the news, but that wasn't the way it happened. The editing made it look like I hit the guy, but I—"

"I didn't see it on the news, I read it in the newspaper." Sam's gaze shifted from Mike to Jim. "I'm sure it was just a misunderstanding."

"Totally." Jim waved his hand. "As we were saying, this boot is a real innovation for adolescent sports medicine, and the customization colors make it fun to wear instead of a chore."

Sam slipped the brochure into his pocket. "Good to know, but I better be moving on."

"Call me."

"Will do," Sam said over his shoulder, followed by his colleagues, and when they were out of earshot, Jim turned to Mike, incredulous.

"What the hell was that about? Is that what you were arrested for?"

"No, something else. But I didn't do it."

Jim pursed his lips. "You were arrested for assault, and you also hit a photographer?"

"No, that's what I'm saying, I didn't do it. I was just at the police station, in connection with Sara's murder."

"You hit somebody in front of the police station? While you're on bail for another assault?" Jim looked at him like he was nuts. "When did this happen? The second time, I mean."

"Yesterday."

"Mike." Jim lowered his voice. "We can't have that if you're gonna sell this thing, and it won't go over with Lyon, at all. He always says, business is all about reputation."

"I know, it'll blow over."

"Okay, but today is a problem." Jim glanced around. "What if someone else recognizes you? The TV news will probably run it again, they always massage that crap. Mike, sorry, but I think it's better if you go."

"Really?"

"Just until this cools down. I don't need to answer to Lyon." Jim met his eyes, pained. "Sorry buddy, you understand. It's only for now."

"Sure," Mike said, wishing he could take another pill.

Later, Mike drove home through the freezing rain, lost in thought. He hated the prospect of selling boots at trade shows, if he could practice again. Maybe if he moved to Connecticut, he could put his old life behind him and start a second chapter. Bob and Danielle could visit him, and maybe it was time for him to go his own way with Emily. Still, on the other hand, it would hurt Emily to live far from Danielle and Bob. They were her only family, and vice versa. Mike wasn't ready to make a decision yet, and there was no reason to rush into anything.

He pulled into the driveway and cut the ignition. He got out of the car and hustled through the rain to the house, but as soon as he opened the front door, he knew something was wrong. A muffled weeping came from the kitchen, and it sounded like Danielle. He closed the door behind him and hurried to the threshold. Bob was standing in the kitchen across from Danielle, as if they'd been fighting.

Mike froze. "Sorry, I didn't mean to interrupt."

"Oh, my." Danielle grabbed a paper towel and dabbed her eyes. "You're home early."

"I can go upstairs. I didn't mean to intrude. Where's Emily? Is she asleep?"

Bob gestured to Danielle, his manner chilly. "Honey, go check on the baby. Make that call, too."

"Okay." Danielle hurried past Mike, averting her eyes. "Excuse me."

"Sure." Mike stepped aside to let her pass, confused. "I can check on Emily. What's going on, what call?"

"I have some papers for you." Bob went to his messenger bag on the chair, opened it, and slid out a stack of legal pleadings, bound with light blue binders.

Mike's heart sank. "Pat MacFarland is suing me, huh?"

"No. We're asking you to leave." Bob handed him the thick stack of papers. "And we're keeping Emily."

Chapter Fifty-nine

"I don't understand." Mike took the papers, stunned.

"The papers are the judge's order that approves our custody agreement."

"What custody agreement?" Mike asked, reeling.

"You remember." Bob's gaze remained even, his tone calm and professional. "The one you signed before you went away."

Mike's mouth dropped open. "That agreement was for while I was deployed."

"No." Bob shook his head, curtly. "The agreement gives us custody of Emily for as long as necessary. It doesn't terminate when your deployment does."

"What the hell are you talking about?" Mike shot back, bewildered and angry. "Emily is *my daughter.*"

"Legally, we have custody of her."

"What? This can't be legal."

"It is completely."

"It *can't* be!"

"Get a lawyer. It is."

"But you're my lawyer!" Mike threw the papers on the table. "Are you *kidding* me? You *know damn well* what we meant!"

"Lower your voice." Bob put up a hand. "I will discuss this with you only if you stay calm. Danielle called the police. They were expecting us later but the station is only five blocks away. Leave or I'll have you arrested for trespassing."

"*What?*" Mike exploded. "I live here! My daughter lives here!"

"You live here only as long as you have our permission. Now, we want you to leave. Your knapsack is packed and in the closet." Bob pointed outside the kitchen. "Take it and go, please."

"I'm not going anywhere without Emily." Mike edged backwards, incredulous.

"Yes, you are." Bob's blue eyes hardened like ice. "You can't give her a good home. You can't even stay awake long enough to babysit. She could've been killed."

"Go to hell!" Mike turned away, bolted for the staircase, and bounded upstairs.

"Mike!" Bob hurried after him. "The police are on their way. You're only making it worse for yourself."

"Emily, Emily!" Mike reached the second floor, rushed to Emily's bedroom, and twisted the doorknob, but it was locked. "Danielle, let me in!"

"Mike, get out!" Bob stalked down the hall toward him. "Leave. If you don't go now, you'll be arrested."

"Emily!" Mike yelled, and Emily started crying inside the bedroom, which broke his heart. "Emily, don't cry! It's Daddy! I love you!"

Emily wailed harder.

"Danielle, open this door!" Mike wrenched on the doorknob, and the door rattled noisily.

Danielle yelled, "Mike, stop! You're upsetting her. Stop it!"

"I'm her father, I love her!" Mike pounded on the door. "Danielle, let me in! She's my child! She belongs to me!"

"Mike!" Bob gripped Mike's shoulder and pulled him back, sending pain like an electric shock zinging up and down his arm. "Stop it, no!"

"Let me go!" Mike torqued his body out of Bob's grasp.

"Mike, stop!" Bob grabbed for Mike, but Mike shoved him back. "How dare you? She's my daughter! You can't take her from me!"

"No!" Bob staggered backwards, falling against the wall. Police sirens sounded nearby.

Danielle screamed, "Bob, Bob!"

"I'm not leaving without my daughter!" Mike yelled to Bob, who was getting up, rubbing his head. "She's mine, not yours!"

Danielle yelled, "Mike, stop it! You're scaring her! Is Bob okay?"

"Open this door!" Mike wrenched the doorknob back and forth, despite the pain. "Danielle, let me have Emily!"

"Mike, no please!" Danielle called back, sobbing. "Please, stop!"

"Danielle!" Mike couldn't give up without a fight. Something told him if he left without Emily, he'd never get her back. The thought shook him to his very foundations. "Danielle, please!"

Bob got to his feet and went running down the stairs. Sirens blared closer, on the street. "Danielle, don't open the door! Be right back!"

"Danielle, please!" Mike pounded the door again. "I'm begging you. Let me have her. I love her. She's mine. I'll take care of her, I promise. I'll make it better, you'll see. She's all I have."

"No! Go away!" Danielle shouted back, and there was a commotion downstairs as Bob ran out the door, hollering to the police.

"Danielle!" Mike wrenched the door. He was running out of time. "Danielle, please! This isn't right it! She's mine!"

"Give up, Mike! Go, you're making her cry!"

"Dr. Scanlon!" came a shout from downstairs. "This is the police, Dr. Scanlon!"

"Emily, I love you!" Mike yelled one last time, as they came charging up the stairs.

Chapter Sixty

Mike drove away from the house, distraught. His heart thundered in his chest, and he was sweating. His stump and shoulders screamed in protest. He tried to catch his breath. He felt like he'd been punched in the gut. He didn't know how Bob and Danielle could do such a thing. He hadn't seen it coming.

I didn't see this coming, I didn't see.

Mike flashed on Chatty, after the attack. The donkey. The grandfather. The grenade. The orange-red blast explosion blinded him. The *boom* reverberated against his eardrums. He put up his hand, shielding his eyes. A car horn blared, and Mike slammed on the brake and veered right, almost crashing into a fire hydrant. Other horns sounded, behind him.

He steered straight, fed the car gas, then pulled over to the curb, heartsick. He slumped in the seat, watching the rain run down the windshield. Emily was gone. The legal papers were in his backpack. He couldn't believe what had happened. He would have trusted Bob and Danielle with his life. He had. Emily was his life.

He reached into his knapsack and pulled out his laptop. He opened it up, turned it on, and waited for it to boot up on battery power, his mind racing. The laptop screen came up, and he scrolled to find a wireless connection. A list popped onto the screen, and he clicked a few networks until he found one that let him join, then navigated to Google and started typing.

He had to get Emily back.

He had a vow to keep.

Chapter Sixty-one

"How can this be legal?" Mike sat in a chair across from his new lawyer, Stephanie Bergen. She was supposed to be one of the best family lawyers in the area, and he was lucky she'd had a cancellation. "This has to be a kidnapping. She's my child, not theirs."

"Give me one more minute, please." Stephanie was reading through his legal papers. She was about his age, but only five foot one, with thick auburn hair cut to her chin and a runner's wiry body. She had a large office, with legal books and journals that filled walnut shelves. The wall above a flowery couch was devoted to diplomas and awards, and next to her neat walnut desk was a curtained window. Outside, the rain was freezing to snow, flying past the panes in icy flurries.

"All right, I'm finished." Stephanie looked up, brushing her bangs away from sharp green eyes. "I'll answer your question, then you can fill me in on the facts."

"I thought the parents always have the rights to the child. So what the hell is going on?"

"Because of this agreement, Bob and Danielle have full legal and physical custody of Emily, and we—"

"I don't have legal custody of my own child?"

"No." Stephanie shook her head, and her thick gold earrings

wiggled back and forth. "You signed the agreement, giving them custody."

"It was supposed to be temporary!"

"Stay calm." Stephanie paused. "That's our argument and your intent, but the agreement doesn't say it's temporary. On the contrary, it provides specifically that they have custody for as long as necessary—"

"It says temporary in the title."

"Yes, but the agreement itself has no term, and the judge's order isn't temporary."

"What judge?" Mike threw up his hand. "When did they go see a judge? How can they do that without me?"

"They didn't. Your brother-in-law filed the agreement you signed, and the judge approved it, so it obtained the force of law. If family members agree to a custody arrangement, a court will approve it, if it's reasonable." The light from a Chinese lamp on Stephanie's desk made her jade green suit look flashy. "The agreement is still in effect, and the status quo is that they have custody, per a judge's order. That's why the police enforced it. You should've had a lawyer when you signed."

"I did. Bob was my lawyer. I trusted him."

"Bob represented his own interests. I never would've let a client of mine sign an agreement like this. We need to schedule an emergency hearing to transfer custody back to you, as her father, and the way—"

"So I have to go to court to get her back? I'll get her back, right?"

"One thing at a time." Stephanie held up a hand. "We have to go to court, and I don't know if you'll get her back."

"It's *not* automatic? I'm the *father.*"

"No, it's not automatic—"

"That's crazy!"

"Please, stop interrupting me." Stephanie smiled in a way that was polite, if not warm. "I know you're upset, but you need to control yourself."

"I still can't believe this is legal."

"It is."

"But it's not fair. It's not justice."

Stephanie shot him a knowing look. "The law isn't always just, unfortunately."

"But it should be. Isn't justice the point of law?"

"Let's stay on track." Stephanie glanced at her oversized watch. "Now, as I was saying, the agreement doesn't provide visitation for you on any regular schedule, so you have no legal rights vis-à-vis your daughter."

Oh my God, Mike thought but didn't say. He was trying to control himself.

"I'll call the court and ask for an emergency hearing. It should only take a day, so keep your schedule clear. Now, in answer to your question, the fact that you are the child's parent gives you the presumption of custody, but that presumption can be rebutted by clear and convincing evidence." Stephanie's tone turned professorial. "The legal standard is what's in Emily's best interests, and the judge will consider sixteen statutory factors in making his decision, which all go to who can provide the more loving, stable, and nurturing home. Understood?"

"Yes."

"You have no home and no job. Is that correct?" Stephanie's gaze dropped to his stump, then back up again, without apparent reaction.

"Yes, but I've only been back a few days."

"That's undoubtedly why he threw you out so quickly. He wants to get to court before you get your feet under you."

"I can't believe he would do that."

"He just did."

"It doesn't seem real." Mike ran his hand through his hair. "I never would've expected this. She's my wife's sister. They're family."

"It is real, and the sooner you realize it, the better." Stephanie folded her hands over the papers, regarding him for a moment, with a frown. "Sometimes you pick your fights, and sometimes they pick you. Litigation is just another kind of war, and a custody fight is toughest of all. Lock and load, Mike."

Mike blinked. It was the way she said his name. It kind of woke him up.

"Now I'd like you to explain to me what's been going on since you got home." Stephanie turned her chair to face her laptop. "Can you do that for me, calmly?"

"Sure." Mike told her everything from Chloe's pregnancy, Sara's murder, the time he fell asleep while he was babysitting, then about the arrest and the reasons he'd hit Pat MacFarland and the photographer. It poured out all of a piece, and he hadn't realized until he told it that he'd been screwing up left and right, burning bridges behind him.

"Well, that should do it." Stephanie turned from the screen and lifted an eyebrow, a faint red line against her pale skin. "I won't sugarcoat this. I'm worried about our case, and my first worry is your drug use."

"It's for pain. I'm only a month post my revision surgery, and it's not like I'm sitting around, elevating it."

"So it's pain medication for your injury. Are you taking a prescribed dose?"

Mike hesitated.

"Level with me. I can't represent you properly unless you tell me the truth. Are you taking a prescribed dose or are you taking a dose in excess?"

"In excess, but I can wean myself off."

"Start right now. I want you to testify that you're taking a prescribed dose, and I want you to be telling the truth." Stephanie picked up a pen and legal pad, then began to write. "I'm giving you a Things To Do list. Number one, I'm writing down the name of a place you need to call, an outpatient program for substance abuse."

Mike recoiled. "I don't need a program."

"I want you to call this place anyway. We're going to get Emily back by showing that you have a willingness to work on your problems and are doing so." Stephanie paused, pen in hand. "You need to be randomly drug tested, from here on out. You don't have a problem with that, do you?"

"No."

"You may even be tested at the hearing tomorrow."

"In court?"

"Yes. Who prescribed your meds?"

Mike's mouth went dry. "I self-prescribed."

"What? How? That's serious."

Mike explained his scheme and his hidden stash of pills, and Stephanie frowned.

"Is it possible that Bob and Danielle found those pills?"

"Yes, they weren't in my knapsack, which they packed."

"We'll have to deal with that." Stephanie started writing again. "Number two, you need to find a nice apartment, furnished. Local. Call TopTrees down the street, I saw they have some. If you can't get it furnished, rent the furniture, right now. I'm writing down the name of a furniture rental, and they deliver twenty-four hours, all my dads use it. The place doesn't have to be expensive, but it has to be family-friendly, with bedrooms for you and Emily. You follow?"

"Yes."

"Number three, you have to get a household up and running. Go shopping." Stephanie checked her watch. "It's only two o'clock. Stores are open late."

"I have all that stuff in my storage unit, from my old house. I have furniture, too."

"No, we don't have time to unpack an entire house. I want you to buy dishes, towels, sheets, and toys, and take some nice pictures of the apartment, especially Emily's room, and email them to me." Stephanie kept writing. "Number four, I want you to call rehab for your injury and set up an appointment."

"That's a long process."

"So?" Stephanie met his eye, sharply. "Now, you said you have feelers for a job. Fill me in."

"There's one in Connecticut that's open right away. I didn't want to take it unless I had to. I didn't want to move the baby away from Danielle and Bob." Mike tasted bitterness on his tongue. "Ironic, huh?"

"Forget that. The judge won't let you relocate without their consent. How are your finances? Can you stay out of work for a month? It would be better for Emily if you could be home with her for a while, and it would look better to the court."

"Okay."

"But number five, for after that period, I would like you to line up some sort of part-time work." Stephanie started writing on the pad again. "What about the job at the trade show? Is that part-time?"

"It could be."

"Firm it up, so we can represent to the court that you're good to go. Also, we have to talk about childcare for Emily." Stephanie paused, eyeing him. "I would like you to consider having Danielle become Emily's childcare provider in your home, on a paid basis, while you are at work."

"No way!" Mike shot back. "She and Bob are the last people I'd ask to do anything. You said it yourself; they wrote an agreement that they knew put them in the driver's seat."

"I understand that, but you have to think about the continuity of care, for Emily." Stephanie's eyes widened, in a frank way. "Wouldn't it be in Emily's best interests if Danielle were involved in her life, going forward?"

"I can't imagine letting either of them be with Emily, ever again."

"Wrong answer." Stephanie shook her head in disapproval. "You're speaking out of your own anger. You're not thinking about Emily. You thought highly enough of Danielle's care to leave Emily with her after you renewed your contract, so what I would like to propose at the hearing is that Danielle take care of Emily. If she's not interested, it will make her look bad, in that she'd only care for Emily if she's legally in her custody. Do you follow?"

"Yes, but it drives me crazy."

"Stop with the crazy. You've had enough crazy, and it doesn't serve you." Stephanie made another note on the sheet. "While we're on the topic, number six, I am writing down the phone number of a therapist. I want you to call him today and set up an appointment."

"The VA provides that, with rehab."

"Then you'll do that too, but I want you to avail yourself of private therapy as well. Stop avoiding."

"I'm not avoiding," Mike said, though he realized she could be right.

"We have to show the court that you're dealing with your emotional issues, and I want to make it clear they're because you're coming back from a war and not reflective of a long-term problem." Stephanie leaned over her desk. "Finally, there's several things I *don't* want you to do. I don't want you to have any further involvement in Sara's murder case."

"It's not uppermost in my mind, Emily is, but why should I abandon it? It's not related to the custody proceeding."

"It affects the custody proceeding. Playing cop on Sara's murder case makes you look like a jealous husband and feeds into a picture that suggests you have deep-seated anger issues."

Mike swallowed hard.

"I'm sorry about the death of your wife, but she's not the one who was murdered, and right now we have to focus on Emily. So no running around to jewelry stores."

"Are you sure?" Mike still couldn't let it go. "It feels wrong to ignore Sara's murder for my own problems."

"You have your priorities backwards. It's wrong to set aside your child's welfare for Sara's murder case. You're Emily's father, and that's why we have police departments. And obviously, stay away from Bob and Danielle."

"Emily, too?"

"Yes, all of them."

Mike felt like hitting something. "I have to stay away from my own daughter? They'll be at Sara's funeral."

"When's that?"

"Tomorrow."

"You may not even be there if we get a hearing scheduled, but if you are, give them wide berth. The same goes for the press, the police, ADA, and Pat MacFarland. Anybody calls you, refer them to me. Agreed?"

"Yes," Mike answered reluctantly, knowing she was right about that, too.

"I'll email you when we get the hearing date, and we'll meet before to prepare you for your testimony."

"Thanks." Mike paused. "But I don't understand something. If

Bob threw me out to force my hand, why don't we wait to go to court? I'd only have more of my ducks in a row, down the line."

"Delay is never good. It looks as if you didn't care, and my instinct is to be aggressive." Stephanie tore off the paper and handed it across the desk. "This is your list. Start now. Get as much done as is humanly possible."

Mike read the list, which was written in block printing, more architect than lawyer. "I'm on it."

"My secretary will give you a representation agreement, which you should sign on the way out." Stephanie gestured behind her. "You can bring a check to the hearing. As I told you on the phone, my retainer is five thousand dollars. Keep checking your email. If I reach the judge, I'll let you know. It will be soon."

"Okay." Mike swallowed hard. "Do you think we'll win?"

"It could go either way. It will depend on how you testify." Stephanie's features softened. "Don't worry. I won't let you walk in unprepared. I got your back."

"If we win, I get to take her home, right? She's mine then, legally, right?"

"Yes, and if we lose, then I'll ask the court to review its order in four months, but I'd probably get six. I'd also ask for visitation, but depending on how we do, worst-case scenario, it's supervised."

"For *six* months, they get to live with Emily? And I only get to visit, with a supervisor?"

"Like I said, worst-case scenario. You have to step up your game if you want your daughter back. Can you do that, for her?" Stephanie met his eye, awaiting his answer, and Mike thought back to Sunday morning, when he'd read to Emily for the first time, and to the vow he'd made to her.

"Yes," he answered, his heart speaking for him.

Chapter Sixty-two

TopTrees was a three-story apartment complex, and Mike hurried to the rental office, his head down against the biting snow and his empty sleeve in his pocket. His stump hurt in earnest, and it was all he could do not to take another pill. He went inside the office, a studio apartment that had been repurposed, and a twenty-five-year-old manager sat behind a generic Staples desk, laughing on his cell phone. He hung up quickly, rising.

"I'm Brian, Dr. Scanlon," the manager said, extending a hand, and Mike shook it.

"Call me Mike. Thanks for seeing me on such short notice."

"Sure, follow me." Brian led Mike out of the office and down a covered walkway. There were three buildings to the complex, which was in decent repair, with olive green siding and sliding windows. "The unit is a two-bedroom, fully furnished. Rent is one thousand and two hundred bucks a month, including utilities, and the security deposit is first and last month. Two numbered parking spaces, no pets."

"Does furnished mean silverware and plates?"

"Yep, everything except sheets and towels. The guy that just moved out of your unit was an accountant, and he took good care of it. How old's your kid?"

"I have a daughter, she's almost two."

"We got kids in the complex, mostly on the weekends." Brian produced a key ring as they reached Apartment 3A. "This is one of the nicest units, full southern exposure." He opened the door onto a clean white box of a living room, with a nubby tan rug and nondescript couch and chairs. The air smelled like piney spray cleaner, but wasn't unpleasant. Mike couldn't help thinking that Chloe would've hated the place.

"Nice."

"Appliances only three years old." Brian gestured to the kitchen, with white cabinets, butcher-block counters, and stainless steel appliances.

"Okay." Mike shrugged. It was the new normal.

"I'll show you the bedrooms." Brian walked ahead, and Mike followed him down the hall, where two bedrooms formed the top of a T, across from each other. Brian gestured at the larger one, which had a generic brown dresser and a queen-size bed. "This is the master bedroom, but check out the kid's room."

Mike followed him into the smaller room, which contained a single bed and another white dresser, and the child-sized desk. "Did you say he had a kid here, too?"

"Yeah, a girl about eight. She was real nice."

"What is this, Divorced Dad Acres?"

"Totally. Here's why." Brian waved at the window, and Mike looked out to see a playground in the corner of the park. Snow dusted the slide, lined the monkey bars, and sat like crescent moons in the seats of the swing set. Next to the playground was a small hill, and people were sledding. He flashed forward to a new life, where he and Emily were spinning downhill on a plastic saucer.

"I'll take it," Mike said, brightening.

An hour later, he was pushing an oversized shopping cart through the glistening aisles of a big-box store, buying sheets, towels, baby shampoo, baby detangler, ranch potato chips, three stuffed animals, Spot books, DVDs, kid's pajamas, diapers, Sippy cups, children's Tylenol, baby wipes, bumpers, and a crib with a matching changing table. His shoulder and stump ached constantly, but he white-knuckled the pain and nausea.

He parked the first cart, fetched a second, and tugged it behind him, stopping for soap, napkins, pretzels, toothpaste, Fantastic, paper towels, and jars of baby food. When he was finished, he steered the second cart to the line and went back for the first one. While the cashier rang him out, he checked his phone for email. There were two, and the first was from Stephanie: **The hearing is scheduled for 12 o'clock tomorrow. Meet me at my office at 10 o'clock to prepare.** Mike's thoughts raced ahead, panicky. He hadn't made any phone calls. He'd have to make them first thing tomorrow morning, and on top of that, he still had to get the apartment ready and take the pictures.

"Sir, may I have your credit card?" the cashier asked.

"Of course, sorry." Mike put the phone down, fished out his wallet, and thumbed his Visa card out with difficulty, then handed it to the cashier. "Here we go."

"Thanks," she said, and Mike picked up his phone and clicked ahead to the next email, which was from Don.

Hey Mike, haven't heard anything new from the police. Have you? Also, I forget if I told you about the memorial program for Sara at school tonight at 7. I'll look for you guys.

Mike felt a deep pang. He would be missing Sara's funeral, so he couldn't skip the memorial program, too. He pressed REPLY and typed, **Don, I will be there tonight but I can't come to the funeral tomorrow. I am so sorry. I'll explain when I see you. Haven't heard from cops. Hang in there, buddy.**

Mike suppressed a wave of guilt. His arm cramped with phantom pain. A pill would have made this so easy, and the craving was so powerful he had to grit his teeth. He put his BlackBerry away and signed the electronic screen while the cashier loaded his stuff into plastic bags, filled the carts, and gestured to another employee in a logo smock for help.

"May I assist you with those carts, sir?" the employee asked Mike.

"Thanks," Mike answered, swallowing his pride. He checked his watch, and it was almost seven o'clock. The only way to make the memorial service on time was to go directly to the school, so he got going.

Half an hour later, Mike was at the middle school, hustling to the entrance through the blowing snow. He was running late, and the building blazed with light because everybody was already inside. Reporters and photographers collected on the curb by the Wilberg Middle School sign, but luckily that was a distance from the door. Still he flipped up his hood and kept his head down, his emotions in check. Chloe had taught here for five years, and a deep longing for her sucker-punched him. He used to meet her here all the time, especially when he was wooing her in the early days, making up excuses to have lunch with her.

You don't really come here for Hot Dog Day, do you? Chloe would ask, smiling.

Hot Dog Day is my favorite, Mike had said, wiggling his eyebrows.

Hush, Mike. Mike?

"Mike?" someone was saying, and Mike looked up from his reverie. A man stood in front of him, a silhouette blocking his path. The man's face was in shadow, and snow flurries swirled around them.

"Pardon me?" Mike asked, puzzled.

"Are you Dr. Michael Scanlon?"

"Yes."

"Then you've been served," the man said, thrusting an envelope at him.

Chapter Sixty-three

Mike opened the envelope, stricken, and inside was a packet of papers folded in thirds. It was too dark to see, and snow flew everywhere, so he hurried to the entrance, stood under the overhang, and read the papers in the light coming through the window. SUMMONS AND CIVIL COMPLAINT, it said at the top, and underneath that, PATRICK MACFARLAND VS. MICHAEL SCANLON. So Pat was suing him, after all.

Mike scanned the paper, an official form that read, **This is a notice that you are being sued**, and the blank had been filled in, **tortious battery, intentional infliction of emotional distress, defamation of character.** He flipped to the next page, where it said, **DAMAGES,** and the blank had been filled in, **in excess of five hundred thousand dollars.**

Mike couldn't read anymore, shaken. He didn't have that much money saved and he didn't know what to do, but he had to go inside or he'd miss the memorial service. He stuffed the papers and the envelope in his jacket pocket, then hurried through the entrance doors, and headed past the WILBERG PRIDE banner toward the auditorium. Its back doors were propped open, and the squeaks and miscues of the school orchestra trailed down the hall.

Mike reached the auditorium, which was standing room only,

and he stood behind a forlorn flock of wool coats and down jackets. Subdued sniffling rippled through the crowd, which brought him back to Chloe's funeral, Phat Phil and Oldstein's memorial service, and even Linda's crying after the attack, all the tears swelling like a tide of sorrow that never ended, but just kept crashing onto shore, washing the world in pain.

The music stopped, and people blew their noses. Mike shifted for a better view of the stage, a sleek curve of maple wood that held Principal Patty Camerone, Vice Principal Joe Swanson, and another administrator, Jason Tremblay, sitting on a line of folding chairs. They had all been friends of Chloe's, especially Patty.

Patty really gets the arts program. Some of the others think if you teach art, you're not a real teacher.

Patty walked to the lectern, a tall woman with clipped graying hair, trim and fit in a dark suit. "Thank you very much, Mrs. Weaver and the orchestra. You did a wonderful job."

Mike scanned the crowd for Bob and Danielle, seething to think they'd be here with Emily. He wondered if they knew about the hearing tomorrow and if they had to go out and get a lawyer. He hoped he'd made them as miserable as they'd made him.

Patty was saying, "You've heard from our faculty members tonight, who knew Mrs. Hambera for a long time. But as our final speaker, let's hear from someone new to the Wilberg community. She's not yet a faculty member . . ."

Mike screened Patty out, looking for Bob and Danielle. He had a fantasy of running down the aisle, grabbing Emily, and taking off with her. He could get her out of the school before they could stop him. He would race to the car, hit the gas, and zoom away.

"I'd like to introduce Ms. Hambera's student teacher, Barbara Kipper." Patty stepped aside as a young African-American woman in a black dress adjusted the microphone. "Thank you, Principal Camerone. I'm here tonight to speak about someone we all know and love, Sara Hambera. We know Sara because she was so friendly and open-hearted . . ."

Mike found himself tuning her out and imagining taking Emily to another state or even another country. Any other man would've done it, no matter what a lawyer said. Chatty would've done it, for sure. Jim would've, too. They were the kind of men who took charge. Mike was the kind of man who asked permission.

Barbara continued, "But there's a lot about Sara you don't know. For example, did you know that Sara was voted class clown in high school? And does that surprise any of you?"

The audience chuckled sadly, but Mike shifted and checked for Bob and Danielle, his anger building.

Barbara was saying, "Teachers touch people's lives in ways they can never imagine, and Sara let us know her not just as a teacher, but as a girlfriend. We all loved to hear her stories about Don, even if he would rather she hadn't told them. Right, Don?" The audience chuckled again, and Barbara gestured to her right with a shaky smile.

Mike followed her motion, and Don was sitting on the left in the front row, his arms around their sons, dressed in clip-on ties and dark blazers. He felt a stab of sympathy for them, then noticed that Bob, Danielle, and Emily sat three rows behind. Emily was twisting around to say something to Danielle, and Danielle and Bob smiled at the same time. Danielle kissed Emily on the head, and Bob fixed something on her coat, then they all smiled again.

Mike watched, conflicted. He felt angry, but he couldn't deny what was before his very eyes, and that was, above all, a family. He looked to the right and left of them, and the evidence filled the seats. Bob, Danielle, and Emily fit in perfectly with the mommies and daddies with kids cuddled in their laps, nestled between them, or held in their arms, already sleeping.

Mike realized he was the one who didn't fit in. He was the one on the outside. He hardly knew his own daughter, and she hardly knew him. He fought his rising nausea and began to feel miserable, not only symptoms of withdrawal. All of the families filling the auditorium were bound by love, and though he loved Emily, she didn't love him. Tomorrow he was going to court to get her back, but he'd have to take her from her family, and he couldn't offer her another one in its place. All he had was himself, and he wasn't even whole.

Mike found himself edging out of the auditorium, turning away, and hurrying from the school.

Chapter Sixty-four

Mike carried the last plastic shopping bag into the apartment, kicked the door closed behind him, and dumped the bag on the rug with the others. He'd bought ibuprofen and he needed it now. He pawed through the purchases until he found it, tore open the box with his teeth, and wedged the lid off with his thumb, then extracted two pills and swallowed them dry. He felt an almost instant relief, which was completely psychological, but it was all he could do not to reach for the Oxys.

He shed his coat and dropped it on the floor, too. He'd gotten his second wind on the way home and unpacked everything. He filled the linen closet with towels, the cupboards with food, and the refrigerator with milk and soda. He unwrapped the new Fisher-Price toys and set them on the floor, laid the Activity Blanket on the rug, placed the *Shrek* and *Madagascar* DVDs on the shelf in the wood-veneer TV cart, and arrayed the *Spot the Dog* books in front. He took pictures of the living room and emailed them to Stephanie.

He hurried with the next bag to the bathroom, where he put the baby shampoo, conditioner, and detangler on the rim of the bath-tub, and piled the new water toys inside, blue plastic pouring cups, a fake fisherman's net with plastic starfish, and hypoallergenic soap that squirted out of a tube. He unwrapped the guard for the faucet, using his hand and his teeth, so Emily wouldn't burn herself on the faucet.

He affixed the plastic hooks to babyproof the vanity, which took forever with one hand, then hurried back to babyproof every door and closet in the apartment, even in his own bedroom. He made his bed, then went to set up Emily's room. He unpacked her bumpers, diapers, and new clothes, then started putting everything away, setting the folded clothes on the side of the drawers, so they didn't topple over.

He retrieved the new night lamp, with a smiling yellow duck for the base, screwed in an eco-friendly light bulb, and plugged it in, shedding a warm soft light around the bedroom. He fetched the new screwdriver and dragged the big cardboard box with the crib into the bedroom. LIGHT ASSEMBLY REQUIRED, read the box. He took a deep breath and got busy.

An hour later, Mike was sitting on the bedroom floor, still trying to build the crib. He'd lined up his screws, washers, bolts, and long metal ribs that went under the mattress, but couldn't get past Step Two. It didn't help that he'd bought the most complicated crib in the universe, apparently a "3-in-1 Convertible." He picked up the directions, which read at the top, **Converts from crib, to toddler bed, to daybed while maintaining its transitional style!**

Mike scanned the diagrams, but they didn't look like the pieces he'd laid out, and there were no other directions in words. There were four sides to the crib, all of white wooden lattice, and since the crib was rectangular, he could easily see the difference between the long sides and the shorter ends, but he couldn't screw the long side to the end, with one arm.

He got up on his knees and tried again. He put the headboard flat on the floor, then rested the long side on it, holding it steady because it didn't have any dowels. But he couldn't hold it and screw it in at the same time, so he tried changing positions. He held the long side in place by resting it alongside his shoulder and tried screwing it in that way, but it kept slipping and the screw popped off. He switched things around, so that the long side was on the ground and the short side was against his shoulder, but it wouldn't line up with the hole, and the end-lattice fell onto the side-lattice.

"Damn!" he said aloud. His stump was killing him from all the movement, his stomach felt queasy, and his mind kept going to the Oxys, bobbing to the surface of his consciousness like a tub toy, guaranteed to float. His emotions were hard to control, maybe because they'd been controlled artificially for so long, or maybe because the stakes had never been this high. Or maybe because he was being sued for half a million dollars and had no one but himself to blame. Or maybe because the side effects of Oxycontin were anxiety, headache, mood changes, confusion, and unusual thoughts or behavior. Also constipation, which was a real treat.

He surveyed the wreckage he'd made of Emily's room, which looked worse in the soft light. The rug was littered with screws, bolts, the mattress and box spring, and the massive box, plus the endless trail of cellophane. He couldn't email Stephanie a picture, but the mess was the reality. He was trying to make an instant home, just add water, but it wasn't working.

Mike checked his watch. It was almost three in the morning, and the apartment was silent and still. Outside the window, he could see the snow falling, growing deeper on the windowsill, and he could feel the temperature dropping. He could stay up all night, but he couldn't make this apartment a home. He couldn't make a bed for his child. And he hadn't even started to assemble the changing table.

He threw the screwdriver against the wall, where it stuck like a bayonet.

"Hoo-ah," he said bitterly.

Chapter Sixty-five

Mike was shown into Stephanie's office, with a fresh shave and a new attitude. It was game day, so even though he'd barely slept, he was ready to go, in a suit and tie. He hadn't taken an Oxy since yesterday, so his stump was killing him, his stomach ached, and he had chills, but he sucked it up and managed a smile. "Hey, counselor."

Stephanie smiled back, rising. "Well, look at you. Somebody's loaded for bear."

"It shows, huh?" Mike slid a hand in his pocket, pulled out the papers from Pat MacFarland, and handed them across the desk. "Before you get too happy, how's this for a revolting development?"

Stephanie scanned the papers, her eyes darting back and forth as she read. She had on a greenish gray suit with an asymmetrical jacket, and a bold perfume that gave Mike the impression she was dressed for court, too.

"They served me last night, at Sara's memorial service."

"Nice." Stephanie kept reading. "Remind me to use that one."

"Can he really sue me, and for that much?"

"Welcome to America, where anybody can sue anybody for anything." Stephanie sat down, closing the papers with a slapping sound. "This, however, is a money grab. They didn't even take the time to file a full complaint. They know you're on the ropes after the criminal charges and they want to start negotiations."

Mike was losing his smile. "I don't have that much money and I'm not about to pay him anywhere near that. I know I did wrong, but come on."

"Absolutely, and we have more pressing matters to deal with today." Stephanie met his eyes evenly. "How are you feeling?"

"The whole truth and nothing but?" Mike didn't want to joke around. He'd said it only because he was nervous. "Ready to get Emily back."

"I know, but it's not a simple case, by any means." Stephanie eased into her desk chair. "Tell me how many things you got finished on your to-do list."

"Besides the apartment?" Mike hadn't succeeded in building the crib or the changing table, but nobody had to know that. "I made all the calls I was supposed to."

"Really, you called the outpatient clinic for drug rehab?"

"I did, this morning, and I left a message to call back. I also went online and made an appointment at the VA rehab, but the earliest they can take me is a month. I called the shrink and left a message for him too."

"Good job." Stephanie sipped coffee from a flowery china mug. "By the way, Bob and Danielle hired Jason Franklin to represent them. Franklin is smart, experienced, and political."

"How much does that matter?"

"We still elect judges in this state, remember?"

Mike let it go. "So what do you think? How are you feeling about our chances?"

"The good news is we got assigned to Judge Shield, one of the old guard, very reasonable and fair." Stephanie leaned over, linking her fingers. "But before I answer you, I want to tell you my trial strategy. It isn't pretty, but it gives you the best chance you have."

"Okay, shoot."

"Let's face it, we have some bad facts to deal with. The other side is going to bring them up in minute detail, but we go first as the movant, and I want to preempt them. In other words, I want to take the sting out of their arguments by raising them first. You understand?"

"Yes, you want to beat them to the punch. But what does that mean, in effect?"

"It means that my direct examination of you won't be comfortable. I will elicit bad information from you, but it's our best shot."

"So you're amputating to save the patient." Mike managed another smile. "I'm familiar."

"Good." Stephanie didn't bat an eye. "All you have to do is answer my questions. Tell the truth. Don't volunteer information. Keep your temper during cross-examination. If you want the judge to see you as a father, act like one. Even when my friend Jason Franklin rakes you over the coals."

"Jason Franklin is your friend?"

"We're lawyer friends, which means we hate each other until five o'clock. Don't let him rattle you."

"I won't," Mike said, with confidence.

"Okay." Stephanie checked her watch. "Let's get started."

Chapter Sixty-six

Mike looked around the courtroom, mentally preparing himself for the hearing, while Stephanie and Jason Franklin exchanged legal papers and Bob and Danielle talked among themselves. The courtroom was older than he'd expected, with a worn marble floor, brass lamps on each table, and sconces that glowed softly on blue plaster walls, making the high-tech black stem microphones, laptop computers, and surge protectors look out of place. The radiators hissed, unable to heat such a large space. The courtroom was used for major trials, and the fact that it was so empty only emphasized its majesty.

"All rise for the Honorable Judge Calvin Shield," boomed a court officer, standing before an American flag and the flag of the Commonwealth of Pennsylvania. "Oyez, Oyez! God save the Commonwealth and this Honorable Court."

Jason and Stephanie took their places as Judge Shield swept into the courtroom, a tall, thin older man with an angular face, whose pure white hair made him look like a church spire in New England.

"Good morning, folks." Judge Shield climbed the mahogany dais and waved everyone into their seats, then sat down, consulted some papers on his desk, and looked up at Stephanie with a quick smile. "Let's get right to business, because we'll be closing early today if the snow keeps up. Ms. Bergen, why don't you get us started?"

Stephanie rose. "May it please the court, I'm representing Dr. Michael Scanlon, who has returned from serving in Afghanistan in the Army Medical Corps, and seeks to modify a court order and obtain permanent physical and legal custody of his minor child, Emily, from nonparents, an aunt and uncle. The child's mother, Chloe Voulette, is deceased, and the child went to live with her aunt and uncle during her father's deployment."

"I've read the papers, so I have the facts." Judge Shield's gaze shifted from Mike to Bob and Danielle, his expression reserved, if benevolent. "Continue, please."

"Your Honor, Dr. Scanlon is the child's natural father and is able and willing to maintain a loving, stable, and nurturing home for her, consistent with Chapter 53, Section 5328. In addition, the statute provides expressly that 'as between a parent and a nonparent, there shall be a presumption that custody shall be awarded to the parent.' That presumption may be rebutted only by clear and convincing evidence, not present in this case."

"I have your argument. Would you call your witness, please?" Judge Shield gestured to the witness box, and Stephanie turned to Mike.

"Dr. Scanlon? Please take the stand."

"Sure." Mike rose stiffly and walked to the witness stand as the court clerk appeared, but when he put his hand on the Bible, he realized he didn't have another hand to raise.

"Uh," the court clerk started to say. "Do you swear to tell the whole truth and nothing but the truth, so help you God?"

"I do," Mike answered, trying not to look at Bob or Danielle, who sat at the other table in navy blue suits, next to Franklin, who was portly, bald, and had a bulbous nose, with thick, rimless glasses that looked wedged into fleshy cheeks.

"Please be seated."

Stephanie stepped forward. "Your Honor, may I approach the witness?" Judge Shield nodded, and she walked toward Mike. "Dr. Scanlon, please tell us briefly about your service in Afghanistan."

"Objection!" Franklin said, rising.

"Come now, Mr. Franklin." Judge Shield didn't hide an amused smile. "Is this going to be one of those days?"

Franklin cleared his throat. "Your Honor, we're prepared to stipulate that Dr. Scanlon deserves our thanks for having served his country well and honorably, with personal sacrifice. I believe that Ms. Bergen is attempting to influence this court's decision by playing on its sympathies and patriotism."

Stephanie started to answer, but Judge Shield raised a hand. "Overruled." He turned to Mike, his soft gray eyes sunk deeply into his gaunt, lined face. "Dr. Scanlon, we appreciate your service to our country, yet we're here to determine what is in Emily's best interests. You understand that, don't you?"

"Yes, Your Honor, I do."

"Fine." Judge Shield turned to Stephanie. "Please, proceed."

"Dr. Scanlon, how long have you been home?"

"Approximately a week."

"And what occurred that occasioned your honorable discharge and release from active duty?"

"I was in Helmand Province, traveling in a Humvee that hit a roadside bomb, and when we exited the vehicle, we were engaged in enemy contact. I sustained injuries to my left arm that required its amputation."

Stephanie nodded. "Did you receive any award or commendation with regard to this incident and subsequent injury?"

Mike hadn't wanted her to ask the question, but she had insisted. Suddenly he flashed on the Humvee explosion, the orange-red blaze. Chatty, unconscious, in the seat. Segundo and the driver trapped inside. Black smoke everywhere. The crack of gunfire. The red muzzle flashes, roadside.

"Dr. Scanlon, you received a commendation in regard to that incident, didn't you?"

Mike came out of his reverie, shaken. "Yes."

"Let's move on, Dr. Scanlon. Where you prescribed any pain medications as a result of your amputation surgery?"

"Yes, Oxycontin."

"Are you taking that prescription, presently?"

"Yes, for pain."

"And does it impair your function in any way?"

Franklin popped up. "Objection, leading."

"Overruled." Judge Shield rested his chin in his hand, eyeing Mike. "Go on."

"Oxycontin causes irritability, some mood changes, and a few other emotional side effects, but it relieves the pain from the swelling."

Stephanie rested a hand on the rail of the witness box. "Are you presently taking a prescribed dose?"

"I am, and I'm in the process of weaning myself off the higher doses required by the acute phase after my revision surgery."

"Dr. Scanlon, are you enrolled in any outpatient program in drug rehabilitation or education?"

"I have called and requested enrollment."

"Are you currently in any therapy to ease your reentry after your tours of duty?"

"Yes, I have calls into a private therapist and am also scheduled to begin a support group for returning vets at the VA." Mike felt it was going well, and Stephanie smiled at him in an encouraging way.

"By the way, Dr. Scanlon, why did you voluntarily renew your contract for a second tour, after serving your first?"

"I renewed because I was requested to do so and knew that I was needed. No other podiatric surgeons were available, at this late stage of the war. I wanted to come home to my daughter, very much, but felt I had to serve." Mike thought it went without saying, but Stephanie wasn't taking any chances.

"Dr. Scanlon, where are you currently living?"

"In the TopTrees complex in Clifton, in a two-bedroom apartment, where Emily has her own room, overlooking a playground."

"Your Honor, may I approach the witness?"

"Yes."

Stephanie took a few photos from counsel table, then distributed copies to Franklin, Judge Shield, and Mike. "Dr. Scanlon, are these photos of your apartment, taken by you?"

"Yes."

"Thank you." Stephanie crossed to the clerk. "Your Honor, I move these into evidence as Movant's Exhibits A through C."

"Granted." Judge Shield examined the photos as the court clerk attached exhibit stickers to them.

Stephanie turned back to Mike. "Dr. Scanlon, before your deployment, you were self-employed fulltime as a podiatric surgeon. Are you returning to that position?"

"No, I intend to work on a part-time basis, marketing a custom-made walking boot to heal sports injuries in children and adolescents. I'm in a position financially where I don't have to work for a month or two, and I want to stay home with Emily full-time."

"I see." Stephanie folded her arms. "Dr. Scanlon, when you return to work, would you consider employing Mrs. Ridgeway to take care of Emily at your home, to afford your daughter continuity of care and ease her transition?"

"Yes, that would be one of the options I would consider, for Emily's sake."

"Thank you." Stephanie picked up some papers from counsel table and distributed them to Judge Shield and Franklin before she strode to Mike and handed him a sheaf. "Dr. Scanlon, please identify these papers for the court."

"They're papers that they gave me after I was charged with simple assault in Wilberg, two days ago, as a result of a fistfight with a former neighbor."

"How did you plead?"

"Not guilty." Mike avoided Bob's eye, though he would have loved to have seen him squirm, since the not-guilty plea was his idea.

"Have you ever before been charged with assault or any other criminal offense?"

"No."

"Can you explain to the court the reason for this fistfight?"

Franklin popped up. "Objection, relevance, Your Honor."

Stephanie whirled around. "Mr. Franklin, if you're prepared to stipulate that criminal charges for assault are irrelevant to this proceeding, I'll withdraw the question and move on."

Franklin frowned. "No, I won't. It's clearly relevant under Section 5329."

Judge Shield leaned forward, his black sleeves billowing over the dais. "Then what's the basis for your objection, Mr. Franklin? Is it relevant or not? You can't have it both ways."

Franklin stepped forward, holding the papers. "Your Honor, the fact of the assault charge is relevant, but the reason for the assault is not."

Stephanie turned to the judge. "That's a distinction without a difference, Your Honor. Why not hear why it happened? There's no jury present, and I trust Your Honor can accord the testimony the weight it deserves."

Judge Shield nodded. "Objection overruled." He motioned to Mike. "Please answer, Dr. Scanlon."

"Briefly, the fistfight was over my late wife, because I found email that suggested my former neighbor had engaged in an affair with her while I was away." Mike hated to admit being cuckolded in open court, but Stephanie said it was the way to go.

"Dr. Scanlon, moving on, why were you at the Clifton police station on Sunday afternoon?"

"I believed I had information that could help solve the murder of Sara Hambera. She was a dear friend of my late wife's and mine."

Judge Shield clucked. "My condolences. It's a tragic case, tragic."

Stephanie waited a moment, then asked, "Dr. Scanlon, did you turn over such information to the police?"

"Yes, I did."

"Did you seek to claim the reward?"

"No."

"When you left the Clifton police station, what happened between you and the press?"

"There was a crowd of reporters standing in my way, so when I tried to go forward, I hit a camera."

"Did you hit or strike anyone?"

"No, I don't think so, and if I did, it wasn't intentional, though it might have appeared that way, the way it was edited on the TV news."

"Finally, Dr. Scanlon, last Sunday morning, when you were home alone with Emily, you fell asleep with her, after reading books to her on the living room floor. Why?"

"I hadn't slept well the night before, and one of the side effects of my pain medication is drowsiness. I have since decreased my dosage and that won't happen again."

Judge Shield lifted a gray eyebrow. "Dr. Scanlon, would you agree to random drug testing, should custody be restored to you today?"

"Yes, of course. Your Honor."

Judge Shields blinked. "Anything further, Ms. Bergen?"

"Nothing, Your Honor. I may call for rebuttal, if need be." Stephanie sat down without looking at Mike.

Judge Shield motioned to Franklin. "Counsel, do you wish to cross-examine?"

Chapter Sixty-seven

"I'll cross-examine." Jason Franklin stood up with a manila envelope in his hands and approached the court clerk. "Your Honor, I wish to move into evidence three bottles of Oxycontin, thirty pills each, at ten milligrams a pill, as Respondents' Exhibits A, B, and C."

Mike told himself to stay calm. Stephanie had prepared him for how to handle it if the pills came to light. She hadn't wanted to ask him about them on the stand, if Bob and Danielle hadn't found them. Her expression remained impassive as Franklin slid the bottles from the envelope and handed them to the court clerk, who labeled them with exhibit stickers, then gave them back to Franklin. The lawyer showed them to the judge.

"Admitted," Judge Shield ruled, scrutinizing the bottles and handing them back. "Let the record so reflect."

"Your Honor, may I approach the witness?" Franklin asked, but didn't wait for an answer as he strode to the witness box and placed the pill bottles on the rail.

Mike blinked, remembering Stephanie's advice. *Wait for the question. Say nothing more than the answer.*

"Dr. Scanlon, do you recognize the three bottles of Oxycontin, entered as Respondents' Exhibits A through C?"

"Yes."

"They belong to you, don't they?"

"Yes."

"You hid them under the mattress in your bedroom in my clients' home, did you not?"

"Yes." Mike felt his face flush with shame, and Judge Shield glanced over, sucking in his cheeks.

Franklin continued, "They're for your personal consumption, are they not?"

"Yes."

Franklin picked up a bottle. "You're aware that Oxycontin is an opiate, a controlled substance as addictive as heroin, are you not?"

"Yes."

"Dr. Scanlon, you obtained these drugs through fraudulent means, didn't you?"

"Yes." Mike couldn't avoid seeing Bob frown in disapproval.

"Dr. Scanlon, you're aware that obtaining controlled substances through fraudulent means violates state law, aren't you?"

"Yes."

"Are you also aware that these admissions in court could subject you to prosecution under the Controlled Substances Act, should this matter be referred to the District Attorney?"

"Yes."

"You're also aware that obtaining controlled substances through fraudulent means violates the medical canons of ethics?"

"Yes." Mike spotted Danielle, shaking her head sadly.

"Dr. Scanlon, didn't you accomplish this by writing the prescriptions, fraudulently pretending to be the patient, and picking them up yourself?"

"Yes." Mike saw the orange-red flash of an explosion, but it vanished into thin air.

"Dr. Scanlon, aren't you admitting to this court that you fabricated the prescriptions and made up the names—" Franklin held up the bottles and read aloud—"Phil DeMaria, Adam Goldstein, and John Jacobs?"

312 | Lisa Scottoline

Mike startled to hear the names echoing in the courtroom, like the Final Roll Call transported to this very spot, and he felt sick to his stomach. "I didn't make up the names."

"Pardon me?"

"The names are men who served with me in Afghanistan. They were killed in action, by a grenade." Mike realized he'd said too much when he saw Franklin's eyes widen slightly.

"I see." Franklin picked up the bottles, reading them again. "When did the explosion occur that killed Philip DeMaria, Adam Goldstein, and John . . ."

Mike missed the end of the question, because he was back at the memorial service. Before his eyes were the four rifles, bayonet-down, driven into the frozen earth. He heard the reading, name after name, of the men who would never answer. *DeMaria? Philip De Maria? Major Philip DeMaria, Jr.?*

"Dr. Scanlon? Please answer the question."

"I forget the question." Mike came out of his reverie to spot Stephanie watching him with concern.

Franklin shook his head. "I withdraw it. Instead, I'll ask, Dr. Scanlon, are you suffering distress over the loss of these men?"

Stephanie stood up. "Objection, relevance."

Franklin faced Judge Shield. "Your Honor, under section 5328, subsection 15, the mental condition of Dr. Scanlon is very much at issue, as is his drug use, under section 5328, subsection 14. I am certainly entitled to explore the extent to which he suffers from post-traumatic stress disorder."

Stephanie stepped forward. "Your Honor, it hasn't been established that Dr. Scanlon is suffering from PTSD, and he testified that he is seeking counseling, in any event."

Franklin shook has head. "Your Honor, it is our position that Dr. Scanlon is in denial over the extent to which he is suffering from PTSD, and that he has misrepresented to this court the extent of his drug addiction."

"Objection, Your Honor." Stephanie raised her voice. "Dr. Scanlon has explained that he takes painkillers as a post-operative amputee. Would counsel prefer he bite a bullet?"

"Counsel, please." Judge Shield raised a hand, as if to silence quarreling children. "Mr. Franklin, I'll allow it, but keep it short."

"Thank you, Your Honor." Franklin turned to the witness stand, his smile fading. "Dr. Scanlon, don't you still grieve your friends who died in action?"

"Yes." Mike clenched his jaw.

"Don't you suffer flashbacks?"

"Yes."

"Don't you feel depressed or sad, at times?"

"Yes."

"Angry?"

Mike was actually starting to feel angry. "Only when called for."

Stephanie rose. "Your Honor, is this keeping it short? Also, if counsel wants an expert opinion, he should have brought an expert."

Franklin turned to Judge Shield. "Your Honor, I'll move on." He returned to Mike. "After Emily almost fell down the steps, didn't you tell my client, Danielle Ridgeway, that Oxycontin was the reason you fell asleep?"

Mike should have seen this coming. Danielle must have told Franklin everything. "Yes."

"Isn't it true that Danielle also told you she was worried about your drug dependence?"

Stephanie rose again. "Continuing objection, Your Honor."

Judge Shield turned to Mike. "Please answer, Dr. Scanlon."

"Yes."

"Dr. Scanlon, didn't you tell Danielle you would not be weaning yourself off your drugs anytime soon?"

Mike swallowed hard. "Yes, but that was before."

Franklin turned away, then seemed to think better of it, and faced Mike. "Dr. Scanlon, when did you call the outpatient drug clinic?"

"This morning."

"So, just in time for court. That was hardly a coincidence, was it?"

Stephanie half rose. "Objection, relevance. Dr. Scanlon has been home for less than a week."

Franklin scoffed, at Stephanie. "That's not an objection, that's testimony."

"Counsel, please." Judge Shield straightened up. "Mr. Franklin, I'm interested in Emily's best interests going forward, in the future."

Mike could have hugged the judge. Stephanie fiddled with her right earring, which she'd told him was her signal that things were going well.

Franklin set down the pill bottles. "Dr. Scanlon, isn't it true that you have been upset by the revelation that your late wife was unfaithful to you?"

"Yes." Mike felt his face get hot.

"You were jealous, were you not?"

Stephanie rose. "Objection, relevance, Your Honor."

Franklin faced the judge. "Allow me a question or two, Your Honor, and the relevance will become clear."

Judge Shield pursed his lips. "Fair enough, objection overruled. I'll wait and see."

Franklin turned back to Mike. "Dr. Scanlon, you became convinced that your wife's lover was also the killer of her best friend, Sara Hambera?"

"Yes."

"And didn't you tell my clients that you were obsessed with finding out who killed Sara Hambera and slept with your wife?"

"Yes." Mike regretted his words when Franklin smiled, as if he'd scored.

"Moving on, Dr. Scanlon, you volunteered for the second tour of duty with the Army, isn't that correct?"

"Yes."

"You chose to stay in the Army for a second tour, rather than come home to your daughter?"

Stephanie half rose. "Objection, relevance, Your Honor. Also, this is hardly moving forward, and Dr. Scanlon has already testified to this point."

Franklin turned to the judge. "I'll modify my question, Your Honor." He faced Mike again. "Dr. Scanlon, when you decided to renew your contract for a second tour, you had absolute confidence in the high quality of the care that my clients would continue to provide Emily, isn't that true?"

"Yes."

"Isn't it also true that my clients have provided Emily with a loving, stable, and happy home?"

"Yes."

"Isn't it true that Emily is happy in their care?"

"Yes, she is."

"Isn't it true that Emily loves my clients, and they love her, as if she were their own child?"

Mike's mouth went dry. "Yes, but I'm her father and I love her, too."

Franklin turned away and faced the judge. "Your Honor, I have no further questions."

Stephanie stood up. "I have no redirect, Your Honor. May we take a break before Mr. Franklin begins his case-in-chief?"

"Make it snappy," Judge Shield answered, with a nod.

Chapter Sixty-eight

Stephanie steered Mike from the courtroom, down the hall, and through a door marked Attorney Conference Room, which was a small room with an old mahogany table and a few hard chairs. She closed the door behind them and turned to Mike, her eyes alive with animation. "Listen, you were terrific! You did great! Way to go!"

"Really?" Mike felt shaky, and his stump throbbed like it was on fire. He pulled up a chair and sat down. "What did I do right?"

"Everything." Stephanie began to pace, too excited to sit down. "Props to your genius lawyer, because our trial strategy worked beautifully. Your direct examination went so well that Franklin had nothing left. Couldn't you tell that? He ran out of gas!"

"You really think it went well?" Mike had been too busy doing it to assess it, and the stakes were so high.

"Yes, the very best it could have gone. I was worried about your cross, but Franklin didn't hurt you at all."

"Good." Mike exhaled, relieved. "Now what happens?"

"Franklin will put on his case. He'll have Bob and Danielle testify, and he's going to rely on the fact that they've had Emily all this time and have provided a good home for her."

"That sounds good for them though, doesn't it?"

"No, if that's all they got, they lose. Remember, you have the presumption as a parent. If it's a borderline case, then you win."

"Wow, really?" Mike felt dazed and happy. "So am I done now?"

"No, remember, the procedure. After Bob and Danielle testify, I may ask you to get back up on the stand, if they've hurt you." Stephanie's expression grew serious. "Just do the same great job you did before, and tell the truth."

"Will do."

"Now, when they testify, don't react if something bothers you or makes you angry. Hang tough. Good to go?"

"Yes," Mike told her, bracing himself.

Chapter Sixty-nine

Mike didn't have to know Bob to see that he wasn't happy in the witness stand, sitting upright with a frown and jerking his chin repeatedly out of his cutaway collar.

Franklin cleared his throat. "Mr. Ridgeway, where are you employed and for how long have you worked there?"

"I'm self-employed in a limited liability corporation, a law firm called The Ridgeway Group. We practice general business law in Erwin and have for almost fifteen years. I employ twenty-one people and intend to hire two new associates this year."

"Mr. Ridgeway, please tell the court how you and your wife Danielle came to take Emily into your home."

"Well, my wife's younger sister passed away while Mike was on his first tour, and we were the only family Emily had. We were her only babysitters, too, and we love her and she loves us." Bob's expression relaxed, but not enough to smile. "My wife Danielle quit her job as my office administrator to stay home with Emily full-time, and Dr. Scanlon was more than happy to have us take her on."

Mike shifted in the chair. Bob's casual tone made it sound like he didn't care, and looking back, he had to admit Emily wasn't uppermost in his mind after Chloe died, especially when he found the booze. His arm throbbed.

"Mr. Ridgeway, did there come a time when Dr. Scanlon formally agreed that you and Danielle should have legal and physical custody of Emily for as long as necessary?"

"Objection, Your Honor," Stephanie said, without getting up. "That calls for speculation about my client's intent."

"Your Honor, I'll withdraw that question and save you the trouble of ruling." Franklin reached for some papers on the table and brought them to the court clerk, who labeled them and handed them back. "I'd like to move into evidence as Respondents' Exhibit D, the custody agreement between the parties."

"Granted." Judge Shield flipped through some papers on the dais. "The agreement was attached as an exhibit to your brief, and I'm familiar with it, so proceed."

Franklin took the agreement to Bob. "Mr. Ridgeway, you're familiar with this, aren't you?"

"Yes, it was drafted by someone in my office, modeled after a form she found. We practice business law, not family law. I know that Dr. Scanlon thinks I wrote it, but I didn't."

Mike blinked, surprised. He'd thought Bob drafted it to screw him, but maybe he hadn't.

"Mr. Ridgeway, the agreement clearly provides that you and Danielle will have custody of Emily for 'as long as necessary.' What was meant by that?"

Stephanie rose. "Objection, Your Honor, as to relevance. This isn't a contract dispute, in which we need to determine the intent of the parties. It's irrelevant whether the parties had a meeting of the minds about when the custody arrangement should end. The only inquiry today is what is in Emily's best interests."

Franklin turned to the judge. "Your Honor, it's relevant because it shows that Dr. Scanlon was more than willing to entrust Emily to Danielle and Bob completely. In fact, he signed an agreement that essentially gave them full custodial rights for an indefinite term."

Stephanie scoffed. "Your Honor, as it states in my brief, Dr. Scanlon didn't intend to transfer his rights to his daughter forever. He trusted his brother-in-law to act as his lawyer with respect to the custody agreement. Moreover, Dr. Scanlon testified that he had faith in the care provided by the Ridgeways. Our position is that it was only temporary."

Judge Shield nodded. "I'll grant your objection, Ms. Bergen. Mr. Franklin, the contract is moot at this juncture. Please, move on."

"Thank you, Your Honor." Franklin pivoted neatly toward the witness stand. "Mr. Ridgeway, moving on, please tell the court about your relationship to Emily."

"It's wonderful. I love her, and I've been, in all practical effect, her father. She treats me like a father and she calls me Daddy."

Mike cringed. Stephanie wrote on a legal pad in block letters, RELAX.

Franklin cocked his head. "Mr. Ridgeway, does Emily call Dr. Scanlon Daddy?"

"No, and she doesn't really know him. She cries every time he holds her and always has."

Mike reddened because Bob was right. Stephanie began tapping the eraser end of her pencil on the table.

Franklin nodded. "Mr. Ridgeway, who paid Emily's expenses during the considerable time you and your wife gave her a home?"

"We did, all of them." Bob frowned again. "I make an excellent living from my practice and I'm happy to do it. Mike said he'd pay us back, but I wouldn't accept it. We're her parents, for all intents and purposes."

Mike was kicking himself. He hadn't had a chance to settle up with them yet, and he should have made it a point.

"Mr. Ridgeway, while Emily was in your and your wife's care, did she incur any accidents or injuries?"

"No."

"Did you ever fall asleep while babysitting her?"

"No."

Mike swallowed hard. It still killed him that he'd fallen asleep on Emily. Next to him, Stephanie wrote, DON'T WORRY, THIS IS GOING NOWHERE.

"Mr. Ridgeway, are you presently or have you ever had any problems with drugs or alcohol?"

"No."

"Are you presently or have you ever had any issues regarding anger management?"

"No."

"Have you ever been arrested or charged with any crime, including but not limited to assault?"

"No."

Stephanie rose. "Objection as to relevance, Your Honor. Again, we have no quarrel with the level of care that Emily has been given while her father was deployed. Our position is that her father is willing and able to care for her, and he has presumptive custody. In the interest of saving this court's time, especially in a snowstorm, we'd be willing to stipulate as much."

Franklin hesitated, facing the judge. "Your Honor, this line of questioning will give the court a much fuller factual basis on which to base its decision, snowstorm or not."

"I'm going to grant that objection." Judge Shield twisted his chair to the witness stand. "Mr. Ridgeway, as a lawyer, you're sophisticated enough to know that you are not on trial here, nor is your ability to care for Emily. In addition, weather aside, the last thing I would do is give short shrift to a matter of this magnitude, where a child's safety and welfare are concerned."

Bob nodded. "I understand, Your Honor."

Franklin said, "Thank you, Your Honor. I have only one question left. Mr. Ridgeway, why do you think that you and your wife provide a better home for Emily than Dr. Scanlon?"

Stephanie rose. "Objection, Your Honor. The witness's opinion on the ultimate question in this matter is irrelevant."

Franklin opened his mouth to respond, but Judge Shield cut him off with a wave. "Denied, Ms. Bergen. You're probably right as a technical matter, but I'm inclined to hear what Mr. Ridgeway has to say."

"Thank you, Your Honor." Franklin turned to the witness stand. "Mr. Ridgeway, please finish your answer."

Bob nodded. "I'm not trying to take away anything from Dr.

Scanlon, but facts are facts. He's had a hard time since he's been back, and the war definitely changed him. Even though that's understandable and he's getting help, we can't pretend that it doesn't affect Emily."

Mike looked down. The war had changed him. He was different now. He knew it inside.

Bob continued, "Emily is happy with where she is, and we don't have any problems like that. Danielle is always home with her, so she had the best possible care, and my wife is her aunt, a blood relative. The truth is, no woman on the earth loves Emily more than Danielle does."

"Thank you." Franklin turned to Judge Shield. "I have no further questions of Mr. Ridgeway, Your Honor."

Stephanie remained standing. "Your Honor, I have no cross-examination of Mr. Ridgeway."

Franklin's head swiveled around in surprise, then he recovered. "Okay, then, Your Honor, if I may, I'd like to call Mrs. Danielle Ridgeway to the stand."

Danielle rose and walked to the witness stand as Bob was excused, and Mike sensed the energy in the courtroom change, perceptibly. Judge Shield seemed to ease back in his chair, his long fingers going to his chin, and the court clerk smiled in a reassuring way. Danielle climbed the steps to the witness box, and when the court officer came over with the Bible, she looked nervous as she placed her hand on its pebbled cover.

"Do you swear to tell the truth the whole truth and nothing but the truth, so help you God?"

"I do," Danielle answered, her voice sweet and soft.

Mike found himself looking at Danielle with new eyes, maybe because she was out of her typical context, and she had never reminded him of Chloe more powerfully than at this moment. She exuded a vulnerability and kindness that she shared with Chloe, and he could feel his heart ache for her, which both surprised and confused him.

Franklin didn't approach the witness stand, implicitly according

Danielle a stage. "Mrs. Ridgeway, please tell us something about the care you've been giving Emily, on a full-time basis."

Danielle smiled, faintly. "I don't understand. Are you asking me what I've done, as a mother? Are you asking me what a mother does?"

Stephanie wrote on the legal pad, SHE DIDN'T KNOW THE FIRST QUESTION WAS COMING? But Mike felt a pang, because he had messed up his first question, too, and he understood what Danielle was saying.

Franklin paused. "Mrs. Ridgeway, let me clarify something before you answer. Both you and your husband use the term father and mother, but you're well aware that you're not Emily's father and mother, isn't that right?"

"Of course." Danielle's face fell. "Emily's mother will always be my little sister Chloe. I loved my sister and I would never try to replace her. It was Emily who started calling me Mommy, and I think of myself as her mother, but these are semantics. To me, I always think about what's best for Emily, and if it makes her more comfortable or more like the other kids to call me Mommy and Bob Daddy, then I'm fine with that. It's always about what makes her feel happiest and most secure."

Mike felt petty for having quibbled with Danielle about the terminology. Stephanie wrote on the pad, DON'T WORRY, THAT DOESN'T MATTER, LEGALLY.

"Mrs. Ridgeway, please tell us briefly the tasks you perform when you take care of Emily."

Danielle nodded. "I don't regard them as tasks, that's the main point to make here. I've known Emily from the day she was born and I've raised her from when she was seven months old. If I listed the tasks, we'd be here forever, and they wouldn't really tell you what it's like to raise her, nor would they tell you what it's like to be Emily and live in our home, as part of our family."

Mike flashed on Sara's memorial service at school, with Danielle, Bob, and Emily sitting with the other families. He couldn't help but think that Danielle was making sense, though he'd never heard her articulate it before. Maybe he hadn't given her the chance.

Stephanie was writing, STAY CALM. I WON'T OBJECT BE-CAUSE IT DOESN'T MATTER.

"Mrs. Ridgeway, can you describe for us your relationship to Emily?"

"I think that, like any mother of a young child, I'm her world." Danielle's tone grew even softer, almost with reverence. "Emily looks to me for all of her basic needs, but that's only a fraction of what children, especially young children, need from mothers. I think those early years are so important. It's not only when a child learns how to walk, talk, and feed herself, but more importantly, it's when a child learns who they are, whether they can trust the world, and whether they're loved."

Mike felt riveted as Danielle spoke, but Stephanie wrote, STOP FROWNING. NONE OF THIS HURTS US. THEY'RE LOSING.

"A mother gives a child self-esteem by being there for her every day, by loving her every day, by taking care of her every day. It's that continuity that makes Emily's life experience so good in our family, especially because she lost her mother."

Mike swallowed hard. Danielle's words rang true, and he understood how important everything she'd been doing for Emily was, and how well she'd been taking care of her.

Franklin asked, "Mrs. Ridgeway, what did you observe about Emily and her emotional state after her mother's death?"

"Emily cried a lot, she didn't sleep. Didn't want her bottle. She was too young to talk, but she would look around a lot, twisting her little head, and I knew she was looking for her mother. I even made some changes in myself, so that she would feel that her mother was still with her, in some ways."

Franklin cocked his head. "What changes did you make in yourself, to benefit Emily?"

"I usually dress more conservatively, but I started to relax my style and wear clothes like my sister's, just to make Emily feel happy and ease her through her grieving process."

Mike hadn't realized she'd changed her style intentionally, to help Emily. Stephanie wrote, CHEER UP! THIS IS TOTALLY BESIDE THE POINT!

Franklin paused. "Ms. Ridgeway, do you think that you provide a more stable, loving, and consistent home for Emily than does Dr. Scanlon?"

Danielle's expression fell into resigned lines. "I know that Mike loves Emily, but the truth is, I believe that Bob and I provide Emily with a family, and in particular, since she is a little girl, I think it's really important that she have a mother."

Stephanie jumped up. "Objection, Your Honor. Under section 5328-b, it is clear that the court may not grant a preference to either party in a custody dispute based upon gender."

Franklin turned to Judge Shield. "Your Honor, Mrs. Ridgeway isn't making a legal argument, and as you say, let's not be overly technical. She's the only person in this courtroom who has hands-on, twenty-four/seven, experience with Emily, and it's valuable for this court to have factual input from her. As Ms. Bergen pointed out, there is no jury present, and Your Honor is more than qualified to determine the weight he would give such testimony."

"Ms. Bergen, I'm going to deny the objection." Judge Shield turned to Danielle. "Please continue, Ms. Ridgeway."

"I was just saying that Emily looks to me for a lot of girly things, like she plays with my makeup and she's beginning to wear my jewelry. Yesterday we played dress-up, which was really cute." Danielle smiled. "I'm not making a legal argument, I'm just telling you how it is between a mother and a daughter. It's very special."

Judge Shield chuckled. "I have three daughters, so I know exactly what you mean."

Mike had to look away, breaking a sweat on his forehead. He understood Danielle's point, and it wasn't something he could give Emily, no matter how good a father he was. She was a little girl and she needed a mother, no matter what the law said. It wasn't just common sense, it was truth.

Franklin paused. "Ms. Ridgeway, knowing Emily as well as you do, can you predict the effect it will have on her emotional well-being if she's removed from your care?"

"Objection." Stephanie rose, but Judge Shield waved her back into her seat.

"Counsel, I'll permit it, on the understanding that Mrs. Ridgeway is not an expert in child care or pediatric psychology, but rather the person with the most knowledge of Emily."

Danielle frowned. "Honestly, knowing Emily as I do, I really fear for her if she loses us. I'm not saying anything negative about her father, but even if he were the best father in the world, it would be devastating to Emily to take her from our care."

Stephanie ignored the testimony, writing, DON'T WORRY. WE'RE WINNING.

Franklin asked, "Ms. Ridgeway, what makes you say that?"

"Emily loves us, and she has finally resettled, after her mother's death, in a new house that she has come to know as her home. I think there would be another round of sleepless nights, nervous upset, and difficulty eating. She'd be miserable. I think she would experience losing me just like losing her mother, as another death." Danielle paused. "Here's what worries me, for Emily. What does it do to a child to lose two mothers in two years?"

Mike held his breath. He'd never thought of it before, but it was true that Emily would experience it as a death, as profound a loss as Chloe, maybe more so, because she remembered Danielle better. He couldn't picture the scene where he walked away with Emily. She'd be hysterical. She'd freak. She'd throw up, like she did before. She'd never stop asking for Danielle.

Danielle testified, "I think it would take her years to recover, especially because at such a young age, it's so hard to explain things to her. I want to do everything in my power to not let it happen, because I want to save her from that trauma." She turned to the judge, her blue eyes shining with sudden tears. "Your Honor, I know you have the power, but I'm begging you, for Emily's sake, please don't take her from her family and her home."

Mike's entire body ached, and he felt sick to his stomach. Stephanie wrote, THIS MAKES NO DIFFERENCE, AS A MATTER OF LAW.

Judge Shield pursed his lips. "I know this is difficult, but I will do the best job I can for Emily, consistent with laws of the Commonwealth. I assure you of that."

Franklin cleared his throat. "Ms. Ridgeway, my last question is this. Dr. Scanlon has said that if he were granted custody today, he would consider having you as Emily's babysitter. Would you do that?"

"Yes, of course. I would continue as Emily's caretaker in any way, shape, or form, because I think I'm essential to her happiness. I would do it for no pay, anywhere." Danielle sniffled, recovering. "I would do anything for Emily. I love her, and she loves me."

Stephanie wrote, WE WIN. THE END.

Franklin turned to Judge Shield. "Your Honor, I have no further questions."

"Your Honor, I have no cross-examination," Stephanie said, rising. "However, I would like to put my client on the stand for a very brief rebuttal, if I may."

"You may." Judge Shields gestured at the witness stand. "Dr. Scanlon, if you will, please take the stand."

Chapter Seventy

"Dr. Scanlon," Stephanie said, facing the witness stand. "Please tell the court why you, as Emily's father, would provide her with a better and more loving home than Mr. and Ms. Ridgeway."

Mike paused, stunned. Time stopped, and everyone froze in place, like figures sketched by a courtroom artist. Stephanie looked expectant, anticipating his answer. Judge Shield was reading some papers, awaiting a self-serving response. Only Bob and Danielle were riveted, their expression horror mixed with resignation, an acceptance that the worst thing you could imagine was about to happen, right before your eyes. He had seen that expression before, but not on them. He'd seen it on Chatty, just before the grandfather threw the grenade. He realized that his answer was about to explode Bob and Danielle's world, and worst of all, Emily's world.

Stephanie cleared her throat. "Dr. Scanlon, did you hear the question? Feel free to tell the court why you, Emily's natural father, would give her a better and more loving home than her aunt and uncle."

Mike's thoughts raced. If he really thought about what was best for Emily, there was only one answer to the question. Bob had been acting as Emily's father, a role he shouldered with confidence and ease. Danielle had been acting as Emily's mother and deserved all the credit for the great kid that Emily was growing up to be. Emily loved them both and didn't know him at all. If he told the truth, he would say that he didn't know himself anymore, either.

The war had changed him, not just by taking his arm and his livelihood. He was a different man now. He abused opiates. He saw explosions where they didn't exist. He felt pain in an arm that wasn't there. He nodded out on the floor and almost killed his own daughter. If he ever got a flashback when he was driving with Emily, he would crash as surely as Chloe would have, when she'd been drinking.

Stephanie smiled, lightly. "Dr. Scanlon, I should have known you're not the type to toot your own horn, and you don't have to. Please, feel free not to answer." She turned quickly to Judge Shield. "I have no further questions, Your Honor. Let's get home before the snow hits."

Judge Shield was frowning in confusion, shaking his head.

Franklin jumped up, waving a hand. "Your Honor, I'd like to cross-examine."

Stephanie scoffed. "Your Honor, there's no testimony to cross-examine."

Franklin strode to the dais. "Your Honor, I'd like to explore why Dr. Scanlon didn't answer the question. It seems like a simple question for somebody who filed emergency papers, bringing us all to court." His gaze shifted sideways to Stephanie, sternly. "Unless he's content to let his lawyer do his talking for him."

Stephanie frowned. "There's no need to get personal. Dr. Scanlon testified ably and he speaks very well on behalf of himself and his daughter."

Judge Shield shifted forward, arranging his dark robes around him. "Ms. Bergen, please sit down. I think Mr. Franklin is entitled to explore Dr. Scanlon's testimony, or his lack thereof."

"Thank you, Your Honor." Stephanie turned stiffly away as Franklin faced Mike.

"Dr. Scanlon, I would like to remind you that you're under oath. You swore on the Bible under the laws of this Commonwealth and even of this country, an oath that I know you take quite seriously.

There's no one in this courtroom who has sacrificed more for his country than you."

Mike's mouth went dry, and his arm exploded in pain. He told himself to stay calm, but he felt chilled and shaky. His heart thundered.

"Dr. Scanlon, please tell the Court why you believe you would provide a better home for Emily than Bob and Danielle."

"I believe that—" Mike started to say, but his voice sounded far away even to him. He thought of what Danielle had said, about their family, about being a mother, about the special bond between mothers and daughters. He pictured himself taking Emily away from her, and he didn't know what would happen to a child who lost two mothers in two years. He loved Emily too much to destroy her.

Franklin asked, "Dr. Scanlon, don't you have an answer?"

Mike had an answer, the truth. He had made a vow to Emily, to always put her first, and he was going to keep his word. He turned to Judge Shield. "Your Honor, I don't think I would provide a better home for Emily than Bob and Danielle."

"What?" Judge Shield leaned over, an incredulous frown wrinkling his brow. "Dr. Scanlon, do you understand what you just said? Did you misspeak?"

"Your Honor, that's an admission!" Franklin shouted, and Stephanie leapt to her pumps.

"Your Honor, Dr. Scanlon means to say that—"

"Ms. Bergen, Mr. Franklin, please, silence." Judge Shield held up a hand and turned back to Mike. "Dr. Scanlon, what are you saying? Just answer the question."

Mike faced the judge, anguished. "Your Honor, I didn't misspeak. I meant what I said. If I'm thinking of Emily's best interests, and not my legal right to her, then she should stay where she is, with them."

"So ordered!" Judge Shield picked up the gavel and slammed it down with a *crack*!

Chapter Seventy-one

Stephanie marched Mike down the hall, hustled him into the Attorney Conference Room, and slammed the door behind them, throwing her coat, bag, and briefcase onto a chair. "What did you just do? What were you thinking? You just lost the case!"

Mike sank into a chair. His head was pounding. Every muscle felt sore. "Don't worry, it's not on you."

"You're damn right it's not on me!" Stephanie's eyes flashed with anger. "You walked into my office with a difficult case. There's very few lawyers who could put that case on, and it went in beautifully. But you sunk yourself! You killed the whole thing!"

"Maybe the law would have given her to me, but that wouldn't be fair to Emily. It wouldn't be justice, really." Mike rubbed his forehead, wishing so badly for a pill. He hurt all over, exhausted from the pain, and he didn't have to white-knuckle it anymore. "I did the right thing for Emily."

"You *didn't* do the right thing for Emily. You didn't do the right thing for her, at all. You did exactly the *wrong* thing." Stephanie's pretty face was mottled, and blotches appeared at her neck. "You only did what you're used to doing. You didn't step up to the challenge. You were afraid that you couldn't do it, so you settled for second-best. I don't know where you got your self-esteem from, but

332 | Lisa Scottoline

you need to get it straight. It's not the war, it's *you*. You answered for you in that courtroom. You didn't answer for Emily. You're feeling sorry for yourself because of your arm, because of everything. You're *afraid* to be a father."

Mike's throat caught. He had no idea how Stephanie knew that, but hearing her say it, he realized it was true.

"Oh, I touched a nerve, did I? You know how I know you did the wrong thing in there? Because *I'm Emily*."

"What?"

"My father was as cold as ice, and I spent half my life wondering why he didn't love me. Blaming myself." Stephanie began to pace back and forth. "I told myself I wasn't good enough. I told myself if I just studied harder, worked harder, did more chores, he would come around. I had ten years of therapy to figure out it wasn't me, it was *him*. And still, I'm not over it. I just cope. You can't undo that damage."

Mike felt shocked. Stephanie's emotions were so raw, she was almost spitting, and she whirled around and pointed at his face.

"That's why I know you did the wrong thing in there. You didn't let yourself down in that courtroom, you let Emily down. She's not old enough to tell you that, but I can speak for her. I'm Exhibit A. You just consigned her to a life of feeling not good enough. Of not being worthy. Of not even *trying* to be the best. She'll settle for second-best because that's all she believes she deserves. Like *you*."

Mike looked up, stricken. He couldn't say anything. It was just how he felt, but he'd hadn't told Stephanie that, either.

"Oh, she cries when you hold her? Your feelings hurt? Too damn bad! It's not *her* job as a child to love *you* unconditionally, it's *your* job as a parent to love *her* unconditionally." Stephanie glared down at him. "Did you even think about the legal implications? The judge could refer this to the D.A., and if he prosecutes, you could go to prison. Not only that, I asked him for unsupervised visitation, and he's going to take it under advisement. I would've gotten that after our case, no question, but you blew it. Now, Emily's with Bob and Danielle, and if I were them, I'd *adopt*. Is *that* what you want? Emily *adopted out* because you don't have the guts to be a father?" Stephanie threw up her hands. "You're really *something*! You got a medal, but you're no hero. You want to be a hero? Be a hero at home. Be a hero for *Emily*."

Mike sat, stunned.

"I'm done, I'm out of here." Stephanie snatched her coat, purse, and briefcase from the chair. "You'd better get going. Now you can make your funeral reception." She swept out of the conference room, letting the door slam behind her. "Good priorities, *Daddy*."

Chapter Seventy-two

It was nightfall by the time Mike reached Don's house and parked behind the line of cars, but it hadn't been a long enough ride for him to compose himself completely. Stephanie's words still rang in his ears, leaving him shaken, not only because they were true, but because they'd come too late. He ached in body and soul, but he resisted taking an Oxycontin. He felt like he had the worst flu in history, the classic withdrawal symptom. The talk at Landstuhl was that opiate withdrawal didn't kill you, but made you wish you were dead.

He cut the ignition and sat in the car as the engine shuddered into silence. Snow fell steadily in heavy, clumpy flakes that stuck to his windshield, obliterating the lights from the houses, darkening the car's interior. He watched it accumulate, knowing if he stayed long enough, he could bury himself inside. He tucked his sleeve into his pocket, slid his keys into his other pocket, then got out of the car.

He flipped up his hood, hurried down the sidewalk, and hustled to Don's front door, which stood open behind the glass storm door. He entered the warm, homey living room, but the crowd was getting ready to go. Only a few mourners were still there, gathering around trays of picked-over sandwiches and excavated casseroles. He didn't see Don, so he walked through it to the dining room.

"Mike? Hey Mike, is that you?" a young woman asked, turning from the dining room table, also covered with leftover food. She had blonde hair and blue eyes that lit up when she saw Mike, but he couldn't remember anything about her except that she was really talkative.

"I'm sorry, I—"

"I'm Nancy Handler, you probably don't remember my name but I was the reading specialist when Chloe taught at Wilberg. I teach there now, and I wanted to say I'm sorry for your loss. I sent a sympathy card but I think you were away. Chloe always remembered me and asked about my mom and she was a super-nice person and I'm so sorry."

"Thank you."

"It's so terrible about Sara, isn't it, and I can only imagine how hard this is for you and Don, and I sure hope the police get whoever did it. Was that you, on the news the other day? I was like, I know him, Chloe's husband, that's him!"

"Unfortunately, yes." Mike cringed. "Do you know where Don is? I'm late to pay my respects."

"Sure, I saw him in the kitchen, and he seems to be doing okay, considering, being strong for the boys. You know how great he is—"

"Thanks," Mike said, edging away. He threaded his way through the guests, looking away from the ones who caught his eye. He didn't know if they'd seen him on TV or knew about his arm, arrest, or custody hearing, and he didn't care. He just wanted to find Don, then go home to his apartment full of toys that wouldn't be used and a crib he couldn't assemble.

"Don?" Mike ran into him when he crossed the threshold into the kitchen, and Don turned around, opened his arms, and gave Mike a hug.

"You made it. So good to see you."

"I'm so sorry." Mike hugged Don back, then let him go. "I'm sorry I wasn't at the funeral, it's a long story."

"I understand, buddy." Don's brown eyes were bloodshot, and he looked uncomfortable in his black suit and tie, but he managed a smile. "I figured it would be too tough for you, after Chloe's. I don't blame you, I got your email. I know you care."

"That's not it, I had a legal thing I couldn't get out of, I'll explain later." Mike knew Don didn't need to hear his problems tonight. "How are the boys?"

"They're upstairs with my parents. They're pretty tired, you know." Don frowned. "You okay, man? You look like hell."

"I'm fine, but can I do anything for you? Is there anything you need?"

"No. I didn't hear anything more from the cops, did you?"

"No, sorry."

"The D.A. and the assistant were at the funeral. They say they have no new leads, but they'll keep looking."

"Did they follow up on the bangle?"

Don shrugged. "They didn't mention it. I don't know if they even got it. I'll call tomorrow and see."

"Let me know what happens, if you can."

"Sure." Don touched him on his shoulder. "I should go up. Last time I checked, the boys were in bed with that cat you gave us."

"Good." Mike felt better to hear it. "Give them my love. Take care. Call you later."

"You, too." Don went upstairs, and Mike made his way back through the dining room, where a group of late-comers were flocking around the table, talking and scooping up the last few sandwiches. He spotted the talkative Nancy putting on her coat and yakking away with one of them, whom Mike thought looked familiar, a tall, well-dressed woman with long, dark hair. He realized with dismay that she was Pat MacFarland's mother.

Mike wanted to avoid her, but the kitchen was too crowded to go backwards, so he'd have to barrel through the dining room. She was facing the table, her back to him, so he had a shot at getting out without her seeing him, especially since Nancy was yammering away at her.

"Karen," Nancy was saying, "I just love that pashmina, I don't know how you always look so great. I never look that put-together, but I should, my mom always says so. How do you know what looks good together? Do you have a personal shopper?"

"No, I prefer to dress myself," Karen answered, to some chuckling.

Mike put his head down and went around the group, while Nancy kept chattering.

"Your jewelry is gorgeous, too, and I love your earrings, and those bracelets are awesome, and so many of them, I love the effect! Where did you get them?"

"My husband gives me one every year, on our anniversary."

Mike had almost passed, but he glanced over and caught a bright flash of gleaming gold bangles like the one in Chloe's jewelry box. He did a double-take, and Nancy saw him, her face lighting up.

"Mike, here you are! I was waiting for you! Forgive my bad manners, I never thanked you for your service. What's the matter with me?"

"Oh, my." Karen recoiled when she recognized Mike, her hooded eyes flaring and her lips parting.

Nancy looked from Mike to Karen. "Do you two know each other? Karen MacFarland, this is Mike Scanlon. Mike, this is Karen. You two should meet, we're all part of the same school community—"

"We know each other well enough," Karen interrupted coldly, in a refined tone of voice.

"Yes, excuse me, I have to go." Mike left for the front door, his thoughts racing ahead.

"Mike?" Nancy called after him. "Wait, did I say the wrong thing? I'm sorry!"

Mike opened the front door into the icy snow, with Nancy on his heels.

"Mike, what did I do? I'm so sorry, I should have thanked you for your—"

"It's fine, Nancy, you didn't do anything wrong." Mike shut the door behind them, his heartbeat quickening. Snow bit his face. "Why is Karen MacFarland at a reception for Sara? Is she a teacher?"

"You sure you're not mad?"

"No, not at all, please, tell me." Mike hurried down the snowy walkway, and Nancy hustled to keep up.

"No, Karen doesn't teach, but she's on the school board, she's a big deal in the district. Actually, she's a Quarles, from the Quarles family."

Mike didn't care about idle chatter. He was trying to fit the pieces of the puzzle together.

"She doesn't use her maiden name, she goes by MacFarland because she likes to play it down, but she's Karen Quarles MacFarland, and her great-great-grandfather founded the Marston Soup Company. The family is super-rich, they were in the Forbes 400 if you saw . . ."

Mike got a hunch, and suddenly everything fell into place.

Chapter Seventy-three

Mike ran to his car through the biting snow, his thoughts flying. The bangle was the key, and if Karen got it from her husband John, then it was John, not Pat, who had the affair with Chloe. And if Karen was a Quarles, John would have a motive to kill Sara. He wouldn't want to risk the affair coming to light because his wife might divorce him, cutting him out of world-class wealth.

Mike chirped his car open just as his BlackBerry started ringing in his pocket, so he slid it out on the fly. The screen read Stephanie Bergen, and he pressed IGNORE. He opened the door, climbed into the driver's seat, tossed the BlackBerry on the passenger's, and plunged his key into the ignition. The engine roared to life, and he pulled out of the space. His Grand Cherokee had four-wheel drive, and the tires rumbled as they churned through the snow.

He twisted the stalk to turn on windshield wipers, but flurries were coming down too fast to be cleared. His BlackBerry rang again, and he looked over. The screen read Stephanie Bergen again, and he wondered if the judge had ruled or something. He took his hand off the wheel for a moment, grabbed the phone, hit a button for the speakerphone, and set the BlackBerry on his lap so he could drive.

"Mike? Hi, it's Stephanie."

"Yes, hi, is it about Emily?" Mike turned right onto the main thoroughfare and joined the traffic, moving maddeningly slowly in the snow.

"No, not at all. Am I on speaker?"

"Yes."

"Where are you?"

Mike wasn't about to tell her where he was going. "I'm home . . . cleaning."

"Oh. How was the reception?"

"Sad." Mike braked behind the line of cars, their red taillights burning red through the snowy curtain. He had to take a faster way to Foster Road.

"I'm calling because I've been thinking about what I said after the hearing and, well, I wanted to apologize."

"No need to." Mike would've felt touched if he weren't so preoccupied.

"Thanks, but I do need to. I'm sorry. I've never spoken to a client that way, and I shouldn't have to you. It was incredibly inappropriate."

"Don't worry about it. It's fine, really." Mike cranked the defrost higher, trying to clear the windshield. He eyed the shoulder and wondered if he could use it to get around the traffic.

"I know you thought you were doing the right thing today. I know you were coming from a good place. I know how much Emily means to you, so it couldn't have been easy. I don't agree that you did the right thing, but I do apologize for raising my voice."

"So you're not apologizing for what you said, just for the way you said it." Mike would have smiled, in other circumstances. Snow was piled high on the shoulder because the road had been plowed, and he wondered if it was still drivable.

"Exactly." Stephanie chuckled. "It's the distinction between form and substance. My form was wrong, my substance was right."

"I agree. You were right." Mike steered onto the shoulder and hit the gas. Snow sprayed from his wheel wells but he kept going, passing car after car.

"Thanks for saying so. Anyway, I've had time to collect my

thoughts and I think we should meet. I want to file something with Judge Shield as soon as possible, and we need to discuss it."

"Okay, when?" Mike gunned the engine, running up the shoulder.

"Do you have dinner plans tonight? I can be at TopTrees in fifteen minutes."

Mike hit the brakes when a white minivan pulled out of a driveway, obscured by the snowfall. Its driver honked her horn, and he skidded to a stop inches from the driver's door.

"Mike? What happened? That sounded like a car. Where are you? Are you okay? I thought you said you were at the apartment."

"I'm almost at the apartment. I'm coming home from the reception." Mike let the minivan cross his path into the lane, then he hit the gas and kept driving on the shoulder.

"Why are you lying to me?" Stephanie's tone turned worried. "You're not going to do something crazy, are you? We can work this out. We can try and turn it around."

"No, I'm fine."

"I don't believe you. I can tell you're lying. Why? Mike, where are you? I'll meet you, anywhere."

"Look, it's not that." Mike knew he'd have to tell her or she wouldn't let go. "I think I figured out who killed Sara, and it's John MacFarland. The father, not the son."

Stephanie gasped. "Mike, don't get involved in this. Stay out of it. Where are you going?"

"I'm driving to MacFarland's now. I'm just going to talk to him. I'm not going to accuse him of anything. I know how to play it."

"No, Mike," Stephanie said, alarmed. "Call the police. Please don't do this. Don't go."

"Relax. I'll be fine." Mike was approaching a high snowdrift that blocked his lane, so he wedged his way back into the traffic.

"Mike, call the cops. You already have an assault charge against you by the son. You want one by the father, too?"

"I hear you, but I'm on my way." Mike shifted into the fast lane, which still wasn't fast enough.

"Stop. Wait. You're jeopardizing any future custody proceedings for Emily."

"Is that true, or are you just saying it?" Mike braked, waiting to go around a stopped car.

"It's true. Please, listen to me. Think of Emily. Call the police, or I will."

"All right, I'll call. Let me hang up." Mike watched brake lights flare in front of him.

"Great. Do whatever the police say. Let them take it from here."

"Okay, good-bye." Mike pressed END, then 911, driving with his thigh while the call connected, then he put the phone back in his lap.

"What is the nature of your emergency?" the operator asked.

"I have information regarding a murder case, the Sara Hambera murder case."

"Please call the administrative number or the tip line, sir. This line is for emergencies only, and we've got our hands full tonight. We have a winter storm advisory."

"Wait, don't hang up. What's the number for the tip line? Can you connect me?"

"Please hold, I'll connect you."

Mike turned right, onto the back streets heading toward his old neighborhood. There was a *click* on the line. "Hello?"

"How can I help you?"

"My name is Mike Scanlon, and I have information that John MacFarland on Foster Road in Wilberg committed the Sara Hambera murder. Can you connect me to whoever's in charge of that case?" Mike drove into the darkness, and snow flew at him from all directions.

"I can't do that, but I will take down your number and have them call you back."

"Is Officer Torno there?" Mike asked, trying another tack. "He knows me."

"Yes, he is. Do you want to speak to him?"

"Yes, put him on. Tell him it's Dr. Scanlon."

"Hold the line, please." There were two clicks, then a man's voice said wearily, "This is Officer Torno. Dr. Scanlon, what's going on now?"

"I'm on my way to the MacFarlands' house on Foster Road."

"Isn't that where I picked you up the other day?"

"Yes."

"What are you doing, sir?"

"I thought it was the son who had an affair with my wife, but it's the father. His name is John MacFarland. He's married to Karen Quarles MacFarland, and I think he killed Sara Hambera so his wife wouldn't find out about the affair."

"Dr. Scanlon, stop. We don't want you going over there, playing town watch, or being a vigilante. We'll send a car out to talk to him."

"I'll meet you there."

"No, don't meet us there. Go home. This is a police matter. You're not to go anywhere near that family or that house."

"I won't, if you send a car. Will you send a car right away?"

"I will go there personally. But you need to go home. Now."

"I will, thank you." Mike hit the gas, his tires spraying snow in wide fans.

He'd be at Foster Road in no time.

Chapter Seventy-four

Mike steered onto Foster Road, but the police weren't there, probably delayed by traffic or weather. Snow fell harder, and everyone was inside, hunkering down. He passed his old house, continued to the MacFarlands', and pulled over across the street, cutting the ignition. The lights were on in their house, though he couldn't see anybody through the front window. He was dying to break down the door and confront John, and the only thing that stopped him was Emily.

He figured somebody was home because there was a black BMW sedan in the driveway, but the snow had been swept off its roof and back window. He wondered why, and in the next minute, he got his answer. John emerged from his front door, carrying a duffel bag and a cardboard box, then he hurried down the porch steps, headed toward the BMW, and chirped it unlocked with his key fob. The BMW's lights flashed, and its trunk lid opened. John loaded the box and bag in the trunk, pressed it closed, and went to the driver's side of the car.

Mike watched, his thoughts racing. John was going somewhere and he'd be gone before the police got here. Mike couldn't let him get away, so he climbed out of his car and hustled across the street. "John, wait a sec!" he hollered, in the blowing snow. "Hold on!"

"You?" John turned beside the BMW, his face in shadow, the porch light behind him. "What are you doing here?"

Mike thought fast. "I want to settle our lawsuit. I brought my checkbook."

"It's Pat's lawsuit, and he's out of town."

"Then you and me can talk, man-to-man, and you can convey my offer to him. Let's go inside, out of this weather." Mike heard Gigi barking inside the house. "Why don't you put the dog away, and we can get this done?"

"I don't have time. I have to go."

"It'll take ten minutes, max. It's quick money, right? If I have to go ahead and pay a lawyer, there's less for Pat."

John shut the car door. "Ten minutes."

Chapter Seventy-five

Mike stepped inside the warm, bright entrance hall, trying to contain the anger that came over him. It infuriated him to be standing in the same room as Sara's killer, but he had to stall until the police got here.

"Feel free to sit down." John gestured to a striped wing chair in the large family room, his expression reserved behind his glasses. He had a five o'clock shadow, crow's feet, and a worn Patagonia parka over his baggy jeans, and Mike couldn't imagine what Chloe had seen in him.

"Thanks." Mike sat down in the chair and glanced around. Framed photographs, table lamps with polished brass bases, and antique end tables filled the family room, which was connected to a large, open kitchen at the back, where Gigi kept barking.

"I'm surprised you want to settle. We heard you pleaded not guilty." John walked to the fireplace, slid a mesh screen aside, and warmed his hands on a low fire, its flames still flickering, hot and orange-red. Mike flashed on the explosion in Helmand, but he shoved those thoughts away. He had to stay in the present and keep his wits about him.

"My lawyer said to plead not guilty, so I did."

"Is it okay with him that you're here, trying to settle?" John picked up a brass poker and nudged the glowing embers, sending a spray of tiny sparks flying.

"He doesn't know. I fired him." Mike kept his voice up to be heard over Gigi's barking. "Where's Gigi?"

"The laundry room. She'll stop in a while. So what's your offer?"

"First, I want to say, I'm sorry. I understand I injured Pat. What did I do and how much did it cost?"

"To begin with, there was soft-tissue damage to his left cheek. Fortunately, he didn't need stitches."

"I'm sorry." Mike felt his heart rate pick up. His thoughts kept turning to Sara and Chloe. It disgusted him to be so near a man who had slept with his wife and killed her best friend. "What happened to his teeth?"

"You loosened the front two. The bill from the ER was almost two grand, and we just got the ambulance bill, for $900." John tended the fire, nosing the poker among the embers. "We haven't gotten the doctor's bill yet, and there was a plastic surgeon, to check him out."

"Surgeons are expensive." Mike felt his hatred reviving like the fire. He had no stump pain, which told him he was becoming adrenalized.

"None of his medical expenses were insured, since he's out of work."

"I understand, and I don't want to go to court. I want this thing to go away." Mike clenched his jaw. Rage constricted his chest. Gigi was still barking.

"That's possible for the right number, and you have to include pain and suffering."

"You know, it's ironic, all this talk of money." Mike found himself on his feet. "I just saw your wife over at Don Hambera's house. They had a reception there, after his wife's funeral. Sara Hambera. She was murdered. I don't know if you heard."

"I did. It's too bad." John kept poking at the embers, and new flames flared a searing orange.

"She was my wife's best friend, so that's a shame." Mike found himself advancing on John, walking over to the fireplace. "Anyway, I understand Karen is a Quarles. I didn't realize that."

"She prefers to keep her privacy."

"I get that." Mike couldn't play games anymore. "I wonder how she'd react if she knew that you had an affair with Chloe. Think she'd divorce you? I do."

"What are you talking about?" John recoiled, the fire reflected in his glasses. "I didn't have an affair with anyone. What *is* it with you and my family? First Pat, now me?"

"I think you're the one, you fell in love with my wife." Mike went with his hunch. "I think you gave her a bangle like the ones you give *your* wife. I wonder how Karen Quarles MacFarland would feel if she knew that."

"I did no such thing!"

"Yes, you did." Mike knew only one way to confirm if he was right or wrong. "Do you know that when Chloe died, she was pregnant with your child?"

John's hooded eyes flared in genuine pain and surprise, which was all the confirmation Mike needed.

Suddenly he felt an agonizing blow to his head. He collapsed to the floor, and the world abruptly went black.

Chapter Seventy-six

Mike woke up lying on his back. Pain seared through his skull. Blood gushed from his forehead. His nose bubbled like it was broken. His side ached, his ribs were cracked. Fire blazed near his feet. He was in Helmand after the grenade blast. He didn't know where Chatty or the Afghan boy were. He had to get up.

"He couldn't let it go. He had to play detective. He brought it on himself. Well, it's over, it's finally over."

It was John MacFarland. Mike recognized the voice. He opened his eyes and saw through a curtain of blood. They were in MacFarland's family room, but they weren't alone. Karen Quarles MacFarland stood in front of the fireplace, yelling at her husband.

"Over, John? Evidently, it's never over! You got her *pregnant*? What were you thinking? How could you make such a colossal hash of our lives? A year later, we're still cleaning up your mess!"

Mike tried to understand what was going on. Karen must have come in and hit him from behind. A heavy brass lamp lay by his side. He hadn't heard her enter because of Gigi's barking. John must have beaten him while he was unconscious.

"I said I was sorry." John sounded more sad than angry. He shoved the wing chair onto its side. "I've said it a million times, and you're not cleaning anything up, I am. I took care of Scanlon, and

I took care of Hambera. You haven't gotten your hands dirty at all."

Mike couldn't think about Sara now. He struggled through his pain to think of a way to save himself. He had no idea what happened to the police.

"I shouldn't have to do anything!" Karen shoved over an end table, and framed family photographs slid to the rug. "You're the one who cheated. You're the one who got her *pregnant*. Can you imagine, if she had your *child*? How could we explain that? My father would disown me! Thank God she died!"

"Karen, don't say that. Don't you have human feelings left, at all?" John picked up a lamp, raised it high, and slammed it to the hardwood with a loud *thud*. Gigi barked louder, frenzied. "It's sad that she died, and the baby. My baby. That's sad, Karen."

Mike realized what was going on. The MacFarlands were destroying their family room to make it look as if there had been a struggle. They thought he was dead and they were going to claim self-defense. The cops would believe them, given his assault on Pat.

"Really, John? Please understand if I don't cry over the death of your mistress and your bastard child!" Karen swept a lamp off the end table. "You're getting weepy all over again, over the wonderful Chloe? You disgust me!"

"Karen, enough." John kicked over the fireplace stand, and the poker and other implements clattered to the hardwood, making Gigi crazy. "Let's call it quits, after this. I'm begging you. Give me a million bucks, and I'll go away. We'll get a divorce, like everybody else in the world."

Mike could barely see them for the blood in his eyes. He couldn't die tonight. He was a father. If he wanted to live, he had to fight. He hadn't fought for her in court, but he'd fight for her now. *Emily.*

"John, I'm not paying you a cent, and we're not getting a divorce until Pat is back on track! He doesn't need us to screw him up more than we already have! You'll get your money then and only then!" Karen tossed a pillow onto the rug. "Look at you! Tears in your eyes, crying over your precious baby! We dodged a bullet, and I was smarter than I knew!"

"What are you talking about?" John stopped knocking things over, and so did Karen, as they faced each other before the dying fire.

"I was there, John. I went over to her house that night to give her a piece of my mind, but she was lying on the floor, bleeding to death. You know what I did? Nothing. *Zilch*." Karen snorted, triumphant. "I watched your mistress die, and it was the smartest thing I ever did. Ha! I even redeemed myself for not getting a pre-nup."

Suddenly John bent down for the poker, snatched it up, and whipped it savagely alongside Karen's head. Her hands flew up defensively, blood sprayed from her cheek, and she emitted an agonized cry. She staggered sideways, but John whacked her again, grunting, and she collapsed to the floor, unconscious.

Mike felt horrified. He couldn't watch Karen be beaten to death. He had to act now or John would kill them both.

John raised the poker to deliver a mortal blow to Karen's head.

Mike seized his chance.

Chapter Seventy-seven

Mike lunged for the brass lamp beside him, scrambled to his feet, and charged blindly at John.

"No!" John whirled around, his eyes wide with surprise. He caught the lamp and shoved Mike off.

Mike reeled backwards, dizzy. Adrenaline dumped into his bloodstream, leaving him shaking. His pain vanished. He edged away from John, backing into the kitchen. "Stop. Don't do this. The cops are on the way."

"Excellent." John dropped the lamp and wielded the poker. Blood and hair stuck to its curved edge. "They'll find you dead. I had to kill you in self-defense. You killed my wife."

Mike looked wildly around for a weapon. All he saw was a Cuisinart. A toaster. A small television. He grabbed a fruit bowl and threw it at John, who ducked it and came at him, swinging the poker back and forth like a scythe.

Mike leapt backwards, shaking blood from his eyes. John took a mighty swing with the poker. Mike jerked back, and it missed him by an inch. The poker wedged in the door of the Subzero, piercing its stainless steel. John tore it out and kept coming. Gigi clawed at the door to the laundry room, then body-slammed it so it rumbled on its hinges.

"Gotcha!" John backed Mike into a corner and raised the poker.

Mike was trapped between the sink and the refrigerator. Suddenly he spotted a knife block behind the toaster and yanked out a knife. It was only a steak knife, no match for the poker.

John whipped the poker at Mike. He jumped out of the way, but the counter hemmed him in. The poker caught him in the stump.

Mike cried out in agony and fell at John's feet, dropping the steak knife. Gigi kept throwing herself at the laundry room door. The banging sounded like grenades going off. Ordnance. Troops in contact. He was back in Helmand. He was going to die.

John stood above Mike and aimed the pointed end of the poker down, like a bayonet.

Mike forced himself into the present. The steak knife was inches from his hand. He'd used a scalpel under pressure. He knew how to screen out distractions. It was his moment of truth. He said his homemade prayer.

John plunged the poker downward. Mike rolled out of the way at the last minute, grabbed the steak knife, and severed John's Achilles tendon with a loud *snap!*

John howled, dropping the poker. He collapsed to the floor, folded into the fetal position, and held his calf. Mike scrambled backwards, knowing John's pain would be unbearable. His Achilles would roll up like an old-fashioned window shade.

Mike jumped to his feet. Blood streamed down his face. He wiped it but it kept flowing. He felt dazed and dizzy. The knife slipped from his blood-slick grasp. John rolled onto his hands and knees and crawled away, toward the family room, trying to get to the entrance hall.

Mike picked up the poker and went after him. John hoisted himself to a stand and hopped toward the front door, dragging his wounded leg. Blood gushed from the cut in his jeans, turning them black. Gigi threw her body against the door, again and again, barking and barking.

Mike stalked John with the poker. John reached the entrance hall, but Mike caught up with him, lowering the poker. He wasn't a podiatrist for nothing. He took a mighty backswing and whacked John in the lower leg, shattering his tibia with a satisfying *crack*.

John collapsed as if shot, writhing and caterwauling on the floor.

Mike felt the poker slide from his grip. John went abruptly silent and still, passing out from pain or shock. Either way, a murderer wasn't getting away. Mission accomplished.

Mike's eyes filled with blood. His arm felt like it was falling off. His knees went suddenly wobbly. His stomach churned. The entrance hall began to spin, whirling around him.

He dropped to his knees, then toppled forward. He fell face down on the hardwood floor. He needed an ambulance and so did John and Karen. Gigi kept barking and throwing her body against the door. The mastiff would break the door off its hinges. She'd attack him when she got out of the laundry room.

Mike reached to his pocket for his phone, then remembered he'd left it in the car. He tried to look around for a phone, but blood ran into his eyes. He couldn't see anything. He felt light-headed. His blood spread in a pool over the hardwood. If the cops didn't get here soon, he'd bleed to death. Gigi body-slammed the door, which sounded like it was splintering.

Mike tried to think. There had to be a phone in the kitchen, but he was closer to the front door. He could crawl to the door and from there to the street. A passing car or snowplow would see him. Or the cops, they had to get here soon.

Mike dragged himself forward, using his right arm and his legs to propel him. He inched toward the door, smearing a gruesome trail. He passed John and kept his eyes on the front door. He didn't know how he'd get the strength to stand up. He'd have to find a way.

The door lay only six feet ahead, but his body was failing. He was so tired. He couldn't go another inch. He knew it was blood loss. He needed to rest. He laid his head down. Chloe must have died like this, her lifeblood leaking away, waiting for help that never came. He prayed she didn't know Karen had let her die.

Suddenly Mike heard a noise, outside. It was the sound of a car pulling into the driveway, then its door slamming closed. Finally, the police.

He filled with hope. Footsteps clattered on the wooden porch and hurried to the front door. He looked up, and a face popped into the window, but it wasn't the cops.

It was Stephanie.

And she was taking off her coat, wrapping it around her hand, and breaking the window.

Chapter Seventy-eight

Mike regained consciousness in a hospital bed, his thoughts foggy. He was alive, and for that he thanked God. The room was dim and empty, and a half-light on the wall illuminated the high-backed chairs, a bed table on wheels, and a plastic pitcher next to a stack of upside-down paper cups. The door was to his right, open a crack to reveal a strip of fluorescent light in the hallway. He heard the sound of nurses, talking.

Mike was in pain, but it felt muted in a familiar way. He knew he was back on painkillers, though they wouldn't get the best of him, ever again. A plastic sensor capped his index finger, reading his vital signs, and the monitor screens glowed blue, with changing white numbers. His blood pressure and heart rate were normal. He couldn't breathe through his nose, so he knew they'd set it. He felt fresh gauze covering his forehead, so he assumed they'd closed his wounds.

He glanced to his left, groggy. The other bed was empty, its mattress bare under the window. Snow fell steadily, swirling around the streetlights, and the sky was as black as onyx, so he knew it was nighttime. His eyes closed, then opened again. His brain struggled to remember how he'd gotten here.

Stephanie.

Mike closed his eyes, remembering that much. She had broken the window, and he wondered if she'd hurt her hand. Exhaustion swept over him, and he drifted into sleep thinking of her, so when he woke up again, it seemed almost natural that Stephanie would be there, sitting in one of the chairs. She was working, making notes on a brief in her lap, her head down.

It was daytime, and the hospital room was light, with a shaft of sun streaming through the window. The metallic rattle of a cart emanated from the hallway, but Stephanie seemed not to hear it, reading with a critical frown. Her hair caught the light, shining a rich, dark red, and she had on a gray-green cable sweater and jeans that made her look less corporate, especially in pink snow boots.

"Hi," Mike said hoarsely, after a moment.

Stephanie looked up with a grin, her green eyes bright. "Well, hello there, sleepyhead."

"What time is it?" Mike tried to orient himself. The clouds in his head were clearing, and he felt more normal than before. He had to breathe through his mouth, and his head ached, but not more than he could handle.

"It's about noon." Stephanie shifted the chair closer to the bed, her papers on her lap. "How are you feeling?"

"Not bad."

"Want some water or anything? It's almost time for lunch."

"No, thanks." Mike wasn't sure if Stephanie was here as his lawyer or his friend, but it didn't matter. He liked it. "It's nice when you're not yelling at me. What a difference a day makes."

"Ha! You redeemed yourself." Stephanie beamed. "You fought for truth, justice, and the American way."

Mike would've laughed, but his throat still hurt from being intubated. "No, not me."

"Yes, you, dude." Stephanie capped her pen and slid it onto the side of her papers. "The MacFarlands are in this very hospital, two floors down, and when they recover, they're both going to be charged with Sara's murder."

Mike felt a bittersweet twinge. It still wouldn't bring Sara back, or Chloe. "How did they prove it?"

"They didn't have to. The MacFarlands confessed, and the scuttlebutt is that the Quarles family pressured them into it, to avoid a trial and bad publicity. By the way, the D.A. told me that John's email was Mac702."

Mike felt a pang, torn. "Does Don know?"

"I'm sure he does, and by the way, I talked to the D.A., and he isn't going to prosecute you for the fraudulent scripts, under the circumstances."

Mike wasn't thinking about himself. "I heard Karen say she'd been to my house that night and that she let Chloe die."

Stephanie recoiled, horrified. "That's terrible!"

Mike's gut twisted. "Can we do anything about that, legally? Isn't that a crime?"

"I'd try, for sure. I'll get a full sworn statement from you, tell the D.A., and see if we can get her to confess that, too." Stephanie thought a minute. "If she won't, though, they might not be able to charge her."

"Why?"

"They can't prove criminal negligence unless they can show that if Karen acted, Chloe would be alive." Stephanie frowned with regret. "We'll try, but if not, your consolation is that Karen will be going to jail for the maximum, already. Can you live with that?"

"If I have to." Mike appreciated Stephanie's honesty, even if it wasn't the answer he wanted. "I'm learning that law doesn't always lead to justice."

Stephanie paused. "By the way, the media vultures are camped outside, plaguing me to put you in front of a press conference. I declined and made a statement on your behalf."

"What did you say?"

"I said you're a great guy, upstanding citizen, blah blah, doctor, blah blah blah, Army vet. The D.A. made a statement singing your praises, too. So you're a hero, dude."

"No." Mike shrugged it off.

"Yes." Stephanie brightened. "You are. It's official."

"What does that make you, then?" Mike smiled. "You saved my life."

"I'm a heroine, but I knew that already."

Mike chuckled. "Did you hurt your hand when you broke the window?"

"Not at all." Stephanie flexed her fingers. "I didn't even break a nail. Did you see how I put my coat around my hand? I got that from the movies."

"Joking aside, thank you." Mike met her eye. "Thank you for coming when you did. You really did save my life."

"You're welcome, but you haven't paid your bill yet. I'm just a collection agent."

Mike smiled again. Stephanie couldn't take a compliment, an intriguing mix of bravado and modesty. "What made you go to the MacFarlands', anyway?"

"As soon as I hung up the phone, I knew you weren't going to listen."

"When did the police come?" Mike had passed out and remembered almost nothing.

"They were right behind me, they got delayed by a tractor-trailer accident. Your friend Officer Torno sends his regards, and your old partner, Jim Haggerty, was here with his wife, last night. He also asked when you're coming back to work."

"For him? I'm not. I'm finished selling things." Mike had thought about it last night, when the pain had kept him awake. "I have to be able to practice again, even do surgery, and it's time to open my own office. I want to be my own boss."

"Go for it. If I can do it, anybody can." Stephanie smiled, and they both turned at the knock that came from the doorway.

Don was standing in the threshold in his green Hambera Construction jacket, and a sad smile spread across his chubby face. "Mind if I come in for a quick visit?"

"Please, do, pal." Mike shifted up in bed, gesturing at Stephanie "This is Stephanie Bergen, my lawyer. Stephanie, Don Hambera."

Stephanie extended her hand to him. "Pleased to meet you, and I'm so sorry about your loss. Sara sounds like a wonderful person."

"She was, thanks." Don kept his chin up, then turned to Mike. "How you doing? You gonna be okay?"

"Good as new. Be out of here in no time."

"Thank God." Don sighed audibly, and his big brown eyes teared up. "I have to thank you. It helps so much to know that MacFarland's going to be punished for what he did to Sara, and to all of us. I'm so grateful you got the bastard."

Mike's throat caught. He still felt guilty for setting the events in motion, and he'd live with that forever. "I'm glad I could do something, anything, to help. We figured it out together, though. We made a pretty good crime-fighting team."

Don nodded, sniffling. "We should keep the friendship thing going, huh?"

"Absolutely." Mike smiled. "Do you golf?"

"No."

"Me neither. We'll just hang with the kids."

Don chuckled, then it faded. "Listen, Bob and Danielle are out there, in the waiting room. They told me what happened with the custody case and all, and well, they want to come in and see you."

"Really?" Mike asked, surprised. He felt ambivalent about Bob and Danielle since court. "Is Emily with them?"

"No, they didn't bring her because they didn't want to upset her. She's with a sitter." Don frowned. "They want to know do you want to see them. Don't say no on my account. I have to go anyway."

"What do you think?" Mike turned to Stephanie, who rose and tucked her papers into her briefcase.

"I think you should see them. The more you talk to each other, the better for Emily, and we need to make nice if we want to get unsupervised visitation. Why don't you let me get them?"

Mike thought a minute, then gave her his answer.

Chapter Seventy-nine

Danielle gasped from the threshold as soon as she saw Mike, her forehead collapsing in a deep frown. "Oh, you poor thing!"

"Mike, Jeez." Bob came up behind her, only slightly less shocked, in street clothes, his trenchcoat over his arm.

"Folks, come in, please." Stephanie pulled over two chairs. "Why don't you sit down, and I'll wait outside."

"No, Stephanie, please stay," Mike blurted out, without thinking. His emotions were all mixed up. Bob and Danielle were family, but they were still the people who'd taken Emily from him.

"Okay, great." Stephanie flashed him a smile and stood off to the side. Danielle sank into a chair, lost in her puffy white coat, which she had on with jeans and furry Sorrel boots. Bob sat next to her, smoothing his trenchcoat in his lap.

"Mike, well, we don't know what to say first." Bob's skin mottled under his fresh shave. "Thank God you're okay, and what you did, figuring out it was John MacFarland, it's just amazing. You were right all along. We shouldn't have given you such a hard time. We're very sorry."

"Yes, we're sorry." Danielle nodded, her eyes filming. She tugged a balled-up Kleenex from her pocket.

"Thanks," Mike said, uncomfortably. "How's Emily?"

"Good, fine." Danielle wet her lips. "We wanted to explain why we asked you to leave the house the other day. We'd like to clear the air."

Mike stiffened, feeling every ache in his face and body. "You explained it in court."

"Yes, I know, but we didn't get to say that we know you love Emily, and I guess, well, we just got scared." Danielle frowned. "You were talking about taking her to Connecticut, and we didn't think you were in good enough shape to do that, so we felt like we had to act, quickly."

Bob rested a hand on Danielle's forearm. "My wife is covering for me, but I don't need her to. It was all my idea. I know I was wrong and I can admit it. I tend to solve things legally. I overreacted, and I'm sorry."

Mike felt something give way in his chest, a sort of a surrender, because he understood them. "I'm sorry, too. For scaring you, and for the way I acted."

"Thank you." Bob nodded curtly, pursing his lips.

"Yes, thanks." Danielle blinked wetness from her eyes. "And there's something we brought you." She reached into her purse, pulled out a white envelope, and opened it up. "I'm sorry I went snooping in your room, that was wrong. I was looking for your pills, but I found these things, and they belong to you." Danielle plucked from the envelope the heart milagro that Segundo had given him, the silver crucifix from Chloe, the gold coin from Lieutenant Colonel Davy, and the battered photo of Emily, then she set them out on the bed table, one-by-one. "When I saw this picture of Emily, I knew you had carried it with you, all through your time in Afghanistan."

Mike's throat caught at the sight of the trinkets. Each one meant so much to him, and he picked up the photo of Emily as a baby, her features still unformed. "She was young here."

"I know." Danielle nodded, with a sniffle. "She's getting bigger every day."

"She is." Mike swallowed hard. "So, can I see her, on a visitation schedule? Unsupervised?"

"I don't think so," Danielle answered flatly, then turned to Bob. "Honey, what do you think?"

Bob cleared his throat, eyeing Mike. "We're not giving you unsupervised visits."

"What?" Mike asked, stricken. He held the photo between his fingers as if he'd never let it go.

"This is how we see it," Bob answered, calmly. "It shouldn't have taken a courtroom for us to hear each other, but it did. I think you heard Danielle and me when you did what you did in court, that is, letting us have custody." He paused, his Adam's apple going up and down. "But we heard you, too, and that's why we want to ignore the court's order. In fact, we're going to apply to modify it. Emily is your daughter, and we've decided that no matter what the judge ruled, you should have complete legal and physical custody of her."

Mike blinked, astounded. "Really?"

"Yes." Bob smiled, in a regretful way. "We know who you are, inside. You lost your way coming back, but you're on the right path now. So what we'd like to do is work with you to help Emily transition to living with you full-time, where she belongs. We can go as fast or as slow as you like. You call the shots."

"Thank you so much." Mike felt like cheering, but he would settle for not blubbering in front of everyone. He caught Stephanie's eye, and she was beaming.

Danielle sniffled. "But I'm hoping that you'll let me babysit when you go back to work. And that you'll stay in Pennsylvania, at least for the foreseeable future."

Mike felt so happy. "Of course I will. I listened in court, too. I wouldn't take Emily from you guys, ever. I think the three of us should raise her together. We're her family. How does that sound?"

"Wonderful!" Danielle's eyes shone. "And from now on, I won't be so bossy about the baby. I know I have been, and I'm sorry about that. And, oh yes, most important of all, we decided that she has to call me Aunt Danielle, not Mommy. Otherwise, it's confusing. Chloe was her mother, her only mother, and I know she'd be so proud of what we're doing today."

Bob nodded, clearing his throat huskily. "I agree, and for my part, Emily has only one Daddy. That's you, Mike. You're her Daddy, not me. You."

Mike realized that Emily had never called him that. He hoped she would someday, but he'd have to earn it, and now he'd have a chance. His heart filled with joy at the sound of the simple word.

Daddy.

Chapter Eighty

"Daddy!" Emily called out, running across the grassy lawn, holding something in her fist.

"Watch where you're going, don't fall!" Mike called back. Emily had grown like a wildflower, already too tall for a pink dress that fit at the beginning of summer, and her curls had gotten lighter.

"She's not going to fall." Bob shifted some boxes in the trunk of his car.

"I know, because I'm watching," Mike told him, with a smile.

"You can't trip on a lawn."

"There could be a hole from a groundhog."

"We don't have groundhogs."

"What about snakes or voles?"

"We don't have those, either."

"Dragons, then."

Bob laughed. It was a running joke that Mike was the world's most protective father. He wanted to keep Emily safe from falls, bee stings, bad boyfriends, and wars, but that wasn't why he was watching her. He was still drinking in everything about her, getting to know her better, every day.

"Dragons. You got me there." Bob shut the trunk with a solid *ca-thunk*.

"Daddy, look!" Emily came running up, and Mike knelt to get down on her level.

"What you got, baby?"

"Flowers." Emily smiled at him, her eyes as blue as heaven itself, her fingers covered with earth. She opened her palm, showing a crumpled mash of thistle and onion grass.

"How pretty, that's great! Thank you!" Mike held out his hand, and Emily shook the smelly pile into his palm. It was the first time she'd brought him flowers, instead of dirty Kleenexes, broken crayons, and empty juice boxes. Maybe someday he'd stop noticing the firsts, or counting his blessings, but he doubted that day would ever come.

"Save dat, Daddy."

"I will."

"Are we goin' to da berfday party?"

"Not yet."

"When is Fenny gonna come?"

Mike loved the way Emily said Stephanie. "Any minute now."

"Where is da party?"

"In another state, called Connecticut." Mike didn't mind that Emily asked so many questions, when he had the answers, which wasn't always. "The party is at my friend's house. Dr. Chatham."

"How old is he?"

"Older than I am. Very old, like forty years old." Mike was looking forward to giving Chatty a hard time. "He has three big girls, remember? They can't wait to meet you."

"Is Uncle Bob and Aunt Danielle gonna come?"

"No, they have errands to run." Mike realized that Emily might be worried. She'd spent nights at his apartment but he'd never taken her away for a day trip. "Don't worry, we'll have fun together."

"I miss Smoochie Kitten."

"I do, too. We'll see her when we get home." Mike had gotten a new kitten and told everybody it was for Emily, which was his prerogative as a father. He visited Jake every time he saw Don and the boys, and it made him happier than he let on. He was a cat man.

"Want more flowers? I know where."

"Where?" Mike didn't want her near the street, though there were only a few cars in sight on this quiet Saturday morning, too early even for leafblowers and lawnmowers. Sunlight dappled the driveway, and the air felt cool and fresh.

"Dere!" Emily pointed to the hedgerow, then waved off a gnat.

"Good. Don't go past that. Gimme a kiss."

"Okay." Emily presented her cheek to be kissed, and Mike obliged, loving its sweaty softness, then she ran off, with Bob chuckling.

"Someday she'll learn that means she's supposed to kiss *us*."

"I hope she doesn't." Mike smiled, rising, and he put the stinky plants into his breast pocket. "That'll keep the vampires away."

"Bob, wait, I found one more box!" Danielle emerged from the front door, carrying a cardboard box.

"I just closed the trunk!" Bob called to her.

"So open it!" Danielle called back.

"Need a hand?" Mike asked, no pun intended. Time and therapy had made him more accepting of his amputation, and he was wearing a short-sleeved shirt that exposed his stump. He felt better and lighter without his prosthetic, which he wore mainly at work. He was running his own practice, and Tony and Dave had come on board, doing the surgeries until he could, someday.

"Thanks." Danielle smiled as she gave Mike the box, then fell into step beside him. Its top flaps were closed, and its contents clinked slightly, like glass against glass. "I'm not even sure where this came from. It might be from your old house."

"What's in it?" Mike checked on Emily, who was crouching on the lawn, yanking up crabgrass.

"Bottles and T-shirts. See if it's anything you need."

"I doubt it." Mike had gotten rid of almost everything. Some of it had too many memories, and the rest he didn't have room for in his apartment, which was another blessing, helping him move on.

"How it got upstairs, I don't know."

"Let me see." Mike set the box on the edge of the trunk, opened a flap, and looked inside. It contained a bottle and old T-shirts, but they didn't belong to him. "It's not my stuff."

Bob opened the other top flap. "Oh, I packed this from Mike's and brought it home. I forgot all about it. The bottle is from Mike's, but the shirts are mine. I used them to cushion the bottle, so it wouldn't break."

Danielle rolled her eyes. "Why didn't you throw it away, honey?"

"It's expensive, and Mike might want it. Mike, you want it? It's really nice Scotch."

"No, you keep it." Mike turned to check on Emily, who was squatting on the lawn, warbling a tuneless song to herself and digging in the dirt. Sunlight caught her hair, making it shine. He found himself thinking of Chloe, his grief coming and going, though he'd fallen in love with Stephanie. He'd learned that the human heart could expand to fit as many as needed, whether that was sound cardiology practice or not.

"Throw it away, Bob," Danielle was saying, behind him. "It probably went bad and it's half-empty."

"Danielle, it doesn't go bad. Why waste it?"

"We have money. Why hoard it?"

"It's The Macallan Estate Reserve, a collector's bottle. This probably costs a couple hundred bucks."

Mike turned at the name, which rang a bell. "What, Bob?"

"Tell her you don't throw *this* away." Bob was holding up a bottle of Scotch with a black-framed label that Mike recognized, shaken.

"Daddy, Daddy!" Emily jumped up, pointing to the street. "Daddy, Fenny's here!"

"Don't run in the street!" Mike called back reflexively, as Stephanie's red Saab pulled up at the curb.

"Hi, Emily!" Stephanie called from her open window. She cut the engine, got out of the car, and reached down just in time to catch Emily in her arms, lift her up, and give her a hug. "Honey pie, I'm so happy to see you!"

Mike walked toward them, then gave each a quick kiss on the cheek. "Stephanie, mind if I borrow your car? I'll be right back."

"No, why?" Stephanie smiled, bewildered, and handed him the keys. "Aren't we supposed to be leaving?"

"We will when I get back. Gimme an hour. I have to take care of some unfinished business."

Chapter Eighty-one

Mike walked through the door at Lyon & Haggerty, and every head turned in the large waiting room, packed because Saturday mornings were the busiest. The seats were full of moms and kids, reading, listening to iPods, or texting away, their thumbs flying.

"May I help you, sir?" asked the receptionist, her ponytail swinging.

"No thanks, I'm here to see Jim." Mike strode past her, opened the door to the hallway, and stalked past the team photos and mounted hockey sticks, calling out, "Jim? You here? It's Mike."

Two female staffers in peach scrubs turned to him. "May we help you?" asked one. "Sir?" said the other.

"I'm fine, thanks." Mike barreled past them. "Jim! Jim!"

"What's going on out here?" Jim asked in surprise, emerging from an examining room, and Mike whirled around to face him.

"We need to talk about Chloe."

Jim's eyes flew open. "Mike, whoa. What do you mean?"

"You tell me. I found a bottle of Macallan in the house. Sorry, *The* Macallan, the same overpriced bottle of booze you keep in your desk drawer. My gut tells me she didn't drink it, you did."

"I went over for the article, I told you that."

"How many times did you go over?"

"Once."

"You're lying. You told me you sip it, but the bottle was half-empty. That means you were over there plenty of times. Why were you over there so much?" Mike kept walking toward him. "And why are you lying about it, if it was innocent?"

"Mike, calm down." Jim edged backwards, gesturing to a staffer. "Melinda, call security. Do something."

"I am calm, Jumbo. You're the one who's not calm." Mike backed Jim down the hallway. "Why are you running away from your old friend and partner? I'm Dr. Mike the war hero, remember? I'm the guy in your brochure. And while I was in Afghanistan, you slept with my wife. *You* could've been the one who got her pregnant."

"No, wait, I couldn't have gotten her pregnant. I took a shot, I admit it, but she said no. Nothing happened, I swear." Jim backed down his new hall. Patients from the waiting room crowded the doorway, astounded. Examining-room doors were opening on all sides, and appalled moms and kids stood in the thresholds watching, among them, a shocked Rick Lyon.

Mike kept advancing. "You hit on my *wife*? What the hell's the matter with you?"

"Sorry, Mike, what can I tell you?" Jim backed himself against the wall of team photos. Mike saw the absolute truth in his eyes.

He felt a wave of sadness for Chloe. She had been so vulnerable, and ripe for someone like Jim to take advantage of her. But something in her had resisted Jim. Mike's impulse was to deck him, but he knew that the moms, patients, staff, and Lyon had heard every word. Tongues would wag all day, and the gossip would be on Facebook by lunchtime. If Lyon believed business was about reputation, Jim was as good as fired.

Mike had hit him where it hurt the most.

In his wallet.

Chapter Eighty-two

It wasn't until almost dark that Mike and Chatty got a chance to talk alone, sitting in chairs on the elevated deck, while the party went on below. Mike held Emily as she snored softly on his shoulder, her body warm and slightly sweaty. She smelled of hot dogs and mosquito repellent, which was somehow sweeter than perfume.

Chatty sipped his beer, smiling. "So you didn't hit Haggerty?"

"No, because I'm a father now. Also I only have one hand and I need it."

Chatty laughed. "Now you're thinking, Scholl's. Besides, the mom network will get on his ass, and Lyon will cut him loose."

"I know, and he's not the guy I thought he was, anymore." Mike was trying to make peace with it, but it would take a long time. "My hitting days are over. I still can't believe you got away with clocking Davy."

"Of course. If he brought me up on charges, he knew I'd tell what he said about the investigation. He wasn't about to open that can of worms." Chatty snorted. "On a lighter note, I like Stephanie. She's great."

"So's Sherry." Mike scanned the party for them, but it was too dark to see. The only light came from yellow paper lanterns strung between the tall oak trees, which made shifting shadows of the partiers. Barbeque smoke hung in the air, an aromatic haze.

"Did you notice that they hit it off immediately?"

"Yes, because they're two of a kind."

"Run for cover." Chatty chuckled, and so did Mike.

"Your daughters are beauties. So grown up."

"Thanks. I'm not ready for Lena to get a learner's permit. I don't want her out of my sight, meeting guys like me." Chatty gestured at Emily. "Meanwhile, my girls love the baby, but I don't know if they understood she's real. They carted her around like their old American Girl dolls."

Mike smiled. "Those big dolls? I saw those, online. They're not cheap."

"No, and you gotta buy the clothes, the books, the DVDs, then take the trip to the store in the city. It's a pilgrimage." Chatty snorted. "I sat next to McKenna on the train."

"Who's McKenna?"

"A doll. I sat with a doll in the club car on an Acela. Think about that. Consider the visual."

"Manly." Mike chuckled. "I have a kitten, did I tell you? Also manly."

"Ha! This is a very manly conversation." Chatty rubbed his chest in his white polo shirt, a bright patch in the darkness. "Only real men can have conversations like this. Men from war."

"Hoo-ah!" Mike said, and they both laughed.

"They're closing bases and Landstuhl, too, did you hear?"

"I heard, because the war's over."

"Right, that's why they're building a hospital at Ramstein."

"One-stop shopping." Mike kept his hand on Emily's back, without really knowing why. "Sew 'em up and put 'em on a plane."

"They're shutting down the 556th, too." Chatty sighed, heavily. "Man, I still can't deal with it. I replay it over and over, but it always turns out the same."

Mike knew he was talking about Phat Phil, Oldstein, Jacobs, and Tipton. "Me, too."

"I think about them, all the time. I think about them *all*. They're always in the back of my mind."

"I know exactly what you mean." Mike thought about them, and everything else. The blood, the wounds, the soldiers, The Kid With The Dragon Tattoo, The Virgin.

"To them." Chatty raised his bottle in tribute, and Mike felt his throat catch.

"Hear, hear."

Chatty set his bottle down on his leg. "I don't sleep well, or not much, really. That's the main thing that drives me crazy, the not-sleeping."

"You gotta see somebody about that. I do."

"That's what Sherry says."

"She's right. Listen to her. Don't avoid it."

"I know, I'm not myself. On the Fourth of July, we went to the fireworks and I started shaking." Chatty shuddered. "I had to come home."

"I hear that. We went to a chick flick last week, and I cried like a baby."

Chatty shook it off. "Too bad Segundo's mom got sick. He really wanted to stick around and see you."

"How's he doing?"

"Great. I love having him, he runs my office like he ran us. He's gonna marry his girl, but he's still a tub. I told him, how you gonna fit in your dress?"

Mike smiled. "Hold on. I have a birthday present for you."

"Scholl's, the invite said 'no presents.'"

"That doesn't apply to me." Mike dug in his pocket, pulled out the heart milagro, and gave it to Chatty. "Happy Birthday, Batman."

"Ha!" Chatty held it up, where it glinted in the light from the kitchen. "Thanks, man!"

"Tell Segundo. Now you'll have all the good luck that it brought me."

"We *are* lucky, man."

"We sure as hell are."

Mike grinned, but it was too dark to see Chatty's smile. The sky had deepened to a soft black, with just a few stars. "Hey, look up. Same sky, different stars."

Chatty looked up. "I should get my goggles."

Mike thought back to the night they sat outside their tent, when he first came back after Chloe's death. "Remember that night?"

"Yeah."

Mike didn't have to explain which night. "Is it crazy to say I'm glad we were there?"

"No, I'm glad we were, too," Chatty answered, after a moment. "Now why is that, I wonder? How can that be? War is *not* a good thing."

"No, it isn't." Mike had thought about the subject many a night, when he was having sleep problems of his own. "Here's what I think. If I hadn't gone over there, I wouldn't be the father I am. I wouldn't be the man I am. War changes everything, and everybody. It changed me, and the sacrifice changed me. I've decided to live my life in a way that honors that sacrifice, and all the sacrifices."

Chatty looked over. "For real, Scholl's?"

"For real, Chatty."

"That's deep. I'll have to mull that over, my friend. I'll have to cogitate on that."

"Be my guest."

Chatty snorted. "Did you get smarter while I was away?"

"No," Mike answered. "You got dumber."

And they both laughed until they cried.

These two heroes, who were finally home.

Acknowledgments

Now to the thank-yous, where I get to thank all of those experts and kind souls who helped me with *Don't Go,* and make clear that any and all mistakes herein are mine.

First thanks go to my medical experts, Vladimir Berkovich, M.D., Lt. Colonel USAR, a decorated veteran who served in the Army Medical Corps in Afghanistan and Iraq. He took his valuable time to answer all of my questions and read the manuscript, making a number of corrections and suggestions. I could not be more grateful to him for his kindness, expertise, and guidance—and more important, for his service to all of us, and his sacrifices in harm's way.

I also want to thank Dr. Marc Baer, D.P.M., who also took the time to read pages of this manuscript as well, and who is a wonderful and caring podiatrist. Thanks to my pal Missy Dubroff, for reading the manuscript and making comments.

I'm a bookaholic, and I want to acknowledge the books that I read on the subject of medical care in combat, which informed the background of *Don't Go.* Primary were some extraordinary textbooks: LTC Brett Owens and LTC Philip Belmont Jr.'s *Combat Orthopedic Surgery: Lessons Learned in Iraq and Afghanistan* (Slackbooks, 2011); Bella May's *Amputations and Prosthetics* (Davis, 2002); G. Murdoch and A. Bennett-Wilson's *Amputation: Surgical Practice and Patient Management* (Butterworth-Heineman, 1996); LTC Shawn Christian Nessen, Dave Edmond Lounsbury, and Stephen Hetz's *War Surgery in Afghanistan and Iraq: A Series of Cases, 2003-2007* (Office of the Surgeon General, Department of the Army, 2008).

I also read some great nonfiction, many, but not all, by returning vets. I would recommend: Milo Afong's *Hogs in the Shadows* (Berkley, 2007); David Bellavia's *House to House* (Free Press, 2007); Peter Bergen's *The Longest War* (Free Press, 2011); Donovan Campbell's *Joker One* (Random House, 2010); Sarah Chayes's *The Punishment of Virtue* (Penguin, 2006); James Fallows's *Blind Into Baghdad* (Random House, 2006); Dexter Filkins's *The Forever War* (Random House, 2008); David Finkel's *The Good Soldiers* (Farrar, Straus & Giroux, 2009); Matt Gallagher's *Kaboom: Embracing the Suck in a Savage Little War* (Perseus, 2010); Dr. Ronald Glasser's *Broken Bodies, Shattered Minds: A Medical Odyssey from Vietnam to Afghanistan* (History, 2010); Dr. Dave Hnida's *Paradise General: Riding the Surge at a Combat Hospital in Iraq* (Simon & Shuster, 2010); Cdr. Richard Jadick's *On Call in Hell: A Doctor's Iraq War Story* (NAL, 2007); Sebastian Junger's *War* (Grand Central, 2010); Robert Kaplan's

Imperial Grunts (Random House, 2005); Jon Krakauer's *Where Men Win Glory: The Odyssey of Pat Tillman* (Doubleday, 2009); Marcus Luttrell with Patrick Robinson's *Lone Survivor* (Little Brown, 2007); Karl Marlantes's *What It Is Like to Go to War* (Atlantic Monthly, 2011); Thomas Middleton's *Saber's Edge: A Combat Medic in Ramadi, Iraq* (University Press of New England, 2009); Patrick Thibeault's *My Journey as a Combat Medic* (IBJ, 2011); Benjamin Tupper's *Greetings From Afghanistan, Send More Ammo* (NAL, 2010); Howard Wasdin and Stephen Templin's *Seal Team Six* (St. Martin's Press, 2011); Bing West's *No True Glory* (Bantam, 2005). I also enjoyed a novel on the subject, *Billy Lynn's Long Halftime Walk* by Ben Fountain (HarperCollins, 2012).

I'm a former lawyer, but family law wasn't my field. One of the country's best family lawyers, Margaret Klaw, Esq., of Berner Klaw and Watson, P.C. in Philadelphia, who also writes for *The Huffington Post*, helped me so much in making sure I got the legal details correct in this thorny issue of family law, which, unfortunately, comes up frequently with returning vets.

Another lawyerly thank-you to a brilliant and dedicated public servant, Nicholas Casenta, Esq., Chief Deputy District Attorney of the Chester County District Attorney's Office, who has helped me with every book so far, including this one. We're lucky to have you, Nick!

Thanks to my old friend Virginia Ayres, for her in-the-clutch help. Thanks to Tom Melvin, genius accountant, who helped me with the financial details herein, as usual. Thanks to Lauren Bowser of O'Brien's Funeral Home, for her expertise and sensitivity.

I want to take a special moment to thank my editor, Jennifer Enderlin, who has encouraged me to stretch with each novel. And big thanks to the brilliant, fun gang at St. Martin's Press, starting with the terrific John Sargent, Sally Richardson, Matthew Shear, Matt Baldacci, Jeanne-Marie Hudson, Brian Heller, Jeff Capshew, Nancy Trypuc, Kim Ludlam, John Murphy, John Karle, Sara Goodman, and all the wonderful sales reps. Big thanks to Michael Storrings, for an astounding cover design. Also hugs and kisses to Mary Beth Roche, Laura Wilson, and the great people in audiobooks. I love and appreciate all of you.

Thanks and big love to my incredible agent and friend Molly Friedrich, who has guided me for so long now, and to the amazing Lucy Carson and Molly Schulman.

Thanks and another big hug to my dedicated and wonderful assistant and best friend, Laura Leonard. She's invaluable in every way, and has been for more than twenty years. Thanks, too, to my girl pack of Nan Daley, Rachel Kull, Paula Menghetti, Franca Palumbo, and Sandy Steingard.

Thank you very much to my amazing and brilliant daughter Francesca, a wonderful writer in her own right, for her love, support, and great humor.

And to my family, for everything.

DON'T GO

Lisa Scottoline

Behind the Novel

• A Letter from Lisa

Keep on Reading

• Ideas for Book Groups
• Reading Group Questions

For more reading group suggestions,
visit www.readinggroupgold.com.

ST. MARTIN'S GRIFFIN

A Letter from Lisa

Dear Friends,

I owe so much to readers like you. Thanks to you, I've built a career writing about strong, smart, independent, and funny women, starting with my Rosato & Associate series, expanding to emotional thrillers, and connecting on a personal level through the humorous memoirs that I write with my daughter, Francesca Serritella. As a writer, I consistently challenge myself to keep my writing fresh; regardless of the genre, my goal is to explore themes of relationships, parenthood, family, love, justice, and morality while providing page-turning and entertaining books.

I think my early novels asked the question: "What is a woman?" Then, more recently: "What is a mother?" And, as the ten-year anniversary of my father's death approached, I really began to think "What is a father? What is a man? What is a hero?" My own father was my personal hero, and that naturally lent itself to writing about a man for the first time, in *Don't Go*.

I loved writing about Mike Scanlon because he is an ordinary man thrown into extraordinary circumstances, yet he remains reluctant to view himself as a hero—in war-torn Afghanistan or on the homefront. Before Mike can accept being anyone's hero he must first learn what it means to be a man and a father. Like my own dad, being a hero does not mean accomplishing superheroic feats. Instead, it means just being consistently present, engaged, and loving. My dad did that for me in spades, and that's why his memory inspired me to embark into new territory—writing my own version of a man, a father, and ultimately, a hero.

With love and thanks,

Lisa Scottoline

Ideas for Book Groups

I am a huge fan of book clubs because it means people are reading and discussing books. Mix that with wine and carbs, and you can't keep me away. I'm deeply grateful to all who read my books, and especially honored when one of them is chosen by a book club. I wanted an opportunity to say thank you to those who read my books, which gave me the idea of a contest. Every year I hold a book club contest and the winning book club gets a visit from me and a night of fabulous food and good wine. To enter is easy: all you have to do is take a picture of your entire book club with each member holding a copy of my newest hardcover and send it to me by mail or e-mail. No book club is too small or too big. Don't belong to a book club? Start one. Just grab a loved one, a neighbor, or friend, and send in your picture of you each holding my newest book. I look forward to coming to your town and wining and dining your group. For more details, just go to www.scottoline.com.

Tour time is my favorite time of year because I get to break out my fancy clothes and meet with interesting and fun readers around the country. The rest of the year I am a homebody, writing every day, but thrilled to be able to connect with readers through e-mail. I read all my e-mail, and answer as much as I can. So, drop me a line about books, families, pets, love, or whatever is on your mind at lisa@scottoline.com. For my latest book and tour

Reading Group Gold

Keep on Reading

information, special promotions, and updates you can sign up at www.scottoline.com for my newsletter.

The Bunnies Book Club of Scottsdale, AZ,
submit their photo for Lisa's book club contest.

Reading Group Questions

Reading
Group
Gold

1. *Don't Go* explores the theme of parenthood, and what it means to be a good parent. Do you think a father can be as good of a parent as a mother? Does the gender of the child change your answer? Why or why not?

2. What do you think caused Chloe's downward spiral after Mike left? In what way did your understanding of her actions change by the end of the book?

3. Do you understand Mike's feelings of alienation from his daughter? Would he have felt this way had his child been a boy? How did Danielle either contribute toward these feelings, or help alleviate them?

*Keep on
Reading*

4. What motivations do you attribute to Bob and Danielle's actions? How did your impression of them change throughout the story? Did you like them? Why or why not?

5. In what ways do you think the war changed Mike as a person? Did you agree or disagree with his decision to return? Do you think he really had a choice? Why or why not?

6. Mike forms an unbreakable bond with his war buddies, yet his longtime friend from home turns out to be less than trustworthy. If he had met his war buddies in regular life, how do you think their friendships would have differed? In what ways do friendships amongst women differ from friendships amongst men?

7. Mike's return home from war turns out disastrously. What do you think Mike could have done differently to make his transition with his daughter better? What ways can our communities and government help our veterans transition back into society when they return? What about helping the families left behind?

8. Mike experiences betrayal from several people he loves the most. Whose betrayal do you consider the most significant? If Mike had not gone to war, how do you think his relationship with Chloe would have been different? How did his feelings toward her change throughout the book?

9. At what point do you think Mike decided to fight back? What do you think are his greatest challenges in raising a daughter as a single dad and a wounded war vet?

10. *Don't Go* is filled with both dark moments and bright moments. What do you think was the darkest moment in the book, and what was the most uplifting?

11. Ultimately, *Don't Go* is about being a hero. What do you think it means to be a hero? In what ways is Mike a hero?

Turn the page for a sneak peek at
Lisa Scottoline's new novel

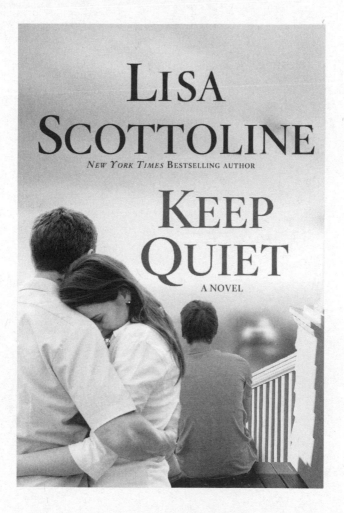

Available April 2014

Chapter One

Jake Buckman knew his son had a secret, because his wife told him so. They didn't know what it was but they suspected it was about a girl, since Ryan had been texting nonstop and dressing better for school, which meant he actually cared if his jeans were clean. Jake wished he and his son were closer, but it was probably too late to turn it around. Ryan was sixteen years old, and Jake couldn't compete with girls, friends, the basketball team, Facebook, Call of Duty, Xbox, Jay-Z, Instagram, and pepperoni pizza. No father could, least of all an accountant.

Jake drummed his fingers on the steering wheel, waiting in front of the multiplex for Ryan, who'd gone to the movies with his teammates. The rift between father and son began five years ago, when Jake lost his job. The accounting firm he'd worked for had gone bankrupt in the recession, and he'd been out of a job for almost a year. They'd lived on his unemployment, his wife's salary, and savings, but he felt ashamed at the brave smile on Pam's face, the snow globe of bills on the kitchen table, and the endless rejection from jobs for which he was overqualified.

He shuddered, thinking back. Since he hadn't been able to

get a job, he'd done something he'd always wanted to do, start his own financial-planning business. He named it Gardenia Trust for Pam's favorite perfume and he'd dedicated himself to getting it off the ground. He'd worked days and nights at a rented cubicle, cold-calling everyone he knew to drum up clients. He'd said yes to every speaking engagement, keynote or not. He'd given seminars at retirement villages, Rotary Clubs, and libraries. In time he became one of the top-ten ranked financial planners in southeastern Pennsylvania, but it had taken a toll on his family. He and Pam had fixed their marriage with counseling, but in the meantime, Ryan had grown up. Only Pam believed Jake could still fix his relationship with Ryan before their son left for college. She'd encouraged him, even tonight.

Go pick him up at the movie, she'd said. *He's expecting me, but you go instead.*

The movie theater was wedged between Best Buy and Nordstrom, and cars idled out front, their exhausts making chalky plumes. Jake wondered if some of the other parents were in the cars, but he wouldn't recognize them anyway. He'd only attended one or two parents' nights, a National Honor Society induction, and assorted basketball finals, because Ryan played varsity. Pam went to all of Ryan's games, having more flexibility in her work schedule, and Jake had told himself that her being there was the same as his being there, as if he could parent by proxy. He'd been wrong. He'd made himself superfluous in his own son's life. His wife was the keynote.

A crowd flowed from the multiplex, lighting cigarettes, checking phones, and chatting as they passed in front of his headlights. Jake looked over to see Ryan push open the exit door with his shoulder and roll out of the theater with his teammates, whose names Jake had made a point to memorize: Caleb, Benjamin, and Raj. They were all tall, but Ryan was the biggest at six foot five and 225 pounds, the scruffy tentpole of a shuffling group of shaggy haircuts, black North Face jackets, and saggy pants—except for the two girls.

Jake shifted upward in the driver's seat, surprised. He hadn't known Ryan and his buddies were going to the movies with any girls and he was pretty sure Pam didn't, either. One girl was a redhead and the other a long-haired blonde, who stood near Ryan. Jake wondered if the blonde was the mystery girl and if he could get a conversation going about it with Ryan on the way home. Pam always said her best conversations with him happened spontaneously, while they were driving around. If so, Jake would plan his spontaneity.

The girls waved good-bye, and he waited for Ryan to notice the Audi. He'd texted to say he was coming, but Ryan hadn't replied, so he couldn't be sure the text got delivered. Jake didn't honk, wave, or do something else dorky, so as not to embarrass himself or suburban fathers in general.

Jake saw Ryan slide his iPhone from his pocket and flick his bangs back, so that the phone illuminated his son's face. Ryan had large, warm brown eyes, a long, thin nose, and largish mouth, his handsome features framed by wavy, chestnut-brown hair, which he kept longish. Everybody said Ryan was the spitting image of his father, but Jake knew that was true too many years and twenty-five pounds ago. Jake was forty-six years old, with crow's-feet, graying temples, and a starter paunch to prove it. He always said that Ryan got his size from his father, but his brains from his mother, which was the best of both.

Jake watched as Ryan looked up from his iPhone, spotted the Audi, and jerked his chin up in acknowledgment, then slapped Caleb's palm and came toward the car. Jake unlocked the passenger door, and Ryan opened it and slid inside, his jacket sliding against the leather seat.

"Where's Mom?" he asked, eyebrows lifting.

"She was busy, so I figured I'd come. How was the movie?"

"Okay. You left Moose home?" Ryan kept an eye on his iPhone screen.

"Oops, yeah." Jake hadn't thought to take the dog, though Pam carted him everywhere. He disengaged the brake, fed the car gas, and headed for the exit.

"I get you didn't want him to come. This car is too awesome." Ryan kept his head down, his thumbs flying as he texted, growing the blue electronic bubble on the phone screen.

"No, it's not that. I forgot. I'll bring him next time."

"Don't. He'll drool on the seats. We must keep the machine pristine." Ryan paused as he read the screen. "You mind if I keep texting? I want to stay with this convo."

"It's okay, do your thing." Jake steered around the back of the King of Prussia mall, where the lights of JCPenney, Macy's, and Neiman Marcus brightened a cloudy night sky. Cars were rushing everywhere; it was Friday night, the busy beginning to the weekend. It should have been colder for February, but it wasn't. A light fog thickened the air, and Jake remembered something he had learned tonight from the pretty weathergirl on TV.

Fog is a cloud on the ground.

He turned the defrost to maximum and accelerated toward Route 202, heading for open road. Ryan texted away, his hip-hop ringtone going off at regular intervals, punctuated by the Apple-generated swoosh. Jake wondered if his son was talking to the mystery girl. He himself remembered racking up huge phone bills when he first dated Pam, at college. He'd fallen for her their freshman year at Pitt and felt unbelievably lucky when she married him. She was a great wife, and he gave her total credit for Ryan being so well-adjusted and popular, despite his naturally reserved manner. He was earning A's in AP courses, got solid SAT scores, and was already being recruited by college basketball programs, some Division I.

Jake switched into the slow lane, heading for the exit. He

wanted to ask Ryan about the girls, but he'd warm up first. "So, how was the movie?"

"Good. Like I said."

"Oh, right." Jake forgot, he had asked that already. "How's Caleb? And Raj and Benjamin?" He wanted to show he remembered the names.

"Fine."

"Everybody ready for the finals?"

"Yep."

Jake was getting nowhere fast. He still wanted to know about the girls, and according to Pam, the trick with Ryan was to act like you didn't care about the answer to the question you'd asked, or you'd never get an answer. So he said, offhandedly, "By the way, who were those girls at the movie?"

Ryan didn't look up from his phone, his thumbs in overdrive. Pink and green bubbles popped onto his phone screen, so he was texting with more than one person, like a conference call for teenagers.

"Ryan?" Jake tried again. "The girls at the movie, who were they?"

"Girls from school."

"Oh. Friends?"

"Yeah." Ryan still didn't look up.

"Nice." Jake let it go, an epic fail, in the vernacular. He pressed a button to lower the window, breathing in the moist, cool air. The fog was thickening, softening the blackness of the night, and the traffic dropped off as they approached the Concordia Corporate Center. They passed glowing signs for SMS and Microsoft, then turned onto Concordia Boulevard, which was lined with longer-stay hotels. He'd eaten enough of their reception-desk chocolate chip cookies to last a lifetime, because even his out-of-town clients were in the suburbs, the new home of American business.

Jake returned to his thoughts. His own office was in a nearby corporate center, and he spent his days ping-ponging between his corporate center and his clients' corporate centers, after which he drove home to his housing development. Some days the only trees he saw were builder's-grade evergreens, planted in zigzag patterns. Lately he felt as if his life were developed, rather than lived. He was a financial planner, but he was coming to believe that too much planning wasn't natural for trees or accountants.

Fog misted the windshield, and the wipers went on to clear his view, and Ryan chuckled softly. "Dad, this car is *sick*. I love how it wipes the windshield automatically."

"Me, too." Jake grinned, feeling the spark of a reconnection. They both liked cars, and last year, when Jake's old Tahoe hit 132,000 miles, he'd bought the Audi, mainly because Ryan had lobbied for one. Jake was a born Chevy guy, but Ryan had built umpteen online versions of the flashy Audi on the company website and designed what he called a "dream machine"—an A6 sedan with a 3.0 liter engine, Brilliant Black exterior, Black leather interior, and Brushed Aluminum inlay on the dashboard. They'd gone together to pick it up, and Jake had given Ryan a few driving lessons in it, when Ryan had the time.

"Dude." Ryan shifted forward, sliding the phone into his jacket pocket. "We're coming up on Pike Road. Can I drive?"

Jake checked the dashboard clock, which read 11:15. "You're not supposed to drive after eleven o'clock. You only have a learner's permit."

"But Dad, I've had it for five months already. I only have one month left before I can get my license. I did fifty-five out of the sixty-five hours, and all the nighttime driving hours and bad-weather hours. And you're with me, you're an adult."

"It doesn't matter, technically."

Ryan deflated. "Oh, come on, there's never traffic on Pike, not on the weekends. I can do it, Dad. You know I'm an excellent driver."

"We'll see when we get to Pike. If there's people around,

no." Jake wanted to keep the conversational momentum going, especially when Ryan's ringtone started up again. "So. It sounds like you're in demand tonight."

"I'm blowing up." Ryan smiled.

"Is something going on, or is it just the usual, women beating down your door?"

Ryan snorted. "Yeah, right. I'm a chick magnet."

"Nobody's a chick magnet, buddy. That's why God invented cars."

"Ha!" Ryan slapped his hands together. "*That's* what I'm talking about! Agree!"

Yes! Jake realized he'd said the exact right thing, and Ryan shifted around to face him, with a new grin.

"When I get my license, you'll lend me the machine, right? I won't have to drive the Tahoe all the time."

"I will." Jake smiled.

"Awesome! Dad, guess what, I'm so stoked. I might have a date tomorrow night."

Bingo! "Really? Who?"

"Wait. Whoa. Hold on, it's Pike Road, we're here. Please, please, pull over." Ryan gestured to the right side of Pike, where the asphalt ended without a curb. "Right over there."

"Relax, remain calm." Jake braked as he approached the street.

"Please let me drive. We're almost home. Look, the place is dead." Ryan waved toward the corporate center. The follow-up ringtone sounded in his pocket. "Can I drive?"

"We'll see." Jake cruised to a stop, letting an oncoming truck pass, then made a left and pulled over, so he could scope out the scene. Pike Road was a long street that ran between the woods on its right and the Concordia Corporate Center, on its left. It was used mainly as a shortcut to the corporate-center parking lots, and during the week, corporate running teams and athletic teams from Jake's high school used it to train. There was no traffic on the weekends.

"Dad, *please*." Ryan leaned over, his eyes pleading, and Jake didn't want to ruin the mood.

"Okay, let's do it."

"Sweet!" Ryan threw open the door and jumped out of the car. Jake engaged the parking brake, opened the door, and straightened up, but Ryan was already running around the front, slapping him a strong high-five. "Thanks, dude!"

Jake laughed, delighted. "Speed limit is forty, but watch out for deer."

"Gotcha!" Ryan plopped into the driver's seat, and Jake walked to the passenger seat, got in, and closed the door behind him. He didn't have to adjust the seat because they were the same size.

"Now. Hold on. Before you go anywhere, adjust the mirrors, outside and in."

"On it." Ryan pushed the button to rotate the outside mirror, then reached for the rearview, and Jake watched him line it up, with approval. His son was careful and methodical, a perfectionist like him. Ryan even enjoyed practicing, especially basketball. Once he had told Jake that it took two-and-a-half hours to shoot a thousand foul shots, and Jake didn't have to ask Ryan how he knew.

"Don't forget your harness."

"I wasn't going to." Ryan fastened himself into the seat with a *click*.

"I have the low beams on. For this street, with no lights, I recommend the high beams."

"Agree." Ryan peered at the dashboard and switched them on.

"Take a second and look around." Jake looked down the street with Ryan, the high beams cutting the light fog. Pike Road was a straight shot the length of the corporate center, then took a sharp curve to the right. Tall trees lined the road, their branches jagged and bare.

"Good to go." Ryan released the emergency brake as his phone signaled an incoming text.

"Don't even think about getting that text. No texting while driving." Jake himself had stopped texting while he drove unless he was at a stoplight, and he talked on the phone only if he had the Bluetooth.

"I know." Ryan fed the car gas. The follow-up ringtone played but he stayed focused on his driving. "That's just Caleb, anyway. He's hyper tonight. He likes one of those girls we were with, the redhead with the white coat."

"I saw her." Jake relaxed in the seat, since Ryan had everything in control.

"Anyway, this girl I might go out with tomorrow night? She's new." Ryan smiled as he drove, warming to the topic. "Her family moved here over the summer from Texas. She rides horses. Barrel-racing. How baller is *that*?"

"Baller." Jake knew *baller* meant good. They passed Dolomite Road on their left, which ran behind the corporate center. "Was she the other girl at the movie? The blonde?"

"Yes." Ryan burst into an excited grin. "Did you see her? Isn't she *mad* cute?"

"I did see her. She's very cute."

"Yo, I'd be so lucky to be with this girl! She's short, but it works on her, you know?"

"Sure. Short is good. I like short. Your mom is short." Jake smiled. Pam was only five foot three, and his mother had called them Mutt and Jeff, back in the days when people knew who Mutt and Jeff were. Jake's mother had died ten years ago of blood cancer, and he still missed her every day. He didn't miss his father at all, though his father had outlived his mother by six years, which proved that not only was life unfair but death was, too.

"Her name's kinda weird, not gonna lie. Janine Mae Lamb. Janine Mae is her first name. You have to say both names." Ryan maintained his speed as they approached the curve, marked by a caution sign with an arrow pointing right.

"I don't think that's a weird name. I think it's pretty. Femi-
nine." Jake made approving noises to keep up the good vibe. The
car's headlights illuminated the caution sign, setting its fluores-
cence aglow. "Lower your speed. It's a blind curve."

"On it." Ryan slowed down.

"So what's she like, personality-wise?"

"She's funny. She has a Texas accent. She says pin when she
means pen."

"Accents are good. Accents can be adorable."

"Agree!" Ryan beamed as they reached the curve, and Jake
felt happy for him.

"So you're going out with her tomorrow night? Why don't
you take her someplace nice, on me, like a restaurant?"

"A *restaurant*? Dude, we're not *olds* like you!" Ryan looked
over in disbelief as he steered around the curve, and Jake met
his eye, bursting into laughter.

But in that split second, there was a sickening *thump*.

They jolted as if they'd hit something, and Ryan slammed on
the brakes, cranking the wheel to the left. The right side of the
car bumped up and down, fishtailed wildly, and skidded to a
stop.

And then everything went quiet.

Chapter Two

"What was *that*?" Jake threw an arm across Ryan, but the accident was over as suddenly as it had begun. The noise had come from the passenger side of the car, toward the front.

"Dad, I'm sorry, I hit something, I think it was a deer." Ryan shook his head, upset. "I didn't see it, I was looking at you. I hope I didn't hurt it or the car."

"It's okay. Don't worry about the car." Jake hadn't seen anything because he'd been looking at Ryan. The car sat perpendicular on the street, its headlights blasting the trees. The airbags hadn't gone off. The windshield was intact. The engine was still running.

"If it's a deer, maybe it's not dead. Maybe we can call the vet. Dr. Rowan is a good guy. He'd come, wouldn't he?"

"Hmm, I don't know. It's kind of late to call him." Jake twisted around and checked behind them. The back of the car had stopped short of a tree and a yellow stanchion sticking out of the ground with a sign that read GAS PIPELINE. He shuddered to think how much worse it could have been.

"Maybe the emergency vet then? Can we call them?"

"Let me go see. You stay here." Jake patted Ryan's arm, opened the car door, and got out, steeling himself for the sight. He'd hit a deer two years ago and still felt guilty. He looked to the right, where the sound had come from. Something dark and lumpy lay off the road, in the raggedy fringe of brush bordering the woods, bathed in the red glow of their taillights.

Oh my God.

Jake knew what he was seeing, in his heart, before his brain let him accept the reality. He found himself racing toward the dark and fallen form. It wasn't a deer. It was a human being, on its side, facing away from him. It couldn't be anything else from the shape. And it was lying still, so still.

Jake threw himself on the ground beside the body. A woman runner in a black jersey and black running tights lay motionless on her side, her skinny body like a limp stick figure.

"Miss, Miss!" Jake called out, frantic. She didn't reply or moan. He pressed her neck to see if she had a pulse, but didn't feel anything. He couldn't see much in the dim light. The woman was petite. She had long hair. Dark blood flowed from a wound near her hairline. Her features glistened, abraded by the asphalt. Road dirt pitted her nose and cheek.

"Miss!" Jake leaned over her chest, trying to hear a heartbeat, but he couldn't hear anything. He turned the woman over on her back to begin CPR and put an arm under her neck to open her airway. Her head dropped backwards. He realized with horror that she was dead.

"Ryan! Help! Call 911!" Jake shouted, horrified. He'd left his phone in the car. He knew CPR. He'd been an Eagle Scout. He prayed the protocol hadn't changed. He bent over and began CPR, breathing into her mouth, willing oxygen into her lungs, counting off breaths in his head. Her lips were still warm, but she didn't respond.

"Dad! Oh my God, oh my God!" Ryan came running up, his

hands on his head, doubled over in shock. "It's a *lady*! *I hit a lady*?"

"Call 911!" Jake stopped breathing for her, shifted position, linked his fingers, and pumped the woman's chest, counting off in his head, praying to God he could resuscitate her. He had to bring her back. She couldn't be dead. This couldn't be happening.

"What are you doing? Tell me she's alive! She's alive, isn't she? No, this can't be! She has to be alive! I'm calling 911!" Ryan shook his head, edging backwards. His breaths came in ragged bursts. He pulled his phone from his pocket, but dropped it, agitated. "Dad, she . . . doesn't look like she's alive! She's alive . . . isn't she? She can't be . . . *dead*!"

"Stay calm, pick up your phone, and call 911." Jake pumped her chest, counting off the beats, trying to stay in emotional control. The woman still didn't respond. He kept pumping.

"Dad . . . no it *can't* be true!" Ryan cried out, bursting into an anguished sob. "I have to call . . . my phone! They can help her!" He dropped to his knees, frantically looking in the dark for his phone, crying and crawling around the street. "She can't be dead . . . where's my phone? I can't find my phone!"

Jake kept pumping on the woman's chest. His efforts became futile, grotesque. He was abusing her body. She had become a corpse. He couldn't believe it. He didn't understand. It was inconceivable. She had been alive a minute ago, running around the curve. Now she was dead. They had killed her.

God, no.

Jake stopped pumping and leaned back on his haunches. Tears came to his eyes. His hand went to his mouth, reflexively stifling himself. He looked down at the woman in the dim light. The sight broke his heart, and he knew it would be seared into his brain for the rest of his life. He bent his head and sent up a silent prayer on her behalf.

"No, no! Where's my . . . *phone*?" Ryan sobbed, scrambling

for his phone on all fours. "I *killed* . . . a lady, I *killed* . . . a lady, I wasn't looking . . . it's all my fault!"

"Ryan, she's gone," Jake whispered, his throat thick with emotion.

"No, no, no, no, she's not *gone* . . . she's not gone . . . what did I *do*?" Ryan fell over, collapsing into tears, his forehead on the asphalt. "Dad, I killed her . . . no, no, no!"

Jake rubbed his eyes, dragged himself to his feet, and half-walked and half-stumbled to Ryan.

"No, no, no!" Ryan cried, his big body folded onto itself, racked with sobs. "I can't . . . believe this. I . . . *killed* someone, I *killed* that . . . lady!"

"We'll get through this, Ryan." Jake gathered him up and hugged him tight, and they clung to each other in a devastated embrace.

"I *killed* . . . that lady . . . *I killed . . . that lady!* I wasn't . . . *looking*!"

"I didn't see her either. I'm at fault too, we both are." Jake held him close, then spotted Ryan's phone glinting in the light, by the side of the road.

"*I killed her!* Oh no oh no . . . what did I do?" Ryan wept and permitted himself to be held, and Jake's thoughts raced ahead. He'd call 911, but if he told the police that Ryan had been at the wheel, Ryan could get a criminal record, since he'd been driving after hours on a learner's permit. It would jeopardize his college admissions, basketball scholarships, everything. And Pam would never forgive him for letting Ryan drive or letting this happen. The open secret of their marriage was that his wife loved their son more than she loved him. Jake reached a decision.

"Ryan, listen to me. We need to call the police, but we can't tell them the truth. We're going to tell them that I was driving, not you. Got it? We'll say I was the driver, and you were the passenger."

"No, no . . . I did it . . . *I killed that lady* . . . she's *dead*!" Ryan sobbed harder, his broad chest heaving. Tears poured down his cheeks. His nose ran freely, his mucus streaming.

"Ryan, look at me. Look at me." Jake put his hands on his son's tearstained face. They had to get the story straight before they called the police. They had no time to lose. A car could come along any minute. "I need you to listen to me."

"I killed her!" Ryan kept shaking his head, hiccuping with sobs. "Dad—"

"Ryan, listen, try to calm down—"

"I can't, I can't!" Ryan shook his head back and forth, almost manically, out of control. "I killed her, I killed her!"

"Ryan, listen!" Jake shouted, only because Ryan was becoming hysterical. "We're going to tell the police I was driving the car, do you understand? I was driving the car and you were the passenger. Got it? I'll do all the talking, you keep quiet. You can do that, can't you?"

"No, no, no, I . . . *killed her*!" Ryan shouted back, his words indistinct, his tears and mucus flowing.

"Ryan, stop. We're going to tell the cops *I* killed her. Do you hear me? You *cannot* contradict me, no matter what they ask you. I'll do the talking, you keep your mouth shut."

"Dad . . . no!" Ryan lurched out of his arms, scrambled backwards, and staggered to his feet, shaking his head. "No, no, Dad. No!"

"Yes, do what I say, it's the only way." Jake got to his feet, hustled to the phone, and picked it up to call 911.

"No, no, wait . . . look. Wait." Ryan plunged his hand into his pocket, pulled out a plastic Ziploc bag, and showed it to Jake, sobbing. "Dad . . . I . . . bought this . . . today. What do I do with it . . . when the cops come?"

"What is it?"

"I'm sorry . . . it's weed . . . I'm sorry—"

"*What?*" Jake asked, aghast.

"I smoked up . . . with Caleb . . . after practice." Ryan wept, his hand flying to his hair, rubbing it back and forth. "But I'm not . . . high now, I swear it . . . I'm not, I'm not."

"You *smoke dope*? Since *when*?"

"I don't do a lot . . . I swear. I did it today . . . but I'm fine now . . . that's not why I hit the lady—"

"Give me that!" Jake grabbed the bag from Ryan's hand. It was a quarter full of marijuana.

"I killed that lady . . . she's dead!" Ryan dissolved into tears, holding his head, falling to his knees. He rocked on his haunches, back and forth, becoming hysterical. "She's dead . . . because of me . . . Dad, what do we do? I killed her . . . I killed her . . . I killed her!"

Jake had to make a split-second decision, wrestling with his conscience. A woman was dead, horribly, but that couldn't be changed. If Jake called the police and told them the truth, then two lives would be destroyed—hers and Ryan's. And Ryan was too distraught to maintain any lie to the police. Even if Jake tried to claim that he himself had been driving the car, the cops would question them both. He couldn't be sure Ryan wouldn't blurt out the truth about who was driving, and if Ryan did, the cops would test him and find marijuana in his blood. They would convict him of driving under the influence and vehicular homicide. He would go to jail. There would be no college, no future, no nothing. Ryan's entire life would be ruined—and all because Jake had let him drive.

Jake's mouth went dry. He couldn't bring himself to look back at the poor woman lying off the road, lifeless. He had no more time to ponder. He was a family man, and he'd lived his whole life being good, moral, and honest. He'd never broken the law in any way. So he knew he was making the absolute worst decision of his life when he stuffed the cell phone and Ziploc bag into his pocket, grabbed Ryan by his coat, and pulled him to his feet.

"Get back in the car, son," Jake said, grimly. "Hurry."

"The tell-all twosome have yet again opened their hearts and homes, cooking up a huge helping of laughs, sprinkled with a few tears and a dash of motherly love—and it all goes down deliciously."
—*Booklist*

St. Martin's Press

St. Martin's Griffin

No one does
EMOTIONAL, POWERFUL, HEARTBREAKING,
or HONEST like *New York Times* bestselling author

LISA SCOTTOLINE

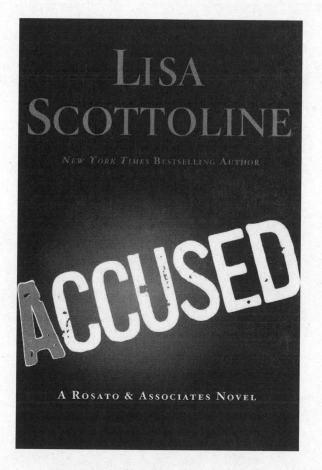